Also by Barbara Hambly

A Free Man of Color

Fever Season

Graveyard Dust

Die Upon a Kiss

Praise for Barbara Hambly's

SOLD DOWN THE RIVER

"Absolutely fascinating . . .
Hambly is a master of atmosphere. Compelling."
—*The Purloined Letter*

"Hambly has created a fascinating set of characters, foremost among them her detective, Benjamin January."
—*News & Record,* Greensboro, NC

"This is a dark, sometimes savage story, powered by disgust for a system so brutal. Hambly's portrait of January's lovely courtesan mother's household is especially chilling."
—*Booknews* from The Poisoned Pen

"Perhaps the best book in the series."
—*Mystery Lovers Bookshop News*

"Intense."
—*Romantic Times*

GRAVEYARD DUST

"Seductive . . . Sweeps from lavish balls on elegant river plantations to voodoo rites in Congo Square and savage brawls in mean waterfront dives. . . . January proves the ideal guide through these treacherous social strata."
—*The New York Times Book Review*

"A richly detailed murder mystery with a little bit of voodoo mixed in for flavor. Don't miss this powerful series."
—*Mystery Lovers Bookshop News*

"Its emotional authenticity, varied cast and rich historical trappings give the novel power and depth."
—*Publishers Weekly*

FEVER SEASON

"A notable writer of mystery fiction . . . This one grips the reader from start to finish."
—*The Washington Times*

"From the highborn Creoles in their river mansions to the uncivilized Americans brawling on the levee, Hambly speaks all their languages, knows all their secrets, and brings them all to life."
—*The New York Times Book Review*

A FREE MAN OF COLOR

"Magically rich and poignant . . . In scene after scene researched in impressive depth and presented in the cool, clear colors of photography, Hambly creates an exotic but recognizable environment for January's search for justice."
—*Chicago Tribune*

"A darned good murder mystery."
—*USA Today*

Barbara Hambly

BANTAM BOOKS
New York • Toronto • London
Sydney • Auckland

This edition contains the complete text
of the original hardcover edition.
NOT ONE WORD HAS BEEN OMITTED.

SOLD DOWN THE RIVER
A Bantam Book

PUBLISHING HISTORY
Bantam hardcover edition published July 2000
Bantam mass market edition / June 2001

LIBRARY OF CONGRESS CATALOG CARD NUMBER:
99-054845

ISBN 0-553-57529-5

Published simultaneously in the United States and Canada

Bantam Books are published by Bantam Books, a division of Random House, Inc. Its trademark, consisting of the words "Bantam Books" and the portrayal of a rooster, is Registered in U.S. Patent and Trademark Office and in other countries. Marca Registrada. Bantam Books, 1540 Broadway, New York, New York 10036.

PRINTED IN THE UNITED STATES OF AMERICA
OPM 10 9 8 7 6 5 4 3 2

For Mom and Dad

Special thanks are owed to Paul Nevski, Bill Coble, Norman and Sand Marmillion, and the rest of the staff of Le Monde Creole in New Orleans and Laura Plantation in St. John Parish, for unbelievable help, inspiration, and friendship in putting together this book. Thanks also to Pamela Arcineaux and the staff of the Historic New Orleans Collection for their patience, friendship, and help; to Laurie Perry for her comments and help on early black music; and to Kate Miciak of Bantam Books.

Thank you also to Jill and Charles, to Neil and deb, to Michael, and, of course, to George.

PARTIAL GLOSSARY OF CREOLE AND AFRO-CREOLE WORDS

One of the problems with the terminology found in accounts of slavery—in Louisiana in particular—is that words have often been transcribed phonetically, and spelling differs from account to account. As usual, my research has spanned so many small sources that the spelling is completely inconsistent. I apologize for this.

Arpent—192 linear feet. Plantations were usually measured in arpents of river-front, extending sometimes twenty, sometimes forty arpents back from the river towards the swamps.

Baron Cemetery (also Baron Samedei, or Baron La Croix)—voodoo spirit of the dead.

Batture—the ground between the levee and the actual edge of the water. Frequently heavily wooded, and piled with snags and debris washed up in high water.

Blankittes (or *blanquittes*)—disrespectful term for whites, used by slaves.

Bousillage—river mud mixed with moss, ground shells, straw, hair, or any other binding substance to make a hard plaster. Also, the act or process of making walls out of this material.

Bozal (or *bosal*)—A slave newly arrived from Africa; in other words, a raw savage.

Brigitte of the Dry Arms—voodoo spirit of death, wife of Baron Cemetery.

Callas—fried rice-balls (frequently dusted with powdered sugar).

Ciprière—the swampy cypress forests that lay behind the cleared plantation lands along the river. Also called simply the swamp by Americans, and the "desert" by French (meaning "a waste place," not as the word is understood in English).

Congris—mixture of chickpeas and rice, or more broadly (in other parts of the Caribbean), any kind of beans and rice.

Damballah-Wedo (or Damballa-Wedo)—voodoo snake-spirit of water and wisdom.

Garçonnière—separate wing of a plantation or town house where the grown sons of the family lived. Sometimes a separate building.

Griot—African word for the village storyteller, bard, and historian.

Loa—voodoo spirits or "gods." *Loa* can be great or not-so-great, powerful or minor, dangerous or benign or even comical, though the line between "good" and "bad" spirits is often less sharp in the African religions than in Western: spirits can be summoned to help with good causes or bad.

Osnabrig (or osnaberg)—short for Osnaberg cloth, a coarse heavy cotton manufactured in Osnaberg, Sweden, usually used for slave clothing.

Papa Legba—voodoo spirit of the crossroads, often conflated with St. Peter, the keeper of Heaven's keys. Guardian of the doorways from this world into the next.

Plaçée—free colored mistress of a wealthy white gentleman. The relationships were usually monogamous and frequently arranged with a contract on business lines.

Quantiers (also quanteers)—a type of extremely coarse rawhide shoes made for slaves by the plantation shoemaker.

Rattoon—to grow cane from stalks planted in a previous season and left in the ground (rather than being dug up and replanted). Rattooned cane tends to come up thinner and is more trouble to harvest.

Roulaison—cane-harvest and grinding season.

Tignon—the head-scarves or turbans whose wear was mandated by law for all women of color, slave or free.

Vévé—voodoo signs or diagrams drawn to summon the *loa.*

Mon Triomphe Plantation

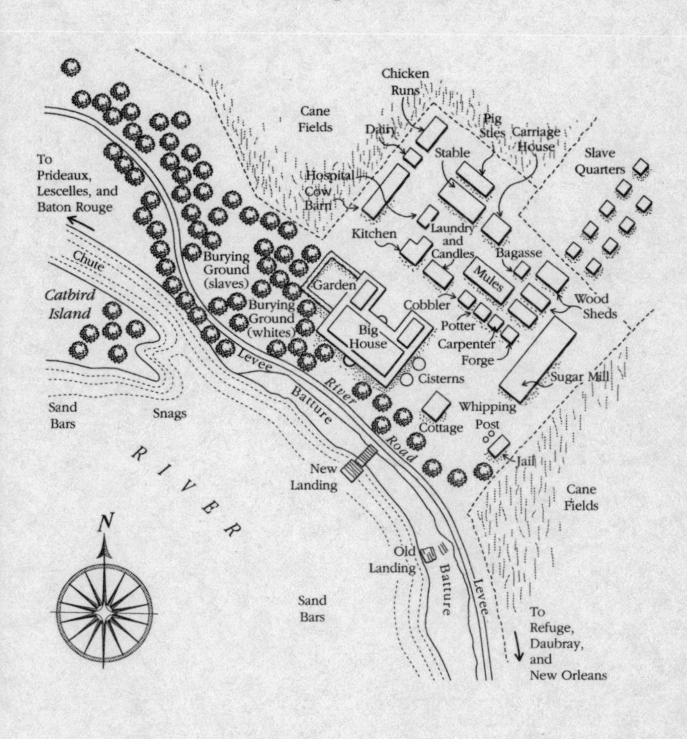

The Big House at Mon Triomphe

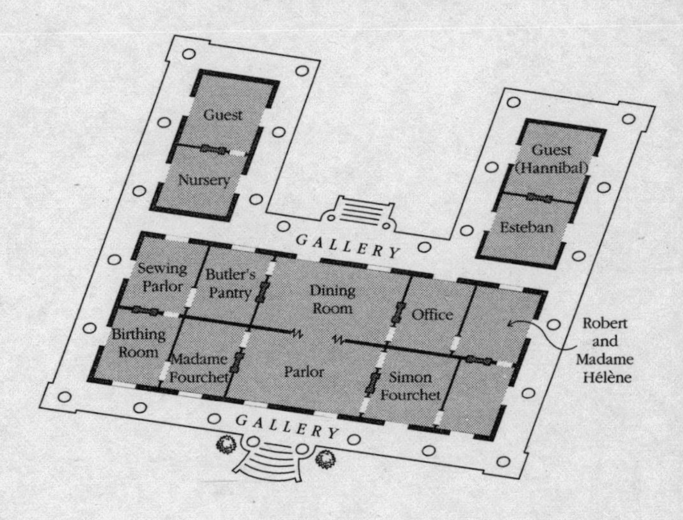

Sold Down the River

ONE

When someone ties you naked to a tree in the yard and beats you unconscious with a broom handle, you don't soon forget it, or him.

"Ben, you remember Monsieur Fourchet," said his mother.

Standing in the doorway of her parlor, Benjamin January felt the hair lift on his nape at the sight of the man beside the window.

In the nightmares, he was taller.

Fourchet turned from the long French door that looked out onto Rue Burgundy, and January saw that he was, in fact, just slightly under six feet tall: more than three inches shorter than his own towering height. That he was wide through the chest and shoulders, but without January's massive strength. In the nightmares his hair was black, not streaky gray and thin, and his face, although creased with a lifetime's rage and cruelty, didn't have the broken network of lines that gouged the sunken cheeks, bracketed the harsh mouth, accentuated the sag beneath the chin.

The eyes were the same. Arrogant, dark, and cold.

But the man had grown old.

"I remember," he told his mother.

"You've grown." Fourchet took a seat in one of the straw-colored chintz chairs of which January's mother was so proud.

Between seven and forty-one I'd belong in a raree-show if I hadn't. January couldn't resist saying, "Monsieur Janvier fed me very well. Sir."

Fourchet hadn't. The slaves on Fourchet's Bellefleur Plantation, where January had been born, had what were called provision lands, small plots where they could grow corn and yams. On most plantations these augmented whatever rations of cornmeal and salt pork the planter saw fit to distribute. On Bellefleur, Fourchet had skimped the women and the children; even out of harvest time, he had demanded extra work after the conch shell was blown at sunset, so that the provision grounds were neglected and choked with weeds. January remembered his aunts and uncles were always being whipped for stealing food.

Fourchet sniffed. "Educated you, too, so your mother tells me."

By the way the man said the words January knew that Fourchet had had his mother, probably many times in the years before he'd sold her to St.-Denis Janvier. Anger rose in him like vomit, and like vomit he swallowed it down. He glanced at Livia Levesque, slender and beautiful still at sixty-four, neat in her fashionable frock of yellow mull-muslin, on her head the tignon that New Orleans statute required all women of color to wear, striped yellow and white to match, and trimmed with lace. Her slim strong hands in crocheted house-mitts rested easy around the cup of pink-and-green German porcelain that held her coffee, and her dark wide beautiful eyes moved from man to man with an alert calculation that held not the smallest whisper of embarrassment, self-consciousness, or anger in the presence of her former master.

The situation simply didn't bother her at all.

"Monsieur Fourchet has come to ask our help, Ben," said his mother. Outside, in the Rue Burgundy, a brewer's dray rattled past, driven far too fast by a young man standing to the reins like a Roman charioteer; two women walking along the brick banquette squealed and sprang aside from the water thrown by the wheels. Even so far back from the levee the hoots of the steamboats could be heard, and the dim stirring of stevedores' shouts and vendors' cries. After summer's gluey horror, the autumn air was crisp. The city was resuming its wintertime bustle and prosperity. "Your name was given him by that dirty American policeman you take up with, but perhaps it's all to the best."

That dirty American policeman was Abishag Shaw, lieutenant of the New Orleans City Guard. Though as a rule—like most of the citizens of the French town, white and colored alike—January mistrusted Americans profoundly, particularly those in positions of power, he liked Shaw and respected him. Still, his mother spoke no more than the truth.

January folded his powerful arms and waited. He had not, he noticed, been invited to sit in the presence of a white man and his former master. Nor had his mother said, *Get yourself some coffee, Ben.*

It was one thing for a white man to share coffee with a velvet-brown mulatto woman. White men did it all the time, in these small cottages at the rear of the French town. The custom of the country. For generations French and Spanish Creoles had taken free women of color as their mistresses, as St.-Denis Janvier had thirty-three years ago freed and then taken her. It was another thing—January could see this in her eyes, hear it in her artfully artless silence—to ask a white gentleman to sit in the same room drinking coffee with the coal-black son of a mulatto and a slave.

In the eighteen months since his return from sixteen years in Paris—years in which he had practiced both surgery and music—January had never been permitted to forget that this house was his mother's, not his.

If Simon Fourchet was conscious of any of this, he didn't show it. Maybe he accepted it as natural that a grown man wouldn't be permitted to drink coffee in the house where he lived, should a white man be seated there.

"There's a secret campaign of deliberate destruction going on at Mon Triomphe," the planter said, glancing up at January from under the grizzled overhang of his brows. "Spoliation, arson, wrecking, ruin—and murder. And maybe open revolt."

Mon Triomphe, January recalled, was Fourchet's other plantation. When Fourchet had sold Bellefleur—years after January, his mother, and his younger sister had been sold and freed—the planter had gone there permanently. It lay upriver in Ascension Parish, some twenty miles southeast of Baton Rouge. Twenty miles, that is, if you wanted to hack your way through cypress swamps and untamed woodland, instead of journeying twice the distance in half the time via steamboat on the river.

Forty-two years ago—in 1793, the year of January's birth—Fourchet had managed Mon Triomphe himself and left Bellefleur in the care of his brother-in-law Gervase Duhamel, only returning there after the grueling hell of the roulaison—the sugar-grinding—was done. Bellefleur had lain close to the small, walled city of New Orleans, to which Fourchet brought his Spanish wife and their two children every year for the Carnival season. They lived in the big house at Bellefleur for the weeks between Twelfth Night and Easter; entertained guests there, something impossible in the isolated fastnesses of Ascension Parish. St.-Denis Janvier, who had eventually bought January's mother, had been one of those guests.

In 1798, when January was five, there'd been a slave revolt on Mon Triomphe. It may have been fueled by rumor, hope, and the example of Christophe's rebellion in the island of Saint-Domingue, though the aunts and uncles and cousins whose cabins January had played in said that it started when a drunken Fourchet beat a young girl to death. Fourchet's wife and daughter died under the machetes of the infuriated slaves. The revolt was crushed, of course, but after that Fourchet sent his sister and her husband to Mon Triomphe, and ran Bellefleur himself.

"It began with a fire in the sugar-mill." Fourchet's harsh voice summoned January back to the present, back to the grim-faced man sitting in his mother's yellow chintz chair drinking coffee, while he himself stood. "We hadn't started harvest yet—you lose half your sugar if you cut too soon—and the hands were still bringing in wood from the ciprière. My sugar-boss managed to get the fire put out, but the beams that held the grinders were damaged. They broke two days later, and that put us back another week. Men found voodoo-marks in the mill, on the sugar carts and the mule harness. The cart axles were sawn, the harness cut, or rubbed with turpentine and pepper. The whole of the main work-gang was poisoned one day, purging and puking and useless."

"And I suppose you put the women out to cut?" said January quietly. "Sir," he added, as he had been taught—as he nowadays had to force himself to remember to say, after sixteen years in Paris of saying "sir" to no one who did not merit it.

Fourchet's dark eyes flashed. "What the hell do you think? We had to get the harvest in, damn you, boy."

"Let M'sieu Fourchet finish his story, Ben," chided his mother, and Fourchet swung around on her with a flaying glare.

Then after a moment he looked back at January. "Yes," he said. "I put the women's gang to cutting the cane as well as hauling it, and kept most of the second gang in the mill. They know what they're doing with the fires. Fool women put 'em out raking the ashes, and smother 'em putting in wood and every other damn thing. We couldn't lose a day, not with the frost coming. You know that, or you should."

January knew. *Can't-see to can't-see,* they'd said in the quarters. The men shivered in the morning blackness as they started their work, and again as they returned from the fields with the sweat crusted on their bodies, once it became so dark their own hands and arms and bodies were in peril from the sharp heavy blades. He remembered loading cane onto the carts by torchlight, and the constant fear he'd step on a snake in the shadows among the cane-rows, or find one had coiled itself into the cut cane. Remembered how the babies cried, laid down by their mothers at the edge of the field, to be suckled when they had a chance. Remembered the men's silence as they stumbled back with the final loads of the day, and how it felt to know that there would be no rest. Only hours more work unloading the heavy stalks at the mill, feeding the dripping sticky billets with their razor-sharp ends into the turning iron maw of the grinder. Remembered exhaustion, and the sickening smell of the cane-juice and the smoke and the burnt-sweet stink of the boiling sugar.

Cold meals and provision grounds gone to weeds and the cabin filthy, hearth piled high with ashes and walls surrounded with trash. He and his sister itching with lice and driven nearly frantic by bedbugs at night because their mother had no time to wage the slave's endless battle against those pests. His mother falling asleep sitting in the doorway, too tired to undress and go to bed.

"Yes, sir," he told Fourchet. "I know."

"Then you should know how devastating this kind of thing can be at such a time. And it's not the first time. God knows blacks are always doing one thing and another to get out of work. Breaking tools, or crippling a mule or a horse. You'd think they'd have the sense to know that a poor harvest will only hurt them in the end, but of course they don't."

No, thought January, silent. *Sometimes they didn't.* Sometimes when you were that tired and that angry you didn't think very straight. When he was a child he'd wanted to kill Fourchet, after the man had flogged Mohammed, the plantation blacksmith's apprentice, nearly to death in one of his fits of drunken rage. Remembered how the drivers had untied the slim youth's body from the post and dropped him to the ground in the stableyard, and how the flies had swarmed around the bloodied meat of his back. Mohammed was a favorite of the children—the hogmeat gang, as they were called—a storyteller and a singer of songs. January had wanted to kill Fourchet and even at the time had known that if the big man died, at least a couple of the slaves would end up being sold to pay debts while the man's son was still a young boy. Maybe all of them.

And he'd known then, for the first time, that taste of helpless fear, the awareness that some things had to be endured for the sake of the slender and priceless good that endurance bought you. Being in hell wasn't as bad as it might be, if you could sit with your family in the hot dark of summer nights, listen to the crickets and the soft sweet wailing of singing along the street of the quarters, in those short lapis hours between supper and bed.

The thought of losing that—even that—was usually enough to make a man or a woman think twice about open revolt.

Still he said nothing. But he felt as if the whole core of him had shrunk and cured to a rod of iron, ungiving and utterly cold.

"Then yesterday morning the servants found Gilles, my butler, dead in the storeroom under the house." Fourchet's mouth hardened. "Beside him was a bottle of liquor, cognac. *My* cognac. The cellaret in the dining room was unlocked, the keys lying beside Gilles's hand."

Bitter hatred froze the old planter's face as he gazed unseeing at the bright slim slat of Rue Burgundy visible beyond the window louvers, remembering whatever sight it was that he had been brought down to see.

"Livia will have told you I used to drink," he said. "And that when I drank, it was as if there was a devil in me."

"My mother never spoke of you, sir," replied January, and the dark eyes slashed in his direction again, then cut toward the straight cool figure in the yellow muslin, sipping her café crème. But since January hadn't actually said, *What makes you think she gave you a moment's thought after she wiped your spunk off her legs and went about her business?* there was nothing with which Fourchet could take issue.

"Just as well. I'd like to say that all the evil in my life sprang from drink, but I don't think even that's true." He took a cigar from his pocket, bit off the end with carnivorous-looking teeth. "For eight months now I have not tasted a drop. Nor will I. But I've spoken of this to no one. Only my wife knows of my decision to put it out of my life, to make some reparation for the harm I've caused. Not so very long ago poisoning my liquor would have been the quickest way to get shut of me." He was silent again, as if he expected praise or admiration for this abstinence—as if every slave on Bellefleur hadn't known to stay out of the master's way when he'd been at the bottle. As if even the scullery maid hadn't held him in fear-filled contempt.

"Well, it's clear to me what's going on this time." The planter shook his head. "I don't think it's revolt—they're taking too goddam long over it. No—someone's set out to destroy my land. To destroy me." His hands balled into fists upon his knees, his face like a storm-scarred stone.

My name is Ozymandias, king of kings, Percy Shelley had written of an ancient colossus, battered and alone. *A shattered visage . . . whose frown, and wrinkled lip, and sneer of cold command. . . .*

Fourchet held the cigar to his lips and glanced at January, not even expectantly, but impatiently. A slave, January realized, would spring at once to the spirit-lamp beneath the coffee and kindle a spill for him.

So, of course, would a gentleman host who didn't want to relegate the task to the only lady in the room.

January fetched the spill, his anger smoldering in him like the ember at the spill's tip. The comparison with Shelley's poem was too grand, he thought. Yet the words would not leave his mind.

"It might just be my neighbors, the Daubray brothers, are behind this, or paying one of my blacks to do it." The dark glance flickered sideways to January again through the curl of the smoke. "I've been in lawsuit against them for near a year now, and the case is coming to court as soon as the harvest's in. I wouldn't put it past them to burn my mill." For a moment the old black glint of unreasoning hate showed through his brooding self-control.

"Sneaking bastards. They know what my land means to me." He puffed his cigar like a caged dragon blowing smoke. "They know I was putting my blood and my sweat into its soil while that lightskirt mother of theirs was promenading the New Orleans docks in quest of a husband, and they know the land is my body and my life. I've done evil in my time, wasted the gifts of God and harmed those it was my duty to protect. But through it all the land was mine. It's the one true good in my life, the only thing I have to show for living: truly my Triumph. They're spiteful as women, the whole family is," he added. "They'd be glad to see me lose it. Glad enough to pay my own field hands to turn against me.

"That's what I want you to find out."

He raised his chin and stared at January, who still stood before him—stood as if this man were still his master. Were still able to beat him, or nail him up in the barrel in the corner of the barn in July heat or February frost. Still able to sell him away, never to see his friends or his family again.

Heat blossomed somewhere behind January's sternum. Ice-heat, tight and furious and dangerously still.

He'd set his music satchel on the floor by his feet upon coming in from the backyard—yet one more of those myriad tiny prohibitions imposed upon him in his mother's house. Neither he nor Olympe—his full sister by that slave husband of whom their mother never spoke—had ever been allowed to enter the house through the long French door from the street.

With the coming of the November cool, balls and the opera were beginning again. Likewise, most of January's piano pupils had returned to town, the sons and daughters of the wealthy of New Orleans: Americans, French, free colored. He'd just returned from a house in the suburb of St. Mary's—quite close, in fact, to where Bellefleur's cane-fields had lain—after talking to a woman about lessons for her son. That angelic six-year-old had announced, the moment January was on the opposite side of the parlor's sliding doors again, "Mama, he's a *nigger*!" in tones of incredulous shock.

Did he think I was going to play a tom-tom instead of a piano?

Now he moved his satchel carefully up onto one of the spare, graceful cypress tables that adorned the parlor, and folded his hands. In the impeccable Parisian French that he knew was several degrees more correct than Fourchet's Creole sloppiness, he said, "In other words, sir, what you want is a spy."

"Of course I want a spy!" Fourchet's eyes slitted and he looked like a rogue horse about to bite. His harsh voice had the note of one who wondered how January could be so dense. "No question it's the blacks. I just need to know which ones, and if the Daubrays or someone else are behind it. This Shaw fellow I spoke with yesterday said you'd be the man."

"I'm afraid the lieutenant mistook me, sir." January fought to keep his voice from shaking. "I'm a surgeon by training, and a musician. I've looked into things when friends of mine needed help. But I'm not a spy."

"I'll pay you," said Fourchet. "Five hundred dollars. You can't tell me you'd make as much between now and the end of the harvest, playing at balls." He nodded toward the piano in the front parlor, where January gave lessons three mornings a week to a tiny coterie of free colored children, the sons and daughters of white men by their plaçées.

"I told Monsieur Fourchet that you certainly needed the money," put in Livia.

January opened his mouth, then closed it, fighting not to snap, *You mean* YOU *want—not* NEED*—the money.* But his mother didn't even avert her gaze from his, evidently seeing nothing amiss in charging her son five Spanish dollars a month for the privilege of sleeping in the room he'd occupied as a child, nor in reminding him of the hundred dollars he owed her.

That debt had come about three weeks ago, when January had gone to play at a ball and, returning late, had encountered a gang of rowdies, Kentucky river-ruffians of the sort that came down on the keelboats. Coarse, dirty, largely uneducated, they were habitually heavily armed and drunk. He'd escaped with his life, and without serious injury, only by refusing to resist, putting his arms over his head and telling himself over and over that to put up a fight would escalate the situation to a killing rather than just "roughing up a nigger." It hadn't been easy.

The custom of the country, he'd told himself later. And he had known, returning from France in the wake of his wife's death from the cholera two years ago, that in the land of his birth he could be beaten up by any white man, that he had no right to resist. It was the price he'd paid, to return to the only home he had.

But the incident had cost him the clothes he wore, clothes a musician needed if he expected to be hired to play at the balls of the wealthy: long-tailed black wool coat, gray trousers, cream-colored silk waistcoat, linen shirt. And it had cost him all the music in his satchel—torn up, pissed on, dunked in the overflowing gutters of Rue Bienville—difficult and costly to replace. The season of entertainments was just beginning, after the summer's brutal heat. He could not afford delay in repurchasing the tools and apparel of his trade.

But he knew, even as he'd asked her for the money, that his mother would not let him forget.

And it was in her eyes now: that avid glitter. Envy,

too, that *he'd* been offered the money, and the task, instead of she.

"I'm sorry, Monsieur Fourchet," he said again, and marveled to hear his own calm voice. "It isn't a matter of money. I—"

"Don't be a fool!" Fourchet's voice cracked into a full-out shout, as January remembered it. The child in him flinched at the recollection of the man's capricious rages, the sudden transitions from reasonableness to violent fury. "Too proud to get your black hands dirty? Think you're too good these days to live with the niggers you were born among?"

"I think—" began January, and Fourchet raged.

"Don't you back-talk me, you black whelp, I don't give a tinker's reverence what you think!" He flung the cigar to the spotless cypresswood floor. "I could get a dozen like you just walking down Baronne Street who'd leap on a dollar to suck my arse, let alone do as I'm asking you to do!"

"Then I suggest you betake yourself to Baronne Street, sir," said January quietly. "I'm sorry to have wasted your time."

"I'll make you goddam sorry. . . !" Fourchet thundered, but January simply raised his new beaver hat to the man, bowed deeply, picked up his music satchel, and walked through the rear parlor and out the back door. He could hear the man's enraged bray behind him as he crossed the yard and mounted the stairs to his room in the garçonnière, and only when he had shut the door behind him did he start to shake.

He was forty-one years old, he reminded himself—forty-two, he added, as of three weeks ago. Simon Fourchet had no power to hurt him, beyond the crass physical violence such as the scum of the keelboats had practiced. The man was seventy years old and probably couldn't hurt him much. *This is the child who is frightened,* he thought, taking three tries to get his new kid gloves off. *This is the child in the dreams, who is unable to walk away.*

He found himself listening, heart racing, to the old man's shouted obscenities as he pulled off the coat and shirt his mother had lent him the money to buy, the armor of respectability that, more even than the papers in his pocket, said: *This is a free man.*

To Fourchet, January realized, he would never be free.

Only jumped-up.

To the Americans who saw him walking well-dressed about the streets, the Americans whose growing numbers were slowly swamping the older population of Creole French and Spanish, it was the same.

He fought down the impulse to change clothes fast and run. With his habitual neatness he made himself fold the coat and trousers into the armoire, and set the shoes neatly under the bed. Clothed in rougher trousers, a calico shirt, and the short corduroy jacket he'd bought while a student in Paris, he descended the stairs and deposited the white shirt in the tiny laundry room next to the kitchen. It was there that his mother caught him, before he could be across the yard again, through the passway to Rue Burgundy and gone.

"Benjamin, I have never been so mortified in my life."

If the statement had been true he would have heard it in her voice, but it wasn't. She wasn't mortified. She was angry. Thwarted and angry.

"Neither have I, Maman, that he'd even think I'd do such a thing as he asks."

"Don't be silly." Her hands were clasped tight, like a little sculpture of seashell and bronze, at her belt buckle. Her mouth was hard as sculptor's work. "I assumed you'd welcome the first chance that came to you, to pay back what you owe me. The quarter-interest in that property the Widow Delachaise is selling is still open for fifteen hundred, and I don't think I need to remind you that because of those new clothes of yours, and all that music, not to mention getting the piano retuned last month, I'm in no position to—"

"No, Maman." January forced his voice level, as he had with Fourchet. "You don't need to remind me."

"Don't interrupt me, Benjamin."

Their eyes met: old wanting, old needing, a thousand griefs never comforted, a thousand things never said. January remembered her—one of his earliest memories—being beaten for stealing eggs for him and for Olympe, when a fox had killed the three chickens that constituted the only livestock they possessed. Remembered her silence under the lash.

"We need that money," Livia said, in a voice that took into account nothing of the other property she owned, or the funds in three separate banks. "You can't possibly think Monsieur Fourchet would use this opportunity to take advantage of your position and kidnap you to sell to dealers, for heaven's sake. If he told that animal Shaw about hiring you, he can't intend—"

"No, Maman," said January. "That's not what I think."

"Then what? It's not as if you know any of those people. And it's not as if you're going to make a sou more this season than last season, teaching piano and playing at balls. Really, Benjamin, I don't know what to make of your attitude."

She looked up at him, her expression and the set of her head waiting for an explanation, and those great brown eyes like dark agate forbidding him to make her wrong by giving one.

Anything he said, he knew, he would still be wrong.

"I'm going for a walk," he said. "Can we talk about this when I get back?"

"I think it's something we need to settle now." She followed him across the hard-packed earth of the yard. "I told Monsieur Fourchet I'd talk to you. You can't judge the man by his speech. You remember how rough-spoken he always was, it's his way. Financial opportunities like the Widow Delachaise selling up don't remain available for long. Monsieur Granville at the bank said he'd hold the negotiations open as long as he could, but they won't last forever."

"I'm sorry, Maman," said January. The cool sun of early afternoon flashed on yesterday's rain puddles, on the leaves of the banana plants that clustered around the gate and along the wall. From the street came the clatter of some light vehicle, a gig or a fiacre, and a woman's voice lifted in a wailing minor key the slurry, half-African gombo patois:

"Beautiful callas! Beautiful callas, hot!" the melismatic notes elongated, embellished like a Muslim call to prayer, as if the words were only an excuse, a vehicle for what lay in her heart.

"I need a little time to think. We can talk about this when I get back."

"And when will that be?" Livia stepped beside him into the open gate. Always wanting the last word. To have his retreat, even, on her terms.

"At sunset," said January, and walked away, not knowing if he'd be back by sunset or not.

TWO

"Rough-spoken, she said." January turned the coffee cup in his hand, and gazed out past the square brick pillars that held up the market's vast, tiled roof. Beyond the shadows, slanting autumn light crystallized the chaos along the levee into the brilliant confusion of a Brueghel painting: steamboats like floating barns, with their black smokestacks and bright paint on their wheel-housings and superstructures; low brown oyster-craft and bum-boats creeping among them like palmetto bugs among the cakes and loaves on a table. Keelboats, snub-nosed and crude, being hauled by main force to the wharves. The blue coats of captains and pilots; the occasional red flash of some keelboatman's shirt; gold heaps of oranges or lemons; a whore's gay dress. Piles of corn in the husk, tomatoes, bales of green-gray wiry moss, or tobacco from the American territories to the north. Boxes without number, pianos, silk, fine steel tools from Germany and England. A cacophony of French and Spanish, English and half-African gombo patois and the mingling scents of coffee, sewage, smoke.

"He beat her, Rose. Beat her with a riding crop—I

was there—and used her as a man would take shame on himself to use a whore. He cracked two of my ribs beating me, and I couldn't have been six years old. Once when my mother got in a fight with another woman, he nailed her up in the barrel in the corner of the barn, a flour barrel you couldn't stand up in. Does she remember none of that?"

Rose Vitrac stirred her own coffee, and with a gloved forefinger propped her spectacles more firmly onto the bridge of her nose. The small thick oval slabs of glass aged her face beyond its twenty-eight years, and gave it an air of aloofness. Behind them her hazel-green eyes—legacy of a white father and a white grandfather—were wise and kind and cynical. "If you take his money," the former schoolmistress pointed out, "you'll be able to get your own rooms. You'll no longer have to live with her."

"Would you do it?" he asked. "Spy on a man's slaves for him?"

"I don't think that I could." A line of men and women passed close to the half-empty arcade, through the chaos of hogs and cotton bales and sacks on the levee, to the gangplank of the *Bonnets o' Blue.* Shackled together, the slaves were bound for one of the new cotton plantations in the Missouri territory, each clutching a few small possessions done up in a bandanna. Afternoon sun sparkled on the water, but the wind that tore at their clothing and at the flags of the riverboat jackstaffs was sharp. One woman wept bitterly. Rose turned her head to watch them, her delicate mouth somber.

"My mother was a free woman," she said. "I was never a slave. I don't think I could pass myself off as one, because I don't know all those little things, the things you learn as a child. If someone wronged me I'd go to the master, which I gather isn't done . . ."

"Good God, no!" January was shocked to his soul that she'd even suggest it.

Rose spread her hands. "I've never been that dependent on someone's whim," she said. Her voice was a low alto—like polished wood rather than silver—and, like Fourchet, she had the speech of an educated Creole, not the French of France. "Not even my father's. And it does something to you, when you're raised that way. When I lived on my father's plantation, after Mother's death, my friend Cora—the maid's daughter—taught me a lot, but just being told isn't the same. I think that's why Lieutenant Shaw directed Monsieur Fourchet to you."

Savagely, January muttered, "I can't tell you how honored I feel."

"But as to whether I *would* spy, if I could . . . Somebody did murder the poor butler, Ben. That the poison was meant for the master doesn't make the servant less dead."

His eyes avoided hers. "It isn't my affair."

"No. Of course not. Justice for a slave isn't anyone's affair."

That this was something January himself would have said—had he not just refused to become involved in Simon Fourchet's war with his slaves—didn't help the slow pain of the anger he felt, and he looked for a time out into the square. A man cursed at the deck crew unloading bales of cotton from the steamboat *Lancaster;* a young woman in the black-and-white habit of a nun stopped with wide fascinated eyes to listen, and her older companion seized her arm and pulled her along. Two boys, white and black, rolled a hoop across the earth of the Place d'Armes just behind the levee, dodging in and out among the brown-leaved sycamores; a market woman in a red-and-purple-striped tignon shouted a good-natured reproof. A few yards farther the hoop bounded out of control, startling a pair of horses being led down the gangplank of the small stern-wheeler *Belle Dame:* a carriage team by the look of them—from somewhere in the bayous of the Barataria country, to judge from the narrow lines of the boat, the single wheel and shallow draft—matched blacks with white stockings, as if they'd waded in paint.

The nearer horse reared, plunging in fear, and the man in charge of them, tall and fair with a mouth like the single stroke of a pen, dragged brutally on the animal's bit to pull it down. For good measure he added a cut across the hocks with his whip, and turned just in time to see the black boy dart to retrieve his hoop, the white playmate at his heels. The fair man's whip licked out, caught the black boy across the face.

The child staggered back, clutching his cheek. Blood poured from between his fingers. His white friend skidded to a halt, stood staring, mouth open, as the man turned away, cursing and lashing at the frightened horses again. He did not even look back as he jerked them toward the blue shadows of Rue Chartres.

The white boy picked up the hoop. He looked at his friend again, in an agony of uncertainty about what sort of support or comfort he should give or should be seen to give. In the end he ran away crying, leaving his playmate to bleed and weep alone.

"Ben."

January turned his head. His sister Olympe stood next to Rose's chair.

January had two sisters. The elder, born two years later than himself, was the daughter of that fellow-slave whom his mother never mentioned: the tall man with tribal scars on his face who sometimes walked in January's dreams. The younger, Dominique, was St.-Denis Janvier's child, their mother's lace-trimmed princess. Dominique had been only four when January had left for Paris to study medicine eighteen years ago.

Dominique, January had long ago noticed, came and went through their mother's bedroom—which opened onto Rue Burgundy, in the accepted Creole fashion—as a matter of course.

Since her departure to join the voodoos at the age of sixteen, Olympe had not entered their mother's house at all.

"It's good to see you." With her awkward, wading-bird grace, Rose moved her rough wooden chair aside to make room, and January brought over another of the several dozen seats scattered around among the tables in the shelter of the arcade. People generally bought coffee from one of the stands in the market and brought it here to sit, but the woman who ran the nearest stand came to the table before anyone went to her, with a cup for Olympe as she was sitting down, and had to be pressed two or three times to take the picayune payment for it.

That was what it was, January supposed, to be a voodoo.

"I hear Simon Fourchet asked you to find the one who wants to kill him," said Olympe.

She was tall for a woman, as January was tall for a man, and like her brother coal black: *beau noir lustre,* the dealers called that ebon African shininess. She wore a skirt of bright-hued calico, yellow and red, like the market women, and a jacket of purple wool. Strings of cowrie shells and the vertebrae of snakes circled her neck and wound in the folds of the scarlet tignon that hid her hair, giving her the voodoo name of Olympia Snakebones. When St.-Denis Janvier had bought Livia and her two children from Simon Fourchet, he'd paid to have them tutored in proper French, which after his years in Paris January spoke without thinking. Olympe, on the other hand, had kept her rough African habits of speech through all her teachers' beatings, sliding *le* and *la* into a single all-purpose *li* and casually slurring and dropping the beginnings and endings of words, as if she took pride in speaking like a field hand. Perhaps she did.

"If Fourchet's looking for one who wants to kill him, he doesn't have to walk farther than the quarters on his own land," snapped January. He was getting tired of everyone's opinions on a subject that he himself considered closed.

"That's exactly where he's looking," returned Olympe calmly. "And what you think's going to happen to those folks when he dies?"

The coffle of slaves clustered the railing of the deck of the *Bonnets o' Blue,* stared back at the swarming levee, the cafés under the sycamore trees around the Place d'Armes, the twin white towers of the cathedral under the sidelong smoke-yellow glare of the autumn sun. Gazing, January knew, for probably the last time. Life expectancy on a cane plantation wasn't long.

Behind him, Olympe's voice went on. "Not four years ago they hanged Nat Turner and near seventy others in Virginia for rising up and killing whites. Every slave-owner in the country has been seeing rebels under his bed ever since. You think getting sold to pay the inheritance tax is the worst that'll befall a man's slaves, if he dies of poison in his own home?"

"You want me to save his life?" January remembered the wet thud of the broom handle on his buttocks and thighs, the agony of blows multiplying as the bruises puffed and gorged the flesh with blood. He couldn't even remember what he'd done to trigger the beating, if anything.

"I'd like you to think about saving the lives of the

hundred or so folks who *didn't* put nightshade into that brandy. However much they might have wanted to."

For that moment, January hated her. He hadn't thought about it consciously, but he realized now that in addition to his sense that Simon Fourchet deserved whatever retribution was coming to him from his slaves—whether incited by his neighbors or not—in addition to his fears of something going wrong, he had been looking forward to a pleasant winter of playing music and being paid for it.

The days of summer heat and summer fever were done. The wealthy of New Orleans—the sugar brokers, the steamboat owners, the bankers and landlords and merchant importers, both French and American—were coming back to town to attend the opera and give parties and marry off their daughters and sons to the sons and daughters of their friends. The militia companies and burial societies, those bulwarks of the free colored community, would be organizing subscription balls and fund-raisers even more entertaining than the galas of the whites. January not only earned his bread through Mozart and Rossini, cotillions and schottisches and *valses brilliantes.* They were the meat and drink of his soul, the fire at which he warmed himself.

For a year he'd lived in pain, after the death of his wife in the cholera. For a year music had been his only refuge.

After that year, there were other refuges in the city as well.

He looked up now, studying Rose's long delicate profile. The cool mouth that was so sensitive beneath the mask of its primness. The way her smile came and went, as if in girlhood she'd been punished for laughing at the world's absurdity. Slim strong hands, stained with ink—she was currently making her living correcting young boys' Greek examinations for a school on the Rue d'Esplanade—and blistered from the chemical experiments that were her refuge and her joy.

A winter of friendship. Of sitting in the markets by the coffee stands with ten cents' worth of jambalaya bought off a cart and talking with other musicians, or walking Rose home through the foggy evenings and seeing the gold lamplight bloom in windows all along the streets.

A winter of rest.

Sugar-grinding. Roulaison. The suffocating heat of the mill-house and the clammy damp of the cabins. The ache of muscles lifting, hauling, dragging armfuls of sharp-leaved cane after not quite enough food and never ever enough rest. The pain that settled into your bones when you couldn't even remember when last you'd slept to your heart's content.

Fear of being beaten. Fear of being sold.

Simon Fourchet's flaying voice and the sense that it would make no difference to anyone if he, Benjamin January, lived or died.

"You think I'd be safe there?" He threw the words at his sister like a lump of dirt. "Maybe Fourchet'll make sure I don't get kidnapped and sold, but that's not going to keep the killer from slipping poison into my food if he guesses why I'm there. And it won't keep me from being beat up by men who think I'm carrying tales to the master. Killed, maybe, if there really is rebellion planned."

"Then you'll just have to be careful," said Olympe, "won't you?"

January visited a free attorney of color whom he knew, who drew up a variety of documents attesting to and reinforcing the already recorded and notarized fact of

January's freedom. Copies were deposited with Lieutenant Abishag Shaw of the New Orleans City Guard, with January's mother and both sisters, and with John Davis, owner of the Théâtre d'Orleans and various gambling parlors and public ballrooms about the city, who for two years had been one of January's principal employers. Two copies went to Simon Fourchet's lawyer.

"Not that it will do the slightest bit of good," said January grimly, "should Fourchet's overseer, or his son, turn out to be a cheat and a slave-thief. Altruism is all very well, and I'm really sorry for those folks on Mon Triomphe, but I'd just as soon not try to convince some cracker cotton-farmer in the Missouri Territory to write to the New Orleans City Notary about whether or not I'm a free man."

Lieutenant Shaw, slouched so deeply in a corner of the big stone watchroom of the town prison, the Cabildo, that he appeared to be lying in the chair on his shoulder blades with his boots on his desk, raised mild gray eyes from the documents, and scratched with businesslike thoroughness under his shabby collar. "Prob'ly wouldn't do you much good anyways, if'n they're like my uncle Zenas—Zenas and his family went to Missouri to grow cotton." Shaw scratched again, and looped a long strand of his greasy ditchwater hair back around one ear.

"Zenas can plug a squirrel through the eye at two hundred and fifty yards and build a house from the ground up includin' the furniture usin' only an ax, but he can't write for sour owl-shit. You think you'll be in much more danger there than you'd be just walkin' around here?"

Shaw asked the question sincerely, and sincerely, January had to admit that in certain sections of New Orleans—the entrepôt and hub of slave-trading for the entire region—he was probably in more peril of kidnapping than he'd be on Mon Triomphe.

"It's easy for you to say. Sir." In his tone he heard his own defeat. The thought of what he was going to do made his stomach clench with dread, but he knew that Rose and Olympe were right. He understood that he could not feel anger that none would give justice to slaves, if he wasn't willing to work for that justice himself.

"I understand that," said Shaw. "And I hope you understand I'd do it, if'n I didn't have certain physical limitations that'd make me middlin' unconvincin' as a cane-hand."

January met his eyes with a bitter retort on his lips, but he knew Shaw. And he saw in the Kentuckian's quiet gaze that yes, this man would go out into the fields to trap the murderer . . .

If he didn't happen to be white. And, as he'd said, a middling unconvincing cane-hand.

So he only said, "What? You don't think you could pass?" and Shaw relaxed and returned his unwilling grin. January reached into the pocket of his neat brown corduroy livery for his watch and tightened his lips when it wasn't there. The watch was silver, bought in Paris after he'd given up work as a surgeon and returned to being a musician. As a surgeon he'd never been able to afford such a thing, for even in France no one would choose a black surgeon over a white.

At least in France, he reflected dourly, he wouldn't have had to go searching through pawnshops for weeks to recover it, after it had been stolen by the same louts who'd cut his coat to ribbons and torn up his music.

Along with his other few valuables, the watch was safe at Olympe's house now. A slave would not possess such a thing.

"Yore pal Sefton'll be along," said Shaw reassuringly. "What do you know about Fourchet's son?"

"Not much." January drew a deep breath, tried to convince his muscles to relax. "He's a few years older than I. Esteban, his name is. I think his mother was the daughter of a Spanish wine-merchant here in town."

"Juana Villardiga, accordin' to the records." Shaw folded his hands over the papers, rumpling them as if they were yesterday's newspaper instead of the proofs that January would need, should his freedom be in jeopardy. The morning was chill, and through the arched doors at the inner side of the watchroom the Cabildo courtyard was dusky still. Two prisoners swabbed the flagstones under the watchful eye of a blue-uniformed City Guard.

January's eyes felt gritty. After spending most of the evening getting the documents drawn up and finding musician friends to replace him in his engagements to play at this or that party until after the sugar harvest—not an easy matter, given the perennial paucity of good musicians in the town—he'd gone late to bed, and in the few hours that he *had* slept, had dreamed of being a child again, and a slave.

"In 1802 Fourchet married again, a woman name of Camille Bassancourt who came here with her aunt from Paris. They had three sons and two daughters—"

"After my time." January shook his head. "We left Bellefleur in 1801. I only remember Esteban."

Shaw used the corner of the top document to pick his teeth, brown with tobacco like a row of discolored tombstones. He was a lanky man who looked as if he'd been put together from random lengths of cane, close to January's height and homely as a mongrel dog. "The girls an' one boy are still livin' . . ." He grubbed in a pocket and consulted a much-scribbled fragment of paper. "Solange is at school with the Ursulines here in town. Robert—that's the boy—an' his wife just got back on the sixth from takin' Elvire, the older girl, to a boardin' school in Poitiers."

Given the man's raspy, flatboat drawl, it always surprised January that Shaw pronounced the names of French cities and individuals correctly.

"Accordin' to Fourchet's lawyer, Camille died in '28." Shaw extracted a plug of tobacco from his trouser pocket, picked a knot of lint off it, and bit off a hunk the size of a Spanish dollar. "Fourchet remarried this past April to a girl name of Marie-Noël Daubray—"

"Daubray?" interrupted January. "Isn't that the name—"

"Of the fellas he thinks might be behind the mill fire an' all? It is." He gestured with the fragment of paper—a bill from Berylmann, a gunsmith on Canal Street, January saw—and concentrated for a moment on reducing the brown chunk in the corner of his jaws to a manageable consistency. "Their first cousin once removed, in fact. Granddaughter of their oldest brother, which is what the lawsuit's about. What's our boy Esteban like?"

"Stiff," said January, the first description that came to his mind. "I haven't seen him since he was twelve, remember, and I was only eight." He leaned back in the chair beside Shaw's cluttered desk with half-closed eyes, summoning back the silent boy who'd stare with such repelled fascination at the naked breasts of the women in the fields. "But he was stiff. He walked around with his shoulders up—" He demonstrated, bracing his whole body in imitation of that tight, silent, awkward boy, and was aware of Shaw's cool eyes flickering over him, reading what that imitation had to say.

"He didn't speak much to anyone. He was clumsy.

You expected him to fall over any minute. You know how there are people that it makes you uncomfortable to talk to? They stand wrong, or they stand too close; it takes them forever to say anything and when they do it's never quite what they mean. That's Esteban. Or it was," he amended, "a quarter century ago."

"Well, Maestro—" Shaw uncoiled his slow height from his chair, dumped the papers on the desk, and glanced across at the wall clock someone had affixed behind the sergeant's high desk. "People don't change that much, boy to man. Oh, you might not recognize who they are, exactly, but unless he works to do somethin' about it, a awkward boy's gonna grow to a awkward man. Same as a girl who's cruel to her pets ain't anyone I'd want to be the mother of my children later on down the road. I don't know how much use any of this'll be to you. . . ."

"All of it's of use." January followed him across the big dim stone-flagged room to the outer door. "Any of it's of use. You have to understand what the pattern is, before you can see where it breaks."

From the Cabildo's front doors they looked out past the cobalt shadows of the arcade and across the gutter to the bustling Place d'Armes. Mid-morning in autumn, and all the world was out enjoying the mild sunshine. The carriages of the wealthy jostled axles with carts of cabbages. A tall old man walked past with a basket of pink roses on his head, and a beggar-woman at her ease on the cathedral steps, her hair a white aurora of chaos, slowly devoured an orange and spit the seeds in great joyful leaping arcs into the gutter. January remembered the rainy gray of Paris in the winter and wanted to fling out his arms and laugh.

Whatever else could be said about it, New Orleans was New Orleans. There was no place like it in the world.

"If it had been clear who's doing the actual poisoning—making the actual voodoo-marks, cutting harnesses and sawing axles—Fourchet wouldn't have come to you. This isn't like coming into a tavern and seeing a weeping woman and a dead lover and a husband with a smoking pistol in his hand. With a hundred and fifty people involved it's not even likely that I'm going to find just one, or two, unaccounted for at any given time."

Shaw's eyebrows lifted. "I figured with slaves in the field you'd at least be able to keep track of where they was."

"That's because you've never tried to do it." There was wry pride in January's voice. "That's what scares the hell out of the whites, you know. Especially out on the plantations. You've got sixty, seventy, eighty grown men, fifty or sixty women—What are you going to do? Keep them in chains all the time? The drivers keep an eye on things and the overseer keeps an eye on things and you know damn well that if somebody wants to sneak away badly enough—if they don't care about getting a beating if they get caught—they'll sneak away. That's what makes them crazy.

"It's a war," he added softly. "Whether or not some of them plan organized rebellion, it's war. And you have to fight for every inch, a hundred times a day. That's why you have to look for a pattern."

"Waffle man, waffle man," sang a strolling vendor. *"Wash his face in the fryin' pan . . ."*

January felt for his watch again. "I can work with the men, live among them enough to hear rumors, at least so that I can find out who was where when. If there *is* a conspiracy, a revolt being planned, I think it'll be pretty clear. But if it's just one man, I'm not sure I'll find our killer—almost certainly not before he kills Fourchet. So I need to know the pattern. Why is this happening *now*? Why not last month or last year? What made the bearable unbearable? That's why you told Fourchet to speak to me, wasn't it?"

Shaw spit in the general direction of the gutter. His aim, as usual, was abysmal. "That's why."

Beyond the levee, the smokestacks of the steamboats poured sullen columns of soot into the dirty sky. At this season they lined the wharves three and four deep, and more tacked around out in the open river, keeping up their head of steam and their boiler-pumps working while waiting for a berth. January felt for his watch yet again, muttered an oath, and looked back over his shoulder at the watchroom clock, then turned back to scan the faces of the crowd.

"Boat ain't due to leave til ten," Shaw remarked, as if he weren't following January's thoughts. "And you know as well as I do they never do."

"Wherever he is," January responded gloomily, "I'm going to strangle Hannibal Sefton."

Fourchet's voice, braying out curses, caught his attention. Looking across the crowd to the levee, January saw the man on the deck of the small stern-wheeler on which January himself and his friend Hannibal Sefton had purchased tickets last night. One of the porters had dropped his valise; the boat's master lashed out with the whip he still held and caught the man a cut across the back. After the brutality he'd witnessed yesterday January had raised an objection to traveling on the *Belle Dame,* but Fourchet would have nothing to do with American boats, and Captain Ney was the only Creole master in town at the moment.

Fourchet's two servants hastily took up the luggage and carried it to the cargo hold. The taller servant took the bags inside. The shorter, given a moment's leisure, turned at the deck railing and gazed back across the square at the cathedral, like a man drinking in the sight.

Something in the way he stood made January remember the field hands yesterday evening on the *Bonnets o' Blue.*

Of course, he thought. Fourchet's butler had just been poisoned. In addition to finding a spy, Fourchet had come into town to look for a new butler.

Fourchet yelled, "Baptiste, damn you!" His voice carried like a crow's caw through the din. The new servant fled after his companion.

January's hand curled into a fist.

"You familiar with Mon Triomphe, Maestro?" Shaw asked. "Ever been there?"

January shook his head. "I was only seven when St.-Denis Janvier bought my mother. I'd never been off Bellefleur. Mon Triomphe was very isolated in those days, but of course now the whole of the riverbank on both sides is in sugar as far as Baton Rouge."

"Well, I got to jawin' some last night with this an' that pilot, after Mr. Fourchet told me as how you'd agreed to go." Shaw spit again toward the cypress-lined gutter that divided the arcade from the open Place; the brown wad of expectorant missed its target by feet. "It did kinda float through my mind as how we's askin' a lot of you, to go up there pretendin' as how you're a slave, and the only ones knowin' you're not is your pal Sefton and Fourchet himself. Now, we know somebody's out to kill Fourchet. And much as I like Sefton you do got to admit *reliable* ain't the word that springs most skeedaciously to mind when his name is mentioned. So I tell you what."

He pointed across the square, to a woman selling bandannas among the fruit stands that clustered beneath the trees. The bright-colored wares were tacked to a crosspole and fluttered like some kind of exotic tree themselves.

"You go buy yourself seven bandannas: red, yellow, blue, green, purple, black, an' white. Accordin' to the pilots, see, the riverbank at the north end of the plantation caved in 'bout three years ago, openin' a chute between it an' Catbird Point. Catbird Island, they calls it now. That changed the current, an' built up a bar just above the plantation landin'—blamed if that river ain't like a housewife with new furniture, always movin' things around. When Fourchet cleared an' cut for a new landin' they left an oak tree on the bank above it, that's big enough that the pilots all sight by it comin' down that stretch of the river."

A woman darted through the levee crowds, a flash of cheap bright calicos between stacks of orange pumpkins and dusty cotton bales, skirts gathered up in her hands. On the deck of the *Belle Dame* Fourchet's new butler pushed his way between the laden porters to the gangway, to seize the woman's hands, to kiss her with a fervent desperation that told its own tale. She was a tall woman, plump and awkward in her ill-fitting simple dress, and as they clung to one another her face bent down to his.

"You be like that old Greek fella," Shaw said, "that was supposed to change the sail of his boat from black to white if'n the news he brung was good. You tie a different bandanna to that oak tree every day, just in the order I said 'em. Red, yellow, blue, green, purple, black, an' white, white bein' for Sunday so's you can remember."

"Don't tell me you've convinced riverboat pilots to remember the order as well." Anger twisted again in January's heart as he watched the couple on the gangway. There was nothing he could do about their pain; Shaw's calm arrangements and placid voice grated at him. "I never met a pilot who could take his mind off the river long enough to remember what color necktie he has on."

"Pilots, hell," said Shaw. "They just told me the tree was there. I paid off the stokers on the *Lancaster,* that makes the Baton Rouge run, and the *Missourian* and the *New Brunswick,* that'll be bound on back from St. Louis a week or ten days from now, and cabin stewards on the *Vermillion,* the *Boonslick,* and the *Belle Dame,* to come here and tell me what color the bandanna is and what day they seen it. It ain't much, Maestro," he added apologetically. "But at least it'll let me know yore still there."

January felt sudden shame at his anger: Shaw was doing what he could to keep him safe. In last night's dreams of childhood he'd been hiding in the barn at Bellefleur, and a monster was after him: a monster that shouted in a hoarse drunken voice, a reeling shadow with a whip in his hand. *Come out, you little bastard. Come out or I'll sell you down the river.*

He'd waked in freezing sweat, as similar dreams had waked him, many nights across the years.

On the gangway the butler and the woman clung together, not speaking. It was the threat every master held over the head of every slave, up and down the eastern coast of the American states and in the new cotton lands of Alabama, Mississippi, Georgia. *I'll sell you down the river.* To the cane plantations of Louisiana.

To Hell.

It occurred to him as he crossed the square toward the bandanna woman that his mother had sold him down the river by the act of giving him birth.

To hell with Fourchet, he thought. To hell with

Olympe, and Mother, and these god-rotted colored kerchiefs and wondering if I'm going to be found as a spy and beaten to death by the other slaves, or poisoned, or kidnapped and sold—or just break the hands that are my livelihood and my joy.

His fingers trembled with anger as he counted out fourteen cents into the woman's palm. Stowed seven bright squares of cloth in his jacket pockets.

Let Fourchet die and rot, Olympe had said to him last night, as he and she had walked from the market back to their mother's house, to tell her of his change of mind. *You're doing this to save every man and woman on the place who didn't try to kill him.*

So he crossed the square to the arcade again, to the thin lanky figure awaiting him in the shadows. Though it was probably impossible over the competing din of the waffle man, the fruit vendors, the stevedores singing a chant as they loaded up the clay jars of olive oil that plantations bought in such quantities, and a German sailor having a shouting match with a woman in blue hair-ribbons, January imagined he could still hear Fourchet's voice, like a carrion-bird's as he rasped out instructions on the hurricane deck to the red-coated, hard-faced master of the *Belle Dame.*

Rose was right about one thing, January thought. With Fourchet's money he would find somewhere else to live. Then he would never be in a position like this again.

Who am I fooling? As long as I'm her son she'll feel she has the right to ask of me what she will.

"A captain bold in Halifax,
Who dwelt in country quarters,
Seduced a maid who hanged herself
One Monday in her garters . . ."

January winced at the light, hoarse voice scraping over the English ballad, slurred and stammering and yet perfectly true.

Shaw muttered, "Oh, Lordy."

Hannibal Sefton was making his way along the arcade in front of the Cabildo to its doors. He did this with great care, caroming off the square brick pillars, one hand outstretched to catch himself against the building's plastered wall, then retrieving his balance only to loop away toward the pillars again. The portmanteau he carried—his violin case strapped to its side—nearly overbalanced him. One of the chained prisoners engaged in cleaning out the gutter caught the fiddler by the arm and rescued the luggage moments before it went into the brimming muck. Hannibal bowed profoundly.

"Bene facis, famulo probo." The fiddler removed his hat and placed it over his heart, then spoiled the effect by coughing desperately. The prisoner supported him, apparently not much put out at the thin ragged form of the white man clinging to his filthy sleeve. *"Medio tutissimus ibis."* Hannibal gestured grandly back at the arcade, took one step in the direction of Shaw and January standing in the doorway, then collapsed in a laudanum-smelling heap.

Across the Place d'Armes the *Belle Dame*'s whistle brayed. Above the square, the cathedral's clock spoke its ten slow chimes.

"Good luck," said Shaw, without irony, and shook January's hand.

January glanced from the unconscious Hannibal across to Fourchet, bellowing down at his new butler, and his stomach tightened. He shoved the last folded bandanna into his pocket, pulled on his gloves, and went to hoist Hannibal bodily to one shoulder, as if he were a sack of meal. Bending his knees he picked up the portmanteau—his own, in fact, for whatever luggage the consumptive Hannibal had once possessed had been sold years ago to purchase opium or medicine—and, thus burdened, crossed the square to the gangplank. A number of the gentlemen on the canopied hurricane-deck pointed at January and laughed, assuming not unreasonably that this was his assigned job in life: to carry his master's luggage and, when necessary, his master. But glancing up he saw Fourchet gazing down at him with contempt in his eyes.

THREE

It was long past dark when they reached Mon Triomphe, and January would have given much—if not quite everything he possessed—to go back to yesterday afternoon and refuse to undertake the journey. Last night's dream returned to him again and again: the staggering shadow that stank of liquor, the sweat of terror at the sound of the whip. Always before he'd waked from this dream to reassure himself, *It can't happen to me now. I'm free.*

He'd installed Hannibal in his bunk in the men's cabin, drawn the curtain, and gone out in quest of the galley, praying that when the fiddler came to he'd be in possession of enough of his senses to recall the story they'd concocted the night before.

The *Belle Dame,* like many of the newer boats on the river, was long and narrow. The galley, situated between the men's cabin and the women's, was barely more than a hall. The saloon up front, which doubled as a dining room, was like the lobby of a modest hotel: worn Turkey carpets on the floor, tables of dark oak, men playing short whist or vingt-et-un. By the murmuring voices, January gathered there were few Americans on board. *Thank God for small favors, anyway,* he thought. The last thing he needed in his current frame of mind was to have his fellow passengers bidding on him all afternoon.

"Will you need help with him?" Fourchet's new butler was already in the galley, fitting out a tray to take around to one of the vessel's two minuscule staterooms. His neatly gloved hands trembled as he arranged the simple china cup and saucer, the small coffeepot and dish of sugar lumps, the napkin and spoon and the plate of buttered pastries; the flesh around his eyes was swollen with tears. Where had she gone, that tall plump woman in her bright dress, after the boat was poled and pushed from the wharf? How would she get through the remainder of her day?

"Thank you, sir, no." January remembered to slur his words and drop the endings, like the field hands did, a mode of speech that had been thrashed out of him by his teachers when he was eight. He had a clear mental picture of the man he was supposed to be, a field hand taken from the quarters and put in charge of the feckless scion of a wealthy family, simply because he was big and loyal and not terribly bright. The kind of slave it would be natural to offer to one's host to help with the harvest, and the kind of man who would accept the change of status without fuss.

"Least I knows where his medicine is," he added, and accepted the coffeepot, the cup and saucer, the horn spoon that the *Belle Dame's* cook gave him, and set them on the tray carelessly, any old how, as he'd seen scullery maids do in the big Paris households where he'd played at balls or taught piano to children.

And like the upper cooks in those Parisian kitchens, the butler Baptiste corrected and tidied the layout, though unlike the French cooks he asked politely, "May I?" and then, "This your regular job, sir?"

January threw a note of helplessness into his voice. "No, sir. Abraham—that's Michie Georges's cook—does trays and such mostly." *And let's remember,* he told himself grimly, *that Michie Georges is Hannibal's imaginary wealthy father-in-law and Abraham's the cook, next time you have to produce names of the household you come from.*

"Line up the spoon with the side of the tray like this." The round, neat little hands made their adjustments without impatience or condescension. "Bowl goes down, not up, so everyone can see the monogram if there is one. Cup right in the center, pot here. They like things to look nice."

"They blessed well better look nice for Michie Fourchet." The doorway darkened with the tall slim form of Fourchet's valet. The man's livery was foppishly neat, dark cravat tied in a severe little bow and thin black curls pomaded smooth. The valet ran a critical eye over both trays and nodded, just a tiny motion, to himself, as if sorry there was nothing to correct. "Any little thing sets him off: forks and knives not aligned, one curtain shut an inch more than the other. Anything. He beat your predecessor unconscious once for having dirty sleeves, when he'd told him himself to dust the ledgers in his office. So keep your buttons polished and your linen spotless."

He glanced at January, sizing him up with that dark sardonic eye: his size, his clothing, the way he'd spoken, the way he held himself—awkward and a little shy, as if fully conscious of the superiority of the two house-servants and even the steamboat's slovenly cook. Then he turned back to Baptiste. "You'd better get that up to him."

"I will do that, M'sieu Cornwallis."

The valet walked away.

"Thank you, sir," said January, as Baptiste picked up his tray.

The butler took a deep breath, nodded, and went out to do his first service for his master.

The cook, looking through the door after Cornwallis's erect figure, said, "Damn Protestant Kaintuck nigger," and went back to the preparation of lunch.

Carrying his own tray back to the men's cabin—a journey that involved sidestepping crated dry goods, barrels of blankets and calico, boxes of spermaceti candles, decanters packed in straw, a small pile of pigs of lead, and a dozen trunks stacked on the deck—January reflected on the fact that the cook, whom the valet obviously scorned for being of almost certainly pure African descent and menial employment, should look down on the valet for his Virginia accent and the religious preferences that accent implied.

During January's childhood, Fourchet had never bothered to convert his slaves. Even the house-servants had only the thinnest veneer of Christianity. St.-Denis Janvier had seen to his religious instruction as well as his education, and January remembered clearly being cautioned about the evils and ignorance of Protestants, a rarity in those days. Since his return he'd been conscious of how many American slaves were coming into New Orleans now from Virginia, Georgia, and the Carolinas, and of how the French-speaking Catholic slaves—even the ones who followed up Mass by attendance at the voodoo dances in Congo Square—tended to shun them.

And vice versa, of course.

Even before he knocked on the door of the men's cabin he heard Hannibal's voice inside. "Of course I'm drunk," the fiddler was saying. "But I'm not stupid, and I assure you I've imbibed enough opium in the course of a misspent life that I've learned to manage quite nicely. Benjamin, *amicus meus* . . ." He propped himself a little on the pillows as January entered, and Fourchet stood back a half-pace from the bunk. "Tell this gentleman about the time I drove Monsieur Marigny's carriage down Rue Bourbon after having quaffed a good four fingers of the finest Kendal Black Drop."

"Drink your coffee." January set the tray on Hannibal's knees, which were so thin they barely lifted above the level of the bunk's meager mattress. "Sir."

He glanced around the men's cabin, confirming his original observation that they were alone. To Fourchet he said, "As someone who's known Monsieur Sefton for two years, I can assure you he's usually less inebriated than he seems. I don't think we need fear his giving away any secrets."

Unless, he thought, *he gets really neck-shot*—something Hannibal did seldom, but did with fiendish timing for those few occasions on which it was most important that he be sober.

Fourchet regarded him with an arctic eye. "I don't imagine you would have been stupid enough to propose an alliance with someone you believed to be as untrustworthy as most drunkards are," he said. "But considering the pains we've taken to arrange a story, as you termed it last night, I'm at a loss to think of a convincing reason for me to offer the shelter of my roof to a sodden reprobate. No matter how desperately he counterfeits sickness."

Hannibal coughed, with a violence and a gluey, glottal note to it that, January thought uneasily, were no counterfeit. The wasting effects of his consumption seemed to have abated with the cooler weather, but with his shirt open and his long hair trailing loose from its ribbon over his shoulders, he still looked like a ghost just back from a night on the tiles. When he regained his breath he said, "Easy. I will have done you a great service, which you feel obliged to repay by taking me in when I'm stricken ill."

"What service? You can't even do up your bootlaces," Fourchet said.

"Then it's fortunate you don't need bootlaces done up. However, I will do you the service of telling you that the gentleman who arranged a half-hour or so ago to go halves with you in the purchase of Chickasaw lands has no more option to title on those lands than I have option to title on the Parthenon of Athens."

Fourchet's eyes widened in alarm. "How do you know what Monsieur LaBarre and I discussed? You haven't been out of this room!"

"I saw you pass the door deep in conversation with him a few minutes ago, and I know there's only one thing Slinky LaBarre holds deep conversations about with strangers, and that's a tract of territory along the Arkansas River that the government is about to negotiate from the tribes. I hope you didn't give him a draft."

The planter said nothing for a time, only tightened his jaw as if chewing something tough and rancid-tasting. January was familiar with the tic. "And what do you know about it?" Fourchet demanded at length.

"Only what I've heard about Slinky from other gamblers, cheats, river pirates, and opium-sodden reprobates in the saloons." Hannibal's voice weakened and he leaned his back against the pillows; January could see the flecks of blood that tipped his mustache hairs. "I'll think of some other service for me to do you if that doesn't suit: the location of one of Lafitte's caches of treasure, perhaps? Or it could be I have title to Chickasaw land myself."

"My family knows how I feel about drunkards and opium-eaters." The savage loathing in Fourchet's voice was deeper than any disgust or contempt. "When we go ashore at Triomphe I'll thank you to restrict your habits to something that can be accounted for by illness, not dissipation."

"I'll commence practicing my coughing immediately." Hannibal gave him the ghost of a military salute.

Mouth almost square-cornered with distaste, the planter resumed his hat and made to go. January said, "If you could spare us a few more minutes of your time, sir?"

Fourchet glanced pointedly at the door, as if to remind him that anyone could enter at any time. This wasn't, January knew, actually likely. No one in their right mind would linger in the passenger cabins of a small steamboat if they didn't have to.

Like most stern-wheelers, the *Belle Dame* was a smallish boat of shallow draft, and what it lost in the smallness of its hold space was made up out of the cabins, galley, staterooms, and saloon. The men's cabin was narrow and cramped, odorous from the proximity of the galley, and Spartan at best. Despite its distance from the boiler room, the walls shuddered with the regular thudding pulse of the engine. Trunks, valises, and portmanteaux that either wouldn't fit in the hold or would be required before many hours had passed heaped the floor in front of and beside the bunks. Most passengers sought the distractions of cards in the saloon, or braved the chill on the hurricane deck above.

Fourchet turned back, nostrils flared with impatience as Hannibal set down his untasted coffee and went into a paroxysm of coughing. "For what?"

"A little information." January knelt, and dug through the valise for the first laudanum bottle he could lay hands on. He had to hold it steady while his friend drank. "Who the members of your household are. Where they were on the night of the fire in the sugar-mill, and when the mule barn caught fire. Who besides Gilles had the keys to the cellaret the cognac was in, and the keys to the mill."

The planter looked about to snap some stricture about the medicine, but drew a breath instead, as if forcibly reminding himself to keep his own affairs in focus. "You've seen Cornwallis," he said at last. "He's my valet, he's been with me about six years. He came warranted honest and sober but I suspect they wanted to get rid of him for some reason, for in the end they let him go for seven-fifty. My son Esteban's valet is Agamemnon—a creeping, sneaking, prissy catamite if you ask me—and Kiki's the cook. The maids are Ariadne and Henna. My son Robert's man and his wife's maid they took with them to Paris, and they weren't even present when the trouble started. Doucette does the sewing. There's Ti-Jeanne the washerwoman, but she wouldn't have had access to the keys of the cellaret, let alone the—"

"I didn't mean the servants," said January quietly. "I mean your family. The people who stand to profit from your death."

The planter's face flamed. "By God, if I have to stand here and take this from a—"

"You don't, sir," said January steadily. "But if your wife was with child, and an accoucheur asked after her health, would you keep it from him if she'd had three miscarriages in the past three years?"

Fourchet, who had opened his mouth to shout him down, checked, and closed it again, listening in simmering silence.

"Would you keep silent about her passing blood, or fainting? I'm a doctor, M'sieu." *Well, a surgeon, anyway,* he thought, but Fourchet didn't have to know that. "I've seen men who do all this and more, and in so doing endanger the lives of those they love by their unwillingness to tell the complete truth."

Footfalls clumped outside the door. January knelt at once and pretended to be rearranging something in Hannibal's valise. Since the cabin did not go all the way through the width of the boat, but backed its inner end onto the wall of one of the staterooms, Fourchet left it entirely, passing in the doorway the man who entered, a stout fair gentleman who nodded a friendly greeting to him and was roundly snubbed.

Nothing discomposed, the newcomer nodded to Hannibal. He asked, "Is all well with the Herr?"

Hannibal lifted a hand in assent and replied in the German in which he'd been addressed. "I'm better now, thank you."

The German gentleman went to his own bunk and fetched a greatcoat. "Might I ask where you are bound, sir? You seem in no fit case to travel."

"St. Louis," said Hannibal faintly. "If I make it so far."

"T'cha, that is not good." The stranger divided his worried glance between Hannibal and January. "Please let me know if I may be of any assistance."

"Fool," muttered Fourchet after the German left. "That's the kind of man who ends up with parasites on his hands and in his house for months, sucking him dry." He had kindled a cigar while on deck, chewing it now angrily as he stared down at the fiddler lying on his bunk. "And serve him right."

Resentment in every craggy line of his face, he dragged up the room's solitary chair and settled in it. "These are they who'd have access to the keys to the cellaret," he said abruptly. "My son Esteban, and through him that sneaking valet of his, Agamemnon. My wife . . ." He could barely bring out the words. "And I presume either of the maids, who could have lifted them from her room if they'd had the wits to do it. My son Robert and his wife weren't back yet from Paris when the mill burned, and they had, as I said, their servants with them: Leander and that good-for-nothing slut Vanille."

"What about your overseer?"

"Thierry? He keeps his own liquor in his own house." Disgust tinged Fourchet's voice, as if he'd sniffed wormwood. "He has no call to have a key. But you know as well as I do the thievery that goes on among blacks. Any one of them could have taken the key."

Well, it would be harder for a field hand to get it, January thought, unless of course he worked out trade or blackmail with one of the house-servants, who generally held the field hands in complete contempt. At that point a copy could be made, if the plantation blacksmith was clever enough. But he said nothing. These were the secrets of the quarters, not to be shared with *les blankittes,* for you never knew against whom information might be used.

Instead he said, "Tell me about the day the mill burned."

"Evening." Fourchet bit savagely on the cigar with one side of his mouth and leaked smoke from the other. "Just at sunset. The men were still in the ciprière. Reuben, my sugar-boss, saw the mill door open and fire inside. He ran in and started beating at the flames, and only fortune saved him, for the mill door blew shut behind him and jammed. We had to open it with an ax, and by that time smoke had overcome him, and the fire spread. We found trash—cane leaves and hay, and last year's dried bagasse—jammed up under the rafter joints, and in the timbers that supported the grinders."

"Who is 'we'?" asked January. "If Reuben was alone and ran in and the door blew shut behind him, how was he saved?"

"One of the pickaninnies. Boy claimed he was gathering kindling—playing in the mule barn more likely, where he'd no business to be—and saw the smoke, and heard Reuben shouting. He and his brother ran to the ciprière and got the men."

January sat silent, gazing at the narrow glaring rectangle of the half-open door and the brown river beyond. It was low water, and gray snags reached up like demon hands, clutching for the hulls and the wheels of the boats. More dangerous still would be those just beneath the surface, mere scratches or ruffles on the glassy flow. Sandbars made slanting riffles, or accrued enough flotsam to build up into islands—the larger side-wheelers veered into the heavy current of the main channel to avoid them, but the *Belle Dame* skimmed "inside" these obstructions, between them and the tree-grown bank. Above the engine's jarring heartbeat, January heard the leadsmen calling the depth: *"Quarter twain. Quarter twain. Mark twain."*

"There were no men nearer?"

"We were behind the harvest, I tell you," snapped Fourchet. "We'd had rain for three days. I had both gangs out cutting wood, Sunday or no Sunday, and most of the yard-men as well. Even the gardener. There was no one about the place except the house-servants."

"And Reuben, evidently."

"He'd been working in the mill on and off all day, making it ready for the grinding."

During the roulaison, the near-universal rule of Sunday as a day of "rest"—which for a slave meant labor on one's own provision grounds instead of for the master's cash crop—was suspended in the interests of the cane. January remembered how the field dust gummed in the cut-cane-juice on his hands, his clothes, his face; how everything was sticky with it.

Suddenly and clearly he had a vision of his father rising in freezing darkness and going outside to wash before joining the men for work, a tall shadow in the banked sulfurous dimness of the hearth.

Where had that memory come from? he wondered. As a rule he had few memories of his father.

"And how long was the grinding delayed?"

"Over a week. Too long—cane'll rot within two days. The sugar goes sour." He blew a vile-smelling cloud. "Reuben spent the day after the fire going over every inch of that mill. That's when he found the hoodoo-marks. The axle-beams of the grinders were charred black, but he said they hadn't been damaged, so he got the grinders running by the Tuesday. Two days later the main gang was down sick, puking and purging. More hoodoo work. I put as many as I could spare from the second gang in the fields with the women, and the women were more use than they at the work. The cane came in full of trash and stones, jamming up the grinders every five minutes. Reuben tried to pull a knot or something free and the mules spooked. The whole business broke and the grinding-rollers came down on him, and what with Esteban having to go to town and get new, and the delay of having a man set them up, we lost another week."

January was silent, trying to piece the images together in his mind. Sick at the thought of those huge toothed iron cylinders, monster jaws drooling the green sticky sap of the cane . . .

Came down on him . . . dear Jesus!

And all Fourchet saw was the delay. The planter pulled on his chewed cigar and brooded about the injustice of it all. On his bunk Hannibal lay with shut eyes, thin hands folded around the empty coffee cup. Above the *thwack-jerk* of the engine, the voices of the slaves on the deck outside could be heard:

"Suzette my beautiful friend,
Suzette my beautiful friend,
Pray to God for me.
I will wait for her,
I will work for her,
I'll carry cane for her upon my shoulder."

And they'll sell you down the river all the same, thought January. He knew the song in another form from town, but among the unfree, music was a thing to be transmuted, quickened or slowed to fit the changing seasons of the heart. He thought of Rose, sitting in the market arcades late last night after everything had been settled, looking out over the levee and drinking coffee. Of the moon near full, above the rising river mists. Of Baptiste's plump woman, running to the gangplank that morning with her bright skirts bunched up in her hands, to see her man one last time.

"You were with the men in the ciprière on the night of the fire?"

"Of course! Where else would I be? Damn blacks won't do a thing unless you're standing over them with a whip."

January opened his mouth to reply and then closed it. At the time—in the days of his childhood, his slavery—the endless, intricate dance of slave and master, of work and avoidance of work, had seemed to him the only manner in which life could be conducted. Looking back on it, he was still amazed that grown men and women should be astonished by their slaves' efforts to evade tasks that they themselves found too hard or too nasty, tasks demanded with no recompense but the simplest of food and the cheapest of shelter and clothing, with the constant threat of losing their friends and families thrown in.

He should, he reflected, never have gone to Paris. Or

else he should have stayed there, no matter how desperate the agony of his grief at his wife's death. He was no longer capable of accepting the custom of the country that at one time had been second nature to him.

A Frenchman would have burst out laughing at Fourchet's indignation.

And would probably have been shot.

"We were all there," continued the planter truculently. "Thierry'd been back at the mill with Reuben earlier in the day, but came out to the ciprière around noon. Esteban was working with another part of the gang, deeper in the trees."

Of course, thought January. Cutting trees wasn't like cutting cane. The main gang would have been split into a dozen little groups, scattered throughout the marshy tangle of cypress, black oak, hackberry thickets, and bramble.

"And the people who remained at the house?"

"Just those I've told you of." The planter hurled the mangled end of the cigar into the spittoon. "Cornwallis, Agamemnon, Gilles the butler, the two maids, the sewing women, the washerwoman. The yard hands like Scipio the potter, who's too old to be out in the woods, the cook, and the woman who makes the soap and candles—"

"And your wife," said January.

Fourchet bolted to his feet, veins bulging in his forehead. "My wife is the gentlest and most honorable soul who walks the face of the earth," he said, in a voice of iron quiet. "You will not speak of her in connection with anything—anything!—concerning this . . . this hoodoo, this vandal, this enemy of mine. She would no more have anything to do with such activities than she would—would—would forswear her faith or betray her country! If you speak again of her as you have, to me or to anyone else, believe me, I will have you whipped."

His hand lashed out and January flinched, but Fourchet in his anger only caught the back of the chair on which he'd been sitting, sending it crashing into the wall. "And that goes for you." He jabbed a finger down at Hannibal. Then with the vast savage violence January had remembered with terror in over thirty years of dreaming, he slammed from the cabin.

His footfalls crashed along the deck, then up the stairs to lose themselves in the promenade above.

The engine clanked in the silence like the labored panting of a wind-touched horse.

"I look forward to making the acquaintance of the gentlest and most honorable soul who walks the face of the earth." Hannibal spoke without opening his eyes. "Any reason for suspecting her of doctoring her husband's tipple? Beyond the obvious one, I mean."

"A woman married to a man who is habituated to violence doesn't need a reason beyond the obvious," said January quietly. "But no. And at the moment I don't suspect her particularly. It's just that she had as much opportunity as anyone else, and more than some, and she's among the group that stands to profit rather than to lose by her husband's death. And then again, if someone cries, *Don't look over there, don't look over there,* I generally can't resist a peek, to find out what it is I'm not supposed to be seeing. On the whole I'd like to know where all the snags and bars lie, if I'm going to navigate these waters."

No man of color—unless in the service of a passenger—being permitted on the rooftop promenade, January spent the remainder of the day watching the river from the cluttered lower deck. Beyond the saw grass and cypress of the batture, and above the low brow of the levee on the landward side, plantation houses seemed to drift by—square, white, ostentatious with pillars and summerhouses if the owner was an American; smaller, plainer, and brightly painted if Creole. When the *Belle Dame* slowed to maneuver among snags, or labored to buck a sandbar, January could pick out clearly the men and women on the galleries: planters' wives in dark neat wools and poplins, servants in plain calico dresses or simple dark livery. Children now and then raced in and out the long French doors, muslin-clad girls and boys in tight-buttoned skeleton suits, whose older sisters would be in the convent in town, whose brothers would be away at school.

And between the houses lay the endless dark green of the cane-fields, buzzards circling lazily overhead. Smoke poured skyward from mill after mill, and from the fields the still air shimmered with voices singing:

> *"The English guns they go bim-bim,*
> *The Kaintuck guns, they go zim-zim,*
> *I say to myself, Run save your skin,*
> *Run to the water's edge, O,*
> *Run to the water's edge . . ."*

The main gangs, the big men, January remembered, leaning on the rail, would be chopping the cane, while the women gathered and carted, and the second gang worked the mill. Fed the cut cane into the grinders and kept the fire going beneath the cauldrons with wood that had been cut and stored up all year against this grueling and terrible season. Once the mill was started, it never stopped. The grinders would halt only for a few moments, to change the mule teams, or to clear knots or rocks picked up with the cane. But the fires were never suffered to go out.

His father was a main-gang man. That much he recalled. Leaning on the rail, he tried to remember that tall quiet man with the tribal scars—country marks, they were called—on his face. But it hurt, like probing an unhealed wound.

Night after hot summer night in his childhood, January had sat on the gallery of the garçonnière, watching the lights across the yard where his mother entertained St.-Denis Janvier. January would watch until the lights went out and sometimes for hours afterwards, waiting for his father to come. He'd never spoken to his mother about the man, nor she to him. But those nights were printed so clearly on his mind, the dim glow of candles in the garrets and town houses visible beyond the roof, and the patterns of the stars in the dark velvet sky. Cicadas thrumming above the whine of mosquitoes, and the shrill cheep of crickets. In those days the ciprière had lain close to Rue Burgundy, a few streets away only.

He didn't remember when he'd quit waiting like that. Didn't remember anything about the last night that he'd done so, or the first night that he had not.

Only eventually, it became something that he no longer did.

"Ben?"

He turned his head to see the butler Baptiste.

"Michie Fourchet sent me to find you, to let you know that your master Michie Sefton's going to be going ashore at Mon Triomphe, to stay til he's feeling better."

January raised his brows and widened his eyes in what he hoped was a convincing expression of relieved joy, and gusted a sigh. "Thank God," he said. "All day I been wonderin' just what we'd do, with him sick and gettin' sicker by the look of it, and us bound all the way to St. Louis. Thank you. And bless your master, for such a kindness."

Baptiste managed a trace of a smile. "I must admit

I'm astonished. Michie Fourchet seems to me to be a—a hard man." He stammered a little over the words. His French was good, if a little Creole in its treatment of articles—he used *je* instead of *mo* to refer to himself, a refinement January was careful, in his new persona, to avoid. "I hope your master will feel better soon."

"Thank you." January shook his head. "It's the consumption, the doctors say. Seems like he get a little worse every year, no matter what they do."

"I know." Baptiste leaned his elbows beside January's on the railing and watched the miniature drama enacted in dumb show on the gallery of a white-pillared house: mistress chiding a sewing-maid, leaping to her feet, rustling into the house; the master emerging, catching the girl by the arm, speaking intently. Kissing her.

Trees intervened.

"My mistress—my old mistress, M'am Grasse—was consumptive also, and there wasn't a thing Michie Pierre didn't try to get her well. In the end he took her to Paris, where the doctors are better, they say." He stared out at the glittering riffle along the water's surface, while from the bow a leadsman called out *"Deep four . . . deep four . . . quarter less four . . ."*

"It help?" asked January, after several minutes of silence.

The little man glanced sidelong at him. "That I don't know. I hoped they'd take us with them—which was what Michie Pierre said they'd do." He opened his mouth to say something more, then closed it.

But they found they needed another fifteen hundred dollars instead.

January could see it, in the tears that slowly filled the elderly man's eyes. But there was nothing—literally nothing—that he could say.

Traveling without interruption, a fast boat could have covered the distance between New Orleans and

Mon Triomphe in five hours. But all the way upriver, the *Belle Dame* stopped at plantation landings, to take on cargo or passengers, to drop off letters and small consignments of goods. January checked on Hannibal twice, and found him as well as could be expected—though bored senseless with nothing to do but pretend to be on his deathbed—and tried to get up a conversation with Cornwallis, only to meet with a cold sarcasm and the kind of mocking double-entendres that couldn't be answered without revealing himself to be a good deal more intelligent than he was supposed to be. Once, in his idle rounds of the decks, January heard the valet describing in detail to the new butler their master's habit of nailing up malefactors in a flour barrel in the barn, and Cornwallis's eyes glinted with spiteful satisfaction at the tale.

January wanted to say, *Don't pay any attention to that,* but couldn't. He knew Cornwallis spoke the truth.

Darkness fell. Mists rose from the river and rendered the moon away to a ravel of shining wool. Smoke from the mills hung thick in the raw air, and through night and fog smudges of gold burned like the maws of ovens, where the mills of every plantation blazed on through the night. January shivered, for it seemed to him they ran awfully close to the shore for low water, fog, and night, but Captain Ney, standing in the open pilothouse in his long coat of scarlet wool, seemed to know what he was doing. "Hell, he was born hereabouts, him," said the cook, when January went to fetch another pot of coffee for Hannibal. "I seen him take her so close to shore you could kiss a girl that was standin' on the batture. One day he may blow her up, for he do like to lay on the speed, but he never snag her."

Following the receipt of this Dutch comfort January reemerged from the galley to the unpromising sight of two rusted smokestacks poking up from the black waters: Here a boat had either been gutted on a sawyer or blown up her boilers. Above him the ship's bell clanged and a voice called, "Give us a little more steam."

At about eight the engine's *thud-thud-thud* altered yet again to a steady shuddering, and the whistles howled as the engine let off steam. From the darkness a voice called, "Mon Triomphe!" and yellow smears of torchlight spotted the batture's indistinct bulk.

Men put out in a boat with towlines. The *Belle Dame* could not maneuver into a dock the way a sidewheeler could. After a few minutes the boat began to move again, with the silent sideways steadiness of dead weight being hauled by main force. The mate, a short bearded man with a Spanish lilt to his voice, yelled, "Let's do this, then! Captain don't want to have to damp the fires."

Voices on the wharf, and the jangle of harness. A lookout would have warned the coachman of the steamboat's approach. January remembered angling for the job of lookout, a task more interesting than pulling weeds or gathering kindling, and being trumped out of it every time by a boy named Gideon, who was older and quick and silver-tongued. He wondered what had become of him.

The batture took shape through the mist. Above the landing loomed the dark baroque shape of a twisted oak tree, gesturing like Demosthenes warming to a Philippic peroration—an ideal place, January thought, to hang his bright-hued bandannas.

Today had been Friday. Tomorrow, Saturday, the kerchief would be black: purple for Christ's blood shed on a Friday, black for the day Our Lord spent in Hell. White for His resurrection—and then red for the red beans everyone in New Orleans cooked on Mondays when they did the wash. After a day of observing what every woman on the river was wearing, he had no doubt that the stokers and stewards would report the colors accurately to Shaw.

His hand sought the rosary in his pocket, the rosary that never left him, and the touch of the blue beads like the grasp of God's reassuring fingers around his own.

Hail Mary, full of grace, the Lord is with thee . . . Pray for us sinners. Pray for us sinners.

Me, and those I'm seeking to help in the house of chains.

Men pelted by him, manhandling the gangplank into position. A rope was tossed across the narrowing space of black water. Captain Ney descended the steps from the hurricane deck and spoke to Fourchet as the planter came around the corner of the boat's barnlike superstructure. The younger man was distant and wary, January saw, as if the captain had indeed grown up watchful of this unpredictably violent man.

In the torchlight on shore, January identified Esteban Fourchet at once—was it possible a man nearing fifty could look that much like the shuffle-footed boy he'd been?—and guessed the narrow-headed leathery gent in dark corduroy to be the overseer Thierry. The neat little fop in a beryl-green tailcoat would be the surviving son of Camille Bassancourt.

It was time to get Hannibal and the luggage, and go ashore.

And let's hope, January thought, as Fourchet's voice slashed the fog like an oyster shell tearing flesh, *Shaw keeps the colors straight in his mind as well, and comes hotfoot if the bandanna says the same color two days running.*

Because if something prevents me from changing the signals, I'll be either dead, or a slave somewhere for life.

FOUR

"This is Monsieur Sefton." Simon Fourchet gestured stiffly as January carried Hannibal, wrapped in a number of blankets against the night's raw chill, down the *Belle Dame*'s gangplank to the rough wharf floating at the river's edge. "He did me a good turn on the trip up from town, saved me from a bad investment. He'll be staying in the garçonnière until he's well enough to go on to St. Louis."

"Thank you," whispered Hannibal, and coughed—for effect, this time. In Paris, January had seen the great Kean expiring as Romeo. So, it appeared, had Hannibal. "I am indebted to you beyond what I can say."

It was sixty feet from the levee to the house, but a green-lacquered barouche waited for them at the top of the flight of shallow plank steps. "Ben, give Lundy M'sieu Sefton's bags and get on the back," ordered Fourchet curtly, as January helped Hannibal into the carriage and tucked the blankets around him. "Lundy, give Ben your torch and follow with the men. This is Baptiste." He nodded toward the new butler. "He'll be taking Gilles's place."

January took the torch from the slim white-jacketed man who bore it, and stepped up onto the footman's perch at the rear of the carriage. Thierry, the overseer, sprang up beside the coachman with a catlike lightness, and the driver's wary flinch told January what he had to expect from this man, when he was working under him in the fields.

"Robert, God damn you, leave the bags alone! We haven't got all night!"

The handsome young dandy sprang nervously away from the luggage pile and Captain Ney, and scrambled into the carriage as the vehicle jerked away.

"What'd you—uh—pay for him?" Esteban glanced back to where Baptiste and the others were picking up the various valises and portmanteaux under the Spanish deck-mate's snapped commands.

"Eleven hundred, from Davideaux."

"Not bad. How—uh—old is he?" They might have been speaking of a pack-pony. "Forty-eight? Um—uh—Things have been quiet here. We got—uh—ten acres cut today, and the new grinder's behaving itself. Oh, and Reuben died."

"Ten? Damn it, boy, those lollygagging niggers should have been able to clear off fifteen! Are you so stupid you don't realize we're weeks behind? Frost could hit us any day! Thierry, God damn you, I'd better see more cane coming in tomorrow or . . ."

So much, thought January sourly, for poor Reuben, dead of shock or gangrene or simply because he lacked the physical reserves to pull him through having his legs crushed by a thousand pounds of falling iron. The stretch of ground between the house and the levee's gentle rise was scattered with the native oaks of the area. Through their dark trunks away to his right January could see the hell-mouth glare of the sugar-mill door, and the shapes moving before it as the women unloaded the cane carts. The men of the first gang—having completed a day in the field that began the instant it was light enough to avoid injury—dragged wood from the sheds to feed the boilers, a long line of half-naked bronze figures struggling out of the night.

The smell of burning sugar clogged his nostrils, the choke of woodsmoke and the thick scents of wet earth and cane.

Home.

Something inside him seemed to be falling a long way into blackness. Cold fear and dreads of things he barely recalled.

His father . . .

". . . damn Daubrays are behind it, I tell you! They have to be! It would be just like that weasel Louis to incite a man's own niggers to revolt. That Mammy Hera of theirs is a voodoo and I wouldn't put it past Louis Daubray to pay to have his own grandmother poisoned, if he thought he could get a half-arpent of land out of it. And that greasy brother of his would know who to ask!"

"Father—uh—whatever else may be said of them, the D-Daubrays surely wouldn't—"

"Don't you back-talk me, boy! I was knocking heads with those lying Orleannistes before you could piss standing! Ever since I married your stepmother they've been trying to find a way to keep me from claiming her father's land. Paying my own niggers to wreck the harvest would be of a piece with their sneakiness."

"D-Did you speak—uh—to the police about that trader, Jones? He'd stick at nothing—"

"Listen, Father," Robert interjected. "In France they were speaking of a new system of physical characteristics by which those of born criminal inclination might be identified. I'm sure if you examined the blacks—"

"Oh, shut up, the both of you." Fourchet flung away his cigar. The carriage drew rein before the steps of the big house, whose long windows glowed through the mists in sulfurous lozenges of muzzy light. "If we examined the blacks we'd find that every Sambo of 'em was a liar and a thief, and what a surprise that would be! Use your brain."

"I was endeavoring, sir, to—" Robert broke off as a tall shape appeared against the luminous rectangle of what January knew—since nearly all Creole plantation houses were built on the same plan—to be the bedroom of the lady of the house. He had an impression of pale hair pulled tight into an unfashionable knot at her nape. Of a small white hand resting protectively over a belly swollen with child. Then she passed into the shadow of the gallery as she descended the steps six feet to ground level, and stepped out into the torchlight once more as January sprang from the back of the carriage.

"M'sieu Fourchet," she greeted her husband in a gruff shy voice.

"Madame." He bowed over her hand.

Over his bent head, his wife's gaze crossed Robert's, questioning and uneasy, and held for a moment before it fled away.

A servant with a branch of candles had come out behind Madame Fourchet, slim and boyish and, like Cornwallis, pin-neat; only when he came closer to take in his free hand the torch January held did January see the wrinkles around eyes and lips that marked him as a man in his forties. Like Cornwallis, the servant wore a small slip of black mustache, and like Cornwallis he was light-skinned, quadroon or octoroon, with some white forebear's blue-gray eyes.

January lifted Hannibal gently from the carriage as Fourchet made introductions and produced again the story of investments averted and money saved. "Welcome to Mon Triomphe, M'sieu Sefton," said Madame, in the hesitant voice of one who has never been sure of her position, and Hannibal extended his hand.

"How beautiful are thy feet with shoes, O prince's daughter," he quoted, and kissed the lace-mitted knuckles. "Forgive me my trifling infirmity. Tomorrow I will prostrate myself to the ground as befits a kind hostess and a lovely woman."

She pulled her hand from his and muttered, "Thank you. It's nothing," and hurried before them up the steps. "Agamemnon, stay and help the men in with the luggage." In the multiple luminance of torch and candles January saw the speculative glance Robert darted from Hannibal to his stepmother, and the burning, bitter glare directed at the fiddler by Fourchet, an undisguised anger that made January's chest clench inside with reactive fear.

The overseer Thierry touched his hat brim and made off in the direction of the mill, his duty to his employer accomplished. He moved, not with a swagger, but with a sidelong swiftness, watching everything around him.

Fourchet led them into the house through his own bedroom, meeting his wife once more in the parlor. This room was small compared to a town house's, as in most Creole plantation houses: sparsely furnished, neat and plain. Over a mantelpiece of cypresswood painted to resemble marble hung the portrait of a young woman clad in the caraco jacket popular in the nineties. A square-faced, dark-eyed boy clung frantically to her striped skirts; a baby in a white christening gown perched on her knee. Next to the mantel a miniature of the same woman was framed in the glittering jet circlet of an immortelle wreath.

Through the parlor's inner sliding doors a child

could be heard piping angrily, "But I want to see! Henna says there's company and they may have something for me!"

A hushed female voice interposed, cut off furiously. "I want to see! I want to *see*! I'll have you whipped if you don't let me see!" and a second, younger child screamed, "Me, too! Me, too!"

By the rather fixed smile that widened onto the face of the other woman who waited for them in the parlor—dark-haired, ripely pretty, and clothed in a gown of figured lilac muslin with gauze bows and enormous "imbecile" sleeves—January guessed that this was the children's mother. "Pardon me," said Robert hastily. He stepped through the sliding doors, closing them behind him.

"M'sieu Sefton," introduced Madame. "My daughter-in-law, Madame Hélène Fourchet."

"If I could write the beauty of your eyes,
And with fresh numbers, number all your graces,
The age to come would say, 'This poet lies;
Such heavenly touches ne'er touched earthly faces.' "

Hannibal's lips brushed her hand, and Hélène Fourchet tapped his cheek playfully with her fan.

"Oh, I just *adore* poetry! Is it Lord Byron? I am most *passionately* devoted to 'The Corsair.' And 'The Bride of Abydos,' of course. Such a thrill goes through my heart . . ."

"English pap," snapped Fourchet. "*Will* you shut those brats of yours up?" For the noise in the next room continued unabated, despite whatever efforts the children's father was putting up.

"Do I understand from what you said in the carriage that you're behind in your harvest?" Hannibal turned to Fourchet and coughed again, with every evidence of great agony valiantly concealed. "I beg that you will let me repay a little of your kindness by lending you Ben here while I'm laid by the heels. You don't mind a day or two in the fields, do you, Ben?"

"To help the good folks who take you in when you're sick?" January did his best to sound like a character in a Chateaubriand novel. "Why, Michie Hannibal, I worked the cotton-fields before this. Won't do me no harm to cut sugar for a while."

"Well done, good and faithful servant."

"M'sieu Sefton, no," protested the young Madame. In the warm amber dimness of the parlor she didn't look much over sixteen, a big-boned, flat-chested girl with a plain triangular face and the sandy coloring that makes a woman appear lashless and washed-out. "Our hospitality—"

"Don't be an ass," snapped Fourchet, and looked January up and down with the same coldness that had been in Esteban's eyes when he'd surveyed Baptiste. "We lost Reuben and it'll be days before Boaz is over his fever. Thank you, sir." He spoke to Hannibal as if the words were being extracted from him with forceps. "I appreciate it. Cornwallis!" He raised his voice like the thwack of a board striking pavement.

The valet, who had evidently finished bestowing the luggage in his master's chamber and the guest room, stepped through the parlor's inner doors.

"Take Ben here out to the quarters and find him a place to stay for a night or two. Tell Thierry he's to be put to work while he's here. And get that Baptiste in here, so Madame Fourchet can teach him his duties."

It was close to nine already, but if the young Madame Fourchet would sooner have had a night's sleep before inducting a complete stranger to a complex set of responsibilities and tasks, she knew better than to say so. Robert, stepping back through the parlor doors in time to hear this, began to protest, "Sir, it's quite late for her to be—"

"Shut up." Fourchet lashed the words at him. "Better tonight than she waste half the day tomorrow when he could be of some use. We need to get this place back into order. Cornwallis, take Monsieur Sefton here to the garçonnière. Good night to you, sir. Esteban . . ." With a peremptory wave at his elder son, Fourchet stalked through the door that led into his bedroom and thence, probably, to his office behind it. Esteban followed, and closed the door with the care of one who fears that a sound will bring the house crashing about everyone's ears.

"I do apologize, Madame." Robert hastened to his stepmother's side as the young Madame led the way through the dining room—cypresswood table, the gleam of glass and flowers in the uplifted shudder of Cornwallis's branch of candles—and she gave her head a quick little shake and hastened her step. "I beg you to forgive my father, and apologize on his behalf."

"Really—" Madame Hélène's strident voice floated behind them, "Robert, you might at *least* have the goodness to—"

The closing door cut her off.

It was a peculiarity of Creole households that the young men of the family, from the age of thirteen or so, were given quarters separate from the family. In town these usually consisted of a wing behind the main town house, or, in the case of the cottages wealthy men bought for their mistresses along Rue Rampart, Rue Burgundy, and the other small streets at the back of the old French town, a room or two above the kitchen, lest a white man find himself sleeping under the same roof as a young man—however nearly related to him—of color. On plantations the garçonnière was usually a separate building connected to the main house by the galleries that surrounded the whole, forming a U that drew the cooling river breezes through. In the case of Mon Triomphe, it was one wing on the downstream, or men's, side of the house. The corresponding wing on the upstream side was, mercifully, given over to nurseries.

"I'll clear this away." Robert followed Madame Fourchet into the second of the garçonnière's two rooms ahead of January and gathered, from the small desk there, a quantity of Parisian journals and newspapers, stationery, wafers, and ink. "I use this room as a study when we're here. And indeed, M'sieu Sefton," he added, setting down the books he'd begun to pick up, "you're quite welcome to peruse any of my library. I rather pride myself on it."

He nervously stroked the neat Vandyke that framed red lips whose pliant poutiness spoke of what his mother must have looked like. "I've been collecting scientific volumes since I was quite a little boy. By the time I was six, I and a friend had made a little steam engine and fitted it to one of the pirogues we had here. A boy's toy merely, but it worked. My mother always said . . ."

Through the French doors, the petulant shrieks of the children floated across the open piazza between the arms of the house.

"Thank you," Hannibal murmured, as January laid him on the tall half-tester bed. Either Cornwallis or Agamemnon had already been in and unpacked the portmanteau and placed Hannibal's violin carefully on the bureau. Four of Hannibal's half-dozen bottles of opium were arranged tidily beside it.

Robert turned again to his stepmother. "I do apologize for my father. He was drunk, to have spoken to you thus—"

"He was not drunk." Madame Fourchet's voice was low and stammering, like an ill-at-ease boy's.

"And I suppose that sober—" began Robert, and stopped himself. Turning back to Hannibal, he finished, "Whatever the case, I do apologize, and bid you welcome to Mon Triomphe. Should you require anything, M'sieu, please feel free to ask any of the servants. And thank you again for the loan of your boy. His help will be invaluable in getting the cane in."

"I'll just get him settled, if you don't mind, M'am," said January diffidently, and Madame Fourchet inclined her head.

Cornwallis lit the candles on the bureau from those on the girandole he bore, then led Robert and Madame out onto the gallery again. "Go on ahead and find Baptiste," January heard Robert say, as they closed the doors. Then, voice low but still audible, "You can't let him talk to you like that, Marie-Noël." The candlelight had departed, and they would be standing, January guessed, in the velvet shadows of the gallery, away from the leaked glow of Fourchet's office window. "He treats you like a servant. Like a dog."

If the young woman replied she did so in a voice too low for January to hear. But he guessed that she only stood with her head bowed and turned a little away. Lips folded close, as they had been when her husband's voice had cut at her before strangers and servants. Pale-lashed eyelids lowered. Heretofore Robert—whose French was irreproachably Parisian—had addressed her with the formal *vous* of a man speaking to his father's wife. Now he called her *tu,* as one would speak to a sister or a friend.

"I've been beneath this roof with you for a few days only, my child, but already I see how it is for you here. It fills me with rage to see him treat you so."

"I have lived with worse." January had to strain to

hear, but could not go closer because the candlelight in the garçonnière would show him up through the French door's glass panes. "Your father isn't so bad as you think." She said, *Vôtre père,* speaking as to a stranger.

Then he heard her footfalls retreat along the gallery. Robert stood where he was for a long time, while Madame Hélène's voice rose from the women's side of the house: "I realize that you're now the mistress here, Madame, but it has *always* been the custom of this house to offer a visitor tea and sweet cakes. I was *most* mortified when you whisked M'sieu Sefton away as you did without so much as a sociable word. Of course I'm sure you had your reasons . . ." And in the nursery wing the older child screamed over and over, "I'll have you whipped! I'll have you whipped! I'll tell Grandpère and he'll sell you down the river!"

"Ben, this is Mohammed." Cornwallis held up his branch of candles and with his free hand gestured to the spare gray-haired man who stood beside him. January, coming down the back gallery steps with the usual slave's luggage of a clean shirt and shaving things done up in a bandanna, had to remind himself forcibly that a youth of twenty will look pretty much the same when he's fifty-three; a boy of seven will be unrecognizable. Besides, why would Mohammed remember one child from the Bellefleur hogmeat gang?

"He'll get you settled." Evidently Cornwallis was not a man to sully his dignity by association with field hands. The valet turned without another word and strode back toward the house, the lights of his candles blurring to golden willy-wisp in the fog.

"You eaten?" Mohammed looked up at him, bright dark eyes as January remembered. The image of the young man he'd carried all those years settled in against the gentle erosion of sunken flesh, wrinkled skin, missing teeth; long years lived in hell while January had eaten good food, learned surgery and music, earned his bread in Paris and New Orleans, and married the woman he loved.

"Yessir. On the *Belle Dame* they had pone and greens."

"Michie Ney's boat." The flex in the older man's voice made January wonder whether he'd at some time had a run-in with that arrogant captain in the scarlet coat. "If you care to stay up a little there'll be some food at Ajax's—Ajax the driver," Mohammed added. "If you're tired I'll take you on to the cabin—I thought I'd put you in with the bachelors, Gosport, Quashie, Parson, and Kadar—and you can sleep if you want. But they're havin' a shout for Reuben, that was sugar-boss here. He died yesterday. Would you care to come?"

"I'll come, thanks," said January.

"What happened?" he asked, as they passed the dark still shapes of the kitchen and laundry, and the ground grew rough and weedy underfoot. Mohammed, who was dressed in a coarse clean calico shirt, wool trousers, and the "quantier" shoes of a yard hand, doused his pine-knot torch in the rain barrel behind one of the plantation workshops—carpentry, pottery, cobbler, cooper—and picked up another stick of pitch-smeared wood from the little stack nearby, to use later if needed. The mill rose ahead of them, fire-lit and seething with life, but January's guide led him around behind a stable and a barn, and past the long sheds where the wood was stored, and so into the dense whispery forest of the cane.

"You got to understand, it started in the dark of the moon." Mohammed's voice came soft out of the pitchy blackness as they trod the narrow rough cart-path between the cane-rows. "And the moon's dark is the time when ill will lies strongest on the land." Mohammed was, January remembered, a storyteller, a *griot.* His earliest recollections of the man were of a young animated face transforming itself from expression to expression, of a quick-frailed banjo and a voice that skipped effortlessly from Compair Lapin's cocky tenor to Bouki Hyena's deep, self-pitying drawl.

"There was a hoodoo marked the mill in anger, and the mill caught fire in the dark of the moon. Reuben was the man put the fire out before it could spread. He was a most careful man, unless he'd been drinking. He thought a lot of himself and was prideful and strong, careful even about where and how he drank lest any should carry back tales to Michie Fourchet. He said he'd checked over the grinders, and the gears beneath them, and the sweeps down below them in the roundhouse where the mules walk. He brought me in to see if the iron had been hurt, and I found no damage. But we did find marks."

January had nearly forgotten how completely the eight-foot walls of the cane shut out air, sound, light, reducing everything to dense narrow slots of rustling gloom. What little moonlight struggled between the razor-edged leaves showed Mohammed's breath, and his own. It was only the walls themselves, and the puddled ditches at the walls' feet, that guided them on toward the woods.

The house, and the mill, and the kitchen and barns and shops—those were the white man's kingdom. Squared and neat, comely as January had been taught to understand beauty. A world where Mozart and Shakespeare had lived, where the surgeons of the Hôtel Dieu had taught him how to set bone and relieve suffering.

But beyond that small neat realm lay the cane. And

beyond the cane, the woods, the ciprière. That world was measured differently. It was a network of interlacing paths, which led to places identified only by the presence of certain trees or certain water: old Michie Lays-Along-the-Ground, they'd called a big oak in the ciprière behind Bellefleur plantation where the slaves had met for dancing in January's childhood, or the Big Slough where the men had sneaked away from their work to catch fish and swim. It was a world of inference and small signs, a world where snakes could be made to talk if you addressed them right and eyes you couldn't see watched you from the shadows. It was a world where *les blankittes* didn't often come.

This was the world toward which Mohammed led him, and as they walked, January was aware, over the murmuring of the cane, of the mutter of other voices, the soft stealthy passage of other shadows on this narrow track.

"Now Reuben was an angry man," the *griot* went on. "He thought that every morning when Allah woke up His first thought was, *How can I make this day harder for Reuben?* And that He set about it before He even had breakfast. Reuben knew all about the marks. But Reuben had his reason for wantin' to stay on Michie Fourchet's good side. If he worked fast and saved the whole of the roulaison, he knew he could get Michie Fourchet to give him back a woman he wanted, a proud strong woman Michie Fourchet had took away from him and give to the butler Gilles. So Reuben checked the mill once, and didn't call up Mambo Hera to come from Daubray, or Mambo Cassie from Prideaux, or even Jeanette here that was daughter of old Mambo Jeanne. He didn't put store in marks. But he forgot how marks sometimes have a way of puttin' store in you."

Far ahead of them, somewhere past the rustling wall

of darkness, January heard singing, the dim ghosts of rhythm utterly unlike the music that for so many years had been his life. The clapping of hands, rhythm that drew at the blood of the heart like the moon draws on the sea. Rags of words, African-French fragments of his childhood: *Azou zouzou ziza, Legba abobo.*

Legba abobo . . .

"Was it the marks made him careless?"

"His anger made him careless," answered Mohammed. "His anger and his greed. And marks like that, made in ill will, have a way of whispering to you when you're thinking of other things. Reuben was angry that the men were sick that day, and he had to do more of the work with a crew not used to the task. The grinders stuck three, four, five times that morning—he was always being called from his work to pull knots of cane, and sticks and branches, free. Always working faster and faster, and not taking care. It was only a matter of time, til something spooked the mules—and they were spooky that week, and wild—while he was at the grinders. The grinders broke free, they came down on him like the lintel of the temple when Samson called on the name of Allah."

"This was yesterday?"

"This was a week ago. But it was clear when they rolled the iron off him he would not live."

Oh, and Reuben died, Esteban Fourchet had said, casually.

After a week of suffering. A week of knowing.

They had entered the woods. From the river the land fell gradually, until the drained and ditched ground of the cane-fields gave place to the ciprière. The roots of red oak and loblolly pine made ridges of high ground, and between them softer wetter earth, cypress, hackberry, live oaks whose branches spread out in all directions under floating veils of Spanish moss that the men would harvest in off hours through the year, to sell for cash. Now and then small scurrying life fled the smell and tread of the men, but with the autumn's cool at least the mosquitoes were few. The summer chorus of frogs and cicadas had long ago stilled.

Others joined them on the pathways. Some bore candles, and others pine torches that dripped gouts of flame; some found their route by simple familiarity. Some had washed and put on what finery they had: bright-colored shirts, or waistcoats of silk or embroidered wool, tattered and patched mostly, or bought brilliantly new from river traders. The women had taken their hair out of its strings, crimped and curly, or braided it up in fantastic shapes which they wore with cocky pride; the men had combed out their hair, or cut or queued it, and put beads on their necks or clappers on their ankles. Others still had just slipped away from night-work at the mill still filthy with the dust and cane-sap of the fields, dark eyes gleaming through masks of grime.

Exhausted, facing another day's work in mere hours, still they'd come to give Reuben his send-off. Maybe not because they'd liked him—by what Mohammed said, few had—but because it was the proper thing to do.

And too, January knew, even in the roulaison few folks of color, either slave or free, would pass up the chance to dance.

Voices wailed from the darkness ahead of them, the slow shuffle of feet and the slap of clapping hands.

"Abobo, abobo,
Ago Legba, ago Legba,
Abobo . . ."

"Could any have got into the mill, to have made the marks?" asked January. *Or tampered with the machinery?* he added in his mind.

"I don't think so." A man fell into step with them, thick-muscled and heavy-shouldered with one of the front teeth missing from his slow, gap-toothed smile. "Reuben, he keep the key to that mill always on a string 'round his neck. See, five-six years ago there was a fella here name Nick, that broke into the mill and tried to do the same thing and break the rollers, and Michie Fourchet had him sold off—and the sugar-boss, too, for not bein' more careful. That's when Reuben got to be sugar-boss, when he'd been just 'ssistant before."

"Nathan's right," added a taller, rangy man with a big cane-knife scar on his forearm. "Reuben always knowed which side of the bread the butter was on. He kept good track of that key and he didn't leave the door open much, either."

Firelight glowed before them through the trees. To the hypnotic, ever-changing beat of hands was added the silky whisper of feet shuffling on the earth. They came into the clearing and January saw what he had not seen since his childhood: men and women ranged in a circle around the clearing, singing as they moved in a slow, swaying line. A low fire burned within the ring and cast gold shawls and handkerchiefs of light across the faces in the circle. Men's faces and women's, children watching from the edges of the clearing with enormous midnight eyes. All swaying, lost, bathed in the music as the saved on Judgment Day would be bathed in light.

The dancers didn't lift their feet, like those who danced in Congo Square in town on the Sunday afternoons of their brief freedom. This wasn't that kind of dance. January remembered one of his mother's friends telling him, "It's 'cause you have to keep touch of the earth." No instruments played—no fiddle or banjo or bones. Only the clapping of hands, the steady beat of open palms on thighs.

An old man knelt in the center of the ring, bowed to the ground, singing. Those in the circle would call out in response, words January dimly recalled from dirges he'd heard in French, in English, in town . . .

"Who'll close my eyes in death?"
"Abobo, abobo."
"Who'll close my eyes in death?"
"Spirit come down."
"Who'll close my eyes in death?"

Slow music rolled over January like the sea's breaking waves, sadness and farewell with the smell of smoke and sugar thick in the misty air. He picked out faces from the shadow and fireglow of the circle, people he'd be living with for days or possibly weeks. Big main-gang men, strong enough to swing an eighteen-inch knife and cut cane tough as bone. Some had come straight from the field to hauling wood in the mill, and so here, with a second and more ragged pair of cut-off trousers on over the first to protect from the sharp leaves, the razor-edged ends of the cut stalks, and a second shirt. Second-gang men, older or smaller, the soot of the mill striped with streaks of sweat. Here and there an artisan or groom stood out in gaudy finery, colors chosen and matched as no white man would choose or match them. Women stood among the trees with their babies at breast, and they too swayed to the music, crooned the responses to the wailing cries.

"Dig my grave with a golden spade."
"Abobo, abobo."
"Dig my grave with a golden spade."
"Spirit come down."
"Dig my grave with a golden spade."

At the edge of the fire's light a tall thin field hand stood with his arms around a beautiful girl in a purple calico dress. Two young boys, brothers by their faces, practiced exaggerated swaying, swinging their bodies in ecstatic double-jointed unison. A good-looking man who'd spruced up with a yellow silk waistcoat slipped and shifted through the torchlight shadows to speak to first one, then another of those new-come from the mill, and January saw something—salt? candles? a bottle?—change hands.

"Lower me down with a silver chain."
"Abobo, abobo."
"Lower me down with a silver chain . . ."

No house-servants, January noted without surprise. Like Cornwallis, house-servants as a rule looked down on the field hands, scorning them as an alien race. And in fact they were. These people had probably all been baptized, but generally that was as far as it went. January's mother, and the other women on Bellefleur, had told him of God and the saints, but they were curious tales, dark and odd and very little like what he heard later from Père Antoine in town.

The music itself, he understood, was what spoke to these people in the wordless words of God.

Only one—a girl, slim and sullen with her dark hair lying in thick corkscrew ringlets over her shoulders—did not sing. Bitter-eyed, bitter-mouthed, she stood apart from the ring, holding a baby in her arms and watching with her back against a cypress tree. In time a heavy-muscled giant in the long-tailed coat and beaver hat of a driver came to her, to draw her away with him into the dark of the trees.

Now and then a woman would shriek or cry out, head lolling in grief, but on one face only did January see actual tears. His attention was drawn to this woman because she was the only person who wore mourning, and her black dress was better fitting, despite her short round body and immense breasts. Her mahogany-black hair had been crimped into long streams, and waved as she rolled her head in a kind of solitary ecstasy, tears flowing from her closed eyes and down her velvet-dark apple cheeks.

"Good-bye, my voice be heard no more."
"Abobo, abobo."
"Good-bye, my voice be heard no more."
"Spirit come down."
"Good-bye, my voice be heard no more."

People came, and people left, as those who'd slipped from the mill vanished again in the darkness, lest the overseer and the drivers note too many gone too long. A big strong woman and a lovely girl, clearly her daughter, gathered seven smaller children—including the dancing boys—and led them away to their beds, with an eighth tucked in the front of the mother's dress at breast. The thin field hand and the girl in purple calico faded into the dark of the woods, hands entwined.

These people were the pattern he had come here to learn, January thought. The warp and the weft of the lives whose telltale break, somewhere, would point the way to the killer whose deed would condemn them all.

And yet looking at them, it was hard to remember that one of these was a killer and a calculating despoiler. All he felt in his heart was a curious and profound sadness, rooted in a darkness his memory couldn't pierce.

They were still singing when he left.

FIVE

There were twenty-five men in the main gang, including three drivers: Ajax, Herc, and Dice. Two of the men, Ram Joe and Boaz, were out sick, Boaz with pneumonia and Ram Joe snakebit. In January's opinion at least three others working in the field should have been laid up as well, for he heard the hum of pneumonia in Lago's breathing, and Java and Dumaka both were running fevers. But the most that would happen with Fourchet was that the men were put back as trimmers, working behind the cutters to lop the cane-tops and slash off the leaves. Of the four men whose cabin he shared, three—Gosport, Quashie, and Kadar—were in the main gang as well.

"Whoo, lord!" Quashie exclaimed, as they left the cabin in predawn mist and cold, and held up his hand as if shielding his eyes. "We got us a *bozal* here! Right off the boat, looks like!" He was the thin tall man January had seen at the ring-shout last night, holding hands with the purple calico girl. Ajax the driver and his wife Hope—she of the nine children—had kept their cabin open long into the night, people bringing in food to share after the shout, but January hadn't seen

Quashie or the girl there. The young man had not returned to their own crowded dwelling until nearly dawn. "It ain't a tar baby, it's a tar daddy!" he told January. "You so black when you come outside the chickens think it's night again, go in to roost!"

"Don't matter none," replied January good-naturedly. "I'm just thinkin' how you so yellow when you step out at night, all the roosters get up an' crow, wake up everybody in the place." He was tired, for he'd sat up long at Ajax the driver's last night, meeting as many people as he could, and afterward had walked down to the bank above the landing in the pitch-black fog, to tie a black bandanna to the arm of Michie Demosthenes the Oak, knowing he'd be too weary to do so in the morning.

And he'd been right.

Quashie contemplated him for a moment, hearing the challenge in his words. Then he said, "And ugly!" He cringed exaggeratedly as they walked along between the rows of shabby wooden cabins toward the open ground that lay between Thierry's house and the mill. "I never seen a man so ugly! Your whole family so ugly, I hear there's a law in town against more'n three of you walkin' down the street at once."

"Now, I don't know nuthin' bout your family," returned January mildly, as they grouped around the two-wheeled rice cart, set up in front of the line of plantation shops just upstream of the mill. "But *you* so ugly I hear you was five years old 'fore you realized your name wasn't 'Damn!' "

As a matter of fact, neither man was ugly—January had heard himself described as good-looking and Quashie was handsome—but the rules of the game had to be observed.

"Yeah, and your mama ugly, too," retorted Quashie, as the men and women around them laughed, holding out their bowls for Minta the cook's helper to fill. "And fat. Your mama so fat when I hump her the other day, I had to roll over two times 'fore I rolled off her."

"Oh, that was you?" January raised his eyebrows in mock enlightenment. This was an old game that wasn't quite a game, and in his childhood years at school, he'd been called hulking and black and dirty, and told he looked like a field hand or a newly-arrived African by sharper-tongued opponents than Quashie. "I wondered about that. She said at first she thought she been stung in the ass by a mosquito. Spent half the night lookin' around for lemon grass to burn, keep them bugs out of her room."

They had barely ten minutes to slop down the congris from the gourd bowls, chickpeas and rice with a little sausage in it to give it heart. The men of the night shift were just leaving the mill, men January recognized a little now from one or another slipping away to Ajax's cabin last night for rice or raisin pudding. Rodney the second-gang driver, in his stylish purple coat and half-boots, counted off the day men as they filed in to take their places, like the damned passing through the glowing mouth of Hell.

Pér me si va ne la città dolènte. Dante's words echoed in January's mind.

Through me the way into the suffering city,
Through me the way to eternal pain,
Through me the way that runs among the lost . . .

"You ever cut cane, boy?" Thierry stepped up to January. His voice was soft, coming from beneath a mammoth wall of black mustache. His eyebrows were long, too, shelving out in a way that should have been comical and wasn't. His eyes were blue.

"No, sir," replied January, lowering his eyes respectfully to the overseer's boots. "Michie Georges, he grew cotton on his place. I worked the main gang there, til they put me to look out for Michie Hannibal."

"Fucking useless shit," said Thierry.

"Yes, sir."

Past his shoulder January saw the girl Quashie had been with last night slip out the back door of Thierry's house, spring down the step, and lose herself into the women's gang. The gay purple calico, newer than the frocks of the other women, glowed in the morning dark like a flower. She avoided Quashie's eye, and the women of the gang stepped aside a little to let her pass.

"They give me some fucking useless cotton-hand . . . Gosport!"

The tall man with the scarred arm came forward, one of January's cabin-mates, steady and pleasant. He'd been sold south two years ago from Georgia, for running away.

"Teach Cotton-Patch here how to use a knife and make sure he doesn't cut his fingers off. You use him for trimming?" The overseer turned to Ajax, who tilted back his beaver hat and nodded.

"We sure need somebody, sir."

So January had been handed a cane-knife, marked down by the overseer against his name.

"Most of the men who cuts the cane wears an old shirt and an old pair of pants on over their regular clothes, 'cause of the dirt." Wearing the same engaging smile that had gone last night with the yellow waistcoat, Harry fell into step with January as the men walked out through the darkness to the fields. The cold was brutal, numbing the fingers and the toes through the cheap heavy brogans the men wore. January could see his own breath. The whetstone slapped his thigh through his pocket, and the dripping gourd-bottle hanging from his shoulder cut into his flesh with its strap. "I brung extra for you, knowin' you'd need them."

Having seen Harry in action last night, swapping candles and the stubs of sealing wax for eggs and salt and string at the shout and later at Ajax's, January guessed the young man had ulterior motives in his offer. There'd been a man like that on Bellefleur when he was young—Django, his name had been. You accepted a gift or a favor, and you owed a favor in return. But looking around him January knew he didn't have much choice about refusing. He'd been given a shirt and trousers of coarse osnabrig cloth—new, heavy, and board-stiff—and a pair of badly fitting brogans from the plantation store, and knew they wouldn't last long with the kind of wear they'd get in the cane-fields. So he made his face look as if there weren't a Harry on every plantation up and down the river and said, "Why, thank you. That's sure good of you."

"Don't mention it," smiled Harry, and handed over a worn pair of pants, too large at the waist and cut off at the knees, and a second shirt, faded and patched. These January put on over his new things, and Gosport showed him how to hold a cane-knife—which he knew, having watched the men as a child, though he'd been far too young to wield one himself—and how to top the armload of cane-stalks the cutter would shove at him, cutting off the unripe portion with quick, flicking strokes and then slashing off the leaves.

"Cane piled on the stubble, trash piled between the rows," instructed Gosport. "Watch out for snakes. When you feel the knife start to labor on the cuts you brace it on your shoe like this, give it a couple swipes with the stone. But you be careful with that knife, understand? You got to cross a ditch, or cross the pile row, you throw your knife over first. That cane's slippery, and if you're not careful you'll see your blood."

"Gonna teach him how to tie his shoes, too?" jeered Quashie.

"He cuts his hand off, *you* want to carry him back?" retorted Gosport, which got a laugh, because of January's size.

They started moving along the rows: the work that would buy acceptance, the acceptance that would buy the right to ask questions.

January hated Simon Fourchet, and the hatred redoubled with every stab of the muscles of his shoulders, with every slice of the sharp cane and razor-tough leaves through the flesh of his hands, with every aching hour.

The men sang as they worked, pacing the rhythm of their strokes:

"Madame Caba, your tignon fell down,
Madame Caba, your tignon fell down,
Michie Zizi, he's a handsome man, O,
Michie Zizi, he's a handsome man . . ."

Or they would sing the African songs, the songs in a tongue no one remembered, the words meaningless now but the music still drawing the heart.

"Day zab, day zab, day koo-noo wi wi,
Day zab, day zab, day koo-noo wi wi . . ."

Buzzards circled overhead, scores of them, tiny as motes of pepper against the blue of the sky as the mists burned away. Rabbits in the cane fled the men, or sometimes fat clumsy raccoons; small green lizards darted to safety, or sat on the thin stalks of grass that the men called maiden cane and watched with wisely tilting turquoise-rimmed eyes. The cane in this field was second-growth cane and a lot of it lay badly, sprawling in all directions and growing along the ground rather than all of it standing straight. The sprawled cane wound among the standing and had to be dragged and wrestled out, stalks sometimes sixteen feet long, a mess of leaves and insects and dust. Dust and cane-juice plastered January's face and he wished Fourchet had died already and all these people, innocent as well as guilty, had been hanged for the crime before he even knew about it, so it wouldn't be his responsibility to try to save them. His shoulders hurt. His hands hurt.

Sometimes if no one else was singing, a man would break into a holler: wailing solo notes that climbed and descended a scale Bach had never heard of. Nonsense sounds, just *"Yay"* or *"Whoa,"* but soaring like hawks with the sense and meaning of the heart. The other men would join in, as vendors in town would sometimes add their wailing to the drawn-out singsong of the berry lady or the charcoal man, catching the notes and twirling them like dancers: elemental music, like rain or wind or the heartbeat of the earth.

Mid-morning the women came out with the carts, gathering the harvested rows. They set their babies at the ends of the rows among the water bottles of the men, with one of the hogmeat gang to keep cane-rats and buzzards off them. At noon the rice cart came, put together by Kiki the cook or more probably Minta: rice and beans, greens and pone, a little pork in the greens.

When it got too dark to work safely, torches were lit and the men set to helping the women load the rest of the cane, and haul it to the mill. Carrying the piled cane up the short flight of steps to the grinders, January was able to see the setup of the mill. The grinders were set on a raised floor above a roundhouse, where the mules hauled on the sweeps that turned the machinery, the three huge toothed iron cylinders chewed the cane, the glinting new metal of one a vicious reminder of the dead man whose soul had been sung across to the other side last night. The green sap dripped and ran into the iron reservoir beneath, to be tipped from there into the first of the battery of cauldrons. *La grande,* it was called, and as each successive kettle was boiled down it was purified with alum and ash and emptied into the next: *le flambeau, la lessive, le sirop, la batterie,* every one smaller than the last, a seething inferno of heat and stink and boiling juice.

Moths and roaches roared around the torches set into the walls, and the smoke pouring from the furnace beneath the cauldrons burned January's eyes, and above everything Simon Fourchet presided, a black-coated Satan bellowing at the men who hauled wood, who stirred the kettles, who dipped out the rising scum of impurities or climbed up and down those steps endlessly to feed the chopped billets of cane into the rollers.

Hell, thought January, stumbling on blistered feet, aching, his mind curiously clear. What window had the ancients looked through, to see that Hell would actually be a Louisiana sugar-mill on a November night?

On his way out to the waiting cane carts for another armful he saw Quashie again, holding the hands of the girl in the purple dress. In the firelight January saw again how pretty she was, eighteen or nineteen years old and clearly the sister of the fourth of the bachelors whose cabin he shared, a second-gang youth named Parson. She was one of the women carrying cane to the grinders and Quashie had stopped her, speaking so low that all he could hear was her name, *Jeanette.* Her gaze, turned up toward the young man's, was filled with a desperate pain in the face of his anger.

Thierry stepped through the mill door. Jeanette instantly dropped Quashie's hands and hastened to gather an armload of cane. More deliberately, Quashie also scooped up a long, awkward bundle of stalks and followed. Thierry did nothing til he'd passed him, then turned casually and licked out his whip in an underhand cut to the young man's calf. Quashie stumbled, dropping the cane, which rolled and flopped everywhere.

The overseer watched the slave, still silent, chewing on the corner of his mustache, while the latter picked it up, a far more difficult task when it wasn't in a pile in the cart. January noticed how careful Quashie was to make sure he got every six-foot stalk.

Thierry let Quashie get a few more steps toward the doors, then he cut him again, this time on the elbow, and with such violence that the young man couldn't keep his grip. The heavy stalks spilled down again around his feet.

For a moment Quashie stood, staring at his tormentor, his hands clenched at his sides. From the mill door Jeanette watched. Then Quashie lowered his eyes respectfully and gathered up the cane again. Blood ran down his arm.

Thierry walked past him to the mill door, took Jeanette by the elbow, and thrust her in the direction of his cottage. The girl glanced back at Quashie once, then went. Quashie didn't look after her, only continued to pick up the cane.

The last of the cane was fed into the grinder a few hours before midnight. Most of the men were released, and the night crew came on, to stoke the fires and tend the cauldrons until dawn. Walking back to the cabin, aching in every limb and shivering as the sweat dried in his filthy clothes, January felt a rush of gratitude that Gosport, who seemed to be headman of the bachelor cabin, had roasted yams and ash-pone in the embers of last night's fire so they'd be ready to eat now. The mere thought of preparing any kind of food before falling asleep was agony.

As the men walked from the mill down the long row of cabins January slipped away from them, into the cane and the darkness, and circled—cautiously, because of snakes—back toward the house.

Moving through the uncut cane-rows themselves was a trick he'd mastered as a child, feeling for where the sharp, leathery leaves would give. You swam through the heavy foliage, slithered. Everyone January had seen that day except the house-servants had those little cuts on their faces and hands, from pushing through those secret ways.

The slight drift of air from the river brought him the smells of food from the big house kitchen—chicken and compotes, biscuits and potatoes and ham—and his belly clenched with hunger that had gone beyond any desire for food into the realm of nausea.

From the fields that day he'd looked back toward the big house, seeing it from the upriver side, and he'd asked at nooning about the high dark hedge. "That's old M'am Camille's garden," Harry had said. "She was Michie Fourchet's wife years ago, Michie Robert's mother. It's all growed over and weeds, though young M'am Fourchet's had Mundan diggin' it up again for her to plant herbs."

"Better herbs than the truck M'am Camille grew," had added Will, a small man—even in the second gang he would have been considered small—with the round head and neat features of Ibo ancestry. An "R" had at some time in the recent past been burned into his cheek with a poker—"R" for "runaway." "Flowers you had to wrap up with burlap on cold nights—I used to be Mundan's helper back when M'am Camille was here—pineapples that you couldn't grow 'cept under glass, and them hedges imported from Italy or Greece."

"You got to admit them oleanders are pretty," said Gosport in his mellow deep voice. "And fine apples—the only Ashmead apples in Louisiana, M'am Camille said. She set a store by them."

The conversation had turned to the merits and shortcomings of fruit pies, but January had kept the information in his mind, and now in the darkness pushed and wriggled his way like a huge cat through the cane that grew close up on that side of the house.

Lights still burned in Fourchet's office, and in the corner chamber on the nearer side of the house that the women of the household used as a sewing room. The dim flush of candle glow flecked the weed-choked beds and neglected paths. Lying on his belly in the hedge's black shelter, January could just make out the intricate pattern of quatrefoil and circle formed by the curved brick walkways. A statue, indistinguishable in a garment of lichen and resurrection fern, presided over a scummed and stagnant fountain. In summer it would stink, January guessed, and be hellish with mosquitoes. Low box hedges had once outlined each minute, fussy bed, and these, too, had been suffered to run wild in neglect, except in one corner where they'd been pulled out, the pattern of the paths simplified, and beds of earth tilled, presumably to sprout herbs in spring.

What had Shaw said about Camille Bassancourt? A Parisian lady who'd come to Louisiana with an aunt. After bearing five children she herself had died—six years ago?—to be replaced by a girl of fifteen or sixteen. January wondered how old Camille herself had been at the time of her marriage, and at her death.

She'd put in this garden, with its impractical Asian lilies, its hedges of Italian oleander, to look at during the eight months of the year when planters' families were required to be on their land. A work of art? January wondered. Or an act of defiance? Clearly Robert's wife Hélène hadn't kept it up. Hélène's French, like her gown, was very Parisian, but with a Creole intonation, speaking of education there rather than birth.

Fourchet's voice rose from the direction of the house. "God damn it, when I say I want—" Followed by a crash.

Cornwallis? January wondered, remembering the valet's cynical aloofness. The maddeningly slow-spoken Esteban? Madame Hélène, whose grating voice and whiny petulance would be almost certain to set off the old man's temper in short order? The young Madame? *He treats you like a servant, like a dog. . . .*

You. Tu.

Belly to the ground, he crawled slowly around the whole of the hedge, peering under the dark skirts of the oleanders and turning the leaves carefully—very carefully, with one of his colored bandannas protecting his fingers—until he found what he had been almost certain he would find.

In the rear corner of the garden a small brick shed had been built, clogged now with trash, old pots and wheelbarrows and broken sugar-molds. Behind it, where the shadows were most dense, twelve or fourteen branches had been stripped of their leaves, and a dozen more cut off and barked, to get the milky sap.

Last night Mohammed had spoken the name of Mambo Jeanne.

In his mind January saw the old woman again. He and Olympe used to go gathering herbs with her in the Bellefleur woods. Under her blue-and-white striped tignon, her narrow, wrinkled face had borne two small scars on each temple—most of the Congo women had them. *Now that one she's a bad one,* he heard her deep, surprising voice, and saw the glossy dark of spear-shaped leaves in her callused fingers. She didn't handle the leaves directly, but wrapped a rag from her collection of rags around her hands, before she'd pluck leaves or flowers or twigs from Simon Fourchet's oleander bushes. *You boil this one, boil it thick, make* obé—*but you throw away the pot you make it in, and you throw away the mortar and the pestle both. You burn the rag you pick them with and you don't inhale the smoke.*

Four-year-old Olympe had nodded gravely, and wrapped a rag around her own stubby little fingers to handle the sprig.

In Italy, January remembered, the pink blossoms were used to decorate the caskets of the dead.

He followed the hedge back to the house's foundations, and kept to the wall under the gallery where he wouldn't be seen in the shadows. Earlier he'd heard Hannibal playing his violin in the garçonnière, a graceful glancing Mozart waltz that was a favorite at the balls they'd play in town. When January passed among the brick piers beneath the house now, however, he could hear Robert's voice, fretful with self-pity:

"But he *will* not listen. I'm sure that, as an educated man, M'sieu Sefton, you've had the same problem. Cotton can't be that different from sugar-cane. Mother made sure I had a very good education—well, as good as one can get in this country. By the time I was twelve I was giving my tutors lessons, though of course none of them would ever admit it. But all these planters *will* persist in their outmoded empiricism. You know how they are."

The jalousies of the French door stood open, and the light that fell through onto the oaks wavered and glittered as Robert made a gesture of resignation and despair. "They 'know sugar' or can 'feel' when the juice is ready to crystallize—like old women prophesying weather through their bones!"

Hannibal may or may not have made a sympathetic noise. There was movement in the shadows beneath one of the large water-cisterns and January froze, flattening himself back under the piers. He was on the downstream side of the house, within full view of the window of Thierry's three-room cottage, and he could imagine what the overseer would have to say about a slave out spying on his betters. Then he heard a woman's giggle, and Harry's voice: "I knew I could count on you, beautiful. . . ."

Robert Fourchet continued with barely a pause, "When I was only ten or eleven I read journals for months and came up with a primitive form of multiple-effects evaporator of the kind that they're even now experimenting with in France. But will my father invest in such a thing?"

The window of Thierry's cottage creaked sharply, bringing January's heart to his throat. He reminded himself desperately that he had to be invisible, here under the house; that in the event of a confrontation Hannibal would defend him. . . . Then a slim shape wriggled through, and dropped noiselessly to the deep carpet of weeds and long grass that grew thickly and patchily among the oaks. It was so dark, away from the house, that January didn't see where that shadow went, but he heard the muted crunch of feet on last year's dead leaves. The cane lay only a few yards beyond the cottage, and at this point stretched to the levee.

Harry's voice, in the dark beneath the cistern, whispered, "It's nothing, darling. Come here." And there was a woman's soft moan of delight.

"Will he even consider using a polariscope to determine concentrations of sugar in the various stages of production?" demanded Robert pettishly. "Heaven forfend! And Esteban is just as bad. All he thinks about is getting away to town, and *not* from any concern about the more civilized things in life, I might add. Tell me, M'sieu Sefton, what is the point of being civilized men—of living in the nineteenth century, in the world where rationalism and scientific methods have finally begun to make inroads against the benighted clutch of outmoded traditions—if no one pays the slightest attention to one's advice? My mother made sure I was exposed to the finest . . ."

The woman beneath the cistern gasped, and whispered, "Again!" January wondered where Harry would get the energy to do anything but fall asleep.

"I suppose one has to feel sorry for him," remarked Hannibal later, when after many more minutes Robert took his leave and January slipped up the back steps to scratch quietly on the garçonnière door. "Or at least I did before that endless lecture on the subject of how dilute sulfuric acid makes a better defection agent for sugar than lime does. He very kindly left me books, lest I be bored."

Hannibal hefted one volume in either hand. Clothed in a linen nightshirt, long dark hair spread loose over his thin shoulders, he looked like a disreputable wood-elf in the chamber's dim light. "Thomas Brown on the philosophy of the human mind, or this roguish little romp of Saint-Simon's on the industrial system. I wonder if Madame Hélène reads?"

"How do you feel about Sir Walter Scott?"

Hannibal shuddered. "It may come to that, God forbid. *Nulla placere diu nec vivere carmina possunt/ Quae scribuntur aquae potoribus.* Are you all right?"

"Compared to what I'll be like a week from today," January replied, surveying his cut hands and filthy clothing, "I'm Bellona's very bridegroom, disdaining fortune with my brandished steel." He flexed his hands gingerly, cursing the stiffness that he knew he'd be weeks getting rid of. "Since you're on your feet I assume the answer to my question is No: You didn't touch any of the liquor in Simon Fourchet's cabinet, did you?"

Hannibal shook his head, and padded back to the bed. "I did set little pans of it about in the storeroom under the house. I tried to set them in different areas, but of course there's no guarantee which particular rat supped which particular dish. *If sack and sugar be a fault, God help the wicked.* They all died, manifestly in the same conditions attending the death of the unfortunate Gilles, of which Cornwallis treated me to the fullest possible description. Cheery fellow. After that I wasn't thirsty for some reason."

"Throw away the dishes." January started to bring up the Hitchcock chair from beside the desk, then remembered the filthy state of his clothes and sat instead on the floor near the bed. "Oleander, boiled up in water. By the look of the branches, it was done several weeks ago. Mambo Jeanne, the plantation midwife when I was a child, told me and Olympe about that one, and I ran across a number of cases when I was in France. There were two children who died of making whistles from its bark."

> *"So mortal that but dip a knife in it,*
> *Where it draws blood no cataplasm so rare,*
> *Collected from all simples that have virtue*
> *Under the moon, can save the thing from death*
> *That is but scratched withal. . . ."*

"More or less," agreed January. "And though Mambo Jeanne died years ago, according to what I've heard her son and daughter are here—the daughter's the overseer's woman. So it might behoove you to watch what you eat and drink."

"Like a Persian Emperor, *amicus meus.*" Hannibal opened the case that lay on the foot of his bed and unraveled his violin from its wrappings of silken scarves. "The same goes for yourself."

"One thing that can be said for living in the quarters," said January dourly. "The food may not be lavish or delicious, but a poisoner would be hard put to pick out a single man to kill."

"It's pleasant and reassuring to know there is good in all situations of life. Why would someone who wished to murder Simon Fourchet take the trouble to set fire to his sugar-mill and his mule barn? Why interfere with the harvest by making the work gang sick and putting red pepper and turpentine on the mule harness?" He experimented with the first few bars of the Largo from Vivaldi's *Lute Concerto* in D, then tightened a string. "Why give yourself away in advance? Wouldn't it be safer to simply dose the man's blue ruin and look surprised?"

"It would," agreed January. "Hence my curiosity about what may actually be going on. It isn't an organized rebellion, I'm almost sure of that. I think I'd have felt it, at the shout last night. Everyone in the quarters is frightened, the way they look at each other, the way the men in the fields speak."

"Could they be lying? Or just not in on it?"

"I don't think so." January recalled what Rose had said, about not knowing the unspoken rules, and thought about who'd spoken to him in the fields, and at the shout. The men and women with the position in the quarters to have led a rebellion had been as genuinely perplexed and afraid as anyone. No one had been wary of a newcomer.

Not rebellion, he thought, at least not on a large scale. Something else that looked like it.

But it was that resemblance that would be fatal to the innocent, if the true culprit were not found.

"Have you had a chance to speak to Madame Fourchet?"

"Only briefly. Madame Hélène, however, has been in here most of the day, keeping me apprised of her new mother-in-law's perfidious and high-handed alterations in household routine . . . and I suppose she has a point. When she and Robert left for France in March, Hélène was very much the woman of the house, both here and in the town house during the winter season. Now, upon stepping off the steamship, she is informed that she's been usurped by a schoolgirl twelve years her junior with little tact and less tolerance of Hélène's sensitive nerves—and not a trace of the schoolgirl admiration which Hélène's beauty and sophistication apparently excited in Madame Fourchet's Daubray cousins."

Usurped of more than her position in her father-in-law's home, thought January.

Il tu traite comme chienne. . . .

"Did Robert know Madame Fourchet before she wed his father?"

"He must have met her, at least. Everyone around here knows everyone else."

"Find out," said January. "And learn what you can about this lawsuit between the Daubrays and Fourchet. If the intention is to damage the plantation, then it might be that . . ."

Nails scratched at the jalousies. January got swiftly to his feet, stiffening muscles knifing him in the side like an assassin.

It was the plump little woman in black, who had wept at the shout.

She stepped back, eyebrows rocketing tignonward as if she were about to demand what a field hand was doing in the big house. Then she glanced at January's face and closed her lips. Looking past him to the bed, she said, "Michie Hannibal?" in the gentle voice that told January that, like every other woman he'd ever encountered, this one had succumbed to Hannibal's courtly and vulnerable charm.

"Kiki, *bellissima mia.*" He set aside his violin and extended his hand. January stepped out of the doorway; Kiki drew her skirts aside lest they brush his clothing, and crossed to the bed.

"I'm just closing up the kitchen now, Michie Hannibal," she said. "I wondered if there was something I could get for you before I do? You barely touched your supper."

"Thank you, no, nothing." He took her fingers in his: Hers were startlingly big and heavy, muscled like a man's. "Kiki, this is my man Benjamin."

"Pleased," she lied, and bobbed the tiniest of polite curtsies. "I've left bread and butter for you in the pantry, in case you do get hungry," she said, turning back to Hannibal with a shy smile she endeavored to hide. From her apron pocket she produced a square businesslike copper bell. "You ring this should you need anything, sir. Agamemnon and Leander, and that Cornwallis"—her sweet-toned voice had a flick of scorn to it as she spoke the Virginia valet's name—"sleep over the kitchen, and I have a little room right behind it. Any of us will hear."

"Acushla—" He kissed her hand. "My slumbers will be the sounder knowing myself so much cared for."

She passed January without glancing at him, only by the tightening of her lips registering his presence at all. January had the impression she was going to instruct the maids to give the floor of the room an extra scrub in the morning.

If Harry and his ladyfriend still reposed themselves under the cistern they'd settled, like the lovers on Donne's moss-grown bank, into silence when January descended the steps. Rather than cross the open ground that lay between the big house and the cluster of kitchen, forge, shops, and stable—illumined still by the reflected glare from the open doors of the mill—he retraced his earlier route under the gallery, around three sides of the house and along the black deadly hedge of Camille's garden, until he could attain the darkness of the stubble cane.

As he went he heard Hannibal begin to play a Vivaldi largo, the sweet sad beauty of the notes a reminder that a world existed beyond the boundaries of Mon Triomphe, beyond the chains of place and time. From the cane's edge he looked back, to the men and women of the night crew still hauling wood along the mill's wall from the closest of the three huge sheds like a trail of torchlit ants. *This is not all there is,* he told himself.

But as a child he had not known that.

Gosport had seen to it that a couple of yams and a pone of ash-bread had been left for him in a basket hung from the cabin's rafter, to keep it from the ever-present rats. Groping for his blankets January noted the absence of both Jeanette's brother Parson—who was in the second gang and on night duty at the mill—and Quashie. When he rose a few hours later, washed as well as he could, and crept through the raw mist of not-quite-dawn to change the bandanna on the branch from black to white, neither had yet returned.

And the evening and the morning were the first day.

SIX

In the iron-cold dark of predawn, the men heard Thierry cursing before they were halfway down the quarters' street. Without a word exchanged among them they passed by the rice cart and went straight on. Even January could tell that someone was going to bleed.

Thierry stood on the steps that led up to the lean-to back room of his house. Through the open door behind him January could see the boxes where the overseer kept the cane-knives, and a portion of the wall above. There was a lamp lit in the room, and the smoky gold light showed up a vévé—a voodoo sign to summon the spirits—written on that wall. January recognized the triangles and stars and skulls of one of the evil *loa,* Baron Cemetery or Brigitte of the Dry Arms. Beneath the sign had been drawn a stylized tombstone surrounded by arrows.

Most of the cane-knives were gone.

After his outburst Thierry was even more soft-spoken than usual, but standing among the bachelors in the main gang, January saw how the man was nearly trembling with rage. "You think maybe you're going to scare us, hunh?" he asked, almost pleasantly, voice smooth as a razor's blade. "Think you'll make things easier for yourselves? Well, let me tell you, before I'm done you're the ones gonna be scared."

He snaked the whip out along the ground, cracked it savagely inches from the nearest man's feet. "You think I don't know who's behind this? Ajax, Herc, you take that Quashie and you lock him in the jail—"

"I didn't do nuthin'!" Quashie fell back a pace as the two drivers handed off the torches they held to others, and stepped up to flank him. "I went right straight back to the cabin when I was done workin'! Ben, Gosport, Kadar, you seen me!"

"I did, sir," put in Gosport, who had probably been unconscious before his head hit his corn-shuck pillow and hadn't stirred until January's return from the oak on the levee. "We was all of us there."

"You lie to me, boy, and you'll get a couple of your friend's licks. That what you want?" The whip cracked the air so close to Gosport's chest it stirred his shirt, though the man—eyes respectfully downcast—didn't flinch. And to Quashie, "Now where'd you dump those knives, my friend?"

"I didn't touch 'em! I didn't—"

"Seems to me you're in trouble enough without lying, son."

"I didn't touch 'em!" yelled Quashie again, as Ajax and Herc took him by either arm. "You think if I was in your house and you sleepin' . . ." His voice faltered and for a moment his eyes met the white man's, as if he were not a slave, as if the man were not the whip in his master's hand.

Thierry regarded him for a moment with a certain amount of surprise, as if a lump of his own excrement had spoken to him. "Maybe somebody you know had somethin' to do with it?" he asked pleasantly. And then, in a voice like an ax in wood, "Jeanette!"

She appeared in the lamplit golden doorway, hair over her shoulders in a cloud like sheep's wool. He hadn't given her time to dress and she was barely breathing with shame as she buttoned her bright calico frock. It was one thing, thought January, for all your friends and all your family and everyone you grew up with to know you shared the overseer's bed, and another to be called publicly to the door of his house at dawn. "Yes, sir?" It was the first time January had heard her voice and in it he heard old Mambo Jeanne's, like woodsmoke and honey.

"You and this boy here been up to something?" Behind the softness there was an edge of terrible danger in Thierry's voice. "You maybe let him in my house while I was asleep, and the two of you threw them cane-knives in the river?"

Quashie's face was like stone.

"No, sir," the girl said.

"I slept real hard last night. You hear anyone coming or going in the night?"

Her jaw set and January remembered how the window had creaked open last night, and the light swift scrunch of feet in the oak leaves. He glanced beside him at Parson, Jeanette's brother. Saw the thin young face set expressionless, giving the Man neither shame nor fear.

"No, sir. I slept sound, too, sir."

He said, "Slut," and turned to glance at Parson. "Your sister's a whore, Parson."

"Yes, sir."

Thierry waved impatiently at Quashie, standing between the two drivers. "Get him out of here. There's ten knives left," he went on, as the young man was led away toward the small brick jailhouse, twisting against their grip to look back at Jeanette. "And if those fifteen that's missing ain't found I'll have the rest of you out chewing that cane down with your teeth."

Eight men were given torches and detailed to search for the knives. Most of the search concentrated on the riverbank, the levee, and the narrow channel that lay between the bank and Catbird Island. Doing the best he could to look as if he were searching for cane-knives, January checked in the grass and weeds around the overseer's cottage itself.

It was built in the old Creole fashion, river mud and moss between studs, the New World version of the half-timber houses of England and France. Two rooms opened onto a gallery that faced the river, with the narrow lean-to built all across the back, the whole of it lying some twenty yards downstream of the big house. Under the window that he'd seen open last night, January found scuff marks in the weeds: There were more a little farther off where the long grass gave way to the mats of oak leaves between the cottage and the cane-fields. He checked in the cane-field itself, as well as he could between the close-growing rows, and found, as he'd expected, various sorts of scuffs and partial prints, but no convenient outline such as invariably presented itself to the Deerslayer when culprits needed to be identified or evildoers trailed across several hundred miles of wilderness. By the unsteady glare of his pine-knot it wasn't easy to tell, and in any case that stretch of cane was a logical pathway from the quarters to the river, and the whole unfree population of Mon Triomphe had probably trodden it during the past week.

"God curse you, man!" Fourchet's roar sliced the

chilly gray gloom from the other side of the house. "I pay you to keep those niggers in line and if you can't do it I'll find someone who can!"

Thierry's reply, if any, was inaudible, but Esteban's voice said, "Father—uh—now isn't—isn't the time—"

"Don't you tell me when I can speak and when I can't, you bastard weasel! I wish to God those niggers had killed you instead of your mother. . . ."

"Michie Fourchet!" a child's shrill voice interposed. Looking around the corner of the house January saw Bumper, Ajax's eleven-year-old son, running toward them through the weeds. The boy was accompanied as always by his seven-year-old brother Nero, a chubby silent shadow. "Michie Fourchet, sir, they found the knives!"

January unobtrusively followed the little group—Fourchet, Thierry, Esteban, and the boys—to the plantation blacksmith shop, unobtrusively because he was joined by most of the other men who'd been ordered to search. By the time they reached the low building that stood at the end of the row of plantation shops, there was a sizable gaggle of witnesses. The cane-knives had been thrust into the forge, coals piled in, and the bellows plied to heat the fire red-hot. The wooden handles had been reduced to crumbling charcoal.

"By God I'll string them up for this!" Fourchet's flushed face looked almost black in the rose-colored glare of the furnace. "The man who did this is going to suffer, and see his family suffer as well, and that I swear to you. . . ."

He swung around, his eye snagging January among the other men at the smithy door. For a moment January feared the planter was so furious he'd start berating him for not doing his job, so he cried in his most gombo French, "My Lordy, could one man carry all them knives in one trip without cuttin' himself?

I couldn't hardly manage one and I'm all cut to bits."

The reminder of who he was and who he was supposed to be caught Fourchet up and made him close his mouth again, and Mohammed, who'd stepped back from the forge to make way for the white men, said, "He wrapped 'em in an old blanket. Look." He held up a ragged piece of cloth that had been thrown in the corner. Thierry snatched it from his hands, then threw it down in disgust. It was one of his own.

Stepping close to the forge again, Mohammed remarked, "He sure wasn't a blacksmith, I'll say that. He's lucky he didn't kill the fire, piling coal on like that every which way."

"Can they be fixed?" Fourchet's voice was quiet now, anger eased as quickly as it had flared. Turning to the door of the smithy, where half a dozen men and women had joined the original witnesses, he yelled, "Out of here! If the lot of you don't have enough to do . . . !"

They scattered. January remained.

Mohammed tonged a blade from the cooling heap that had been carried to the table near the door. Laying the metal over the anvil he gave it a smart rap with one of the smaller hammers: The sharp edge fractured like flint.

"Now, wait a minute, you gonna start breakin' these, too—"

"He's testing the temper, you imbecile," snapped Fourchet at the protesting overseer. "That one was ruined before he touched it."

"I'll check and fix as many as I can, sir." Mohammed turned the blade doubtfully back and forth under the weak yellow glow of the smithy lamp. "We'll need handles for all of 'em, though."

January caught Fourchet's eye and the planter said,

"Ben, you're no good in the field, we'll leave you here for that. I'll send Random over with wood and a knife and he'll show you what to do. Thierry, get the rest of the men started with whatever knives are left. The others can haul wood til we have those ready to go." He jerked his head back toward the long sheds of cordwood, looming in the dawn gloom. "You men who made the search, get yourself some food if you haven't.

"Boy—" This was to Bumper. "You go to the kitchen and tell Kiki to start cooking up some glue. Get Ti-Jeanne to give you rags to wrap the handles. And put out the flag on the landing. Esteban, go to town and get fifteen knives. We'll make do til you get back. Understand?"

"Yes, Father."

"And I mean you get back *today.* No lollygagging in town, or stopping for a cup of coffee with your—"

"I'll be back today, Father." Esteban's jaw muscles jumped in the firelight and he spoke the words between his teeth without meeting his father's eye.

"See you are."

Though the warm radiance of the forge still colored his face January saw how pale the old planter had turned, once the flush of anger ebbed. Pale and a little shrunken. His hand trembled as it rested on the brick sill of the forge and it remained there, almost as if supporting him, for some moments.

Then Fourchet turned, and walked into the misty white of dawn.

"So who is this hoodoo?" January measured the length of the charred and crumbling handle of one of the damaged knives against a billet of the wood that Random, the plantation carpenter, had brought from his shop, and settled himself on a bench just inside the smithy door to shape it. After a few minutes' wary observation, Random apparently concluded that January was competent to wield tools. He went back to his shop to cut more lengths for the handles. "You spoke of a hoodoo at the dark of the moon. What's going on here?"

"Don't think we're not nearly crazy tryin' to figure that out for ourselves." Mohammed blew out his breath in a sigh. Outside, a driver cursed at one of the wood-haulers, whose path from sheds to the mill doors ran along the wall of the mill just opposite the smithy's entrance. "It's somebody crazy. It's somebody who don't care what happens to him, it's got to be. Not care what happens to him, not care what happens to anyone else. Which makes me think it's somebody not on the place."

"Who, 'not on the place'?" January marked where the rivets would affix the handle to the shank, and carried the wood to the drill bench. "How is that?"

"You don't think with the hoodoo, and them tools broken—you don't think with what happened to Michie Fourchet's first wife and their child—they wouldn't come after everyone on the place if he was to die?" The blacksmith shook his head, and then grinned a little, as if against his own will. "The sorry thing is, you could go up and down this river and ask every solitary person you meet, white or black, if they'd like to murder Simon Fourchet and I bet the answer you'd get is 'yes.' You ever worked a drill? Just like that, yes.

"Michie Fourchet is on bad terms with nearly everyone in the parish," the blacksmith went on. "It's nearly come to shooting with Rankin, that cracker farmer lives over toward New River. Michie Fourchet killed Judge Rauche's eldest son in a duel not two years ago, in an argument over the location of the bar that silted up near the old landing, of all the boneheaded things.

That trader that comes by here, False River Jones, Fourchet chained him in the jail here last September, and threatened to horsewhip him if he ever saw him on his land again—though every planter on the river's threatened to horsewhip Jones one time or another."

While he spoke the smith carried each blackened steel to the anvil and struck it lightly, testingly, with one of the smaller hammers, then held it to the milky daylight that trickled in now through the smithy doors.

"And if every slave with a killing grievance against his master did as he wished, after that master had sold him off down the river, or beat him for what he didn't do, or sold away his wife or his child . . ." His jaw stiffened with old wounds, old memories, and he shook his head.

"But that slave would know, wouldn't he," said January, pausing in his stroke at the old-fashioned bow-drill, "that coming back to get revenge on the man that sold him, would mean hurting every other person on the place."

"That's why I say," said Mohammed, "whoever's doin' this is crazy."

"And are there any?" asked January. "That he sold off, who might come back? That had their families sold?"

Mohammed thought about it, tapping and striking, testing the metal, shaking his head with a look of pain—as he himself did, thought January, when he'd enter a home and find that the children were suffered to bang on and mistreat the piano, until its hammers were broken and its keys out of tune.

"Well, ten years back he sold off Zuzu, that was Lisbon's wife, and their children." The smith fished, casually and accurately, back into his *griot*'s memory for details like the verses of a song. "There was some to-do over that, but they're only down on Voussaire plantation, and Lisbon sees them when he can. Michie Fourchet sold off Tabby, that was Yellow Austin's wife, about a year ago, to a guest that came through, a broker from New Orleans who took a fancy to her."

As St.-Denis Janvier did, thought January, *to my mother. "That man's gonna buy your mama."* He still remembered hearing the other children whispering, around the cabin door that night. *Gonna buy your mama, and sell you off in New Orleans.*

He tried to remember if his father had been there then, and couldn't. "He take her children as well?"

Mohammed shook his head. "They're still here—Tanisha and Marbro; that's Marbro." He nodded toward the first of the woodsheds, where the hogmeat gang was picking up chips and bark. "The little one there playin' with that piece of cane." As January watched, an older child showed the boy—who looked about three—how to blow pebbles through the slender stalk; Bumper came up and hustled them back to their duties. Already Ajax's son seemed to have grasped the concept of how much work had to be done. He seemed also to have learned from Ajax how to go about it with a laugh.

"M'am Fourchet's taken Tanisha into the house, teach her to sew like her mama," Mohammed added thoughtfully. "They do set a store on the light-skinned ones. I think the dark frightens them, dark like you, and dark like me. But Yellow Austin, he moved in with his sister Emerald and her husband, and they do well, and besides"—he rested the hammer gently on the anvil's horn—"the night the mill burned, Austin was working out in the ciprière, and I've talked to three men who was standing beside him when Bumper came running with news of the fire."

January brought the drilled handle back, and worked the bellows while Mohammed heated rivets.

From the forge door the damage to the mill didn't appear to be much. Smoke-blackening in areas under the eaves of the steeply slanted roof, and around the small windows high in the walls. Fortunate, he thought, that the fire had been checked early, for along this side of the mill was piled all the scrap lumber and broken packing boxes cleared out from the carpenter's and cooper's shops, mixed in with worn-out baskets and shards of oil jars or damaged clay cones such as the sugar was cured in. Hashed in with all that was an almost unbelievable quantity of cane-trash: leaves, cut ends, bits of maiden cane, weeds, dirt.

He frowned, and with the air of a man speaking a sudden revelation asked, "Well, couldn't you—couldn't you figure out who's doing this by asking, I mean, who was where when the mill burned? You say Austin was with these three other men, I guess in the second gang? Since Austin's in the second gang? So if the second gang was out in the ciprière . . ."

"You do got a head on your shoulders," said Mohammed, and January looked flustered, as if he'd never been told this in his life.

"Aw, my mama always said I was the dumb one."

"Well, maybe your mama wasn't payin' attention." The smith's eyes twinkled. "You don't do bad on a drill. You have the rhythm of it, like music." He tonged a rivet into place and upset it with a few neat hammer-taps, so that it held the handle tight. "I tell you this," he added, picking up another blade and cutting the old rivets free, "I've been asking, and I've tried to get as many people as I could trust to ask, and it's like trying to catch fish in your hands. It was near dark, and foggy, and yes, the second gang was in the ciprière cutting wood, two miles from the mill when the fire broke out. But I think, who can watch who in the dark and the fog?"

His powerful hands flipped the next handle's wood over, and with a nail-gouge marked it for the rivet holes; his dark eyes turned somberly inward, seeing what only he could see. "And every time Gosport—who is a good man, and can be trusted—says to me, 'At the time the fire broke out I was with Samson and Balaam, and I saw Dumaka and Laertes and Boaz together, and Dumaka tells me he spoke to Lando only a few moments before,' I think: *Gosport could be lying. He's only been on this place two years. What do I know of him before then?* Dumaka could be lying, or mistaken. I think I know, and then it turns out that I don't."

Random returned, and started shaping the handles as they were marked and drilled. Of the fifteen blades that had been thrust into the forge, five were completely unfit for use and ten were questionable. The day was now bright outside, the mist gone, the breeze from the river fresh and chill. Fewer hands passed the doors hauling wood, as other tasks became possible, and from the direction of the fields January could hear the men singing, the women's voices answering them as they went out with the carts. Lisbon—one of the steadiest and oldest men of the second gang—called out, "Giselle, you holdin' up the line, what you doin' there?"

Roulaison.

"What about the vévés?" January asked. "First in the mill, and now in Michie Thierry's house, and other places, you said."

Mohammed's glance cut sharply to him, but Random said, "The signs turned up all over. On the brick piers underneath the house, and in the mule barn, and in the house, too. When Michie Robert came back from Paris, first thing he did was have the big house searched, and all the barns. They found hoodoo marks on the backs of armoires, and behind the curtains."

"Same as the one in Michie Thierry's house?"

"Exactly the same. The coffin and arrows, and all those triangles and the skull."

January was silent for a time, body swaying with the rhythm of the drill. "I think I'm getting the hang of this," he said. "That bit stayed in the wood and didn't go after my fingers, that time."

And Random laughed.

"Funny thing about those vévés, though," said Mohammed. "Here, Ben." He threw him a piece of red chalk. "You go make an X on that wall there. Now look." He took the chalk himself and did exactly as he'd told January to do, demonstrating to Random what January already knew—that, particularly when he's writing in a hurry, a man will mark a wall not much above nor much below the level of his own eyes. "Now, I don't know how far off the floor those marks in Michie Thierry's cottage are," the smith said, returning to his forge. "But I saw the ones they found in the butler's pantry, and in Michie Fourchet's office, and they were maybe as high as my eyes, maybe a little above. Whoever's makin' these marks—" He gestured with a damaged knife. "It wasn't Quashie. He's too tall."

Over the course of the next two hours, during which Ti-George the scullery boy appeared with a stinking pot of isinglass, mastic, and turpentine glue to wrap the knife handles—Kiki apparently disdaining the thought of bringing it to field hands herself—January pieced together a rough chronology of the hoodoo's depredations on Mon Triomphe. As Fourchet had said, the first sign of trouble on the plantation had been the fire in the sugar-mill, which had broken out on the evening of the second of November—All Souls' night—shortly after darkness fell. It was difficult to get a definite idea of where anyone was when Reuben had first seen the blaze in the mill, but the drivers in each gang were definitely accounted for. The main-gang men leading the mules were accounted for. Little groups—unless they were all lying together, as Gosport had lied for Quashie that very morning—accounted for one another.

Of the main gang, a man named Pancho had definitely been missing ("He has a broad-wife over at Lescelles, though," pointed out Random, "he was gone most of the day."). Harry had definitely been missing ("Well, *Harry*!"). No one specifically remembered seeing Quashie, and no one remembered seeing a man named Taswell, who was as inoffensive as a milk-cow and occupied primarily with his wife and children. The second gang was more difficult to pin down, owing to the more diffuse nature of their work, but everyone had a general idea of having seen everyone else in the gang too recently before the fire started for anyone to have run nearly two miles to the mill and back.

If everyone was telling the truth.

"Jasper and Scipio were out with the main gang," provided Random, speaking of his fellow artisans, the plantation cooper and potter. "Besides, they're both married, they have children. . . . They had no call to do such a thing."

Didn't they? thought January. What might be a catastrophe to one man, a hammer-blow to his pride, might to another be simply the way of the world. The custom of the country.

On the other side of the low rise of the levee a whistle shrilled. The black smokestacks of the steamboat *Vermillion* could be seen past the big house and the oak trees, bound south from St. Louis and pulling out of the big current at the sign of the white flag on the wharf. January wondered whether one of the strikers or the firemen would report to Shaw that that morning, Sunday, the bandanna on the tree branch was white.

Like that old Greek fella.

"I tried to find out some about the house-servants." Mohammed wrapped a strip of rawhide, glued on one side, carefully and tightly around one of the new handles, set it aside on the table outside the smithy door. "You'd have thought I was Benedict Arnold out trying to sell the country to the British. Catch Michie Cornwallis talking to a yard-man: hmph!" He grinned.

"You need to have a try at Leander," suggested Random, returning the blacksmith's grin, "now he's back from Paris—That's Michie Robert's man," he explained to January. "My lord, that man gossips! You want to know the colors of M'am Hélène's stockings, that's the man to ask."

"Leander wasn't here at the time of the fire in the mill," said Mohammed. "Nor when the breakfast pots were poisoned."

"Couldn't you figure out who did it by who was around the rice cart? Who fixes that? You say Jeanette's mama was a voodoo."

"So she was," agreed Mohammed. "And lord, you'd have thought Michie Fourchet was going to give birth, the way he carried on! But you've seen yourself Jeanette doesn't leave Michie Thierry's house til all the men get their day's work, and she goes straight to the women's gang. The men have already eaten by then. Minta brings it out, but she's got to help Kiki with takin' breakfast up to the big house, so most mornin's the rice cart just sits out with a board over the top of the pots. Anybody could come and stir something in."

"And Kiki? . . ."

"Has her own reasons to want to see this hoodoo

caught," said Mohammed quietly. "Gilles was her husband."

"They fixed?" Thierry's shadow blackened the smithy door.

"Fixed as I can make 'em, sir." Mohammed finished wrapping the handle he was working on and rose, drying his hands on a rag. Thierry took the first knife they'd worked on and whacked it savagely into the doorpost half a dozen times, so that January winced. But the blade held up. The overseer turned it in his hand a moment, then tossed it carelessly back among the others.

"Ten was all you could save?"

"I'll show you the others, sir: edges cracked, metal split. And these won't last long, beggin' your pardon."

"Fuckin' hoodoo." Thierry tapped the handle of the most newly repaired, feeling the slight tacky give of the wrapping, then ambled into the smithy to look at the blades that were past use.

"It'll be a good hour, sir, 'fore the glue sets up on those we fixed."

The overseer regarded the smith with narrowed eyes, as if gauging how much truth was in the statement, then glanced past him at the confusion around the doors of the mill. Baron the mule-drover was leading new teams down the short slope into the roundhouse. Through the arched windows between the brick piers that held up the floor of the grinder, January made out dim comings and goings as Rodney checked the harness. Mohammed and Random had agreed that the first time the mule harness had been rubbed with red pepper and turpentine was the day of the poisoning, when the grinders broke as the poor beasts had bolted. After that the harness had been contaminated twice more—two nights after the fire in the mule barn, apparently during the night, and again on the night Gilles had died. On those same occasions other harness had been cut, and cart axles sawed.

Equipment was now guarded by Baron and his son Ulee, as their personal responsibility.

Through the low arched windows Fourchet's voice could be heard, savagely informing someone or other that those mules were a damn sight more valuable than he was, and smarter, too. Thierry's eyes squinted up a little, and the anger in him resonated with his employer's like the drone-string on a banjo.

"Ben, you get on back to the field and tell Ajax to put you to work." Thierry tossed him the first of the knives, the one he'd struck at the doorpost with. "Stop at the mill and tell Rodney to send another nine here to pick up the knives as soon as they can be spared."

"Right away, sir." January put from his mind the seductive image of his own fist smashing into the man's dark lean face as the overseer strode away toward the path that led to the fields.

As he limped along the wood-haulers' path—cursing the poor fit of his shoes—January pieced the days together in his mind. Trying to see a pattern in them, of who could have gotten to the harness, and the mill, and the barn, and the rice cart; who could have gotten into the house and when. Who knew enough about poisons to kill the drinker of the cognac but only make the main gang sick. Where the oleander had been cooked. Where the turpentine and pepper mixed.

Off the place entirely?

How visible would a stranger have been, slipping up through the cane-fields from the old landing in the dark? But how could a stranger have known that everyone would be away and busy, that foggy afternoon at the dark of the moon?

In the blazing heat of the sugar-mill Fourchet was yelling, "Get the hell out of the way, you black fool!"

at one of the men who skimmed the black foam from the boiling cane-juice in *la grande.* The man leaped aside to make way for the barrel in which the foam would be settled and dried to add to cattle-feed. "You think we got all goddam day? All goddam week? Stupid bastard apes . . . What in hell you want?"

He glared at January, his furious eyes blank black pits of rage, and January knew very clearly that Fourchet would think no more of striking him than he'd think before striking one of his slaves. January waited a moment, eyes downcast, before saying, "Michie Thierry sent me to let the men from the main gang know the cane-knives are fixed, sir, and they can get back to the cuttin' if you have no more need of 'em here."

"Need 'em?" bellowed Fourchet. He flung his cigar end to the ground. "We need 'em everywhere, you brainless *bozal*! I'll send 'em back when we've got the next run cooking properly! Fucking niggers don't know the difference between—"

"I'll tell Michie Thierry that, then, sir." January bowed. He flinched at the thought, but added, "And if you're free just for a moment, sir, there's somethin' regardin' the knives gettin' broke." And, ready to duck, watched Fourchet's hands and body. He saw the planter's hand tighten on the sugar-paddle, but Fourchet stopped himself, glanced around the mill with those bloodshot, bestial eyes. "Come outside. Rodney!" The dapper little driver bounded over from *la lessive,* which men were just filling from the second after another round of boiling and skimming. "You know how much ash and lime goes in when this mess is skimmed? Good. When I come back in every man jack here better be working or there'll be sore backs."

He shoved the paddle into Rodney's hand and stalked from the mill, January at his heels. They pushed through the women unloading cane and rounded the downstream end of the mill where the brick walls of the jail sheltered them from view of the confusion at the mill doors. Only a few yards away, the dark cane rose in a knotty wall.

"What is it?" Fourchet bit the end of another cigar as if it were personally responsible for all the woes that had beset Mon Triomphe. "What have you found?"

"First, sir, that I think you're right—I don't think it's a revolt being planned. They're giving themselves away, giving too much warning."

"Hmph," muttered Fourchet. "I told you as much." But in the slight relaxation of his shoulders January saw the portrait of the dead woman, the dead child, on the parlor wall, and thought, *He was afraid for her. Afraid for Marie-Noël.*

"Secondly, I don't think Quashie was the one who damaged the knives." And he related what Mohammed—and he himself—had already observed about the height of the voodoo marks on the walls. "It automatically rules out a number of people."

"It does, does it?" Anger flooded back into those bitter eyes, a rage at the world so deep it had forgotten its origins, had it ever known them. His shirt beneath his black wool coat was sweat-sodden and his grizzled hair hung in lank and dripping strings. "Then you'd better automatically rule him back in, because Robert's man Leander saw him around the front side of Thierry's cottage. After midnight, which is when those other niggers swear he was tucked up like an angel in his bed! So how about that?"

January shut his teeth hard and took two deep breaths before replying. No wonder Esteban couldn't get a sentence out of his mouth. Already after two days he'd found himself less and less willing to go anywhere near Fourchet if he didn't have to, an attitude, he knew, that wouldn't help his inquiries. "Did Leander see Quashie take the knives, then, sir?"

"You think my son lets his man stand around the gallery half the night staring into nothing? The boy's a self-conceited pup and his man is worse, but at least he knows how to keep a servant at his work."

"Then Quashie might have been there for another purpose? Waiting for someone, maybe?"

Fourchet's eyes slitted. After a long time he said in a quieter voice, "I told that bitch she was too good for him. And Thierry's worth more to me than the brats that field hand would sire on her. He'll sire 'em on someone else, they all do."

"Perhaps Quashie was waiting for someone else, then, sir."

Fourchet opened his mouth to snap something at him, then let his breath out, and came down off his toes exactly as a fighting cock settles back when its opponent is taken from the ring. Some of the fury receded from his face, and his mouth untwisted from a grimace to a bleak and weary line.

He looked at the cigar in his hand, then looked around for a light. January reminded himself that Fourchet didn't know he, January, carried lucifers in his pocket—and cursed himself for that impulse to appease the man by producing one.

What the hell is wrong with me? But he knew the answer to that.

"God knows I've done ill enough in my life," Fourchet said. "I've tried to make amends where I can." Turning abruptly, he strode back to the mill doors, as Thierry came around the other corner, whip coiled beneath his arm. Herc was behind him, his round baby face wooden, and they were clearly headed for the low brown brick box of the plantation jail; Fourchet said, "Thierry," and they stopped. "Doesn't look as though Quashie had anything to do with them knives."

The overseer stared at him, then past him at January, bleak blue eyes like glass. "You don't mean you believe anything this—"

"It's none of your lookout what I believe or don't believe, or why," Fourchet snarled. "For now I don't think Quashie did it, and let it go at that. So you just give him a couple of licks for wandering around outside at night, you hear? Now I've got to get back to the mill. God knows what that imbecile Rodney's been dumping into the boiling while we've been out here wasting time in talk."

He shoved the unlit cigar into his mouth and stalked back into the mill, a rigid bristling figure: January could hear him shouting at Esteban for not skimming *la lessive* quickly enough, and did he want the sugar to sour on him?

Thierry said, "Cunt fool," in his soft mild voice and slapped his whip on his boot. Then he glanced up at January. "So. With me, Cotton-Patch. Let's get that nigger triced and laced so's the both of you can get back to your work."

January hesitated, helpless and angry that, accepting his story as truth, the planter had decided to have the man whipped anyway, simply to prove to everyone that he could. . . .

"Step along, boy. I said give me a hand, unless you want a dose of the same."

Fourchet had already vanished into the darkness of the mill. In any case January knew that no white man would countermand his overseer's orders in front of—and certainly not regarding—a slave. He said, "Yes, sir," and followed Thierry and Herc to the jail, hating himself and Fourchet more completely at every step.

SEVEN

It was one of the most savage beatings January had seen administered in his life. Quashie fought like a devil, screaming curses at him, at Thierry and Hercules from the moment they entered the jailhouse, kicking, biting, ramming with his head and trying to catch and strangle one or the other of them in the short slack of his chains.

"Hold him," Thierry panted. "Hold him, God damn you!" and Herc stepped in to obey, so January had to follow—follow or destroy whatever chances he might have of finding the true killer before Fourchet's inevitable murder triggered wholesale retaliation against everyone on the plantation.

A laudable end, he reflected angrily—more praiseworthy than simply the desire to be spared whipping himself—but the result for Quashie was the same.

He did the best he could not to think about what he was doing, while he held the young man's arm in an iron grip. Tried not to hear the leathery thump of balled fists hammering into belly, groin, face.

"Strip him," said Thierry, when he finally stepped

back. Sweat rolled down his jaws but he spoke as if to a baker about an order of bread. "Trice him up."

Quashie was still trying to fight as January and Herc manhandled him outside, though his knees were water and they had to carry him. The whipping frame stood in front of the jail, about thirty feet from the doors of the mill. The women unloading the cane carts, the men hauling wood stopped work, clustering uneasily, and a voice from within the mill shouted at them to *Move on, damn it!*

With a cry, Jeanette dropped the bundle of cane she carried, ran across the open ground. Thierry caught her by the arm, slapped her face, shoved her away so hard she fell. "Get back to work."

Jeanette remained kneeling, trembling, staring mutely up into the face of this white man who had her every night.

"Boy isn't anything to you, is he?"

Her eyes fell and she got slowly to her feet. "No, sir," she whispered. "No. He's nothing to me."

Quashie took the flogging in silence. January wasn't sure at what point the man passed out.

"Leave him there," Thierry ordered when he was done. "Herc, fetch me a bucket of water to clean this." He gestured with the gore-clotted whip. "You, Cotton-Patch, ain't I told you an hour ago to get them knives and get back to work?"

"Yes, sir." January was shaking with self-loathing, with rage, with emotions he thought he'd left behind him in childhood. "Right away, sir."

He went around the downstream end of the mill rather than the upstream side on which the smithy lay, walked about halfway along, then staggered into the cane to vomit. There wasn't much—it was a few hours yet short of time for the rice cart to come at noon. Then he went on to the forge and collected the knives, and returning to the mill doors found Herc with the nine first-gang men released to return to the fields.

Across the yard, Quashie still hung silent from the rawhide ropes on the frame.

Thierry was nowhere around.

"I'll join you in a little while," said January to Herc.

"If Michie Thierry asks me who cut him down I'll have to tell him." Hercules's round face was grave. January remembered him from the shout, taking the sullen pretty unweeping girl away into the woods with him. Trinette, someone had called her at Ajax's house afterward. The dead man Reuben's wife.

"That's all right. You can tell him you tried to stop me, too."

Herc nodded. "All right."

January walked across the yard and with two quick strokes of the cane-knife cut the ropes, caught Quashie over his shoulder, and carried him past the downstream side of the mill and along the quarters street to the twelve-by-twelve cabin the five men shared.

When he took the gourd from beside the door and stepped out again to fetch water from the cistern to wash the blood from the young man's back, he was met by Jeanette, a dripping bucket in her hand.

"Thank you." He took it from her, and she followed him up the two plank steps and into the cabin. "The flies will have got to him. Could you run to the kitchen, ask Kiki if there's brandy or whiskey, even rum?"

"Kiki wouldn't spit on a field hand's back to wash it." Jeanette jerked her head toward the big house. "They none of 'em would. Besides, Gilles died of drinking liquor in the big house. I be back." She turned and he heard her dart down the steps and run, light as a deer.

She was gone many minutes. January washed down

Quashie's lacerated back as gently as he could and laid a spare shirt over it, to keep out dust and flies. The quarters were silent. Chill sun slanted through the door onto the gray floor-boards, accentuating each shadow with crystalline brightness. The smell of cut cane, of burnt sugar and wet earth, were a universe of childhood griefs. Yet curiously, here in this cabin he felt a strange sense of deep peace.

His own actions had shocked him, his acquiescence to Thierry's tyranny, though he still had no idea what he could have done and yet retained his position as a slave among slaves. He felt deeply soiled and shamed, and at the same time—to his intense embarrassment—afraid of facing Thierry's anger for cutting Quashie down.

This is slavery, he thought, as if he were telling Ayasha about it back in Paris. He scratched in his armpit, the first louse, he realized philosophically, of what would be many, before roulaison was done and everyone had the time it took to keep clean. *This is what I'd almost forgotten.*

This was the world he'd been saved from, at the age of seven, by a Frenchman's lust for his mother. He'd been grateful for it—even at the time he'd been grateful. But for months, sitting in the classroom of the St. Louis Academy among the sons of colored women by their white protectors, or walking along the close-walled streets of the French town, or falling asleep in the narrow confines of the garçonnière of his mother's house on Rue Burgundy, he had missed the smell of the earth, the silence broken only dimly by the singing of the men in the fields.

"I'm sorry." Jeanette's shadow darkened the doorway again. "I knew where Rodney keeps his liquor, but it's been since the dark of the moon that the *onisówó*"—she used the African word for a trader—

"been by, and I had to get this from Harry." She held up a cheap clay bottle of something probably even Hannibal wouldn't have touched unless he was desperate.

Harry, reflected January as he daubed the liquor on a clean rag and gently squeezed it over the puffed and bleeding welts, was the kind who always had a cache of whatever others wanted and would trade for. He wondered what she'd paid for it, or promised to pay.

"Did Gilles buy from the *onisówó,* too?"

She nodded. He saw where Thierry's slap had left a bruise on the side of her face, puffed up now. Saw also a half-healed split in her lip, and a small fresh scar on her chin, the kind a woman gets from her own teeth when a man belts her hard. She was still an extraordinarily pretty girl, slim-boned and strong, her close-wrapped tignon making her head seem small, like a deer's.

"Gilles used to trade candles from the house—not the fresh ones, but the ones that'd already been burned—and coffee grounds and tea leaves after they'd been used. Only somebody stole his stash and drank it up, way before False River Jones was due back."

"He ever steal from Michie Fourchet's liquor before?"

She nodded. "About two years ago." She settled herself on the rough plank floor by the cot—of course there were no chairs—and very gently touched Quashie's hand. "We thought Michie Fourchet was going to kill him. Kiki nursed him, though she was Reuben's wife then—and Reuben, he wasn't pleased. Gilles was laid up three days, ribs broke and everythin'. He should have known better. Should have known that liquor was like gold to Michie Fourchet. Everything he touches, everything he owns, is like gold to him, that other people can't touch."

Her lips tightened. She'd been working in the fields, and her old dress was kilted up to show long, slim legs. The stink of dirt, of cane-juice and sweat on her was not unpleasant to January, only an accounting of who she was. "Gilles wasn't like most men, though. You know how most men, they get liquor and drink it all up and get silly and get sick and then they're fine. They wait til the next chance comes along, and if it don't come along, they say, 'Damn fuck I'd like a drink,' and it's gone from their minds the next second. But Gilles . . ." She shook her head.

"He was the sweetest man in the world, Michie Ben. Kind and good and friendly. And funny—he could always make us laugh. Most of them house niggers, they don't care whether we live or die out here. But he'd sometimes sneak food to those women that was nursin' or about to give birth, or give the children worn-out stuff from the house, blankets and things. But if he couldn't get liquor, liquor was all he thought about until he could."

January was silent, recalling some of the insanely stupid things Hannibal had done, in the course of their two years' acquaintance, when he couldn't get money for opium.

"I was glad when he could finally marry Kiki," Jeanette went on. "She may be stuck up, but nobody deserved bein' married to Reuben."

And January remembered what Mohammed had said, about Reuben's carelessness. About his wanting to win from Michie Fourchet a woman who'd been given to someone else.

"Michie Ben, you better get on back or you'll get a whippin'. I'll stay take care of Quashie a little."

As she spoke she touched Quashie's hand again, where it lay limp on the corn-shuck mattress. The tenderness on her face was free of any shame or fear. Confident, like a child, not in the world, but in the knowledge of love.

Ayasha had been like that, thought January—the beautiful Berber woman who had been taken from him by the cholera. Like a summer tree, rooted in and watered by love. And Jeanette's eyes told him all he needed to know about Quashie's love for her.

"You left Thierry's house to meet him last night?"

She nodded. "I got out the parlor window. He keeps the door keys under his pillow. He has a couple drinks, and sleeps like a dead man. Quashie waits for me in the trees by the levee."

To comfort you, thought January, *knowing you come to him from another man's bed.* Shakespeare, and Marvell, and all the other poets had missed that one, when they'd written about the nature of love.

"You left the window open?"

"Yes. I had to go back to him, you see. He likes to fuck in the mornin' as well as at night. That's how the hoodoo got in, isn't it?"

"I think so, yes."

Her eyes filled with fear and she swallowed hard. "Please don't tell him that. Don't tell anyone," she added, when he shook his head. "Michie Ben, you know how these things get around. That Leander, he's like a magpie squawking. Cornwallis, too."

"It won't get past me," promised January. "How long were you at the levee?"

She thought about it a moment. January remembered his silver watch, safe in Olympe's bureau drawer, and remembered too how long it had taken him to learn to think in terms of anything shorter than morning and afternoon. As a child, the first six months of his lessons he was always late.

"The moon was just about straight up overhead when I got there," she said at last. "Maybe not half-way down to the trees on the other bank, when I left."

About two hours, thought January. Plenty of time to load up an old blanket with as many knives as a man could carry in a single load, even if the hoodoo hadn't been watching for the exact moment of her departure. "You didn't see anyone as you were coming or going?"

"If I had," said Jeanette, with a grim twist to her mouth, "you think I'd have left or come back?"

"And you didn't go in that back room after you came back from the levee?"

"No. There's no need for me to, and it's cold in there." She glanced at him under her lashes, still afraid to trust even a man who'd risked Thierry's wrath by cutting Quashie down.

"Mohammed tells me your mother was a hoodoo. Did she teach you any, you or Parson?"

He knew she'd deny it, and she did, shaking her head immediately and vigorously. "Oh, no. She died when we were only little, Parson and me."

It might even have been the truth.

"There anyone else on the place who'd know the hoodoo marks?"

She hesitated a long time. "I think Hope knows some, Ajax's wife. And Emerald, and old Fayola. Auntie Zu knew, that was Lisbon's wife. Well, everyone knows a little, you know? Enough to keep witches away from the door anyway, and make juju bags an' that. But not the big stuff. Not like what was wrote on the wall. I saw Mama make signs like that, but she never taught me, nor anyone else as far as I know."

And that, too, might have been the truth.

"He all right?" asked Ajax, when January returned to the fields. January nodded. "You want to watch yourself," cautioned the driver. "You think Thierry won't beat another man's boy, but you're wrong. He told me to lick you if you got behind."

"Thanks for the warning," said January. "I'll remember."

Ajax put him into the row behind Gosport again, topping the cane and trimming the trash, and piling the stalks in the stubble as the cutters advanced. They were still working ratooned fields upstream of the house. Rats darted and rustled among the sprawled stalks, and now and then a man would pull back with a cry and the brown-patterned buff sinuosity of a snake would flick out of sight.

The sun grew hot, and moved in the sky, and the hawks overhead watched for rats.

At noon, when the boys brought the rice cart out, Harry ambled over to January and said, "That working out well for you, the extra pants and shirt?"

January nodded, grateful for the protection from the sharp leaves and also from some of the chafing annoyance of field-dirt creeping into his clothing. But he braced himself, hearing in the other man's voice that the next words out of his mouth would concern payment of some kind for the gift.

"You like to give me a hand tonight with a little project I've got going?"

January wanted to ask him when or if he ever slept. Instead he said, "It can't be tonight. I'm working night shift in the mill. Thank you," he added, as a little boy named Cato handed him a gourd bowl of dirty rice with sausage in it, and his water bottle that he'd brought down from the end of the row.

"Tomorrow night, then? Old Banjo tells me it'll be clear for a couple nights and the moon's still full."

"Tomorrow night," January agreed. Harry strolled jauntily away to flirt with one of the girls by the cane cart; January shook his head.

Because he was to work in the mill through the night, when full dark fell January was allowed longer for supper than the men who'd be working for only a few hours. This was so that he could get a few hours of sleep, but after eating and washing, and shaving as well as he could in the rain barrel behind the cabin, instead of immediately seeking his bed like a sensible person, he went to the levee to change the bandanna on the tree from white to red, knowing he'd be too exhausted to do so when released from work at dawn.

As Harry had said, the night was clear. The full moon's milky light glittered on the river, as it had glittered last night for Quashie and Jeanette. North and east, and all along the dark shore, red dots of light marked other mills, other men who labored through the night, and between them tiny sprays of sparks traced the passage of the steamboats, hugging the ebony banks.

Coming down from the levee January saw in the moonlight the narrow trail away into the thickets of buttonwood northeast along the river, where the trees divided it here from the cane. Earlier in the day, one of the men had spoken of the slaves' graveyard that lay by the river upstream of the house. Curious, January turned his steps in that direction. In time he came to the small cleared space between the levee and the trees, opposite the woods of what was now Catbird Island.

Side by side, two dark mounds marked the newest graves. Rough-nailed white crosses at their heads bore painted inscriptions: REUBEN. GILLES.

As if, thought January, *in another five years anyone would care.*

No marble angels here, as there were in the great

walled necropoli in New Orleans. No brick tombs to be whitewashed every November second, by families who picnicked between cleanings and hung up immortelles of beads and tin. If a slave knew his grandfather's name he was lucky.

And yet there was peace here, a sleeping quiet, all anger and all pain laid to rest. January recalled what the Romans had said, that Death was Freedom for a slave.

Gilles's grave had been decorated with broken bits of white china—the remains of two cups and a plate, it looked like—and with bottles driven neck-down into the soft earth. Broken horn forks and spoons, the bright-colored lids of tin boxes, stumps of red candles and sealing wax, broken strings of cheap beads, fragments of lamp chimneys. Reuben's grave was bare.

These fragments of pottery were the only markers many of the older graves had, like Lilliputian fences, or eroded teeth rising out of the sunken earth. The cheap paint on the few crosses left standing had long been rinsed away, leaving only phantoms of names in places—PUSEY, said one. Someone had cut the letters deeper with a shell fragment or a knife. LAVINNIA, said another. In most cases, there was now nothing at all.

Forgotten. Twenty or thirty or maybe only fifteen years of living in hard work, loving where they could, trying not to hurt others or be hurt themselves, and for what?

January wondered who they were, and what they'd died of; whether they had left children in the hogmeat gang to mourn them or whether those children had been sold away already; whether these women themselves had been sold away from children, and husbands, parents and friends whom they would never see again. When he was a child he'd often asked himself, *Do* les blankittes *REALLY think a woman'll forget the husband she loved if she gets sold to another place, assigned a new husband? Do they* REALLY *think that bearing new children makes the memory of the lost ones fade?*

But now he knew the answer. And the answer was: *Yes, they do. Most of them.* And the others—he'd overheard them, at the parties he played for in town, at the quadroon balls and receptions—would only say, "Oh, she's still sad 'cause she misses her husband back in Virginia, I bet," in the same tones, *exactly* the same tones, in which they'd say, "Poor puss! She's still looking all over the house for her kittens that I had to have the coachman drown. Just breaks my heart."

The soft clink of glass somewhere nearby. January whirled and called out "Who dat?" doing his best to sound like a man nervous in the dark.

"Just me." It was the cook Kiki's voice, a light sweet soprano, like Rhineland wine. "You want to be careful, here alone in the dark, Ben. The witches'll ride you." She stepped from the velvet abyss beneath the trees, a white blur of tignon and apron against the black of her dress, her hands, her round decisive face. She carried her apron gathered up, and the clinking came from it.

"I got a blue bead and mouse bones tied round my ankle, and some pepper in my pocket. I should be safe."

"No one is safe." She moved past him, and knelt beside Reuben's bare grave. "Not with the anger of the dead."

"Is that why you're here?" He nodded at Reuben's cross. "To keep him quiet?"

"I'm here because I owe him." She took fragments of a broken oil jar from her apron—those oil jars that were bought in such numbers on plantations, not for the oil but for their massive usefulness as containers—two smashed plates, and five or six medicine bottles, caked and crusted with dirt. "Everybody had something to put on Gilles's grave, look. Even the field hands." She shook her head. "Reuben. . . . Not even Trinette, who was his woman, put so much as a broken teacup here, to show where he lies once the headboard falls over and the name washes out. It may be only what he earned in life," she went on, methodically working the bottles mouth-down into the soil around the edge of the mound. "But it isn't right."

"Jeanette tells me he was your husband."

"Four years." The moonlight showed the little pinch of the mouth that women sometimes get, speaking of bad times survived when the distance from those times widens a little. "God forgive me, I could have treated him better than I did, for all he was a hard man."

"Michie Fourchet gave you to him?"

"Isn't it Michie Fourchet who gives every woman to every man here?" She didn't raise her head, but he felt her glance at him under her long lashes.

He took up another bottle, to stick into the earth on the other side of the grave, and chipped away a little of the dirt sticking to it with his nail. The label had faded, but he recognized the shape of the bottle: Finch's Paregoric Restorative Draught, a staggeringly powerful opiate much favored by Hannibal, who was a discerning connoisseur of such things. Glancing down he saw that the other bottles were the same.

"Where'd these come from?"

She glanced up at him again, and he saw his own awareness of what they were reflected in the irony of her eye.

"Look around you at these graves here," she said. "Every bottle you see is one of these. *White lady medicine,* the field hands call it. There's a mound of them higher than your knee, behind the shed in the old garden."

The women's side of the house, thought January. Easily reached if you went down the back stairs and passed under the brick piers that supported the nursery wing, keeping to the oleander hedge so that you wouldn't be seen from the house. The empty bottle hid in the folds of your skirt.

I'm at a loss to determine why anyone would think I'd offer the shelter of my roof to a sodden reprobate. . . .

The boy is a fool like his mother.

"Did you know her?" he asked, holding up the bottle. "Ma'am Camille?"

Kiki's mouth twitched a little at his deduction, and she only said, "No. I came here five years ago. She was dead by then." She worked a brown curved shard of oil jar into the ground, adding, "By the number of those bottles out there, I wouldn't be surprised if those children of hers that died, the ones that poor nurse Zuzu was sold away for not looking after, didn't die of something else."

She got to her feet, and shook out her skirts, standing back to admire the look of the grave. January stood, too, and he had to admit he felt better, seeing the bare turned mound properly decorated, the points of the broken china like a protective hedge against the angry ghost.

"Was he so bad?" he asked, as they walked together along the trace back toward the house. "Reuben?"

She glanced at him again, and her mouth made that same little pinch, as if tasting the memory of her own blood. She said, "He was an angry man, like Michie Fourchet. Maybe that's why he understood Michie Fourchet as well as he did." In the moonlight she looked tired, and there was a haunted expression in her eyes, as if she listened behind her for a heavy step and muttered curses. "Once, after Michie Fourchet broke up the marriage, and let Gilles and me be together, Reuben found Gilles when Gilles was drunk and beat him, as if he thought that would make me turn against

Gilles and return to him. Reuben was stupid that way. Stupid and mean, and dangerous."

"But you cared for Reuben after he was hurt."

She averted her face. "He was my husband," she said. "A man who's been your husband once, in a way he always is. Like your child is always your child, living or in death. Surely you know that."

Ayasha. The way she used to sit in the window of their rooms in Paris, listening to the workmen's voices down in the estaminet, seven flights below at the bottom of the canyon of the street; brushing out her long black hair. One day, January hoped, he would marry Rose, when the broken trust in her healed, that shrank from any man's touch. The thought of her was tender in him, like the scent of flowers, the wry glint of her eyes behind her spectacle lenses and the astringent beauty of her voice as they walked along the levee together. But Ayasha would always be his wife.

"Yes," he told Kiki. "I know."

As they came out of the trees the alto groan of a steamboat's whistle sounded from the landing, and January saw the carriage swing around from the side of the house. The lamps from the gallery twinkled on its brass and the emerald lacquer of its sides, as Musenda the coachman drove down to the landing to fetch Esteban, returned with a box of new cane-knives from New Orleans.

EIGHT

On his return from the graveyard January slept for an hour. Quashie still lay unconscious, though Jeanette had gone. Waking on his corn-shuck pallet, January listened for a time to the young man's breathing, and by the grimy light of a half-burned kitchen candle checked the dressing he'd put on the bloody welts. Then he went to work in the mill, hauling wood and stoking the fires in the vast roaring brick furnace under the kettles.

There was no singing in the mill. During the day the brick walls picked up the endless creaks of the iron grinders, the groan of the timbers that supported and turned them, and the wet sticky crunching of the cane as it was devoured. Even in the dead-night hours, when the grinders were still, the fires beneath the kettles roared with the thick greedy panting of a vast beast, and the smoke gripped and grated at the throat. The heat was dizzying; more than once January saw Simon Fourchet stop in his cursing, his pacing, his watchful gauging of the boiling juice, and lean against one of the rough wooden pillars that held up the high roof, pressing his hand to his side.

Watch and boil and skim; add lime and ash and tilt the heavy kettle to pour the rendered juice into a kettle smaller still. Rake away the wood-ash and charcoal from one door of the furnace and thrust in wood at another. Exhaustion and sweat, and stumbling out on blistered feet rubbed raw by ill-fitting shoes into the icy cold of the night to fetch more wood from the sheds, to feed the fires' greed.

By the flaring holocaust light the toothed wheels, the soot-blackened timber cage of the raised grinders seemed more than ever some Dantean vision of torment. *He was an angry man,* Kiki had said of the one who had been her husband. *Stupid and mean.* Yet the thought of those huge timbers snapping, the squeal of the mules already infuriated by the irritants rubbed into their harness . . .

Just how long, January wondered, would a cypress beam four inches thick have to burn, that it would snap when the mules spooked?

He paused in the chilly darkness outside the hot hell-mouth of the mill, studying the timbers, and the grinders, and the now-empty roundhouse visible through its low arched windows below. The milling equipment hadn't changed much since his childhood on Bellefleur. The grinders were essentially enormous spindles, their bottoms resting in sockets in a huge trough into which the squeezed cane-juice ran down, the timbers that ran up their central axes disappearing into a wooden frame above. The two side wheels were simply mounted in the frame, but the axis of the central roller was in fact the axle of a geared wheel, rotated by another geared wheel that was in its turn powered by the mules walking in their circle in the chamber below. It was one of the outer rollers whose timber had broken, weakened by the fire, and the weight of it lurching free had cracked the axle of the central roller as well.

The timber of the surviving roller was fire-blackened, but it seemed little damaged. January raised his eyes to the walls and rafters of the mill. These bore out his earlier impression that the fire hadn't spread far or lasted very long. He could see where the bagasse and cane-trash had been shoved into joists and cracks and crannies; maybe an hour's work, he thought, and nothing so high or so awkwardly placed that a woman, or a man without particular strength or agility, couldn't have been responsible.

Danny, the second-gang driver in charge of the night crew, looked over in his direction and January returned to work, dragging his rough little wood cart the length of the mill to the first woodshed, loading it up and dragging it back, with the hot gold sullen glare of the fires showing up through the high smoke-streaked windows and reflecting on the faces of the men.

More smoke than fire, thought January. Though he knew from years of work at the clinic of the Hôtel Dieu in Paris that in fact smoke and heat could kill, as surely as flame itself. He thought again about Trinette, sullen and pretty and unweeping with her baby in her arms. About Herc putting his arm around her, leading her away into the woods. She was Herc's wife now, he had heard them say at the wake following the shout, and, as Kiki had said, had not put so much as a broken teacup on Reuben's grave.

Where had she been, he wondered, when the mill caught fire?

Or had Reuben's death been only a stepping-stone, a way of making sure of exactly where Simon Fourchet would have to be every night for the remainder of roulaison?

Morning came and the main shift took over. "You be out in the field by the noon bell, you hear?" In the open ground between the mill door and his cottage,

Thierry counted the night-shift men and women over with his eye by torchlight: January, Okon, Balaam, Danbo, and Black Austin from the first gang, plus the second-gang kettle men and Yellow Austin who looked after the machinery. "If I have to come roust you, you're gonna wish I hadn't."

Rather than return at once to his cabin, January took a pine-knot torch and walked slowly back around the downstream side of the mill, where the path to the sheds didn't run. Here were heaped the long piles of trash and broken barrels and cracked sugar-molds, all trampled and mixed up with dirt where they'd been dragged clear of the wall during the fire. There were barely ten feet between the cane on that side and the mill wall. They must have to keep a close eye on it, he thought, when at harvest's end they burned the cane-trash in the fields.

He found the broken grinder there, teeth snapped off and the iron cracked by its own falling weight. There were black stains on it, too, of what could have been a man's blood.

As he'd guessed, the timber had been sawn nearly through, and the cut place smeared with soot and lampblack to cover where the wood shone bright.

"Marie-Noël Fourchet is the great-granddaughter of Alysse Daubray, one of those fearsome Creole matriarchs whose rule terrorizes half the plantations between here and the mouth of the river, and nearly all of New Orleans society." Wrapped in a robe of quilted lettuce-green silk that appeared to have been borrowed from Robert, Hannibal set aside his violin and picked up the cup of cocoa from the bedside table. As January had approached the house he'd heard the sad sonorous strains of "Espagnole" through the shut doors of the garçonnière, and had seen several of the house-servants lingering close to listen. The walls were thin. Drifts of sound filtered in from outside.

Footsteps creaked by on the gallery: Agamemnon taking coffee to Esteban's room next door. Across the piazza, little Jean-Luc screamed hysterically, "That's mine! That's MINE!" and the even-littler Fantine shrieked as if she were being murdered.

"The Daubrays own forty arpents of riverfront immediately south of here," Hannibal went on, "which after the Creole custom was equally the property of Alysse's children, to wit Gauthier, Enid, Corinne, Louis the Worthy, and Hippolyte. Gauthier as eldest son married early and profitably, and his son was Raymond, only a few years younger than his uncle Hippolyte. In true Creole fashion *la famille* lived together beneath one roof for a number of years, which is one of the best arguments I've ever heard for primogeniture."

"Napoleon has a great deal to answer for," January remarked.

"Perhaps too many of his friends asked him to provide for younger sons. Be that as it may, Gauthier's wife and Mama Alysse did not get on—apparently Gauthier's wife didn't get on with anyone—and by common consent shortly after the slave revolt here in '98, Gauthier and his bride obtained permission from the rest of the family to build another house about three-quarters of a mile upstream of the main Daubray residence, and slightly more than that distance downstream of here. They called this refuge Refuge, and evidently such was the animosity between Gauthier and the rest of the clan that Gauthier, instead of leasing family slaves to cook and clean, bought them out of his wife's money. In time they bought cane-hands from the same source of funds, and even built their own mill rather than use the family one."

"I'm not surprised." January leaned one massive shoulder against the doorjamb, looking out through the jalousies into the piazza between its enclosing wings. The new-risen sun sparked on the French doors of the dining room, and made a bright splash on Madame Fourchet's silvery dimity as she emerged to stand leaning with her elbows on the gallery rail, looking out toward the kitchen and the fields, telling over her rosary beads. "Given the Creole system of keeping land and family together and everyone living and working under one roof, I'm a little surprised there aren't more murders in such households."

Madame Hélène came out of the dining room talking, and cornered her new mother-in-law against the railing: "Of course, as mistress of the house now it's up to you to discipline the servants however you see fit, but *I've* always found that . . ."

"It's worth looking into," remarked Hannibal. "In the case of the Daubrays, homicide was apparently considered on both sides. Gauthier got family permission to work about fifteen arpents as a semi-independent fief, always with the understanding that he'd come to Daubray on Christmases and Easters and pledge fealty to Mama. Son Raymond spent a lot of time in New Orleans gambling and drinking and getting into duels, and at the age of nineteen showed up at Refuge one morning with a completely unsuitable wife—according to Madame Hélène she was Irish and made hats—and an infant, the girl Marie-Noël. Gauthier died a year or so later—of outrage, presumably—and Raymond spent about seven years running his fifteen arpents' worth of Refuge into the ground with unsound business practices, foolish decisions about planting, and too few slaves. I don't know anything about cane, but Robert assures me that the fields weren't replanted at all in that time, the cane just growing again and again from the same roots, which I gather isn't something that answers."

"It isn't." On the gallery, the conversation between young Madame Fourchet and Madame Hélène had developed into a lively quarrel, with all the talking evidently on Madame Hélène's side. In her gown of swagged bronze-gold silk and blond lace lappets, she resembled nothing so much as a gorgeously plumed pheasant pecking a half-grown partridge chick. "The cane comes up thinner and thinner each year and won't stand. It falls and grows sideways and is almost impossible to harvest, and is so thin it's barely worth grinding when you do. But digging it out and replanting takes a tremendous amount of labor. You need slaves."

Robert came out of the dining room. His wife seized him and thrust him at Marie-Noël in the hopes that he'd back up her contentions, whatever they were. January caught the words ". . . worthless maid must have cut off a piece of it . . . I distinctly ordered fourteen yards and there's barely twelve in the package! Now what am I going to do with twelve yards of pink silk?" Robert's eyes sought Marie-Noël's, and the girl quickly turned her face away.

"In due time, and to no one's unbearable surprise, Raymond got himself killed in a duel," Hannibal went on. "The unsuitable Irishwoman having already been gathered to her ancestors, little Marie-Noël returned to Daubray to be raised as a poor relation—mending her cousins' ball dresses and running their errands for them and cleaning out the kitchen grates à la Cinderella for all I know. At this time the beautiful Camille was still alive, though I think she'd gone to live permanently in New Orleans by then, and in any case Marie-Noël was only six. Robert was eighteen, and went with his mother. He did not return to Mon Triomphe with any regularity until the time of his marriage seven years ago to Hélène Prideaux, whose father had some sort of business dealings with the good Michie Simon, though they subsequently ceased to speak to one another."

"So Marie-Noël Daubray would have known Robert Fourchet only as a handsome young neighbor who regarded her as a child." January thought of Robert saying *Tu,* of the way their gazes had crossed, and Marie-Noël's had fled.

"Well, she *was* a child. And still is, by any standards but Creole. In London she wouldn't even be out." Hannibal picked up his violin again, sketching the outlines of an old galliard, like an artist noodling the shape of an eyebrow or the refraction of a rose through a water glass while his mind was on other things. *Is it not strange,* Shakespeare had said, *that sheeps' guts should hale souls out of men's bodies?*

"But time's wheel turns. At some point it apparently occurred to our delightful host that a) legal claim might be made on the fifteen arpents' worth of Refuge through the person of its sole heiress, and b) that said sole heiress might be tired of cleaning kitchen grates and mending flounces for the daughters of Louis the Worthy."

"And he rode over and they put their heads together."

"As Cinderella would probably tell you, even a prince who only recognizes your footwear is preferable to a lifetime cleaning out grates."

On the gallery Madame Hélène gesticulated angrily, the argument evidently not going her way. Robert stood back, shaking his head in silence. If Madame Fourchet resembled a half-grown partridge chick being pecked by the opulent pheasant, then Robert was a trim little grass-parrot, fastidious and overwhelmed.

At Daubray, thought January, the girl must have had her fill of tantrums and abuse. But even Cinderella had not been married to a furious and violent man four times her age. Madame Hélène burst into noisy tears and stormed away toward the sewing parlor that faced the ruined garden.

"Of course I haven't heard the arguments for the other side, but apparently Gauthier *did* get a legal sequestration of the Refuge lands in writing from Alysse. Who is of course now claiming that she never signed any such document. *Grammatici certant et adhuc sub iudice lis est.*"

How had it answered, January wondered, to wed in April, and in November to be confronted with a daughter-in-law more than ten years one's senior who had had no notice that her place as head of the household had been usurped?

Robert turned, and caught Marie-Noël's arm as she would have left. He said something to her, apparently urgent, by the bend of his body, the gesture of his free hand. She shook her head, withdrew to the length of his arm and hers, but he would not release her fingers. In the garçonnière's other room—Esteban's room—a man's voice said passionately, "He doesn't run my life!"

Marie-Noël met her stepson's eyes, and after a long moment he let her go. She turned and hurried along the gallery and down the steps to the piazza, and hence across to the kitchen. From the sewing parlor Hélène's voice cried, "You uppity slut!" and there was a woman's cry of pain.

Robert watched Marie-Noël until she disappeared

into the kitchen. Then, visibly bracing himself, he walked down the gallery to see what his wife might be up to now.

When the work ended for the day, instead of seeking his mattress, January paused at the bachelors' cabin only long enough to wash, then continued along the quarters street in the clear blue wash of the winter moonlight to Harry's cabin at the far end. A couple of yellow candles burned, filling the place with the stink of tallow, and as January paused in the doorway Harry was saying to Ti-Jeanne the washerwoman, "Good. These are good." He held up to the candlelight one of the objects from the sack on the little table, a golden-brown russet apple. Going to a corner of the cabin he removed a loose board from the floor and, kneeling, felt around the space between the floor and the ground below, eventually leaning down to the full extent of his arm.

He drew up a small sack of coarse hemp—January guessed he'd had it buried under a brick beneath the house for protection. Indeed, though many planters would argue that the cabins were raised on piers, and floored with plank instead of earth, for reasons of health and cleanliness, in fact they were so built to curb the slaves' propensity for burying stolen goods under their floors.

Harry brought out a twist of paper containing salt, which he put into Ti-Jeanne's hand. "Now, if you should happen to find a couple of wore-out pillowcases that they're going to throw away anyhow, I think I could probably talk Ned into parting with one of his cat's kittens, when she gets old enough to mouse good."

There was no one named Ned on Mon Triomphe.

The nearest Ned January had heard of lived on Lescelles, the small plantation immediately upriver—his cat Ikà was a mouser noted throughout the parish.

Harry knelt again to replace the sack and the board. He shared the space with his brother Bello and Bello's wife Cynthia, they and their baby daughter sleeping now behind a hanging made of thick osnabrig sheets and presumably long inured to Harry's huckstering. Other than having more chickens than anyone else in the quarters, tucked up in the African fashion in baskets dangling from the rafter-ends outside to keep them safe from rats, more pigs in the sty behind the cabin, and a half-dozen strings of bright-hued beads hung on a peg near the hearth, there was little sign of Harry's activities in the dwelling.

"M'am Fourchet, she set a store by those pillowcases," said the washerwoman worriedly, and Harry nodded with an understanding smile.

"Maybe a shirt, then? Or a couple handkerchiefs? I hear Michie Robert has a lot of fine shirts. He won't miss one. That's my sweetheart." He kissed the stoop-shouldered, gray-haired woman, and she giggled like a girl.

"You are bad." Passing January in the doorway she grinned up at him. "You watch out for that Harry, Ben, because he's as bad as they come." She sounded pleased.

When she'd gone, Harry picked up another loose board and retrieved another sack. This one contained a powder-flask, bullets, and a small box of waxed linen patches. He wrapped up the apples and handed the sack to January, except for two left on the table—presumably for Bello and Cynthia—one that he stuck in his own pocket, and another he threw to January.

"Best apples in the parish," he said, as they slipped outside and went around to the pigsty in back of the house. "M'am Camille, she had the trees brought in special, like everything else in that garden of hers. Here." He stepped over the fence and reached under the roof of the pig-house, bringing out a Kentucky long-rifle with its lock wrapped carefully in greased cloth. "Sweet as candy. Pigs love 'em."

"That what we're huntin' tonight?" asked January, fascinated. "Pig?"

"Nuthin' in the world like a good pig," replied Harry cheerfully. "And Tim Rankin's are the best."

While sugar plantations lined the river from its mouth to Baton Rouge, January was aware that most of the whites of the river parishes were, in fact, not of the planter class. Along New River, and Bayou Conway, in the Achtafayala country and on the nameless little bayous of the ciprière, lived a scattered population of small farmers, Scots-Irish or Welsh or descended of the old Acadians of Canada, crackers who raised a haphazard selection of cotton, corn, and yams and lived largely on the increase of their herds of cattle and swine. Most kept a few slaves—Aniweta, one of Harry's girlfriends, was broad-wife to a man whose master lived over on New River—but on the whole they had as little to do as possible with tillage or agriculture. They were, January had found, a curious combination of autodidactism and ignorance, squalor and pride, and he mistrusted them wholeheartedly.

"From what I hear," said January, "Tim Rankin's dogs are the best, too, and he won't take kindly to one of his hogs takin' a little walk out in the country."

"Ben . . . No wonder Michie Hannibal's daddy-in-law put you nursemaidin' him. You worry more than any man I ever met. You worry so much it's a wonder you don't chop your hand off cuttin' cane."

And Harry led the way off, through the ciprière.

In January's childhood, when Louisiana had been Spanish land, the ciprière had stretched unbroken, mile after mile of marsh and pond and oak ridge, as far as you could walk in a day. Indian tribes, Natchez and Chickasaw and Houmas, had wandered it. Runaway slaves had established whole villages in it and had lived in peace for years, and so in places it remained. But after an hour on the winding trail, with the moon's thin dappling filtered by moss and cypress branches, January smelled the stinks of settlement, the sweetish revolting stench of hogs and the murkier pong of outhouses nobody had bothered to clean in decades, and among the oaks the milky light showed a straggly field of cotton, the stumps left in where the land had been cleared.

Beyond that squatted the usual squalid cracker dwelling of boards and bousillage, sagging on its piers and possessed of not a single glass window, though by its size it was clearly the home of the master, not a slave.

There were no barns. Crackers tended to let their stock live as untrammeled a life as they did themselves, though a kind of shed offered minimal shelter to a couple of mules. Near that, as he and Harry circled through the silent woods, January glimpsed a rough zigzag of split rails, and heard the mumbling grunts of swine.

"Once we get goin'," said Harry, producing a caneknife and chopping down a sapling which he stripped and topped with the deftness of long practice, "we gotta go fast. I'll take care of the dogs."

"You just do that." What the hell, January wondered, had he gotten himself into? But it was all a way of buying his way into the community, a way of listening. . . .

If he didn't get himself killed for the benefit of some benighted barter of Harry's.

Had he been picked because he was a new boy and dumb enough to go along with one of Harry's schemes? Or simply because he was big enough to lug a dead hog at a run through the woods?

Harry had slipped away into the ghostly silence of the woods. A few moments later January heard the dogs, first barking, then barking and crashing through the trees on the far side of the house. Keeping hold of the stripped pole with one hand and the sack of apples with the other, he darted from the cover of the trees, pulled open the crude gate of the hog pen, and tossed the first few apples out a couple of yards away. He poked and prodded the pigs in the pen until they were on their feet, snuffling and grunting as he fed one of them an apple. Then he retreated toward the woods again, breath coming fast, dropping apples which the pigs, with the gourmandise of their kind, trotted out to devour.

The crash of a gun in the undergrowth nearly made January jump out of his skin. A hog squealed and dropped, kicking, in the tangle of laurel and hackberry, and Harry called out in a triumphant whisper, "Got him!" Distantly, the dogs still barked.

"You could have got me!" January had been about four feet from the quarry, and having fought the British under Andrew Jackson he knew all about the accuracy of the average rifle.

"I didn't, though." Harry bent down with his cane-knife and slashed the hog's throat. "Not a bad shot for moonlight." January recognized the cane-knife as one of those he and Mohammed had repaired the previous day, and wondered how that one had been extracted from the "fixed" pile without Thierry's knowledge.

"Let's get this boy out of here. They'll be along any minute."

He was tying up the pig's feet as he spoke and sliding the pole between them. January groaned inwardly, guessing what kind of evasion procedures would follow. He was right: They set off along the path, the pig borne between them on the pole with its blood dripping copiously; crossed a small bayou and continued through the woods with the ground getting lower and marshier around their feet. In summer the night would have been alive with frogs and crickets, the air a humming torture of mosquitoes. Winter had stilled the land, and January breathed a prayer of thanks for small favors. Distantly he heard the baying of dogs in the woods—more than before, he thought.

"I swear I never met a man who worries as much as you!" Harry shook his head. "It'll just be Rankin and his brothers and the Neys. Old Jules Ney and his boys live just on the other side of Lost Bayou. They're the ones you have to watch out for, not Rankin. Watch it here." They had stepped into water again, one of the wide sodden sloughs that dotted the ciprière. The water was freezing: January could only be grateful that snakes and gators would be asleep at this season.

"Are these Neys any relation to that charming gentleman who owns the *Belle Dame*?"

"That's them." They waded among the sedges and cypress knees. Then, at the point where a dirt road passed the slough beneath a low-limbed oak, they turned on their tracks and worked their way back, emerging from the marsh at the same place they'd gone in and following the blood-trail back to the bayou, with the baying of the dogs growing louder all the time. "We'll leave our friend here in the back of Disappearing Willie's cave. It'll be safe there and it's cold enough in that cave to freeze water, nearly. The

Neys are a bad bunch. If you get caught by them out without a pass, you tell them you belong to Michie Fourchet and not to a guest of his. They'll pass you along to Captain Jacinthe on the *Dame* if you're not careful, and you'll end up for sale in someplace you don't want to be."

"*Here* is where I don't want to be," said January through his teeth.

"That's just what you think now."

The watercourse grew narrower and more winding and the darkness more dense as the cypresses crowded in close and the moon sank. It was, January guessed, only a few hours until first light, with the prospects of a full day in the cane-fields to come. *This had better be worth it.*

In time they reached the oak-hummock in the midst of the waters that housed Disappearing Willie's shack. Disappearing Willie, the friendly little Ibo who had long ago lost his position of assistant gardener to M'am Camille, had, in addition to the brand on his face, more whip scars on his back than any man on Mon Triomphe. He wasn't surly or quarrelsome or disobedient or a thief: Simply, he could not be broken of the habit of running away. He'd never be gone long—two days or three days or four days. Willie had any number of hideouts in the ciprière, and seemed to consider a whipping the reasonable price to pay for a few days' liberty in the woods.

"He's crazy if he thinks Fourchet isn't going to kill him one day," January remarked, as he helped Harry suspend the hog in the damp-floored hollow cut in the bank beneath the shack. Harry was right—it was icily cold there, and at this season there was little danger the meat would spoil before the entrepreneur could dispose of it. "I've seen how crazy it makes Fourchet if anyone—a slave or one of his sons or whoever—goes against him. One day Willie's going to come back from hiding out and Fourchet's going to beat him to death."

"I think he knows that," said Harry. The cave was guarded by a couple of boards propped over its low opening to keep foxes and gators out. He took a couple of tallow candles from his pocket and lit them—he had lucifer matches, not flint—his breath glittery smoke in the light. January's wet clothes clung to his body and he shivered as he worked. "I sure wouldn't do it. But I think Willie figures, *So what?* Where else is he going?"

Harry finished tying the hog's feet to the rough beam driven from wall to wall, and regarded January in the candle-gleam. Without his habitual engaging smile his face seemed older—he was barely twenty—and tired. "What else is he going to do with his life, 'cept enjoy a couple days here and there, and put up with what it costs him? Isn't that what everybody does?"

Was it? Stepping out of the wet dampness of the cellar, January looked across the cobalt glimmer of the bayou, of black lumpy cypress knees and gray moss like chalk smears on the velvet gloom. He thought of the men who'd knocked him down in the street, slit his clothing with their big Green River knives and tore up his music, who would have happily beaten him or killed him. . . . The white oafs in the taverns, whom he had to call "sir."

It was the price he paid to sit at the dinner table with Olympe's children and listen to his brother-in-law tell them stories about High John the Conqueror by mellow candlelight. What he paid to have coffee with Rose in the arcades of the market by the levee, or to walk across the Place d'Armes in the multicolored delight of autumn mornings when everyone was out with their market baskets in the freshness of the air.

He'd lived in Louisiana for twenty-four years, before leaving for Paris. When he thought—when he *knew*—

that remaining in Paris in the wake of Ayasha's death would destroy him with grief, he'd known also what it would cost him, to come back to the only family he had.

What had his mother paid, he wondered, for the freedom she'd bought for herself and her children? Had she loved the tall black man with the country marks on his face? Was that why she never spoke his name?

Or had she had any choice?

Velvet silence. Bitter cold. The far-off smell of smoke from every mill along the river and the green musky scent of the water, only inches from the entrance of the cave.

And then, suddenly, much nearer now, the baying of the dogs.

"Shit," said Harry, not much discomposed. "We better split up. I'll see you back at the quarters."

"Wait a—!"

But Harry was gone.

And the clamor was far too close, now, for him to dare shout, *I don't know the way back, dammit!*

Somebody yelled, "There he is!"

NINE

January bolted straight into the water, plunged and floundered for the opposite bank. The bobbing lanterns were some distance off, where the trees thinned into a muddle of cypress knees, muck, and reeds, and his pursuers wasted time seeking dry ground before they realized there wasn't any; this gave January time to reach the woods. He cursed himself for having followed Harry blindly, without asking the way, and cursed Harry even more. In the lowering moonlight every oak, every hickory, every swamp-maple and thicket of hackberry looked just alike, and as unfamiliar as the landscape of China or the surface of the moon.

Even following the bayou didn't help, for there was no way of telling which way a bayou "ran." They didn't "run" at all, most of the time, or sometimes seemed to flow in one direction, sometimes in another, depending on the river's rise. In any case it was too dark to tell. The voices called to one another in French, beyond the barking of the dogs: It was the Neys and not the Irish Rankins. *"They'll sell you where you don't want to be,"* Harry had warned.

But running through the moonlit woods, memories

came back to January, of childhood stories told by old Uncle Zacky about Compair Lapin and how he'd outwit Bouki the Hyena and Michie Lion by running along fence-rails, or doubling on his trail, or wading through water . . . *All he'd have to do was lick his four paws and JUMP up in the air. . . .* He could still see the agile old man's delighted, ridiculous imitation of the act.

And he smiled, understanding that Uncle Zacky hadn't been telling them about a rabbit at all. He'd been telling them about this. How to avoid dogs. How to get to safety, and leave the whites behind scratching their heads. And as he doubled on his own trail, and JUMPED up in the air to grab the branch of an oak—as he scrambled along the limbs of the tree to the limbs of the next, watching below for water to land in—January felt in his heart the exhilaration of knowing he was going to get away.

Of knowing he'd outwitted *les blankittes.*

Striding through the woods in the last of the moonlight, hearing the voices, the furious barking fading behind him, he wanted to sing. Nonsense words, alien words, slave-song African words he remembered his father singing:

"Jinga bunga bungala bunga,
Jinga bunga baby . . ."

His old piano master, the ramrod-spined Herr Kovald, who'd worked so hard to make him master of the beauty of Mozart and Bach and the floating wonderfulness of Pachelbel, would die of offended indignation.

"Jinga bunga bungala bunga,
Jinga bunga baby."

There were songs for singing when you set forth on Quests for Enlightenment to the Temple of the Queen of the Night, January thought, and there were songs for singing when you'd just outrun a bunch of white men with dogs who'd sell you down the river if they caught you.

He followed the sinking moon til he came into the cane-rows, then worked his way along the ranks of silent rustling spears toward the river. The cane was thin, snarled and matted underfoot, cane ratooned so many times it was practically indistinguishable from wild grass, and this told him where he was: in the back fields of what had been the Refuge lands, fields the Daubrays hadn't yet brought back into productivity even after all these years. After a narrow belt of this he came into replanted acres, and worked his way riverward, til he came out of the cane nearly on top of what had been the big house, Gauthier Daubray's Refuge.

Cane was planted almost up to its walls. The oaks that had stood between it and the river had been felled. The house itself was a "house of twenty," as the Senegalese builders would have called it, meaning twenty cypress timbers had been hewn to support its floors on the brick piers that raised it above the ground. The dense shadows that cloaked its silent gallery hid every detail of its swampward side, but January saw that the tiny garçonnière was shuttered fast, the pigeon coop boarded up. The cistern still stood beside the kitchen, however, and January ran a little water from its rusted tap, catching the icy flow in his hands. This wasn't particularly satisfactory, and he closed the tap and went to the kitchen to see what had been left by way of gourds or cups.

The kitchen door was closed but unshuttered. January took from his pocket the candle stub he, like

Harry, habitually carried, and the little tin box of lucifers. By the new-sparked light he made out vacant shelves, bins emptied of their contents, dough troughs and an old rice cart. . . .

And the mark of the *guédé,* written in red chalk and lampblack upon the wall.

The sight of it shocked him so that he nearly dropped the candle. A triangle topped with a cross, and stylized serpents. The skull and coffin of Baron Cemetery. Trailing lines scrawled over the floor, creeping like serpents toward the hearth. January fished automatically in his pocket and touched the blue beads of his rosary, whispered the first few words of the Avé, as a child would have ducked for shelter into the folds of the Queen of Heaven's blue robe.

Then, candle held high, he walked to the hearth, and examined the ashes there.

There were a lot of them. The fire had been kept going a long time. Its ashes were white and sunken-looking, but clearly not anything like ten years old. A few weeks, he thought, no more. The dark of the moon.

The moon's dark is the time when ill will lies strongest on the land.

The table had been used, too, though it had afterward been cleared and cleaned. He knelt to search underneath and found an assortment of fragmented leaves and stems, which told him this had been done at night, in bad lighting. He wrapped these in the cleanest rag he could find and tucked them in the pocket of his shirt. In the midden outside, behind the kitchen, he found buried a pot, a knife, a cutting board, and a thick wad of mushed and boiled leaves.

Oleander. He picked the leaves up gingerly, bandanna wrapped around his fingers. She—or he—had made the poison here.

Reuben's new wife Trinette? he wondered. Who had not left so much as a broken teacup at his grave?

Jeanette, who'd been Mambo Jeanne's daughter? But surely she'd have poisoned Thierry first of all.

Zuzu, who'd been sold away when the children in her care died? Her husband Lisbon?

Or was all this the work of the Daubray uncles, concealed from the wagging tongues in their own overcrowded family house?

But no white, he thought, would have invoked the *guédé*'s blessing on their act. Would they?

Coming back to the kitchen he looked around again, and saw, beside the door, a dozen tiny holes in the wood of the jamb. When he held the candle close they looked fresh, as if someone had stabbed the wood with an awl. Some were enlarged, as nail holes are enlarged when a nail is pried or twisted out; one contained a broken-off point of what looked like wood.

There had been a couple of long splinters, he recalled, on the kitchen floor among the leaf fragments. He unwrapped the rag from his pocket to make sure. A little more search near the door showed him a three-inch splinter of cane-stalk, sharpened to a point with a knife.

This too he wrapped up in his rag.

He'd hoped to find something salvageable in the kitchen, something he could trade to Harry for information or goodwill, but there was nothing. Whoever had come here to make poisons had brought his or her own pot, knife, and cutting board; chalk and lampblack. The small door at the back opened only into a cabinet, a shedlike back room stocked with wood for the kitchen hearth so the cook wouldn't have to fetch it from the main sheds by the mill. There wasn't even a kindling hatchet left.

By the wavering candle-glow the vévés seemed to watch him as he came back into the main kitchen. The wriggling snake-trails reached out after him when he turned his back. Field rats had taken residence here: They skittered along the shelves, waiting him out with scant patience, like party hosts whose guests have lingered overlong.

Half numb with fatigue, January made his way through the thickets of cane that, with a kind of spite, the Daubray cousins had planted where Gauthier's lawns had once stretched to the river. He reached the levee, and from that shallow ridge looked at the moon, round and bright as an alabaster dish just above the trees of the western bank. The Refuge landing was a black tongue among black cypresses, jackstaff still pointing bravely at the sky, and beside it a crumbling boathouse crouched, a velvet shadow-beast lapping at the luminous water's verge.

In the dense chill of predawn January walked along the levee, thinking about Reuben and Trinette, and Lisbon's wife Zuzu. Of Fourchet himself, and young Marie-Noël Daubray. But his tired mind kept straying to Rose Vitrac, asleep in that shabby room on Rue de la Victoire near the wharves, looking young and vulnerable with her spectacles set on a pile of books at her bedside and her soft brown hair spread in waves about her on the pillow in the dark. And from those thoughts, his mind reached out to his father, and the green-black fields of cane that had once grown an hour's walk or less from the center of New Orleans, back when New Orleans had had actual ramparts where the Rue des Ramparts now ran.

He climbed the bluff above the Triomphe landing, untied the red bandanna there, and replaced it with a yellow. Thought for a passing moment about Abishag

Shaw, and shook his head at the gangling backwoodsman's familiarity with the myth of Theseus.

A steamboat passed in the darkness behind him, amid a shower of uprising sparks, like American fireworks on the Fourth of July. Among the oak trees the big house slumbered dark and still, the kitchen shuttered fast, the overseer's house a coal-lump of malice against the beating glare of the mill. As January watched, a light flared in its window: Jeanette making coffee for the white man whose concubine she was. *Thou shalt not muzzle the ox that treadeth out the grain.*

Sorrow and rage filled him. Bitter helplessness, and fear that edged daily toward the uncaring violence of outlawry and revolt. *How dare they?* he thought. *How dare they do this, to her, to Quashie, to me? To everyone here?*

The rage and rebellion that had scorched him since he'd helped punish Quashie boiled to a blistering head in him, poisoned by the knowledge that revolt *was* useless. As Nat Turner and all who'd followed him had found. Rebellion *would* only make matters worse. You couldn't fight them.

But like the skirl of bright unbidden music, he remembered half a dozen white men running madly about with their dogs in the bitter-cold woods, blaspheming and blowing on their fingers while they looked for his trail, like Bouki the Hyena when Compair Lapin ran off with his supper or his shoes or his wife.

You can't defeat the army, he thought. *But if you lie quiet in cover you might save yourself and win a skirmish or two.*

He was singing softly to himself as he came down the levee, as the first bell of morning sounded.

At noon, January lay down on the strip of waste ground at the end of the cane-rows and fell asleep as if he'd been struck over the head, not caring that it meant missing his dinner. Harry, he noticed—in the two seconds of consciousness between recumbence and blackness—didn't. In fact, Harry disappeared the moment Ajax yelled "Rice cart!" and didn't reemerge from the cane, sleek and pleased with himself, until seconds before the men were choused into the rows again. Time enough to rendezvous either with one of his many girlfriends or, more likely, with someone from the house or from one of the nearby houses.

He's got to be a machine.

They were cutting quite a ways downriver of the house, and back towards the ciprière. January had to fight to keep his mind from drifting, a dangerous thing when you were swinging half a yard of edged metal full force, the dust of the fields gummed with cane-juice to his hands and face and hair. Lack of sleep slowed his mind, and that was deadly. Hunger, too, now that he had no choice but to be awake. The singing helped, the rhythm of it focusing the mind without distracting it. Now and then some shouted phrase, some wailing fall of the music, would lift and turn his heart. Then down the line one of the women called out, "Look alive!" and he heard the crash and rustle of a horse, riding through the scattered stubble and trash.

Thierry, he thought, his stomach clenching, but it wasn't.

"What on earth is the meaning of this?"

Two men, mounted on bay hacks that January recognized as expensive. The younger rider was about January's own age, large and fair and portly, and clothed in a coat of costly malt-colored wool: His neckcloth was striped a vivid gold, and a tad too fancy for riding one's acres in. The older, perhaps eight years senior, had the same square chin and the same fair hair, though what was thick and mostly still flaxen, lying on the shoulders of his companion's inappropriate coat, was thin and graying on the older man's head; the man himself was narrower, smaller, and more compact. The difference between a hank of jerky, thought January, and a fat-marbled roast with *sauce Béarnaise.*

"Tell your men to stop," ordered the older man, drawing rein beside Ajax. "You're on Daubray land."

Ajax doffed his beaver hat at once, respectfully avoiding the mounted man's eyes. "Michie Louis, sir, it'd give me great happiness to oblige you, but Michie Fourchet'd skin me alive if I did." The driver's scarred, ugly face wore an expression of wholly specious concern. "He told us off to cut these fields today, and I can't go against what he said. Bumper!" he called, and his son, with the inevitable Nero at his heels, dashed up, water gourd dripping from his hand. "You run back to the house and get Michie Fourchet fast, so he and Michie Daubray can work this out between them."

The two boys fled, and Louis Daubray looked annoyed because the driver had refused to be bullied. The younger man, whom January guessed to be Hippolyte, said, "I told you he'd try something like this." And smote the field dust from his sleeves. "Well, look at the bubbies on that one," he added, small gray eyes twinkling in their pouches of fat, and he gestured with his quirt at Ajax's daughter Eve, working her first season at the cane carts with her mother in the women's gang. "Wonder what old Simon would charge for the pleasure of breaking *her* in?"

"Tell your men to stop," ordered Louis pettishly again, and gestured around him. "Your master may *claim* that this is his land, but it is indubitably *my* cane."

"Sir, the fact is I don't remember whether we planted this cane or you planted this cane, so you may very well be right." Ajax bowed again as he spoke, hat in hands and voice carefully neutral. "But I can't go against Michie Fourchet's orders—"

"You very well can, when his orders are in direct contravention of the law!"

"He gets any more mad," murmured Gosport, in the thick African patois that was barely French at all, "he'll pop right up off that horse and spin around in the air," and there was a silent ripple of laughter among the men.

"Little bitch put him up to it," muttered Louis Daubray, shading his eyes and gazing in the direction of the house. "Under that piety she always was a schemer."

"She'll find her claims—*if* she wins them—come a little more expensive than she thought," remarked Hippolyte. "If she hasn't found so already. The first time he takes a knife to her dresses, or starts smashing things she treasures . . ." He shook with a sudden chuckle of reminiscent laughter. "Do you remember the night old Simon took a hammer to Camille's pianoforte? And her staggering along the levee all done up in that ridiculous yellow ball dress, waving her opium bottle and screaming to all the boats to take her back to France?"

"That sour little puritan wouldn't care about her dresses, and if she ever fancied anything in her life other than the Bible I'd be surprised," muttered Louis. "That's the only reason Simon hasn't driven her off yet. She treasures nothing: no novels to tear up, no pianoforte to take a sledge to, no glass birds and music boxes to stamp, no lace to rip . . . What, sir, is the meaning of this?"

For Simon Fourchet had appeared at a hand-gallop across the stubble, hatless, gray hair jerking behind him in the breeze.

"The meaning of this, you mangy weasel, is that it's harvest . . ."

All work in the cane-rows had ceased by this time, men and women both gathered around the cane carts, listening as unobviously as they could. Finding himself next to Jeanette, January touched her shoulder gently, asked, "Is there someone on Daubray who'd know how to make gris-gris?"

"Mambo Hera," the girl said promptly. "Even my mama was afraid of Mambo Hera." Like most of the women, she'd stripped off her coarse woolen jacket and hiked up her skirt almost to the thigh. Sweat gummed her calico shift to her breasts and ran down her cheeks from beneath the tignon that bound up her hair, making cedar-red tracks in the mousy dust. "Before she got so crippled she was them boys' mammy—Michie Louis and Michie Hippolyte. My mama said in her prime she had the Power, more than any other woman in this parish. I remember Mambo Hera when I was just little: She was a scary woman in those days."

"But not now?"

"She's near ninety," put in Disappearing Willie, who stood just behind them. "And this past summer she had a palsy-stroke, and doesn't get around much. She's near blind, too."

"When she looks at you with those white eyes it still seems like she looks right through you, though."

Maybe, thought January. But somehow he couldn't imagine a dim-sighted and crippled nonagenarian accomplishing even the modest scramble up to the timbers of the mill, or slipping through Thierry's window to fetch a blanketful of knives to dump in the forge.

"I think all of 'em was scared to death of her," Jeanette went on. "M'am Enid's daughters, and Michie Louis's, and all of 'em over to Daubray. All except Mamzelle Marie-Noël—M'am Fourchet, I should say."

"It was the labor of my men who planted this cane here last season, and three years ago," Louis Daubray was shouting, waving his quirt before Fourchet's face. "My men who cleared the trashy wasteland that was all that was left here of the ruin our cousin had made of family land . . ."

Gosport was right, thought January. If Daubray got any more riled he would fly off his horse like a badly made toy.

"Mama would take me over there, and I'd see the girls, M'am Enid's daughters Aimée and Rosine, that were always dressed so pretty, and Michie Louis's daughter Loië. They were fifteen, sixteen then, and Michie Robert and all the other boys would ride over to court them, all but Michie Esteban, of course. The girls, they'd give Mambo Hera sugar and candy and sometimes they'd steal things like tobacco or earrings, when their mamas would get them from off the steamboats, to bribe her to make them gris-gris to get this boy or that boy they wanted."

"Don't think I'm not aware that you'd rejoice if my crop failed!" Fourchet stormed at the two Daubrays. "And don't think I don't know that it hasn't stopped at rejoicing! I know perfectly well you were on my land the night my mill burned . . . !"

"Don't be ridiculous!" Hippolyte, who'd been lounging in his saddle eyeing Eve and Jeanette and the petite sullen-faced Trinette, straightened with a jerk. "I was pursuing that pestilent thief of a goods-trader whom *you* permit to tie up and set up shop on *your* land!"

"And who saw you, eh? I've heard all about how you followed Jones halfway down the river, but who was with you?"

"Do you call my brother a liar, sir?"

"But Mamzelle Marie-Noël," Jeanette went on softly, "she'd go by in her old made-over gown that she'd turned herself, just holding her Bible and her beads in her hands, and she wouldn't even so much as look at Mambo Hera. And Mambo Hera'd look after her and laugh."

". . . making free with the goods that are stolen from the rest of us! Why, I shouldn't be surprised if Jones gives you a cut of what he receives."

"Liar!" Fourchet lunged from his saddle, hands reaching for Hippolyte's throat. "Pig of a liar!" Hippolyte's horse, not surprisingly, threw up her head with a squeal of indignation and reared, blundering into Louis's mount, and by the time Ajax, January, Gosport, and Hope had grabbed bridles and steadied would-be combatants from clambering down to take up the challenge on the ground, the immediate danger of assault was past. "I will send my friends to call on you, you perjuring filth, and in the meantime get your fat bottom and your scrawny brother off my wife's land!"

"Should you find any friends the length of this river willing to call on me or to perform any office whatsoever on your behalf, I will own myself to be astonished beyond speaking, and this is our family's land, and no possession of any thieving bastard of our cousin's Hibernian drab!"

"I thought *you* was good at the dozens, Ben," remarked Gosport, coming up beside January, after Hippolyte, Louis, and Fourchet had been separated once again. "But I would *purely* love to hear those two go at it!"

"And you get back to work!" screamed Fourchet, lashing at Ajax and the field hands with his quirt. "Idle, stupid blocks . . . !"

"Not on my land you're not!"

Fourchet lunged at *les frères* Daubray one more time and Ajax caught him back, expostulating with him to the extent that Louis and his brother were able to depart without the appearance of flight. The driver then had the task of respectfully talking his master out of pursuing the brothers through the cane and flogging them with Ajax's whip ("If you want to take it, sir, of course, but it'll leave me without anything to beat these lazy niggers here with. . . ."), by which time Louis and Hippolyte were out of range. Trembling, Simon Fourchet leaned against his driver's shoulder, his red face suddenly white and his hand pressed to his chest, looking as he had following yesterday's outburst of rage at the smithy. January had the impression of a horse that has been galloped too far and too hard, wind-broken, unable to run again.

Hope broke away from the slow-moving cane cart, picked up one of the water bottles, and brought it silently to the old man. The water spilled as he took it. "Thank you," Simon Fourchet said quietly, and drank. As the planter remounted and rode away January braced his knife on his shoe for two quick passes with the whetstone, and returned to cutting.

Just before sunset three more riders appeared along the cart path, rough-clothed men on scrubby horses. "Lordy lordy," murmured the gap-toothed Nathan, "it's Sheriff Duffy." He dropped the billets onto the cut row, scooped the trash over onto the trash row, and nodded back toward the ape-browed, sharp-eyed unshaven man in the lead. The men riding with Duffy were of the rough cracker class, spiritual brethren of the original owner of the hog that now hung in Disappearing Willie's cave up Lost Bayou, though one of them, January recognized, had to be related to the *Belle Dame's* cold-eyed master.

"Got a restraining order here," said Duffy in quite proper though thickly accented French, and extended a folded piece of paper. When Fourchet only crossed his arms and regarded the lawman with stubborn contempt, the man with the Ney eyes took it, handed it to the planter, and repeated the words. His French was, if anything, worse: the backwoods patois of French Acadia, but a native's French.

"You may inform your master, M'sieu Ney," retorted Fourchet, ignoring Sheriff Duffy completely, "that by tomorrow I will have Justice Rauche issue another such order against that thief Daubray and his whoremaster brother, forbidding them to set foot upon my wife's land."

"That's as may be, sir," replied Duffy stolidly. "But for the moment you're to remove your men—and leave the cane."

"So Daubray may send his slaves to pick it up and grind it?" Fourchet spat the words, turning for the first time to stare at the sheriff with cold, half-mad eyes. He shifted his gaze to Ney. "Inform this American that I charge him to leave a guard here, lest my cane be stolen in the night by the same thieves who have poisoned my slaves and attempted to torch my mill and my barn."

"Simon, don't be a fool! That cane will be worthless in a day—"

"Tell him, Guy!"

Guy Ney sighed, and obeyed, evidently well aware who was going to get landed with the job of standing guard over nine acres of rotting cane—and he was correct. When Ajax and Hercules had organized the men and dumped the loaded cane back onto the ground, and both gangs walked back between tall green rows followed by the empty carts, January looked over his shoulder and saw the fair-haired Acadian sitting his horse, rifle propped on his thigh, among the stubble and cut rows and trash.

It being only an hour short of dark, January had hoped that the men would be released back to the quarters. This was an optimistic hope at best. Fourchet marched the men to another section of the fields just downstream of the mill, and started them to work, though in the daylight remaining they'd barely fill the carts one time. Exhaustion, hunger, and lack of sleep made January feel like his body was being raked through with steel harrows, but he made it through the twilight, and helped load the last of the carts by the flare of torches the suckling gang—the women pregnant, or too old for heavy work—brought down.

Knowing he'd be working until the moon was high hauling wood, he took the ash-pone and beans Gosport had put together that morning for tonight's supper, and carried it to the smithy. Mohammed was just concluding his prayers for the night, kneeling on the dirty little square of faded carpet facing east. January recalled seeing the blacksmith so thirty-five years before, and asking him about it—it was the first time he had heard the name of Allah.

"Tell me about Lisbon," said January, "and about how Zuzu happened to be sold."

The *griot* nodded, as if the question did not surprise him. "They was married ten, twelve years, Lisbon and Auntie Zuzu," he said. "Lisbon was born on Bellefleur,"—January carefully made his face blank, with a little knit of his brows as if he had never heard of the place before—"the plantation Michie Fourchet used to own just outside New Orleans, just a year or two before the uprisin' here. Zuzu was brought in when she was sixteen, from the Locoul place down in St. John Parish. She was a flighty girl, always givin' this man and that man the eye, but she was good with children. She'd had a child herself by that time, and M'am Nanette Locoul saw how she watched over that baby, and the babies of the other women on the place. Zuzu was put in charge of the nursery down at Bellefleur, when Mamzelle Elvire was born, and just before Mamzelle Solange came along two years later, Zuzu and Lisbon married. She had four children by Lisbon: Nan, Roux, Sidonie, and Beau, Beau dyin' of pneumonia before he was two—it was a bad winter, that year. They did say as how Roux wasn't Lisbon's child but Boaz's, for he was mighty light, like Boaz, and both Zuzu and Lisbon are dark, but Lisbon loved Roux like his own."

"Did he love Zuzu?" January settled his back to the doorpost of the smithy.

Torchlight reflected through the mill windows etched the shift of lines and wrinkles on the smith's face as Mohammed sorted through the truths of that question. "They got on well," he replied at last. "As to how much they loved each other. . . . When first she came, Zuzu walked out with Cicero, and Boaz, and Johnny, who was one of the footmen on Bellefleur in those days, and as I said she had a roving eye."

He rolled his prayer carpet neatly as he spoke and stowed it inside the door of his little room, built off the back of the smithy. With the path to the mill running a dozen feet from Mohammed's door, January didn't wonder that he hadn't heard someone enter the smithy from the other side and work the bellows; he must have long ago gotten used to noises, in the roulaison.

"But Lisbon was a driver, and a good one. He's slowed down some now after havin' the lung fever two years ago, he never quite got over that. Now, the way Michie Fourchet buys good service from men is to give them the women they want: as he gave Kiki to Reuben, and then later Trinette, after Gilles and M'am Marie-Noël both asked him that Kiki and Gilles could be together."

"And I suppose," remarked January dryly, recalling Kiki's words, and Jeanette looking up at Thierry from the dust of the whipping-ground, "that what the woman wants doesn't enter into it."

Sitting down easily beside January with his own supper, the blacksmith met his eyes, not answering for a time: *You know as well as I do.* Then he said, "Michie Fourchet has never been a man to admit he'd paired up the wrong couple." He offered January salt pork and rice, and water from the covered jar beside the door, sweetened with a little sugar, and January gave the smith one of his yams.

"Even his own son, who hates that wife of his and the children she bore him. Kiki and Gilles were clever, asking him to let her be with Gilles on the day he'd brought M'am Marie-Noël home after their wedding. Reuben had hit Kiki bad that day and marked her face, but even then Gilles had to put it right, saying, 'You know, sir, how Reuben has changed, how he used to be a better man than he was when you first gave Kiki to him.' "

And in the shifted note of the *griot*'s voice, January heard another voice, lighter and more cultured, with the accent of town. Gilles's voice, speaking out of the past, from beyond his grave.

"Meaning Reuben had changed, not Michie Fourchet had made a mistake in the first place. He was clever, that Gilles."

Clever, thought January, except where liquor was concerned.

The path from the woodsheds was quiet now as the men ate their suppers. Up by the front of the mill a baby cried, and a woman's soft voice shushed it—Trinette, January identified the sweet soft lisp. Herc's wife. Reuben's wife, after Gilles's "cleverness" had won Kiki from him, though the ten-month-old child she carried to the fields to work with her, and to the mill at night, was definitely the lighter-skinned Hercules's child.

"Well, whatever Zuzu thought of the matter, Michie Fourchet gave her to Lisbon because he wanted Lisbon's good work, and the pair of them got on well enough. Like I said, there was good reason to think Roux was Boaz's son rather than Lisbon's, and everybody knew for sure that Lisbon fathered girls on Quinette and Heloise. And now and then Zuzu and Lisbon would have it out, like all married couples. But the true thing is that both of them loved the children she bore, loved them dearly.

"She loved M'am Camille's children, too. For all her faults Zuzu was a woman of great love. Whatever Michie Robert says, this wasn't true of M'am Camille. She was a beautiful woman, and a brilliant one, but M'am Camille wasn't happy, especially not after Michie Fourchet sold his place Bellefleur. His sister died, who'd been running Triomphe ever since the uprising here in 'ninety-eight, and Michie Fourchet fought with her husband at the funeral and told him never to come back. And the town was growing. Men offered Michie Fourchet a lot of money for the Bellefleur lands. So he sold Bellefleur, and most of the slaves from it, and moved the rest of us up here to Mon Triomphe."

January was silent, remembering that place, that world of his birth. Remembering in his childhood how close the ciprière had lain, a wildness of marsh and silence, endless in all directions, save for just around the little walled town.

Mohammed mopped the last of the beans with a fragment of corn-bread. "M'am Camille had been all right mostly," he said, "when she'd been able to go into town to the opera, and to buy books and see her French aunt and her friends. Out here I think she felt alone. Well, a lot of us did, that had friends, or abroad-wives or husbands in town, and in the plantations round about town. M'am Camille, she'd always been hot and cold towards those three children of hers, holding onto them tight one minute then pushing them off the next because she had to get dressed for some party, or wanted to play her piano or read. She left Michie Robert in school with the Jesuits and came into town to see him whenever she could—to see him and to see her friends—but the little girls she mostly ignored, and it was Zuzu that raised them. All she wanted was to go back to France. It wasn't a good time."

"No." January thought of his own anger at being separated from the music he loved. At feeling his hands grow stiffer and more clumsy each day, and seeing the tide of days flow between himself and Rose, days that could be sweet and were instead bitter with hard work, isolation, and fear. *No novels to rip up,* Hippolyte Daubray had chuckled. *No glass birds and music boxes to stamp. . . .*

As if he'd passed her ghost on the levee last night, January saw a woman in a yellow dress staggering beside the river with an opium bottle in her hand, screaming to the boats to take her back to France. And Camille had to come down from the levee sometime, he thought. And there was only the house to go back to when she did.

"Zuzu kept the girls away from their father as much as she could," went on Mohammed, "for he'd take out his hate of his wife on them. When Mamzelle Solange was two or three, M'am Camille bore another son." Glancing aside at him January saw the untold half of that tale in his eyes: how it must have come about that she conceived them, to a man she would never have willingly bedded.

"A year later she bore another, and the first one a stout boy by then, crawling all around the place with Zuzu after him, laughing. M'am Camille was jealous that little Toussaint would go to Zu rather than to his mother. She used to slap Zuzu, and once or twice thrashed her with a cane-stalk for being uppity, when she'd catch her playing with the children. She'd seldom play with them herself. Then one summer little Toussaint died, laid down on his bed in the nursery taking a nap. It was like Zuzu had lost one of her own sons. The boy'd had no fever, though there was some sickness in the quarters that summer, like there always is. And two weeks later the baby died, too, the same way: was alive when Zuzu laid him down, and when she came back into the room he was dead."

Down at the front of the mill Danny the night driver's scratchy tenor sang out, calling, "Time to pick it up again, boys," and from the direction of the quarters the men who'd gone to their cabins straggled back along the path by the mill wall, talking to one another and laughing: January heard Parson say, ". . . so fat they hired her out to schools for a globe . . ." and wondered where he'd picked up that fragment of Shakespearean insult.

It was time, he knew, to go back to work.

"And that's when they sold Zuzu?"

Mohammed nodded. "M'am Camille took on somethin' desperate, of course, and Michie Fourchet was drunk for near on to two weeks. Michie Esteban and Michie Robert ran the plantation. Zuzu was sick with grief, swearin' she'd sooner have died herself than see those two babies come to harm, but for spite Michie Fourchet sold her off separate from her children: Sold her for a field hand, too. M'am Camille never got over it," he added, brushing the last of the cornmeal crumbs from his hands.

"Yet they only sold her down to Voussaire."

The blacksmith nodded. "Nan and Roux went to Lescelles, just upriver from here, but it's a little place. They was sold away from there this summer, to a dealer. But Sidonie's still on Daubray itself. Pretty, she is, and just married this spring—isn't she, Lisbon?" For the driver himself had come walking along the path from the quarters, a stout spry man arm in arm with a young woman named Zarabelle, with whom January had seen him at the shout.

"Sidonie?" Lisbon smiled with gap-toothed pride. "She's so pretty the roses take shame and ask her pardon when she walks by."

"Prettier than Zarabelle?" teased Harry, ambling along the path just behind them, and Lisbon and Zarabelle laughed and nudged each other the way that lovers do. "You better watch out, or one day she'll go down to Voussaire and sit down with Zuzu for tea. . . ."

"Now, whoa, how fair is that?" objected Lisbon. "How is it women can sit and talk about men, and they get all prickly and hot when they think men are talking about them? What if I went and had tea with Syphax, and talked to him about Zuzu?"

"Syphax is Zuzu's husband?" January fell into step with them as they headed along the trash piles toward the lights of the roundhouse windows.

"Her latest," said Harry, which made Lisbon laugh.

"You wouldn't happen to know," asked January, in a softer voice, as Lisbon and his ladyfriend moved out ahead of them and left him and Harry in the dense shadows along the wall, "whether Zuzu knew any juju, would you?"

Harry paused, mobile eyebrows flicking up. "You don't think Zuzu might be our hoodoo?"

"I don't know," said January. "I'm sort of curious."

He saw something alter in the young man's bright intelligent eyes. Something in the back of them, as if he were sorting out a hand of cards. "You curious enough to do another little favor for me tonight? Because it so happens," Harry added, with an ingenuous smile, "that I'm headed on down to Voussaire myself tonight, as soon as I can bribe Herc to let me slip away."

TEN

"Somebody told you *I* was a mambo?" Auntie Zu made a shooing gesture with one big bony hand. "Shush!"

January had already taken note of the stoppered bottle on the shelf in the corner of Zuzu's cabin, nearly invisible in the shadows thrown by the single tallow dip, before which sat a saucer filled with white sand and molasses, and of the sieve that hung beside the door.

"They did tell me you might be the one to take the fix off me," he said apologetically, and shifted his aching shoulders. Carrying twenty-five pounds of pork five miles through the twisting paths of ciprière and canefield was no joke. "I don't know who put it on me, whether it was just Mamzelle Jeanette, or Mambo Hera on Daubray, or maybe somebody else. . . ."

"That Harry," sighed the woman, and shook her head. "What'd you find . . . ?"

"Ben," he supplied, to the questioning tilt in her voice. "I'm the one staying at Triomphe while my gentleman gets better enough to travel."

She nodded, evidently familiar with the story. There

was enough coming and going between Triomphe and Daubray, and Daubray and Voussaire, to have spread that piece of information over half the parish.

"When I unrolled my blankets last night I found a chicken-foot in 'em," January went on. "I didn't tell nobody, because—well, you're in a new place . . . But I can see I could have got somebody angry at me. I did help trice up another man, Quashie, for the overseer to whip, but if I hadn't . . ."

"Jeanette's man," sighed Zuzu. She shook her head. From what Lisbon had said of her, and Mohammed, January had expected a pert if aging strumpet, but Auntie Zuzu was tallish, thin as a slat, and plain—and none of it made the slightest difference when that big mouth smiled, and those bright black roving eyes sized him up with playful ravenous joy. She was in her mid-thirties and missing a few teeth, her black frizzy hair braided in dozens of strings, and like every other field hand on every plantation up and down the river during roulaison was ill-washed and worn-looking. The cabin bore signs of hasty and perfunctory cleaning, and when Harry had knocked, Zuzu had been in the process of bedding down three weary but relatively clean children.

"If it's a chicken-foot I'd say it's just Jeanette." Aunt Zuzu went to the shelf where the bottle sat, and took a couple of jars, which she carried to the doorway. "And I can't blame her for being angry, for all you didn't have any choice about what you did. Get me a dipper of water, would you? Thanks." January followed her outside, carrying a dripping gourdful of water from the jar.

The quarters on Voussaire were quiet. Dim splotches of orange light marked where the women had come back from the mill, whose fires still blazed at the far end of the muddy street, and January could hear a woman's voice from somewhere nearby: "And the bear say, 'Who is this High John the Conqueror, that everyone say is the King of the World?' And he laid in wait for him behind a bush. . . ."

His father had told him that story, January remembered, smiling. And like this unknown woman he'd given Compair Bear a big gruff deep voice, and had rolled that line of it over on his tongue, how the bear lay in wait for High John the Conqueror . . . and came to some serious grief.

"Here." Aunt Zuzu took his hand in hers: rough warm fingers, cramped and clumsy from a day's work with the cane. She sponged water over it, and January smelled in the flickering darkness the vague sweetness of crushed flowers. The light from the doorway limned her profile, and through the aperture he could see the children sitting up and watching their mother from the room's single bed. A boy of eight, a boy of six, and a little girl just big enough to walk, three pairs of great shining dark eyes. Zuzu took his other hand and washed it, too—honeysuckle on the right, January guessed, and verbena on the left, just as Mambo Jeanne had taught Olympe when Olympe was barely bigger than that little dark-eyed girl.

Here again, thought January, he walked in the world *les blankittes* didn't know about and couldn't know about, the nighttime world of the quarters and the pathways and the ciprière. The world of Compair Lapin and magic dogs and the platt-eye devil and tales about little boys and their wise grandmothers. The world beyond the big house. He sensed it all around him in the quarters, that secret life. Smelled sausage and rice cooking for tomorrow's dinner beneath the gritty sweet of boiling sugar, and heard voices mutter over small barters and bits of gossip, the cluck of chickens hanging up in their baskets for the night and the slosh of water behind the next cabin as someone washed the field dirt from her hair. Through the black wriggly outlines of the oaks, he could glimpse the lights of the big house, where Monsieur Voussaire and his family consumed the cook's roasts and tarts and sauces, before Monsieur and his son or sons returned to supervise the night-work at the mill.

All those people he saw on their galleries from the deck of the *Belle Dame,* thought January, the women in their bright dresses and the children playing with dolls and toy guns. Women who were lonely, maybe, whose husbands treated them like dogs and who had no family they could turn to for protection. Men who drank to ease an anger they could not bear. He felt as if the whole night sang to him and he understood its mingling song, about time and lives and change, but his heart and his body were too sore and too weary to take it in.

"There," said Aunt Zuzu. "If you find anything else, you bring it on here to me and I'll take a look at it, but I think you won't. And don't blame Jeanette for being mad. You see someone you love get hurt like that, you hit out at whoever you can. It does no good. . . ." She shook her head, her face grave and sad and her eyes, as Rose's sometimes were, gently amused. "But sometimes it's all you can do. And you," she added, her tone changing to playful annoyance as Harry appeared once more in the dark of the street, "you don't go around tellin' half the parish I'm a witch, you hear me? I have enough trouble gettin' people to respect me as it is."

Harry was with a big bearded balding man whose sooty clothing and leather apron identified him as the plantation blacksmith; the smith stepped over to Aunt Zuzu and gave her a mighty hug around the waist, and the two of them kissed. "Got that pork ready to salt away?" the smith asked, and Aunt Zuzu nodded.

"I'll get it cookin' 'fore we go to bed. Tom!" she

added, furious, as a child squealed in the house and the oldest boy attempted to hide something in the blankets. "You let your brother alone! I swear . . ." She sprang up the step and into the cabin, and there was a great flurrying of bedclothes and protesting denials.

"Gettin' late," said the smith. "This boy here and his keys!" And he poked Harry, who tried to look innocent.

"Keys?" Zuzu came out of the cabin again, a tube of maiden cane in her hand and an expression of indignation on her face. "One day somebody's going to dig up under that house of yours, Harry, and they'll find copies of all those keys to this smokehouse and that brewery and the other place all over the parish—"

"Never!" protested Harry. "Never! Besides, if I didn't keep up with getting new keys every time Michie Fourchet got a new cellaret or a new lock on his salt-box, how'd you get rum or cinnamon or whatever when you need it?"

"I can buy whatever I need from False River Jones," Zuzu replied haughtily. "I don't need the likes of you spreading stories around about me." She held up the maiden cane, evidently the forbidden toy, and dropped a long thin thorn into it, which she then blew, like a dart, at the door of the cabin across the way.

"You as bad as they are," grinned the smith, whom January deduced to be her husband Syphax.

"Worse," said Zuzu. "I can't hit the broad side of a barn with one of these, and Tom pegged one of Michie Randall's carriage horses in the hock with it the other day and nearly started a runaway. I thought I'd die laughing. And just as well Harry did lose the key to that cellaret when he did," she added, glancing over at January, bringing him back into the little group, as if he were a longtime friend. She gestured with the confiscated blowpipe. "I asked him for a little whiskey about three weeks ago, when I needed some for a conjure and it was before the trader comes. He said he'd lost the key to the cellaret—"

"I *did* lose that key!" protested Harry, with a nervous glance at January.

"Oh, like Harry ever loses anything!" joshed Syphax.

"And what do you think?" said Zuzu. "Just a little while later it turns out the liquor in that box was all poisoned, and a man there, a friend of ours"—and her face grew suddenly sad—"died of it."

January was very thoughtful as he and Harry walked the five miles back through the ciprière to Mon Triomphe.

Mon Triomphe
Ascension Parish
19 Novembre 1834

My beloved,

I am well. Monsieur Simon Fourchet, whose man I now am, is a stern man with a reputation for harshness, though I have myself seen him act with kindness and generosity towards those in need. His young wife is gentle and just, and I am treated well, and am making friends among the other servants here. Please do not feel concerned for me.

Every day and every night I think of you, I pray for you, and hope that somehow we can be united again, even for a short while. I miss you more than I can say and hope that you are well and are happy.

Living in the country is strange and very different from town but I am learning how to go on here. Most unsettling is the absence of Mass, though every night Madame Fourchet leads the house-servants in prayers, which is a great comfort to me. Many of the field hands do not seem to be Christian at all.

There is great trouble here because one of the field hands, or maybe more, has been burning and breaking things mysteriously at night, and all here are in a state of fear. I pray that all matters will work out well.

Take care of yourself and tell Aurette and Leon that their papa loves them. And know too that I love you.

Your husband,
Baptiste.

"Can you get that to her?" Hannibal was handing the stiff sheet of cream-colored paper back to the butler as January came up to the garçonnière door. In the morning's brittle sunlight the fiddler looked greatly restored by four days of bed rest, though he was still in his nightshirt and the green silk dressing gown he'd borrowed from Robert, his long hair tied back in a neat queue.

"I think so, sir." The butler glanced at the doorway to make sure who was standing there, and lowered his voice anyway. "One of the field hands let me know there was a—a chance he could get a letter to a trader, who'd take it to town." He folded the page and tucked it into the pocket of his dark livery. "Thank you, sir. If there's anything I can do for you, please let me know."

"Poor old duffer," remarked Hannibal, when the butler had gone. "I wrote as he asked me, but I didn't have the heart to tell him that if his master sold him off he'd almost certainly have sold off his wife as well. I wonder what he traded to Harry to get him to take the letter to False River Jones?"

He returned to the bed, where a tray lay in a glint of silver and china in the bars of brightness from the door. "Help yourself," he said. "The lovely Kiki has clearly made it her mission in life to fatten me up." And indeed, there were enough muffins, grits, butter, eggs, ham, and coffee on the tray to breakfast half the Achaean host before the walls of Troy.

"At a guess," said January, sitting on the floor by the bed and taking the fullest possible advantage of the offer, "he lent him the keys to the new cellaret—at any rate that's what Harry had the blacksmith at Voussaire copy for him last night. And apparently that wasn't the first time."

Hannibal whistled through his teeth. "So much for the notion that the field hands couldn't have had access to the liquor."

"I always knew there was the possibility," said January. "Harry isn't doing a thing that hasn't been done before, and by smarter men than he. But unless there's something else going on—something I haven't heard about between Harry and Fourchet—I doubt Harry would have done it. Harry's whole position depends on things remaining *in statu quo* . . . for everyone except Harry. He might poison Fourchet if he felt threatened, but burning the barn and the mill, damaging the knives, calling all kinds of attention to the activities of the slaves—this has him terrified, and rightly so. I'm more interested, myself, in the fact that this False River Jones seems to be back in the area, if Harry's bargained to take a letter to him."

He fell silent as footfalls creaked along the gallery—the maid Henna's, by their light quick decisiveness—and faded as they turned the corner and passed into the dining room. The sharp, cold wind that had sprung up last night whispered and rustled in the oak trees and made a constant roaring in the cane just downstream of the house, a warning of cold to come. After changing the bandanna on the oak from yellow to blue, he'd slipped up to the garçonnière in the dead of last night and slid a note under Hannibal's door, asking that he be sent for that morning.

"If you'd like to sleep for a few hours on the floor I think I can contrive to keep Robert out of here," offered Hannibal, pouring him out a cup of coffee. "Keep your voice down, by the way—Leander sometimes listens on the gallery."

"Thank you. I might take you up on that later." January cradled the porcelain in his huge hands, grateful for the warmth of it, for the rich scent, for the stillness and rest. After four days his back and arms had quit aching every single minute and he could sleep through even the nibbling of the bedbugs in the unaired corn-shuck pallet, but the pain had settled into his wrists and hands. His fingers were stiff and raw with blisters—it would take weeks, he reflected bitterly, before he'd be able to play the piano again—and his bones hurt for sleep. In the few moments over the past four days when he wasn't sound asleep or wishing he could be, he missed Rose desperately, and, though he felt childish for doing so, missed his piano nearly as much. Missed the godlike logic of Bach, and Vivaldi's wry grace. Missed the peace they brought to his mind and his heart.

Missed—he realized now—the person he was when he played, and the calm thoughtfulness of living without fear.

"And was the company of this charming nursemaid worth carrying twenty-five pounds of pig meat five miles on foot in the middle of the night?"

"Oh, yes," said January slowly. "Though I'd be very surprised if Zuzu turned out to be the hoodoo. What was even more valuable was Harry's gossip on the way down to Voussaire and back: where people were on the nights of the two fires; why Reuben chose Trinette to replace Kiki when Kiki was given to Gilles; any number of things about the Fourchet family that are none of my business . . ."

"And you're about to learn another," remarked Hannibal. "Are you aware that Esteban's a boy-lover?"

January paused in the demolition of a fifth muffin, startled, then nodded, as pieces fell into place in his mind. The awkward man's unmarried state, still at the age of forty-plus living in the garçonnière. The sour flex of Simon Fourchet's mouth when he'd ordered his eldest son not to waste time in town, and Esteban's stifled reply. The smooth pomaded prettiness of the valet Agamemnon. "It doesn't surprise me. Who told you?"

"The long-eared and loquacious Leander," replied Hannibal. "And a few days' observation of the man and his valet together. There was a row last night when Madame Hélène happened to mention to her father-in-law that when Esteban was in New Orleans to purchase the new grinder—and to meet the homecoming Robert and his family—Esteban visited a gentleman of the town named Claude Molineaux, according to Leander a dear friend of long standing. Fourchet had ordered Esteban some time ago to sever the relationship, which I gather dated back to the era when the family lived on Bellefleur. As usual when those whose lives he's planned refuse to go along with the program, Fourchet was furious. The word *will* was apparently uttered, and that deadly phrase, *Continue the family.*"

He coughed, his educated French and small, delicate

hands a reminder, like a reproach, of the family duties Hannibal himself had long abandoned, whatever they had been.

"So tell me what it was you learned from the lovely Mamzelle Zuzu."

"Not much," said January. "But while I was there one of her children misbehaved in a way that set me thinking, and when I came back here, instead of going to sleep like a sensible person I took a torch and searched through the trash piles on the downstream side of the mill, near the windows of the roundhouse where the mules walk. And I found this."

He held up a billet of maiden cane, a pale brown segmented stalk about thirty inches long. Putting it to his lips he blew at Hannibal's face, and the fiddler blinked at the stream of air.

"It's large for a child's," remarked Hannibal, immediately grasping the thing about it that January had first noted. He held out his thin hand. "I manufactured similar implements of destruction back at our place in County Mayo, of course. The favored missiles were dried peas from the kitchen, but our gamekeeper's son used squirrel-shot and could down a bird at thirty feet. He cut them long, too. This one's like a Kentucky rifle."

"Well, Aunt Zuzu's son Tom used thorns—darts. Like these." From his pocket January produced the rag-wrapped scraps and fragments he'd collected from the floor of the kitchen at Refuge, and picked forth the two long splinters of cane. They were of a size to fit neatly into the cane blowpipe: Blowing with all his force, he drove one of them into the opposite wall so deeply that Hannibal had to work it loose.

"Arma virumque cano," murmured the fiddler, coming back to the bed with the missile.

"And by the arms you may know the man," said January somberly. "Or at least take a good guess at him."

"I'm surprised you found this at all." Hannibal perched on the bed, turning the blowpipe over in his hands. "It looks exactly like the rest of the cane-trash to me."

"Except that it's maiden cane, not sugar cane," said January. "It grows in the fields but nobody harvests it—hence the name. Sometimes it gets into the bundles, if it's growing too close with the sugar, but in that case the ends would have been cut on the diagonal, where a man cuts down with a knife, or upwards to top the bundle. You see both ends of this were severed straight across—it's shorter than cane so it wouldn't have been topped at all. Aunt Zuzu said her son had spooked Michie Voussaire's carriage team with a dart."

"Hmm." Hannibal dropped a little bolus of muffin crumbs into the reed and puffed it at the bureau mirror; his damaged lungs barely generated the force to clear the long barrel, and afterward he coughed. "And considering the mule harness had been tampered with—and believe me, if I had to work all day with red pepper and turpentine rubbing my arse I'd be ready to bolt—" He twirled the stalk idly. "Could a white man remain unseen long enough to watch for when the rollers stuck?"

"If he wore rough clothes and a hat, maybe. If no one saw him close. There are some field hands who're fairly light-skinned, but not many. It's *just* possible, but only just. The cane stands within a few yards of the downstream wall of the mill, and with a spyglass you could probably watch through the door to see when the rollers jammed. By the same token, the mule barn stands just beyond the mill. You can reach it in moments from the cane, going around the backside of the mill between it and the quarters. It wouldn't be difficult on a foggy evening, when everyone's in the ciprière or the fields."

"And the mule barn is where all the damage to the harness occurred. Shall I keep this?"

"If you would. And if you would," added January, as the fiddler rose and went to secrete the pipe—and January's little bundle of leaf fragments and darts—in the rear fastnesses of the armoire, "do you think you could contrive to send me with a message to a fictitious relative in New River? I'd like to stop by the Daubray kitchen and ascertain first, whether Hippolyte Daubray actually did pursue False River Jones five miles down the river on the night the mill caught fire, and second, if Harry, or any other of Fourchet's servants, has any kind of close connection with the Daubrays."

"Consider it done." Hannibal settled himself at the desk, trimmed up a quill, and began to write in the looping, beautiful Italianate hand so different from a Frenchman's upright and rather pinched script. *"Inceptis gravibus plerumque et magna professis/Purpureus, late qui splendeat, unus et alter/Adsuitur pannus. . . .* Curse," he added, fishing around in the drawer. "No wafers for our Robert. *Such a* SHOPGIRL *embellishment for a work of literature.*" He mimed the dandy's finicking horror at the idea of those newfangled, brightly hued lozenges of flour and gum, and started to rise to get a spill from the embers of the fire.

"I think it might be best," said January, bending down to touch a fragment of kindling to the flame and carrying it back to the desk, shielded in his hand, "if you were to feel well enough to go back to town for a day. Or so ill you felt in need of a trusted family doctor."

He lit the candle on the desk and watched as Hannibal melted the sealing wax, touching drops neatly to the inside of the folded sheet, then pressing it down and adding several more drops on the edge and the in-turned ends. Wind whistling through the French doors on both sides of the room made the flame lean and flicker. "It shouldn't be too difficult to learn about M'sieu Claude, and about whether Fourchet expressed his disapproval of his son's choice of friends in his will."

"I'll speak to Fourchet about putting out a flag on the landing in the morning." Hannibal blew gently on the wax to harden it, and superscribed the letter to *J. Capulet, Verona Plantation, New River, Ascension Parish.* "Will you stay for a nap, or is M'sieu Ajax likely to flog you for being late back to your office?"

January stepped to the French doors on the downstream side of the room that looked across the gallery toward Thierry's house and the cane beyond. The sun stood high above the oaks. "Since your note didn't specify how long you needed me for, I think I can push it another hour or so." It was a seven-foot drop to the ground from the gallery on that side; he crossed the room to the door looking into the piazza, mentally gauging whether Kiki would be preoccupied with getting the rice cart loaded up and preparing the noon dinner for the big house. "I'll be back . . . Damn," he added, as Cornwallis appeared from the dining room and strode out onto the gallery.

"Well, *you're* the one who's always going on about how he's practically a member of the family," Fourchet's valet was saying to Agamemnon. "*Surely* you'd be able to keep track of a small thing like that."

The smaller man, in his neat black suit and dandified cravat, was nearly spitting with rage. "There is a difference," he said, "between keeping a master's things in good order, which *some* people in this household don't seem to be able to do, and knowing every receiver of stolen goods along the river. . . ."

"For God's sake, can't you quarrel someplace else?" January muttered. "If anyone asks," he added, over his shoulder to Hannibal, "come up with a really pressing reason why you're sending me over to Catbird Island for half an hour or so."

"Catbird Island?" Hannibal looked baffled. "There's nothing over there. Why would any man send his valet to an empty hunk of mud like that?"

"You heard False River Jones was camped there and might have a message for you from a beautiful widow on the other side of the river." January leaned on the doorjamb, angling his eye to the slats of the jalousie. "Get off the gallery, you lazy heretic," he added. "Don't you have any work to do at this time of the morning?"

"Why wouldn't this lovely lady just have written me?"

"Her sons," provided January, inventing freely. "They aren't eager for their mother to bring in an unknown stepfather, lest the fruits of that new union diminish their own inheritance. So she sends a winged messenger across the Father of the Waters. . . . Thank God, Cornwallis has gone in. Ring that bell Kiki gave you if he comes out again before I'm under the house. I'll be back here to take that nap before I return to the fields."

ELEVEN

There were two sorts of islands in the Mississippi River: low ones, built up from sand or gravel bars in the channel as they accumulated silt and towheads brought down by the river's rise; and high ones, carved off the bank when in heavy storms the river cut new channels behind points of land. Catbird Island was of the latter type. Though the water in the chute was low now, it was very strong, and January felt the pull of it as he waded breast-deep through the muddy flood. Were the river only a little higher a skillful pilot could probably take a small boat like the *Belle Dame* inside the island, between it and the bank, avoiding the massive current mid-river. Personally, January wouldn't have wanted to be on the boat.

Clearly the pilot of the *Lancaster* wasn't so sanguine about his skill; the long side-wheeler was just negotiating the bars on the outside of the island as January came around the little cove on the downstream side. He stayed in cover behind the inevitable snarl of snags that built up at the tops and bottoms of islands where the current veered, wondering which stoker or striker or deckhand on that boat had been paid off to go to

Shaw and say, "Wednesday? Yeah, we passed the point above Triomphe landing that day—that bandanna on the tree was blue."

All is well, King Aegeus. Thy son lives.

Catbird Point had originally been triangular, but once it became an island the action of the current against its outer side had built up a little bar there, with a sheltered cove behind. The belt of weathered gray deadfalls protected it from the sharp chill of the wind, but January still shivered as he pulled his clothes back on. If Harry had been telling poor Baptiste the truth about False River Jones being in the neighborhood, this is where the trader would camp.

The only thing January saw in the cove, however, as he emerged from the thickets of loblolly and cypress, was the scuffed dimple of an old campfire in the sand. Even before he reached it he could see it was weeks old, the earth tamped by subsequent rains. Presumably False River Jones had set up shop here on his last visit. But as January approached, he saw the fresh tracks of a woman's feet, crossing the damp earth.

She'd made no attempt to conceal them. Maybe her conscience was clear, or maybe she'd come here at night, her mind on other things. Her feet were narrow, her shoes the brogans that masters gave to slaves, newer than most but still patched, broken, and worn. The tracks led directly to the masses of snags along the island's outer edge.

Drawn up under them was a boat, a shallow-bottomed pirogue little larger than a canoe. After a few experimental pokes with a stick, January reached in and drew forth a red-and-blue blanket of the kind that had been found in the smithy, dirty and worn. Two cane-knives were wrapped in it, not broken ones but the new ones Esteban had bought in New Orleans. There was also a cooking pot containing a couple of gourd cups, a dozen partially burned candles—both tallow and wax—and a bandanna wrapped around flint, steel, and tow.

January wrapped these things and replaced them. A few yards' search in the woods yielded a bundle hung from a tree. This contained a loaf of bread, two apples, a piece of salt pork the size of his fist, and a slightly smaller chunk of cheese. The bread was a day old. The apples were Ashford russets from Madame Camille's garden.

Stealing a little at a time, he thought, wrapping the food and hanging it once again. *Waiting for a cloudy night, or rain, to get away.* He wondered where the boat had been acquired.

But even if you had a boat, where would you go? Upstream, through Baton Rouge, Natchez, St. Louis? He shivered at the thought of trying to row a pirogue through those vermin-nests of river pirates and slave-stealers, day or night. Across the river, and so on foot through the western parishes and on into Mexico? You'd have to be a powerful oarsman to keep from being swept away in the big current.

Or you could just go south to New Orleans, and hope to blend into the mangle of free colored and freedmen, and runaways that nobody bothered to look for. Get a laborer's job with somebody who wasn't going to ask. Try to get someone to forge papers for you. Maybe get a ship, to Philadelphia or New York.

The sun stood directly overhead. He stripped again and waded the channel, dressed in the thickets of the batture, and climbed the steep clay bank, to stand with the cold steady wind flapping and pulling at his clothing, looking down over the dark green acres of cane in the heatless light. The cane-rows churned like the ocean before a storm, and in the distance he could see the men, like ants in long grass, and, antlike, the coming and going around the doorway of the mill. Around the side of the house the rice cart appeared, the boys of the hogmeat gang leading the oldest of the mules out along the cart track into the field. Though it had been in January's mind to stop at the kitchen and speak to Kiki, he knew it was time and past time to return to work.

Quashie and Jeanette, at a guess. She'd have access to the knives. But as he descended the levee and walked toward the fields, he reflected that it might just as easily be someone else, someone who had another reason entirely to be arranging flight at a moment's notice.

Someone had lain in wait, thought January, making his circuitous way among the mule paddocks and sheds toward the kitchen after dinner. Had watched for the moment when the rollers would jam. Someone had prepared the blowpipe and the darts, had boiled both oleander to poison the master and some lesser poison to guarantee that the mill would be shorthanded, that the cane would be full of trash, rocks, roots.

Someone who'd written signs to summon the dark spirits to the poison's making.

A slave. Or someone who had been a slave.

He glanced around him uneasily, lest Ajax or Thierry or even one of his cabin-mates see him and demand where he was going when he was due back for the night work at the mill.

Maybe Harry *had* lost his spare key; maybe it had been stolen. But someone had to have gained access to the pots of grits and congris and sausage that the men ate before they went out to the fields. Kiki was just as likely to chase him off with a broom as to answer his questions. Still, it was worth a try.

But as he ducked around the back of the laundry January saw the unmistakably short, stout, black-clad figure of the woman he sought slip quietly from the kitchen door with a bundle beneath her arm. Still hidden in the shadows himself, January saw her look furtively around in the glimmer of the moon's rising light.

Meeting Harry? But on any number of occasions Kiki had expressed her contempt for all the field hands—including January—and her complete disdain for Harry.

Meeting False River Jones herself with coffee grounds or used tea leaves to sell?

Kiki set out at a swift walk, the night's chill wind jerking at her shawl, flapping her skirts. January followed, through the velvet dark between stable and carriage house, past the rude huts of pigsties and chicken runs, until she disappeared into the cart track between two rows of the wind-thrashed cane. It was easy enough to follow her then, a row over and a little behind, the noise of his own body shoving through the thick leaves masked by the roar of the wind. A short ways into the fields, Kiki lit a lantern: The gold light bobbed between the clattering stalks. To their right the quarters lay, lightless houses and weedy plots of corn and yams, huddled against the thrashing wind.

When they reached the ciprière the wind was less, though the tops of the trees tossed and muttered, and even down below the air was achingly cold. A half-mile in, close by the place where the ring-shout had been, was a hut used sometimes by those Fourchet sent out to burn charcoal for use in the forge, and sometimes by the men who gathered Spanish moss. Its single window was shuttered, but most of the moss and mud that chinked the walls had fallen out. January could see the lantern's light inside like a pile of gold needles in the dark. The one knot-hole big enough to see through didn't give a very good view, but he saw a few rough bales of moss stacked along the opposite wall, and a black-skirted knee and foot.

Kiki was sitting on the moss.

Waiting.

January knew, at this point, that the supper hour was well and truly over and he would be beaten by Ajax when he returned to the evening's work at the mill. For Hannibal to protest would mean the loss of his position in the work-gang, and with it the loss of any chance for further information.

Stealthily he backed into the shadows of a hackberry thicket and thought, *This had better be worth it.*

And waited, while the moon sailed high over the heaving trees, and the ghosts whispered in the darkness. Waited, to see who would come.

Frost on the way, January thought. His bones twinged with the reminder that he was no longer a young man. *If not tonight, then soon.* Maybe the attempts on Simon Fourchet were only anger, against his merciless drive to make the crop. Maybe the break January sought in the pattern was too small to see, a flaw in the mind of a man or woman pushed to personal extremity, like the hairline fracture in a steamboat's boiler that one night will bear the pressure of the steam no more. It wasn't as though the planter hadn't pushed his slaves to murder and rebellion before.

His land, Fourchet had said. All that he had to show for his life, and everything that was precious to him. Devotion to it had cost him the life of the woman whose portrait still hung on the parlor wall, and the life of the daughter she'd borne him. Had cost him the love of Madame Camille, fleeing to New Orleans in the wake of her babies' deaths. Would they have lived, had they had the services of a doctor in town?

He thought about the pirogue, waiting in the

darkness of the snag-piles on Catbird Island, and of the butler lying dead in the storeroom, a glass in his hand.

Voodoo marks on the walls . . .

The smell of blood.

January's head came up as he scented it, sudden and raw as the wind momentarily slacked. Then he heard her moan.

He strode to the hut and hurled open the rickety door. Kiki raised her head from the floor where she'd fallen when the convulsions overtook her. Her skirts were hiked around her waist. The thick pad of moss and rags over which she'd been squatting, now drenched with blood and fetal matter, made clear to him why she had come. Mute eyes, huge and terrified, met his, then she doubled over again. An animal sound was wrung from her, hoarse and dreadful.

"What did you take?" Without waiting for a reply January plucked aside the towel that covered her basket, unstopped the half-empty gourd of brownish liquid inside, and sniffed it, not even needing to taste. Quinine. Of course she'd have access to the plantation medicine chest, and there was never any telling how strong the bark was, when you boiled it.

There was a rain barrel behind the hut, at this season clear even of mosquitoes. The water was fairly fresh. Among the packets and boxes in her basket there was powdered tobacco, which he mixed—carefully—with gourdful after gourdful of water, forcing her to drink. She vomited twice, January holding her shoulders, the smell of the blood nauseating in his nostrils but familiar. How many times, during his six years at the hospital in Paris, had he dealt with women in similar case?

He'd known women to take anything, any sort of poison, to purge unwanted pregnancies: foxglove, ipecac, arsenic. He was preparing a third dose of tobacco-water when Kiki raised her head—hair sweat-matted around her face, dark eyes huge and sunken in the candlelight—and gasped, "Paper. Herbs. The basket." And vomited again, and again, as if all her guts and soul would come up as well.

They were powdered up in a twist of paper and January wasn't certain what they were—fragments of honeysuckle at least, and a smell of licorice. But he mixed them with a little water, and held the gourd for Kiki to drink.

She retched, gagged, fingers digging into his biceps like iron vises. She had kneaded pounds of bread every day for years, and her grip was like a blacksmith's. Then she lay back, gasping, in the crook of his arm, and began to weep.

Gently, January lifted her, carried her to the moss bales. He tucked her skirt up out of the way and laid more of the rags from her basket under her bottom to absorb the last of the blood. The mess of bloodied rags, moss, and aborted flesh he gathered together and carried outside, locating a charcoal-burner's bucket and upending it over the sorry little heap to keep the foxes out of it until he could come back and bury or burn it. By lantern light, the fetus had looked to be about three months along. A dangerous time to abort.

When he came back Kiki had pulled her skirt down over her legs. She lay breathing shallowly, eyes closed, tears running from them down her plump cheeks. January took off his coarse jacket and tucked it around her, then used his clasp-knife to cut the cords on one of the moss bales, piling the wiry gray masses around her like a rude blanket. Kiki groaned, and whispered, "Gilles."

"Was it Gilles's child?"

She opened her eyes, not surprised at the question. He gave her the gourd he'd filled from the barrel; she drank thirstily. Not the cleanest, he thought, but she'd lost blood and it was exactly what she'd have drunk back in the quarters.

After a time she nodded, and wept again without a sound.

January turned away, and sorted through the basket on the table. There was slippery elm there, and willow bark. It wasn't part of a surgeon's training, but he'd learned from Olympe and, long ago, from old Mambo Jeanne. He hunted through the little hut til he found a tin cup, which he filled with the last of the water in the gourd and set over the lantern's candle, so that the bark could steep. As he worked he felt Kiki's gaze on his back, and saw she had turned her head a little to watch him work.

She whispered, "He'd have sold it. Michie Fourchet would have sold it."

January couldn't argue.

"Gilles was so good. And it made him so happy, when I told him I was carrying." She shook her head. " '*She gonna be a beautiful gal,*' he said. '*She gonna look just like you.*' " She closed her eyes, and laid her forearm over them, not sobbing, but with the tears still flowing down.

Still January said nothing. He knew—they all knew—what generally happened to *beautiful gals* who were not free. The water hissed and bubbled in the cup. He wrapped a corner of his outer shirttail around his hand and brought the cup to her, helped her sit up to drink. "We'd better be getting back," he told her. "You're chilled, and you've lost blood. I'll get you to your cabin and then come back here and bury the child. Should anyone find it, with you sick tomorrow, they'll guess." It meant a day in the fields with little more than an hour's sleep, but he had no thought of not helping her. For a slave woman to induce abortion in herself or anyone else was punishable by whipping, an act of robbery from her master.

Kiki sighed, and struggled to sit up. "I won't be sick tomorrow," she said. There was infinite weariness, an endless chain of days on which she had been strong, in her tired voice. "Nobody will know."

"They'll know if you faint dead on the kitchen floor. Can you put these on yourself?" January handed her the long rags she'd folded as clouts to absorb the bleeding and, though he'd performed the most intimate care of her less than an hour ago when she was semiconscious, now turned his back on her, and let her tend to herself. "Tell 'em you broke a jar and cut your foot, and need to stay off it for a day, and let Minta do the cooking."

"I do that and the whole family'll die of poisoning, not just Michie Fourchet."

January laughed, and turned back in time to see her rising shakily to her feet. "No, you don't." Again, he picked her up, not easily, for she could not have weighed less than two hundred pounds, but without trouble. He had worked with the dying and the dead, both as a surgeon in Paris, and before and after those years during the fever summers in New Orleans. He had learned the knack of lifting bodies. "Which is the best way back to your cabin?"

The candle in the lantern was flickering out, so he left it on the table with the basket. The gibbous moon stood high, shedding sufficient silvery light through the bare trees to find their way back to the fields. January hoped he'd be able to return as easily to the hut when he'd left Kiki at her quarters.

It worried him, until they emerged from the woods, and saw the yellow fountain of upwelling fire from the direction of the quarters; heard the shouting, and smelled the smoke.

TWELVE

The fire had started in the woodsheds. By the time January reached Kiki's small room attached to the rear of the kitchen, wind had carried burning fragments to the roofs of the cabins. "Dammit, get into line!" He heard Fourchet's snarled bellow, and the crack of whips. "Get the goddam buckets—!"

"Dear God." Kiki's eyes were wide with shock. When he set her down to open the door she clung to the doorpost, staring back at the flames in horror.

"What do you have for burns?" January scooped her up again, carried her into the little chamber and over to the bed she had shared first with Reuben, then with Gilles. Though none of the field hands had spoken of it, the presence of the healing herbs in the basket told him she did at least some doctoring. "I'll need bandages, beeswax . . ."

"There's wax in the kitchen." She started up from the bed and he pressed her back by her shoulder, met her eyes. "Oh, for God's sake, Ben, I've cooked dinner for twenty people five hours after I birthed a child."

"Well, somebody else got the fire going tonight. You have sassafras? More willow bark?" He'd already gone to the hearth, thrust a stick of kindling into the banked embers, and breathed on it gently, adding more kindling as the yellow flame licked up. The brighter light showed him her medicine box beside the bed. "May I?"

She nodded, and he flipped back the lid, sniffed the tiny bundles wrapped in worn clean sheeting. "Make yourself a tea of these and take it," he ordered, setting willow bark and briory on the bed beside her. "Then lie down and stay down. I'll be back as soon as I can."

Bandages and herbs in his pockets, he set out for the quarters at a run.

Ajax's house, first in the line and nearest the mill, was a torch—even as January arrived the driver flung himself out of the flames, naked and gasping, with his two-year-old daughter Milly clasped to his chest. Rodney's little son Bo lay screaming on a blanket near the cane, his mother Ancilla crouched above him, frantically pouring water over him from a gourd. The child's shrieks made a keening, hideous background to the greedy din of the fire.

Rodney's cabin was ablaze and Dan and Minerva's just beyond. It was just past midnight and most of the inhabitants of the quarters had sunk into the first depths of heavy sleep—Giselle and Emerald were running along the dirt street, pounding on doors, thrusting into dark cabins to drag their friends out of paralyzing slumber and shove them to safety. Someone had gotten to the plantation bell: It was clanging furiously, the iron racket penetrating the dreams of the unfree as no other sound could.

"Get the buckets and make a line for the river!" Fourchet was yelling. "Get the trash away from the walls!"

January slung his coat into a safe corner near the mule barn, caught up a rake, and joined the gang of women frantically clawing the piles of loose trash—

cane-tops and leaves and fragments of dropped wood—away from the walls of the first woodshed, the one nearest the mill, which had not yet caught. The second and third, stocked and ready with enough wood to complete the sugar-boiling, lay downwind. If the wind didn't shift, the first shed and the mill would be safe. He saw Thierry, in shirt and boots and no trousers, thrusting and shoving men toward the burning sheds: "Pull the walls out! Save the wood!" Looked beside him and saw Madame Marie-Noël, dressed with a shawl around her shoulders, wielding a rake beside the nightgowned housemaid Ariadne. Saw Esteban and Robert, both in their nightshirts, running from the direction of the house.

Men were already forming up a line past the smithy and the mill, across the open square and Thierry's house, through the oaks and over the levee to the river. Nearly two hundred yards, buckets being passed from hand to hand, while Herc, stumbling and naked, shouted a second gang into order to clear the trash from the walls of the mill. Frenzied mules brayed and kicked in their barn, the horses in the stable, maddened by the scent of the smoke. Another woman shrieked "Claire! Claire!"—Juno, January identified her: He'd seen the baby Claire only that morning, one of the swaddled infants along the edge of the field. . . .

Through the battlefield scud he glimpsed Hannibal in night-gear and Agamemnon trouserless in a ruffled linen shirt, running past with hooks and axes to join the women in the quarters. In the milling mass, the blinding smoke, they doused Random and Charity's house, Rachel and Chevalier's, with the contents of every rain barrel they could find, desperately trying to keep the fire from spreading along the line. Water flashed in the red glare as January ran to join the gang pulling at the rickety wooden walls of the third shed, the one nearest the quarters, dragging the burning wood out and dousing it.

Fourchet yelled something, plunged in with a small gang of men to drag at the woodshed walls. His hat was gone but he was fully dressed—when had the man last slept?—and his gray hair framed a face twisted with fury and desperation. January was beside him, shrinking back from the hammering heat of the flames, when someone yelled, "It's coming down!"

Looking up, January saw the wall of burning logs above them crumple. It seemed to take forever, as time does in a dream, the light growing brighter and brighter as the flames poured down onto their heads. Thinking about it later he realized how easy it would have been to dodge out himself and leave Fourchet standing. The old man had certainly earned that kind of death.

But whether because he'd spent his adult life tending burns and trauma, or because the Virgin Mary had, in fact, put in his heart the forgiveness he had grudgingly asked for—or simply because he could not let another man die three strides from him if he could help it—he hooked one massive arm around the planter's chest and shoulders as he plunged back, dragging him bodily from under the collapsing logs.

"Father!" Robert was shouting, clutching at Fourchet from the other side as they stood panting in the maelstrom of men. "Father!"

Fourchet started to speak, then doubled over, choking, face flushed dark in the firelight.

"Get him out of the heat." January scooped the old man effortlessly up in his arms—after Kiki he was nothing—and carried him back toward the barns. "Sit him up. Let him breathe. Keep him still." Confusion swirled around them, the fire's roar blending with the sinister, breathing rattle of the wind in the canes. The scattered wood and slumped walls of the third shed were little more than a shapeless bonfire now, pouring rivers of flame at the hard bright watching stars. In the quarters Ajax's house collapsed, then Rodney's, like shacks built of cards to which some malicious child had applied a match.

The child Bo's screaming was silenced. January heard a woman crying, howling her grief. For the first few moments he thought Fourchet too would die, and cursed that he had no medicines, no preparations of any kind. He could only grip the broad flat shoulders in his hands, and feel the old man's desperate spasms as he fought for breath.

"His heart?" Robert knelt beside him, pressed a silver brandy flask into his hand.

January nodded. Esteban yelled, "Save the wood! Save the wood!" and Herc staggered past carrying a young man from the second gang—Marquis was his name—who'd been burned in the collapse of the third shed.

"Get him a blanket," said January. "Anything, keep him warm—"

"Get that devil's piss away from me!" Fourchet spat out the mouthful January had given him and sat up, eyes crazed in the flaring light. "You're trying to ruin me! Thrust me back into hell . . ."

"Get him hartshorn," said January. "Baptiste, run back to the house and get hartshorn and a blanket, fast!" The butler, his coat awry and his white shirt smutched everywhere with soot, bolted for the house like a dog coursing hares.

"Here." Someone pressed a medicine bottle into January's hand; he looked up and saw Kiki, who shouldn't have been on her feet.

"Water." The ammoniac reek of the hartshorn was far too strong to drink. Everyone looked around, but the rain barrels and cisterns and jars of drinking water had mostly been dumped on the barn walls, and the mill. January settled for holding the bottle under Fourchet's nose. The planter coughed violently, but opened his eyes, and his breathing seemed to be more steady. He tried at once to sit up and January forced him back against the barn wall. "It's being taken care of, sir."

"The wood . . ."

"It's being taken care of. Can you breathe?"

Someone put a blanket into his hand and he wrapped his former master in it: a slave's quilt, strange gaudy colors, unfamiliar shapes. Other voices behind him, lost children calling for their mamas, women crying their children's names. Juno calling "Claire! Claire!" over and over like a machine.

For the first time January looked around him and saw Kiki, and Robert, and Cornwallis, and Harry. Trust Harry to find a way of looking like he was doing something without putting himself in any position of risk. To Cornwallis, January said, "Who's the nearest doctor?" Then he remembered to glance at Robert, as if seeking white advice.

"Dr. Laurette, in Baton Rouge." January guessed there were American doctors in Donaldsonville across the river, but guessed too that Fourchet would no more submit himself to an American doctor than he'd trust an American steamboat master—and no wonder. Robert continued, "I understand that the most modern medical thinking these days is that a patient should be given brandy immediately, to stimulate the system, followed by mild electrical massage of the hands and feet. There's a doctor in New Orleans—"

"You're not going to give me brandy and that's final," snarled Fourchet, silencing his son. "Or stinking opium, like your mother. Marie-Noël . . . Marie-

Noël . . ." He sank back against the wall again as Baptiste came dashing back from the house with blankets and—thank God for the man's good sense—a glass of bromide diluted in water. January applied this to Fourchet's lips.

"Michie Georges—Michie Hannibal's father-in-law, sir"—January dipped a nervous little bow to Robert and reminded himself to say *li* instead of *il*—"he gets took like this. I'm sorry if I done give myself big dewlaps over it, sir, and spoke as I didn't ought to, but the doctor back in town, he tell me what-all to do and he say, 'Don't you take no back-chat from *nobody* or your master a dead fish.' "

"No, it's quite all right." Still looking put out at having his advice refused, Robert screwed shut his brandy flask and pocketed it. He'd pulled on trousers under his nightshirt and was barefoot, his hair rumpled and his face now blackened with smoke and soot. Madame Fourchet came up, flaxen hair hanging in confusion down her back and her arm wrapped around her swollen belly as if in pain; January got quickly to his feet and offered her his arm, and she shook her head and waved both him and Robert away.

"I'm well," she said. "Thank you." In the firelight, she looked alarmingly white about the mouth. "What about the children in the quarters? Was anyone badly hurt?" She'd lost her shawl in the confusion and January saw that she wore no corset under her dress, not even the shaped stays of maternity. Only a thin shift, and the dress itself had been merely caught together at the waist and nape with its buttons, the laces pulled any old how, as if she'd dragged them tight herself.

"I want to see, I want to see!" Jean-Luc came dashing from the direction of the house in his nightshirt, pursued by Madame Hélène's maid Vanille. Now that things were a little quieter, January could hear Fantine screaming like a steam whistle from the gallery outside the nursery. "Is Grandpère going to die? Did all the slaves get roasted? I want to *see*!"

The blaze was dying down as the wood was scattered and doused. The reek of burned cane was thick among the gritty stink of smoke. In the confusion the bagasse shed nearby had taken fire, too, and being too far away to further ignite anything was blazing unchecked and unregarded. Women and children drifted through the mirk from the direction of the levee, buckets in hand, like the damned stumbling out of Hell. From among them Rodney ran to his wife, stood like a man stunned above the silent body of their son. Ajax and Hope clung together, Hope weeping as she held their many children close. Thierry cursed and struck a man.

Ajax took a deep breath, and called out, "Let's take a count," as January and Harry between them lifted Fourchet to carry him back to the house. "Make sure there's no one missin'. Soon as it gets light let's get cuttin' saplings, make a shed for what's left of the wood so it won't get wet next time it rains. . . ."

It occurred to January that he'd just saved the life of one of the few men whom he had actually ever dreamed about killing.

When he'd seen Fourchet safely put to bed, with Robert and Madame and Cornwallis in attendance, January returned to the plantation hospital. Kiki—duly limping on a bandaged foot—was there already, mixing poultices and applying dressings to burns.

Rodney's Bo and Juno's Claire were dead. The young man Marquis had some bad burns but was already talking sensibly and trying to make a joke or two with his friends through the pain; Emerald had broken her wrist getting Chevalier's daughter Princesse out through the cabin window after the door caught fire behind her. Dumaka, sick with pneumonia in his cabin, had been overcome with smoke and dragged out by his wife Fayola.

In all, ten men and two women had suffered various degrees of blisters, burns, and scorches. After making sure all were cared for and sending Kiki to bed, January collected a shovel from the storeroom beneath the house, and walked out through the cane-rows to the moss-gatherers' hut, where he buried all evidence that a woman had aborted her child there. Then he climbed the levee and changed the blue bandanna to green. By that time it was dawn.

"When we catch the nigger that did this," Thierry was saying, as he and Esteban surveyed the wet heaps of cordwood, the charred ruin of the sheds, "I'm personally going to skin him—or her—and make a tobacco pouch out of the pelt."

An acre of cane, ground and boiled, consumed nearly twenty cords of wood. Throughout the year, once the cane was in the ground and the corn planted, cutting wood in the ciprière was a constant, getting ready for the next roulaison.

Approximately four hundred of the plantation's six hundred acres of cane still stood uncut, and at a guess—surveying the long wet row of scorched logs, half-charred salvage, debris collected from the ruins—January estimated there were about a thousand cords of usable wood. Or would be, once they dried out.

In the quarters, the slaves sifted through the smoking remains of the six burned cabins in quest of cook-pots, cups, shoes, blankets. The younger children had already been parceled out among the women, bundled in borrowed blankets wherever beds could be found. Juno and Ancilla slept, broken with weeping.

The wind had died down. The morning was cold.

Nobody was keeping track of anybody. January climbed the back steps, and scratched gently on the door of the garçonnière.

"Inire, amicus meus! As the lady said in the play, *All strange and terrible events are welcome, but comforts we despise!"*

"Are you all right?"

"Tolerable." Hannibal had washed the soot and filth from his face and hands but his nightshirt was still black with them, and he looked beaten with exhaustion. He was propped on the bed-pillows with a tray across his thin knees, sipping cocoa and contemplating a French porcelain plate of untouched rolls. "God bless Baptiste. He brought these—he tells me the beautiful Kiki was injured in fighting the fire. Did you take note of who was dressed and who wasn't?"

"As if our friend wouldn't be clever enough to strip before the alarm sounded?" January listened for wheezing or gasping in the fiddler's speech, but other than the rough huskiness characteristic of consumptives he sounded well. In himself he could feel the rage like a low-grade fever, a small steady pulse that nevertheless let him speak quietly and evenly. "What time did it start, do you know?"

"About midnight. And I'm pleased to announce definite proof that neither Esteban nor the beautiful Agamemnon is the hoodoo, as they were together—discreetly quiet, I'm grateful to say—in Esteban's room next door at the time the fire started, and for at least an hour and a half before."

"Good," said January. "I didn't look forward to explaining it to Fourchet if his son turned out to be the culprit. To say nothing of the fact that I'm almost certain our culprit is a slave, or was one at one time. It saves you the trouble of getting details of the will out of Fourchet's lawyer, too."

"Well, I'd still be curious about that. Where there's a will, there's a relative, and it doesn't do to discount that fact. Robert was in here after supper explaining political economy and the shortcomings of the factory system to me—knowing how desperately I crave enlightenment on the subject of workers' housing in Paris—and went to bed at about ten. I heard Esteban turn in shortly after that, I assume when the night men took over at the mill. About five minutes later Agamemnon scratched on Esteban's door, presumably to help him off with his socks, and remained until people started shrieking 'Fire!' "

"Cornwallis was dressed," remembered January, casting his mind back to the confused images of blackness and flame. "Baptiste was dressed. . . ."

"Baptiste has barely had time to change his linen and wash his face," said Hannibal. "Fourchet doesn't hold with half-dressed servitors trotting out to the mill to give him his coffee halfway between midnight and morn. And Cornwallis has been sleeping fully clothed, in a chair in his master's room these past several nights, and catnapping during the day—an excellent way to remain unaccountable for your exact whereabouts at any given time. If all the field hands were supposed to be in their cabins except those actually working in the mill, you might be able to inquire among them. . . ."

"And I'd get lies," said January. "Nobody in the quarters is going to mention it, if someone was absent. And if Harry's behavior, and Quashie's, and mine for that matter, are anything to go by, there's a world of clandestine coming and going. God knows what it's like when everyone *isn't* dead tired."

He passed a blistered hand across his face. "Not that any of the field hands could provide a word of evidence if they wanted to about whether their cabin-mates were awake or asleep, present or absent, thirty seconds after they themselves lay down. I didn't see Quashie, I didn't see Trinette, but that means nothing—I didn't arrive on the scene until well after the fire had taken hold, and if I'd started the fire the first thing I'd do is take off my britches, rumple my shirt, and mix in with the crowd, doing my best to—".

"My dearest cousine, I was *horrified* to hear," a man's rich voice broke in, muffled by the garçonnière walls but still audible from the direction of the dining room. January's eyebrows rocketed into his hairline and he got soundlessly to his feet, crossed to the French doors, and pushed them open in time to see, through the dining room door, a glimpse of the malt-brown coat Hippolyte Daubray had worn two days previously in the cane-fields of Refuge. "And now the good Cornwallis informs me that your husband is ill? How *dreadful* for you!"

The voice retreated deeper into the house. January slipped through the French door and drifted down the gallery, positioning himself at the corner of Esteban's room where he could look through the door of Fourchet's office, through the office, and through the open door into the old man's bedroom beyond. He couldn't see Fourchet himself, but had a good view of Daubray, looming in all his refulgent splendor with Marie-Noël standing, abashed and silent and with an expression of unexpressed pain on her face, at his side.

"My dear Simon, I am *appalled*!" Hippolyte leaned forward, presumably to clasp his erstwhile foe by the hand. "Pray forgive me, and give no further thought to our little contretemps of Tuesday. I wouldn't dream of pressing a duel on a man—"

"Since it was my challenge, I'll be the best judge of that," snapped Fourchet. "I daresay—"

"Father," said Esteban's voice. "M'sieu—uh—Daubray—uh—hasn't come to discuss the duel."

"Of course not," cut in Daubray. "I came merely to offer whatever assistance it is in my power to extend. We are, after all, in a sense family."

"Then as family," said Fourchet, "you can help my men bring over the cut wood from the sheds at Refuge."

"At the least possible computation it is half ours," added Madame Fourchet, straightening up and regarding her cousin with those calm gray eyes.

"The hell it is, woman, it's *all* ours!" bellowed Fourchet. "Every stick and scrap of it! Of all the puling, mealymouthed—"

"My dear cousine!" Hippolyte threw up his buff-gloved hands in mimed dismay. "Had we but known! But of course, it was the first that we used for the sugaring. We had such a *very* large crop this year, you know, and the sheds at Refuge were closest to our mill. Not that there was much there, of course, only a few dozen cords—"

"There was a shed fifty feet long and twelve wide, chock full of it!" roared Fourchet. "I went over myself and saw it!"

"Then sell us an equal amount of what is in your own sheds," cut in Marie-Noël steadily. "If you admit to having taken what was mine, it is the least that you owe."

"Of course!" Daubray clasped his hands before his breast. "Of course. We can certainly spare you a thousand cords to get you started—until your men can get more cut—but since we're also going to have to pay *our* men to cut extra, the lowest possible price we could ask is five dollars a cord—"

"Five dollars!" Fourchet's blankets—all January could see of the man—jerked as if yanked by a string. Both Marie-Noël and Esteban leaped forward, hands held out to restrain him from leaping at his enemy's throat. "You scoundrel, I could pay my own Negroes fifty cents a cord!"

"Dear heavens, fifty cents! As little as that?" Hippolyte rounded his piggy pale eyes as Esteban hastily poured his father a glassful of bromide-and-water from the carafe beside the bed. "Well, you're known throughout the countryside as a man who gets the most work out of his hands. Why, we have to pay ours at least two dollars a cord during the year—"

"That's a lie," said Marie-Noël. "You pay your men fifty cents as well."

"My dear cousine, I had hoped that a man's attentions would have schooled your manners a trifle," sighed her cousin, with the air of a man teasing a chained dog and hugely enjoying the sport. "Of course I was talking about the extra men we'll have to hire to cut wood to make up the difference. Though it seems to me . . ."

At that point Baptiste mounted the back steps with a big kitchen tray in his hands, filled with ham and eggs, cakes and pancakes, compotes and pitchers of cream. As he entered the pantry door he glanced in January's direction and January, conscious again of his soot-grimed and filthy clothing, knew the gallery was no place for a field hand to be loitering. The butler said nothing, but January knew he'd better not be there when Baptiste came out. He descended the steps, turning over in his mind the distance from Daubray to Mon Triomphe across the contested acres of Refuge, and how a man might come up from the river through the cane-fields south of the house to within a dozen yards of the woodsheds, unseen.

There was, of course, no question of looking for tracks anywhere near the sheds themselves. The ground was a vast gumbo of mud, slopped water, trampled ash, and burned wood. On the sides of the sheds that faced the mule paddock, the quarters, and the cane-fields, however, January found the scorched fragments of three or four oil jars, and in a weed-grown ditch by the first row of the cane a whole jar, the oil film still slick on its cool clay inner curve.

He straightened, considering the black charred heaps of the burned sheds and the intact, half-empty shed closest to the mill. In the dead of night it would be easy enough to move the jars from the storeroom under the house. Probably rolled, he thought—they contained about forty liters each and would have to come around the back of the kitchen, laundry, hospital, and barns. But they could be concealed in either of the two farther sheds, probably for a couple of days if hidden deeply enough behind the wood. Even a woman, or a man as slight as Agamemnon, could have managed easily given sufficient time.

Easier still, of course, if the jars had originated elsewhere.

As he'd earlier ascertained, when inspected by daylight the paths between the cane-rows downstream of the house bore the scuffed tramplings of dozens of passages. The weeds and cane-trash, and the closeness of the rows, prevented him from distinguishing anything that resembled the print of a man bearing a heavy weight, or of a woman rolling one; moreover, he wasn't sure how long such a mark would have lasted in the rough weeds. All of the prints he was able to make out were the brogans and quantiers of slaves.

He emerged from the cane into the bright morning

sunlight in time to see Quashie limp stiffly from the burned ruins of the quarters and intercept Jeanette. The girl, who was helping Hope poke through what remained of Ajax's house, straightened and reached to embrace him, then drew back—his back was still a mass of bandages and crude dressings, smutted and filthy with soot.

He took her in his arms.

Would they have fled together, wondered January, had they been able to find each other in the confusion? He saw how the girl's hands gripped the young man's muscular arms, how Quashie's head bent down over hers. Clearly, neither had been prepared.

Kiki was in bed when January knocked at her door. She called out, "Come!" and he ducked under the lintel; it was low, less than six feet, like most of those in the quarters. The single room, seen by daylight, was swept and neat. Pegs in the wall supported clean aprons, and a dozen white tignons lay folded on a shelf. Beside them gay dresses of red and blue calico had been put aside, in favor of mourning black. On the inside of the door a circled cross was chalked in red, to keep witches away, and in a corner three strands of blue beads and one of shells hung before a stoppered calabash gourd. Herbs hung drying from the rafters. The blanket on the bed was red German wool, worn and faded but infinitely warmer and cleaner than those of January and his four cabin-mates. The faint scent of the turpentine used to discourage bedbugs ghosted on the air. There were sheets on the bed as well, the perquisite of house-servants the world over, and a pillow in a pillowcase—very worn but neatly mended with yellow thread—behind her back.

"You have no idea," said the cook with a tired smile, "how good it is to just lie here." She held out her hand to him. "Thank you, Ben."

"You feeling all right, Mamzelle Kiki?" He checked the small kettle that hung half-filled over the hearth, the tin cup on the table whose dregs breathed faintly of willow and briory. "Can I get you anything? Do anything for you?"

"You can make us a little tea." She pointed to the dented canister on the mantel. Used tea leaves from the house, another perquisite. But during his years in Paris, before January had forsaken the ill-paid surgery of the Hôtel Dieu for a musician's life, he'd routinely bought used tea leaves from the cooks of the rich.

"What'll happen now?"

"They got a flag out on the landin', for Michie Robert to go upriver lookin' for cut wood. They don't get wood, Michie Fourchet is ruined."

"Good." There was bitter pleasure in her voice.

January thought about the fetus he had buried, and recalled her words of the night before: *I cooked dinner for twenty people five hours after birthing a child.* She who had no child now. *He'll only sell it. . . .*

Kneeling, he tested the side of the kettle with the backs of his fingers. Finding the water almost boiling-hot, he tipped it into the teapot with the leaves. "What's gonna happen to us—to the field hands—is we're in for hard work if nuthin' else. Maybe worse. Maybe a lot worse."

She said nothing, only sat with her hands clasped around her knees under the faded blanket, the bronze rosebud of her mouth set with the steadiness of one who understood early in life that she had to be strong. He found part of a sugarloaf and a cutter, arranged the chunks neatly on a small plate which he brought to her, balanced with the cup in his big hands. By the way she turned her face aside, January knew instinctively that she had not let even Gilles see anything she thought or felt.

After a moment she said, still not meeting his eyes, "This scares me, Ben."

"It scares me, too." He poured himself tea, a little bitter but drinkable. "Michie Hannibal, he told me this mornin' what a English fella, a Michie Bacon, said one time: It is the nature of extreme self-lovers, that they'll set a house on fire just to roast eggs. And that's what we're dealin' with here. Someone who don't care who gets hurt."

"That's fitting," said Kiki, her voice metallic calm. "For if ever there was a man who didn't care, it's him."

January sighed, and gazed out through the door of the little back room, which faced, not the big house among its peaceful oaks, but the yard between kitchen, laundry, hospital, and the little shop where an old slave named Pennydip made candles and soap. Beyond, the new sun glared harsh and heatless on the cane, a dark green wall that drank sweat and life and spirit.

Mon Triomphe.

My Victory.

"Even so," he said, caught between his earlier anger and a vast weariness. "You sow the wind and you'll reap the whirlwind—and the whirlwind doesn't care whose child lies asleep in its path. Six families just lost everything they had. Every white man in the parish is now thinking *Rebels,* and getting ready to kill. Two children are dead, and men and women are crying in pain, because somebody wanted to hurt Fourchet. And yes, he deserves to be hurt. But whoever boiled up oleander bark and dumped it in Michie Fourchet's liquor, they knew other people might drink that liquor. They knew your husband might be one of 'em, and from all I can hear tell he never hurt a soul in his life. But they wanted what they wanted more than they cared about Gilles or you or Reuben or Rodney, or what'll happen if *les blankittes* decide this is a revolt. They were like

Baptiste's master, who sold him off because he'd rather have that eleven hundred dollars, thank you very much. Whoever this was, he sold your husband down the biggest river of 'em all, for the pleasure of seein' Fourchet ruined and dead."

Sharp and clear, the plantation bell began to ring. January flinched, a thousand memories cutting at him from whenever the bell rang at the wrong time of the day. The queasiness he hadn't experienced since his childhood; the dread of whatever *les blankittes* had decided to do.

Kiki put back the blankets and started to rise: "You got a bandage on one of your feet?" he asked.

She pulled up her nightdress to show him a surprisingly dainty foot for so heavy a woman, ankle delicate as a young girl's.

"I stepped on a piece of cane in the dark, if anyone asks," she said.

He answered her fleeting smile with one of his own, and handed her a black dress from the shelf. She slipped it on over the white calico of the shift and buttoned its big black buttons.

"Just remember to limp, then." He took her arm and helped her to walk down to the open ground between the mill and the overseer's house.

THIRTEEN

Thierry stood on the rear steps of his cottage, whip lying loose against the leather of his boot. The last feathers of the night's deadly wind stirred the skirts of his coat. Bumper, dust-smeared and scared-looking, still banged at the bell; Esteban and Robert, rifles on their arms, flanked the overseer, their eyes blank as smoked beads. From around the corner of the garçonnière the house-servants filed in a line, the three maids clinging close beside Baptiste, whom they already seemed to have taken to as a father or an uncle. The valet Cornwallis—the American and the Protestant—strode ahead, haughtily alone.

Madame Fourchet could be seen in the shadows of the big house's gallery, still in her soot-damaged shawl and gown. Taller and more opulent, Madame Hélène was beside her, little Jean-Luc yanking furiously at his mother's grip on his arm. Fantine was still screaming.

This sound fell curiously distant and detached, against the silence in the yard, when the bell ceased.

In the mill, the rollers were still.

"Now you listen to me." Thierry's soft voice cut the hush like rusted iron. "We had about enough of these little games. You think we don't know that some of you know who set those fires. Some of you know who damaged the knives, and set the fires in the mill and the barn. Know who's been writin' hoodoo to scare each other with. You think we don't know, but we know."

From the crowd's edge January watched the faces, the flicker of eyes meeting eyes. A gust of smoke from the mill doors blew over him, and an exhalation of heat, like the belch of Hell. No one spoke.

Thierry shifted his weight, like a dog setting itself to spring. "So I'm tellin' you. Whoever knows anythin' about the fires, or about them juju marks, or about the knives—you come forward right now. Juno—Ancilla. The man you're protectin'—*they're* protectin'—killed those kids of yours. You gonna let him get away with it?"

Ancilla cried out and pressed her face to Rodney's shoulder. Juno, an older woman, listened with a countenance of stone.

"All right." Thierry nodded as if he had expected this. "You want it this way, it'll be this way. Ajax, Herc, line 'em up."

Bumper's tiny sister Milly started to cry. The men shuffled and milled, frightened and not certain what was wanted of them, looking at Ajax with questioning eyes. But the big driver just pushed them into line, so they went, each trying to garner a minute advantage in placement as the drivers pushed each gang into order: "Stand 'em straight, goddammit! Single file! I gotta draw you a picture?"

They formed up in lines, by gangs: main gang, second gang, women's gang, suckling gang. Old Pennydip, who watched the toddlers during the day, clutched her charges around her, face working with terror. "Get those brats in line, dammit!" bellowed Thierry, the unexpected roar making everyone jump.

"If they can't walk they go with their mamas, now how hard is that? House niggers over there. Baptiste, don't you know what a fuckin' line is? Now number off."

January had guessed already what was coming, and discreetly worked himself into a position a few places from the front of the main-gang line. The other men mostly hadn't had the advantage of a classical education.

His number was eight. Gosport was ten. Nathan was twenty, that gap-toothed friendly man remarkable only for his ability to whittle the best toys in the quarter for the children.

In the second gang Philippe was ten, Ti-Fred twenty. The four women taken were Flora, Ajax's daughter Eve, Chuma, and Cipria. Among the house-servants they were Baptiste, Agamemnon, and Vanille, Madame Hélène's maid.

And if you touch the children, thought January, cold fury twisting in his chest, *I will personally step out of this line and break your neck.*

But even as he thought it he felt something in him falter, something in him ask, *Will you really? What good would it do?* And he knew it would do no good at all.

After a long moment of standing and looking at the weeping youngsters of the hogmeat gang, Thierry seemed to realize—if he had not before—what would happen, should he decimate them as he was about to decimate their seniors. He turned away, and with his whip signed to Ajax and Herc to separate out those whose numbers were ten, or twenty.

"Now every one of those people is gonna be whipped." He spoke calmly again, surveying the crowd that had already begun to fall out of line, to clump and cling and seek comfort among themselves. "And it ain't me who's makin' it happen. It's *you.*" January saw Esteban flinch and turn toward Thierry; saw him put aside what he was going to say. Saw him glance away from Agamemnon's horrified look of appeal.

"For the last time—Who started the fire in those sheds?"

A rising ripple of voices, a deadly muttering. Angry, and yet knowing already that a dozen lashed was better than what would happen if all rose up. January felt the violence like the breath of heat from the mouth of the mill. Felt every man look again at Ajax, and at Herc.

The two drivers folded their arms, impassive as statues, on either side of their charges. Behind Thierry, Robert and Esteban shifted the rifles in their arms.

From the river the hoarse whistle of a steamboat sounded, an upstream boat putting out of the main channel toward the landing where a white flag flew from the jackstaff; Robert Fourchet turned his head. "You better get on, sir." Thierry spoke without taking his eyes from the slaves. Gauging them. Understanding that the moment for rebellion had slipped past. "We can handle it from here."

Robert started back toward the house.

"Rodney, get your gang back into the mill," ordered Thierry. "We got little enough wood there as it is, let's not waste it. Ajax, Herc, take those folks and lock 'em up. 'Ceptin' for Ti-Fred. He's first."

Esteban wavered, looking as if he might speak, but it was Mohammed who stepped forward out of the milling crowd.

"Michie Thierry, sir." The blacksmith bowed. "Michie Esteban. Beggin' your pardon, sir, but Baptiste, he's the one nigger on this place who can't possibly have done or known anythin' of this. He only came here six days ago, not knowin' a soul, sir. Him and Ben."

"Why, I guess you're right, boy." Thierry stroked his mustache and nodded as if with deliberation.

"Guess maybe you better take Baptiste's place. Ajax," he added, as, without so much as a hesitation, the smith crossed over to the little knot of the selected. "Maybe we better get M'sieu Quashie in there for good measure. Somehow I just can't believe there's any hijinks here that he don't know about."

"God damn it, you got no fuckin' right—!" Quashie, who had dodged along behind the crowd at once to speak to Jeanette, jerked his arm free of the driver's grasp. At once Esteban raised the muzzle of his gun.

"Me, too!" screamed Vanille, and threw herself forward as Herc began to push and nudge the prisoners toward the squat brick jailhouse. "Me, too! I wasn't here, me and Leander, we wasn't even here when the mill burned! M'sieu Robert, M'sieu Robert . . . !"

Robert paused a step, already several yards off in the direction of the house. By the levee the steamboat whistled again, maneuvering in to the wharf. Thierry looked from Robert's face to Esteban's, and let out a crack of rude laughter.

Trying not to look as if he were trembling with relief, Leander bustled self-importantly to his master's side. "Best we get going, sir." He cast a spiteful glance back at the maid, with whose airs and self-importance he'd shared the small servants' quarters of a packet-boat from France not many weeks ago. "I've got your bag all packed, Michie Robert, and you know how Michie Ney hates to wait with a head of steam in the boilers."

Robert allowed himself to be led away. Grinning behind his mustache, Thierry said, "What about it, Esteban?" and the older son opened his mouth, then closed it again. Even as there wasn't a man in the quarters who would have come forward with information about another's transgressions, by instinct and custom and habit ingrained just as deeply, no white man was going to tamper with another white man's authority before the slaves. It was simply something that wouldn't happen.

Thierry grinned at the shocked betrayal on Agamemnon's face, and nudged Esteban with a conspiratorial elbow. "Don't worry, I won't scratch him up much! I'll skin his back for him but I won't touch his arse!" And turning to Ajax and the main gang, he commanded, "Get that boy triced and then get those niggers back to work! We got wood enough for a day's fires yet! And you," he added to January, as January started to lead the limping Kiki back toward the kitchen. "You get out to the field right smart, understand? Your master gave you to us for payment while he's here and you ain't done two days' solid work yet."

"No, sir," agreed January, bobbing his head and trying to look frightened, and gritting his teeth til his jaw hurt. "Yes, sir."

Kiki stumbled with a gasp and a cry, and grasped at his arm for support. As January scooped her up into his arms he could feel the steady rhythm of her breath, not the shallow quick panting of pain. Meeting her eyes for an instant he saw no pain there either, only complicity, and he was hard pressed to keep his smile hidden. "I be out there right quick, sir."

"Whew, look at him tote that load!" he heard the overseer jest behind him. "Now, that's one strong black boy!"

"What can I do?" Kiki asked, as January laid her down on her bed again.

"You can tell me how many jars of oil they had stored under the house. The small jars, forty liters or so."

"Eight," said Kiki immediately. "Maybe ten. Michie Fourchet used to have me just pour out the oil so we could use the jars for drinking water, but Madame says, there's no point wasting it. . . . Only of course we *do* pour it out, as soon as we need a jar for something. But there's eight or ten at the north end of the storeroom under the house."

January nodded, and glanced through the door again, as Pennydip climbed slowly up the brick step into her little shop, her thin back bent nearly double under the weight of her years. Ti-Jeanne the laundry woman hurried up after her, helping her inside.

"Can you get into the laundry room between now and Sunday night and have a look at the clothes before Ti-Jeanne puts them in to soak?" he asked. "Our hoodoo was working fast and working in the dark, and you and I have both emptied enough wash-buckets to know that somethin' almost always gets on you, of what you throw around. Will you do that?"

Kiki's eyes widened as she realized what he was talking about. "I'll do that," she said. "The house-servants and the family both. But what then? What if I find something?"

January was silent, knowing what she meant. Understanding her, because he too had been a slave, and he knew what all slaves know: that once you pass information, *any* information, along to the Man, it's out of your hands. *Les blankittes* are going to do about it what they will. It will be the worse for someone, and maybe not the person you thought.

He said softly, "We have to do something, Kiki. There's two children dead this morning."

"Children die all the time, Ben." Weary defeat stained her voice and he remembered the bloody scraps of flesh he'd buried not eight hours ago.

But that had been her choice. Juno and Ancilla, Bo and Claire had had none. He could only shake his head and repeat, "After last night, we have to do something."

He came around the corner of the kitchen in time to see the coachman Musenda bring the carriage to the rear of the house. The natty Leander emerged onto the gallery from the French doors of the room Robert shared with Madame Hélène, burdened with a small portmanteau and a valise. As the valet hastened down the rear steps and loaded the luggage into the vehicle, Robert himself came out, and at the same moment Madame Fourchet emerged from the dining room, in a clean dress now, properly corseted and combed.

Their eyes met. She turned quickly to go back inside, but Robert reached her in a stride and caught her hands. There was desperate urgency in every line of his slim shoulders and straight back as he bent his head toward hers.

". . . fear that something terrible may happen in my absence," he told Marie-Noël, as January stepped neatly under the shadows of the gallery and circled the house so that he stood almost beneath them. "You saw the marks on the walls, beneath the house, in the very room where you sleep. My darling, my darling, I fear for you. . . ."

"You have not the right to call me that."

"I know. Yet though you were only a child when first I knew you, I feel as though we have known each other for years. Can't you feel it? Don't turn away, my darling! Deny that you feel it if you can!"

"I deny it." Her voice was unshaken but so soft that January could only guess at what she said.

He heard the boards creak as Robert stepped back. "Then I can only beg you, take care."

"I will take care of him," she replied. And her footfalls retreated swiftly along the gallery, to the doors of her husband's office and so through to the room where Simon lay.

January slipped quickly through the door that led

into the storerooms beneath the house. It was cold there, a long shadowy earth-smelling chamber whose low ceiling made him stoop his great height. The Senegalese builders who'd put the house together had founded it on piers of brick, each pier widening into a pyramid underground, so that the bricks drew up the groundwater and the storeroom was always slightly damp and cool. Long wooden wine racks stood at the upstream end, the bottles held in place by boards pierced and hinged and locked like stocks. Presumably Harry had copies of those keys, too.

The oil jars stood next to the wine rack. There were a half-dozen of the larger ones, three feet tall, standing in another corner, full of drinking water for the household. All over the quarters, in addition to everything else, women and children were patiently stirring blocks of alum in similar jars of rain water to purify it, to replace what had so casually been hurled on the flames.

Of the smaller jars, still sealed, only six remained. The earth floor around them was much trampled, but he saw where the jars had been tipped on their sides and rolled to the door.

"And I suppose," snapped Madame Hélène's voice, so close to the storeroom door that January nearly brained himself on a ceiling-beam, straightening up in shock, "that it never occurred to you to bid good-bye to your *wife*?"

"Madame, the boat awaits me." Robert's voice was toneless. "I could not stay to seek you."

"You stayed long enough to have a little tête-à-tête with that snivelly child."

"You are speaking of my stepmother, Madame, and your mother-in-law."

"I am speaking of a sly, encroaching hussy who entrapped your father—"

"Madame," said Robert, "we've spoken of this

before. I see nothing to be gained by hashing it through again."

"You mean you're so enamored of that pious mealy-mouthed hypocrite that you won't hear a word against her! Well, good luck in getting any farther than that glove of hers you have secreted in your desk drawer! You'll have your work cut out to add her to your tally of mistresses! And good luck with your father if he ever finds one of the love-notes you've been sending. . . ."

"Madame. . . ."

January had edged his way, silent as a huge black cat, to the door of the storeroom. Even standing far enough back that he could not be visible, he could see Robert and his wife clearly, in that narrow ribbon of brightness: the lively green of that wasp-waisted frock-coat, the woman lush as a peony in her lappets and swags and curls. Robert had taken her wrist in a crushing grip, twisting her arm to one side; his own countenance, icy with fury, almost a stranger's.

"I have sent nothing to my stepmother," he said, very quietly. "And you'll find if you go to my father with such a lie it will go the worse for you, and for me, and for our children. Do you understand?"

Hélène said nothing, but her red mouth worked a little, between the desire to have the last word and the inability to formulate any reply sufficiently witty and cutting to hurt that cold and erudite front. Into that silence children's voices broke, Jean-Luc screeching, "Papa, bring me something! Bring me something from Baton Rouge!" and little Fantine adding her shrill whistling screams to the din. Tiny feet clattered furiously on the gallery, followed by Marthe's heavy tread.

Robert's face twisted in revulsion. He shifted his grip on his wife's wrist, and bent to kiss her hand. Jean-Luc swarmed down the stairs, grabbing his father's coat. "Can I go? Can I go? I want to go!"

"Is there anything you'd like me to send you from Baton Rouge?" Robert asked Hélène.

Hélène snatched her hand back. "I hate you!" January heard her feet creak on the boards of the steps, and then of the gallery, as she ran away back to the nursery. The children continued to clutch their father's coattails and scream until Marthe dragged them away.

"Shush now! Your grandpère's sick! Shush!"

Neither shushed. His own mother, January reflected, would have taken a cane-stalk to him if he'd displayed manners like that.

Robert climbed into the carriage, on whose rear perch Leander stood elaborately admiring the wainscot of shadow on the whitewashed brick of the kitchen, laundry room, and candle shop. Musenda's voice called out "Away, girls!" to the carriage team, and there was a scrunch of wheels and hooves, a gay retreating jingle of harness. January crossed the damp uneven earth of the storeroom floor to the front entrance, which looked out beneath the gallery stairs, and saw the bright-painted green-and-black vehicle come around the side of the house and head down to the levee, where the *Belle Dame* steamed impatiently at the plantation wharf.

On the point above, the green bandanna flickered in the wind.

The short winter daylight was beginning to wester when little Obo, the smallest of the hogmeat gang, came running out to the field with the message that Michie Hannibal wanted January back at the house.

"Man, he got to know somethin' about Michie Hannibal that Michie Hannibal don't want known," jeered Kadar good-naturedly, as January straightened his aching back.

"Yeah, he say to him, 'Hey, you send for me about sunset, so it'll be too late for me to go back out,' " amplified Taswell with a grin.

" 'Oh, and have some chicken ready for me, too,' " added Laertes, and January swiped his hand dismissively at them.

"Chicken?" he said disbelievingly. "Aw, if I knowed anythin' to blackmail Michie Hannibal with, I'd ask him to set me up with Ariadne," and that got a general laugh, for the housemaid was as haughty as she was pretty. In point of fact January guessed why Hannibal was sending for him. Across the cut acres, the smokestacks of a downriver steamboat could be seen gliding along the levee, and January guessed the flag had been put out again, and Hannibal was bound away for New Orleans.

This indeed proved to be the case. When January reached the garçonnière, Cornwallis was just finishing strapping up Hannibal's valise; the valet looked out through the French doors and said in a dry voice, "We're doing fine, Ben," accompanied by a glance that brought a hot flush to January's face with his consciousness of the field dust in his clothing, the stink of sweat that, in spite of a wash in the stable trough, still permeated his flesh, the muck on his coarse shoes.

"Ben, thank you for coming." Hannibal rose from the chair, where he'd been doing a good imitation of a man too exhausted by the effort of dressing himself to continue to pack, and staggered artistically to the door. January caught his arm to steady him and, with the neatness of a gentleman turning a lady in the waltz, guided him out onto the gallery. "You be good, and mind what Michie Fourchet and Madame Marie-Noël tell you," admonished Hannibal. "I should be back tomorrow evening, or the day after at the most. It shouldn't take me very long to see Dr. Aude-clay." His eyes flicked back toward the room and Cornwallis, as he twisted the name of Esteban's lover into childish pig-Latin.

January inclined his head to show he understood. A hush hung over the house and grounds—on his way in from the fields January had heard the crack of the whip, and coming past the jail had seen Ajax just untying his own daughter Eve from the whipping frame. The girl was still on her feet, though she held tight to Ajax's arm. January guessed she'd had only a few strokes. Thierry was already walking toward his house.

Tired from a day's hard work.

"I wish you would take my excuses to Michie Capulet in New River about coming to see his sister. I've spoken already to Madame Fourchet about letting you go tomorrow." January yanked his mind back with an effort as Hannibal handed him the letter he'd written, and a pass. The packet of papers felt thick and January thumbed them apart. There were three passes. Two were dated simply November, the numerals left blank.

January nodded again. "I surely will do that, Michie Hannibal. Now, you take care of yourself on that boat, and when you get to town you go straight back to Michie Georges's and lie down. You still look mighty peaked."

"I assure you, *amicus meus,* I'll be fine. As the great Homer says: *Quid plus me oportet Shavum quaero.*" The fiddler spoke the Latin phrase as though it were a quote, but in fact it was a query: *Is there anything further I need to ask of Shaw?*

January manufactured a hearty chuckle. "Lordy, Michie Hannibal, you're as bad as Michie Georges, with all them foreign tongues. What's he say, that business about *iurisconsultum consulere* and findin' *condicionem testamentum domino?*"

Hannibal laughed, as at a quaint mispronunciation of words—which were in fact *seeing a lawyer* and *provisions of the master's will.* "We'll make a scholar of you yet, Ben. *Testamentum locumquae acti?*" *The will and the status of the lawsuit?*

January nodded. "And—what's he say?" He furrowed his brow. "Oh, *Quid scire Shavus de Fluvius Fictus.*"

The steamboat groaned at the landing: the *Heroine,* a far larger boat than the *Belle Dame.* The steam was more than a signal, for the water pumps on most boats were operated by the engines, and a vessel that lay too long at wharf had to damp its fires or risk a boiler explosion. Hannibal clapped January fraternally on the bicep and said, "*Solus pro virili parte ago.* Mind yourself while you're here." He turned to take his leave of Madame Fourchet, who had emerged from the dining room looking tired and worried. She smiled shyly as he bent over her hand.

"Mine eye hath played the painter and hath steeled
Thy beauty's form in table of my heart."

He even managed a creditable translation of Shakespeare into French.

Marie-Noël drew her hand back, uncertain—probably, thought January, she'd had enough poetic flirtation from Robert—but something about the bright twinkle in Hannibal's eye informed her that this tribute to her moderate prettiness was tendered in gratitude and friendship, not in entreaty for response.

She smiled, and blushed, and looked aside, and didn't know what to say.

"Until I return, oh beautiful lady. Thank M'sieu Fourchet for his hospitality for me, and please convey my best wishes for his swift recovery."

He descended the steps to the waiting carriage, as Robert had done earlier in the day, Cornwallis following with the portmanteau behind. From the back step January watched the carriage swing around the end of the garçonnière wing, and so past Thierry's house and out to the levee in the long gold slant of the westering sun, leaving him alone.

Alone on Mon Triomphe, he thought.

Behind him he heard Fourchet hoarsely cursing Cornwallis for not bringing him his cigars, and distantly, the sound of Eve weeping as her father led her back to the shelter of a friend's cabin.

Alone and, for all anyone there knew, a slave.

He put the thought from his mind as well as he could. The address Hannibal had given as his own was, in fact, Shaw's. Given the fiddler's fragile health, should anything adverse occur, January would simply be "returned" to the "family."

He was safe, he reminded himself. He was in no peril. All he could do now was trust.

Trust that Hannibal would reach New Orleans more or less sober, and remain sober for as long as it took to locate Shaw and find out who Claude Molineaux was and whether his dealings with his dear and lifelong friend Esteban Fourchet went any farther than dear and lifelong friendship. Trust that Shaw would know something about Fourchet's lawsuit against the Daubrays, or something concerning the elusive False River Jones.

Trust that he himself wasn't so exhausted, so numbed by work and lack of sleep—even shirking a few hours a day as he was—that he wasn't missing something vital, something that he should be seeing.

Trust, he thought, turning away and walking back toward the fields, that some disaster wouldn't befall his hapless friend and leave him stranded here, sold down the river into this small domain ruled by death.

When he looked back later on that chilly glittering afternoon by the river, he reflected that not only was his trust betrayed on all four counts—a good round average, for a black man relying on Fate's good will in Louisiana—but he missed even considering the biggest catastrophe of all, lying hidden under the calm surface of the next forty-eight hours like a snag in the river that rips the heart out of a boat, and slaughters all on board.

The worst was that it was one he should have foreseen.

FOURTEEN

"Ben." Kiki must have been watching the back of the house, for she stepped from the kitchen as he made his way through the yard and toward the field path once more. The shadows were slanting over but January guessed there was another hour and a half of work in the full daylight, plus whatever twilight, torch-lit labor Thierry would decree.

The scents of new biscuits, of long-roasting pork, of chicken and garlic surged over him like bathwater as he crossed the yard to the brick loggia under the kitchen gallery. His stomach flinched and he hated Fourchet anew. "What is it?" Kiki's foot, he saw, was still swathed in bandages. She even remembered to limp on it until they got away from the house.

"A couple of them that Thierry whipped." She spoke quietly; spoke too as if he'd never made the pretense of being an ignorant field hand, and she had never scorned him. "Would you have a look at them? They're bad off."

January nodded. He'd planned to look in at the hospital. "You got prince's pine in that satchel of yours? Ground holly? Sassafras?"

"I don't have ground holly but I know where it grows."

"Get me some, if you would, please. Make a strong tea out of the roots, the color of coffee if you can get it that dark." He followed her to her door and took the packets of herbs she handed him.

"I used willow bark on them already. Ti-Fred and Vanille are running a fever, it's them I worried about most. That Vanille, she's too thin. She has too much white blood in her to be tough."

She'd been raised too gently, rather, thought January, as he climbed the steps of the rough-built cabin that served as a slave hospital. This was probably the first real beating of her life.

Most of those Thierry had lashed throughout the day had already returned to their cabins. January never ceased to marvel at the physical toughness, the matter-of-fact stoicism, of those who'd been born his brothers and sisters in bondage. Of those who'd been burned in last night's fire only Marquis remained, moaning softly in the wet sheets propped around him. Throughout the day the children in the hogmeat gang had come out to the fields with the latest bulletins: *He beat Quashie fifty strokes an' Quashie never made a sound, but Jeanette, she sat behind the kitchen an' cried an' cried. Agamemnon, he fainted dead away after five strokes. Mohammed, he prayed when Thierry beat him, yelled out loud to his Allah-God to help him.*

Two of the women, Flora and Chuma, had simply pulled their blouses up over their bleeding backs and gone out to the field to finish their workday. January had seen them loading the cane cart on his way in to speak to Hannibal.

Ti-Fred, as the first man beaten that morning, had gotten the overseer's first anger and first strength. He lay on his belly like a dead man, barely breathing, face and hands clammy with shock. In the next cot Boaz, a man of about January's age, lay far gone in the pneumonia that his body was too exhausted by a lifetime's overwork to resist. Quashie, on another bunk, was motionless as the image of a dead god. Two beatings in five days, thought January, checking Boaz's pulse, then Quashie's, with a sickening sense of despair. For Quashie it was truly, now, flee or die.

He examined Marquis's raw, blistered skin for sign of infection, and added another chunk of wood to the fire in the cabin's little hearth. The last one. Thierry must have raided even the hospital's small store to feed the mill furnaces.

Madame Hélène's maid Vanille was weeping, feverish exhausted tears, the kind of broken sobbing that feeds on itself. A small pot sat on the grate above the hearth flames—there was no pothook—and January poured water into a gourd and washed his hands again. In a second gourd he made up a sassafras wash, and set the little kettle of willow-bark tea closer to the flames to warm again.

"Michie Robert?" whispered Vanille, when January carefully removed the poultice from the young woman's back.

"Ssshh, shush. You'll be all right."

Vanille pressed her face into the corn-shuck mattress and began to cry again as he trickled the warm water over her flesh. He counted the stripes—ten lashes. Nothing, to a field hand. "He didn't speak a word," she whispered. "He let me be beaten and he didn't speak a word."

January thought of the valet Agamemnon, turning anguished eyes toward Esteban. "Did you think he would?" he asked gently, and she shuddered.

"He should have looked after me," murmured the girl. The smell of sassafras was a strong clean sharpness, summery against the smells of sweat and blood. "He should have spoke. He did before, when M'am Hélène would get mad. He said, 'Don't you take it out on her, 'cause you hate M'am Fourchet.' Why didn't he speak now?"

"Is she jealous about the love letters?" January patted lightly with a clean cloth, spoke in his softest voice, in his best French, masters' French, house-servant French. Under the gentle warmth of the rinse the gashed skin grinned in red slits. She would always carry these marks; they would lower her price if she were sold, maybe prevent her from being bought for a house-servant at all. "The love letters Michie Robert writes?"

"It was that woman in Paris. First her, and now M'am Fourchet. She thought he was all hers, when his papa made him marry her. But there was that woman . . ."

"A mistress?"

"A whore," whispered Vanille. "If she's a mistress, he'd have given her someplace nice. After he went out three, four, five times, M'am Hélène followed him in a cab, she and I together. We followed him to this dirty house in a dirty part of town, and saw them through a window. Saw her on her bed, and Michie Robert sitting by her, holding her in his arms. M'am Hélène was so angry she cried. When he gave her diamond earrings—same as he gave his sister when he left her at that school—M'am Hélène said, *Did you give a pair to your old whore, too?* 'Cause she was old. Old and ugly, in that torn-up lace wrapper. And he hit her."

She laid her forehead against January's arm, tears hot against his flesh. She had been bought in town, January remembered hearing someone say, and like Kiki, was "proud." She had no one on the place to turn to.

"When he went out again she beat me. And she beat me the other day, when she saw him talking to Madame. Now he's not here to stop her, what'll happen to me?"

What indeed? January felt sickened. In this soured and unhappy household it was indeed the slaves who reaped the whirlwind of their masters' sowing: men and women who had nothing to do with the reproaches and rage passed from generation to generation, who would happily have been anywhere else, leading lives of their own.

And there was worse to come, if he didn't find the killer.

Under his soothing touch Vanille was sinking into drowsiness. He had best, he knew, put the astringent solution of ground-holly root on her wounds before she slept. Gently he covered her back with Kiki's poultice again, to keep the flies off, and crossed again to the kitchen. As he approached it he saw Jeanette by its door, glancing around her at the other doors that let into the yard—the laundry and the candle-room. A moment later Kiki herself appeared in the doorway. She handed the girl a large basket with a towel tucked around it, and what looked like a rolled-up quilt.

Jeanette slipped around the corner and was gone.

"I'm sorry." Kiki went to the hearth, moving slowly and painfully still, and with a crane-hook brought forward a small pot that had been boiling over the flames. "I was about to bring you this out to the hospital when Baptiste came over and told me Dr. Laurette's come from Baton Rouge on the boat that Michie Hannibal took to town. He's that fond of meringues, Dr. Laurette, and Madame thought it'd be nice if we had some."

Her round face was gray with weariness, and, January thought, there remained at the back of her dark eyes some of the haunted look they'd worn in the firelight last night. He recalled Jeanette's scornful words, *She wouldn't spit on the back of a field hand to wash it,* and thought about the poultices laid not only on Vanille's back, but on Quashie's and Ti-Fred's in the hospital from which he'd just come.

She had spoken of children. Was it that loss which had touched her, finally? Or simply the understanding that what was happening could break into violence at any moment, and destroy them all? Her hands twitched—not quite a tremor—as she poured the tisane into a gourd.

"Michie Fourchet going to be all right?" he asked.

"Dr. Laurette thinks so." Kiki handed him the gourd. "He bled him good. Laurette's a great bleeder; I think he wants to be a soldier in his heart. Most of the time I look at these *blankitte* doctors that bleed everyone no matter what's wrong with them and I think they're crazy, but for Michie Fourchet, it makes him weak and keeps him quiet, and right now quiet is what he needs. Dr. Laurette gave him some bromide, all mixed with sassafras and sugar to kill the taste of it—it's better than hartshorn, they say."

As Kiki talked she broke eggs into a white Germanware bowl, neatly separating the whites from the yolks, and scraped a little sugar from the loaf on the table. "How do you use it?" She nodded at the gourd. "Ground holly? I never heard of that."

"It's an astringent, mostly," said January. He sloshed the liquid—it was dark, the color of strong tea. "It keeps wounds clean better than brandy or rum. My sister learned of it from an old Natchez woman: My sister's a voodoo. Olympia Snakebones. Watch it," he added, as Kiki's hand twitched again and the pinch of cream of tartar she was carrying to the meringue bowl scattered fluffily over the table.

"I'm all right." Kiki braced herself on the corner of the table, rosebud mouth caught together tight. "It just . . . takes me sometimes."

"You shouldn't be up."

"I'll be all right. You go out and take care of Vanille. I'll get Minta to do the washing up tonight and lie down as soon as supper's done."

Yesterday's clear hard cold seemed to be breaking as January walked back to the hospital through the chill, slanting light. Rain coming. Clouds piled in the southern sky. *He'd only sell it.* And, *I cooked dinner for twenty people . . . after giving birth to a child. . . .*

What had become of that child?

When January emerged from the hospital again the shadows were long across the yard, and under the dark of the gallery candlelight showed in a window or two, like sleepy-lidded eyes. Had Marie-Noël Fourchet burned the letters Robert denied he'd written her? Or did she take them out of some compartment in her desk sometimes and read over words of tenderness that her husband never spoke?

Did she believe them? A middle-aged whore in a dirty part of Paris. An odd choice, for a man as fastidious as Robert Fourchet.

On the whole, he thought, it was likelier that she'd burned them. Marie-Noël didn't look like a foolish woman. And she'd be a fool to think Madame Hélène wouldn't search til she'd found them, in order to throw them in Simon Fourchet's face.

But sixteen is an age that treasures scraps of comfort.

He worked through the night in the mill, hauling wood, stoking fires, thrusting cane into the grating iron teeth of the rollers and later piling cut stalks along the downstream outer wall of the mill, so that it could be carried in easily once the mill was running full-out again. Thierry went up to the house just after supper and returned in a savage mood, wielding his whip as if he suspected every man and woman present of destroying the wood stores in order to threaten his position as overseer. It was a relief when the overseer went off duty a few hours before midnight. Esteban stayed later. He worked without shouts or curses, frequently consulting the silent, ashen-faced Rodney about the appearance of the boiling sap, and when it should be skimmed, or struck, or moved from kettle to kettle.

"Will you be all right?" January overheard him ask Rodney at one point during the evening, and the bereaved father nodded.

"The work keeps me from thinkin'."

Esteban lifted a hand as if he would have touched his driver's shoulder, then thought again, and turned away.

The men on the night gang generally had three or four hours' sleep before they were due back in the fields again. After slipping up to the levee to change the green bandanna for a purple, January had intended to take an extra hour before setting out for Daubray with his pass and his story about a letter that needed to go to New River, but instead was wakened at full daylight by Harry and Disappearing Willie bringing Quashie back in. "Thierry made him go out with the main gang cuttin' this mornin'," explained Will, gently laying the young man down on his cot. Quashie was unconscious, ashen and waxy-looking; his hands, when January pinched his fingernail, were icy cold.

Harry silently disappeared, and returned a moment later with a gourd containing a little whiskey. January sniffed it but concluded that its quality was such that it couldn't possibly have come from the big house, and held it to Quashie's lips. "Thank you," he said later, when Will had gone out to find Jeanette. Harry waved away the thanks.

"I hear tell you're headed for New River with a letter," said Harry, following January down the cabin steps and around to the back, where the bachelors' communal washing facilities—a trough—faced their weed-grown patch of yams, corn, and peas.

"I wouldn't be washin' up extra fine to impress Ajax." January dug his fingers into the little firkin of soft soap he'd brought out with him, and scrubbed the water over his face, hair, and naked chest.

"You goin' by way of Daubray?"

"I might be."

"Arnaud, that cooks for Michie Louis, might give you something in the way of lunch, if so be you was to stop at the kitchen there and hand him this." From under his shirt, he pulled a rough bundle wrapped in rags. He must have gotten it from his cabin at the same time he got the whiskey.

"Be a pleasure," said January.

From his pocket, Harry produced a small sack of salt—the scrunch of it, and the smell, unmistakable—and said, "And if so be you'd just give this to old Mambo Hera, from Trinette, I'd be obliged."

The moment he was out of sight of the house January opened the bundle. It contained about two yards of the pink silk Madame Hélène had been so enraged about a few days before. He shook his head.

The bag contained only salt. It was high quality and clean, presumably from the big house salt-box.

Just what I need, thought January, shoving both parcels under his arm again. *To get stopped by the patrollers with this on me. . . .*

Since he was supposed to be going to New River, January took the field roads through the cut cane-stubble, waving to the women loading the cane carts as he passed. But as soon as he was out of sight of the big house he veered south. Rats scurried unseen through the weed and maiden cane; buzzards wheeled lazily, watchful black dots against the hazy blue. The day was warmer and clouds stretched horizon to horizon now, with more to the south. Alone, January let the peace of the country fill him again, and wondered what Rose was doing, back in town, or Olympe, or his enterprising nephews and nieces. Flexed his aching hands and wondered how long it would take his fingers to regain their lightness on the keyboard, and whether his mother would let him take away the piano St.-Denis Janvier had bought for him, when he took his share of Fourchet's money and got his own rooms elsewhere at last.

Wondered if he would one day be able to induce Rose to share them with him.

He had not lived alone in twelve years, he realized, save for those two nightmare weeks in Paris following his wife's death.

Arnaud, the Daubray cook, a trim little man with a dapper salt-and-pepper beard, received Harry's bundle with alacrity. "What people waste!" he cried disapprovingly. "My Katie can get herself a whole bodice out of these bits!" Ayasha had been a seamstress, so January could tell that though Harry had snipped and cut the shell-pink fabric to give the impression that it was scrap, it was not, in fact, waste—and what woman in her right mind would discard that much fabric that could so easily be made up into something else?

But Harry had been wise, for the cook promptly launched into a sincere diatribe about theft, while counting out small bits of lead from jar-seals and broken pipe-fittings—evidently his agreed-upon payment for the silk. "Now, it's one thing to trade with real leavings, like that silk or coffee beans that's been used, or tea leaves," he said, clicking his tongue. "But those field hands will steal anything—*anything*."

January, who'd been careful to dress in the wool trousers, blue calico shirt, and corduroy jacket of his earlier incarnation as a respectable house-servant, nodded gravely. "I can understand them stealing food, if their master's a harsh one," he said, mirroring exactly the cook's more educated—though certainly not Parisian—French. "But stealing things to sell them to a river-trader like this M'sieu Jones I hear so much of . . ."

"Good Lord, False River Jones!" Arnaud raised his hands in an appeal to heaven. "There are times when I believe the man is employed by the Devil himself, to tempt field hands to theft and flight."

"Flight?" January thought of the pirogue waiting under the snags at Catbird Island.

The cook wrapped up all his little scraps of lead—a chunk nearly the size of a woman's fist—and handed it to January. "Half the runaways on this river," he declared, with the air of one driving home a point, "start out with Jones bringing somebody word of their woman or their child or their mother up in Baton Rouge or down in the city. Now, you sell a young buck, or a likely girl, and they get over it, mostly. Field hands do." With his clean clothes and shaved chin, as January had expected, Arnaud had assumed him to be a house-servant, in league with him against the coarser spirits of the cane-patch.

So he nodded a self-evident agreement and donned an expression of admiration for the man's philosophic wisdom.

"They do," continued Arnaud, "until they're down at the levee in the middle of the night trading off a tablecloth or a china cup or half *my* store of tea for a gourd of liquor! And such liquor—my lord! And all it takes is Jones asking, 'You wouldn't be Plautus from Four Corner plantation, would you? I have a letter from your girl there,' and the next day the boy's moping and thinking about how everything was wonderful back on Four Corner, and nobody made him work there, and they fed him chicken and biscuits there, and off he goes. And I ask you, what good does it do?"

"Not any," said January, in the voice of one aggrieved by the misbehavior of inferiors. "Not any at all."

"I mean, they have to know they're going to be caught and brought back. They have to know that that part of their life is over. They're never going back there. They're never going to see those people again. Why not just accept that fact and go on?"

January remembered the tears of one night in childhood, when a boy he'd been best friends with—Tano, his name had been—was sold away. He'd wept and wept, sick with the thought that he'd never see that friend again. That for all intents and purposes, Tano was dead. Gone. Sold down the river.

"Why not?" he agreed. "You'd think the decent people around here would do something about Jones, wouldn't you?"

"They've tried." Arnaud shook his head, and with a few quick strokes sliced bread for them both, and cheese and apples. "Near to three weeks ago, Michie Hippolyte heard Jones was back, working his way down the river, and set out to trap him. I could have told him it was no use. Anyone could. It's my belief the field hands heard of it, though Michie Hippolyte kept quiet about his plans, and only took Michie Roger—that's our overseer—and Michie Evard his cousin with him. But the field hands, they eavesdrop and listen and spy. Would you believe it, just the other day . . ."

January listened patiently for another hour, contributing his mites of agreement and gossip, until he ascertained that Hippolyte Daubray, his overseer, and his cousin, had in fact been seen to depart for their hunt on the night of the Triomphe sugar-mill fire. By dint of careful questioning he learned also that the middle-aged dandy had been "out hunting" when he was supposed to have been supervising the harvest on the afternoon and evening of the seventh, when the mule barn had burned, but the rest of the timing was not so certain. Having seen him, January couldn't imagine that stout sybarite dressing himself in a field hand's rough garb and hat to sneak up and spook the mule team in the roundhouse in the middle of the morning, but, he was aware, appearances could be deceptive indeed.

"An unpleasant situation all around, M'sieu," Arnaud sighed. "That girl, that Marie-Noël . . ." Across the yard a knot of young ladies of the Daubray household were visible on the back gallery, bright chattering creatures like tropical birds. They were sewing—fancy stitchery, it looked like from here—and one of them sent a maid hurrying across the yard to the kitchen for lemonade. Once he heard their laughter.

"I understand her jealousy." The cook counted out lemons with a grimace of regret. "Particularly of M'sieu Louis's daughters. They are so beautiful, and Mamzelle Marie-Noël is—well—not. Michie Louis, he did everything he could to prevent the match. He even sent her away to New Orleans to keep her from marrying that awful man, for it was clear as day all he wanted was claim to Michie Raymond's house and lands. But she schemed to get M'sieu Fourchet wound around her thumb, saying no and then saying yes, and he went nearly crazy trying to find out whether that wife of his was dead or not. A bad hat *she* was, gettin' drunk and actin' up and leavin' him and her children to go back to France as she did. And a good thing, too, that she did turn out to have died, for I would not have put it beyond him to have murdered the poor woman. A drunkard and a brute," Arnaud added, in a tone rich with satisfaction, "and one day that girl'll find out her mistake, if she hasn't already."

"Still," said January thoughtfully, "if one wished to get a letter to someone on the river . . . Where would one find this Michie Jones?"

"Oh, he's due back any time." The cook scowled his disapproval, and sent the maid off with her wickerwork tray of lemonade, cakes, and *marrons glacés*. "He generally camps on the far side of Catbird Island, or sometimes up Bayou Prideaux, that little bayou between the Prideaux lands and Lescelles."

Before departing, January asked to be taken to Mambo Hera's cabin, and with visible distaste Arnaud pointed out a tiny annex on the back of one of the barns, just opposite the long shabby rows of the pig-houses. "She asked for that place," he apologized. "M'sieu Louis, and M'sieu Hippolyte, offered her a room above the kitchen where it was warm, but she wouldn't have anything but a place among her animals. It makes it most awkward to look after her. . . ."

"Thanks," said January. "I'll find my way."

As he crossed through the stable yards he could see her already, a little bundle of faded gaudy rags in the shadow of the annex's tiny gallery. Close by the kitchen he saw another old woman plucking chickens and telling stories to the littlest children, the toddlers too old to be carried to the fields with their mothers but too young to do any kind of work, but no one, apparently, had any idea of burdening Mambo Hera with such a task. She sat alone on her bench, staring out with eerie contentment in her cataract-blind eyes, as if she lived on air alone and the sounds and scent it brought her.

And January shivered as she turned her face toward

him—as she twisted her wry little neck to look up, for she was bent nearly double with arthritis. And he understood what Jeanette had meant, when she said this woman had Power.

Even had he not been told who she was, he thought, he would have known. She was a priestess. Not as Marie Laveau was in town, heiress of traditions adapted and mingled in this new world. Not like Laveau's disciple Olympe, who had studied with the old mambos and learned the ancient medicines and the ancient ways.

Mambo Hera *was* the ancient way.

She said, "Who this *alejo* come walk up my path?" and her voice was thin and high and mumbling over toothless gums. Her nostrils flared, scenting him; he saw thought pucker the wrinkled flesh on that little skull that seemed barely bigger than his own great fist. "Stranger come walking from Triomphe, where they're cooking the sugar. . . . Stranger come from town? Come on the boat?"

January realized he must have the smells of the steamboat's soot, of the town market's spices, imbued still in his clothing, along with the light sweat of a few hours' walk. He replied, "I've come down from Triomphe, yes, Mambo. A woman there asked me to give you this." And he took the little bag of salt from his pocket, and held it out to her. The old woman extended a hand so balled and broken with arthritis that the palm was gouged with healed wounds from her own nails, but she pinched the bag between finger and thumb, and secreted it in her clothing. Her hair was thin, a myriad of white braids framing old country marks on her temples; under the creased and wrinkled lids the opal deadlights seemed indeed to see.

"Trinette?" she asked, and January said, "Yes."

"That Reuben died?"

"He died."

She nodded, satisfied. "How did he die? I made a ball of black wax and pins for her, and the ashes of a thrush's wing; told her bury it under the threshold of his house, where he'd walk. I burned a black wax candle for her in the dark of the moon, stuck all through with pins, and the last pin fell out when the moon was full. Was that when he died?"

"Yes," said January. "That was when he died."

As he worked his way back through the cane-fields of Refuge, examining the ground along as much as he could of the border between the two properties, January glimpsed Gauthier Daubray's empty house from afar. Seen by daylight, it had originally been a gay pink, faded now but still somehow reminiscent of a single camellia among the monotony of the cane-fields.

January had a good deal of sympathy for Marie-Noël Fourchet: for the young girl's desire to escape Daubray at almost any cost, and for her present difficulties. Yet he had been reminded, in the past week, that there are worse fates than to live with your wealthy relatives under a roof that doesn't leak, and to eat the bread of captivity accompanied by liberal helpings of the chicken of captivity, the ham of captivity, the gravy of captivity, and the *marrons glacés* of captivity while suffering no worse fate than to mend your beautiful cousins' dresses and watch them catch husbands while you had none for yourself.

Since the confrontation between the Daubray brothers and Simon Fourchet, no cane had been harvested in the Refuge lands. It would have been easy to make one's way through it to the fields of Mon Triomphe, and so almost to the walls of the mill itself. However,

January found no evidence that anyone wearing a white man's boots had done so.

He hadn't Shaw's abilities as a tracker, but in default of other evidence it was increasingly clear to him that the hoodoo was someone on Mon Triomphe, whoever else might be paying or urging that someone to mischief. The one exception to this hypothesis might just be False River Jones. And he would know more, or be able to guess more, after he'd seen the man himself.

It had been three days since January's last visit to Catbird Island, so he worked his way riverward through Refuge's straggly fields til he came to the levee and the snag-tangled, tree-grown batture beyond. Far off he could hear men singing, maybe the gang from Mon Triomphe or maybe the Daubray gang, the rhythm punctuated by the chop of knives.

"Way-o, Madame Caba,
Way-o, Madame Caba,
Way-o, Madame Caba,
Your tignon fell down,
Your tignon fell down."

Blackbirds flitted and dove through the cane. A rabbit sat up and looked at him, soft gray-brown with its little white shirt-front, as if it were going to a ball in town. When the green wall before him lightened he waited, seeing the moving stacks of a downriver boat gliding by. From those slow-moving decks there was nothing to do but watch the banks, and someone would almost certainly point him out: "Hey, there goes some nigger just standin' wastin' time on the batture. . . ." From its tangled shelter he could see them, two Americans in tobacco-brown coats leaning on the rail, spitting into the churning water. A waiter hurrying along the deck with a tray of coffee things. He saw how the man stepped aside in contempt from one of the stevedores on the deck—because he wore rougher clothing, January wondered, or because he was Congo black, African black, and the waiter was fair of skin, quadroon or octoroon?

All going south, to New Orleans.

Why? January blinked sleepily at the sun-glitter where water rippled over a sunken bar. Who were these people, standing at the railings, looking at the banks? What were the patterns in their lives?

When the boat had gone by (*Oceana,* said the red-and-blue letters on her wheelhouse) he made his way for a mile and a half along the batture, sheltered from view by cypresses and willow logs, thanking God that it was winter and there were few gators around. A corn-snake slipped across his path, sluggish with the cool season, and he remembered how Olympe would trace the vévé for Damballah-Wedo in the earth of Congo Square, to summon the Serpent King. Sometimes she'd draw two snakes framing a pillar, sometimes instead of a pillar an elaborate column of crosses and stylized flowers—other nights only a few stars. Shaw had asked him once about this: Like a white man, Shaw thought these things always had to be done the same way to be "right." But the spirits changed, and their signs shifted, and it all depended on what mood Olympe was in and what she felt that spirit of water and wisdom required—January felt he had grown up understanding this.

When he reached the old landing behind its silted-up bar, he examined it with particular care. You couldn't get a big side-wheeler in behind the bar anymore, but there was ample room for a pirogue or a keelboat—probably even for a small stern-wheeler, if you had a pilot who knew the water. An ideal place to put in if you wanted to come up along the cane-rows and make mischief with the woodsheds.

But as far as January could tell, examining the damp earth around the mossy and dilapidated wharf, nobody had done that within the past four or five days.

He was close enough now to the house that he could hear the women singing as they unloaded the cane at the mill. He removed his coat and shirt, shivering a little in the cool afternoon, and rolled up his trousers to his knees, so that he wouldn't return mud-spattered and scratched from what was allegedly a peaceful trip out to New River with a letter. Watching and listening all around him and expecting every moment to hear Thierry call down from the levee, "What the hell you doin' here, boy?" *(And what the hell would the overseer be doing on the levee at this time of the day?)* January crawled and crouched and dodged from tree to tree, from snag to snag, up the half-mile or so of bank, past the new landing, through the older willows around the little headland where Michie Demosthenes the Oak stood gesticulating with his purple bandanna at the passing boats *(Everything fine here, Michie Shaw),* and around to the foot of the Catbird chute.

Behind the shelter of the headland he stripped off his trousers and boots, and waded across to the island.

There were tracks there. A white man's boots, coarse and heavy and square-toed. He recognized them at once: Thierry's. He'd seen such tracks now for days in the fields and around the muck of the burned sheds. Fresh, coming and going. That day, the mud not even dried. No older than lunchtime.

He shuddered at the thought of how easily he could have run into the man.

He followed them around to the little bay at the end of the island, knowing with heartsick certainty what he was going to find.

The overseer's tracks crossed and recrossed the margin of the concealing snags and brush, but January could see with a single glance at the ground that Thierry had found the boat. He saw where it had been dragged from its hiding place, saw the digs and gouges in the damp clay where the bottom had been stove in—probably, thought January, squatting to examine them in the slanting afternoon light, with an ax. There were long sharp gouges in the mud where the protruding shards had plowed, when the boat had been shoved back.

A little ways into the clumps of snags January found the dented and useless pot, the smashed cups and gourds. The candles were in fragments; the blanket, bread, and cheese lay scattered, sodden and stinking of piss.

For some reason he remembered the gang of keelboat toughs slicing his coat off him with their skinning-knives, shredding his music into the gutter.

That same viciousness. That same easy demolition of what had taken such time and such heartbreaking effort to procure.

The basket Kiki had given Jeanette had been torn from its tree branch. It had contained two loaves of bread, a quantity of salt meat and a small sack of cornmeal, another pot, three more apples from Madame Camille's garden, and three tin cups.

Three. January knelt by the damaged and mucky mess. The pillowcase that had wrapped the food was far too old to have come from the big house, but he recognized the neat yellow mending-stitches along its edge.

He'll only sell her. . . .

He searched the rest of the island for signs of False River Jones and found none.

The afternoon was drawing to a close. Keelboats and

flatboats showed like chips of debris on the quicksilver river, coming down the big current, the dark squat shapes of the great paddle-wheelers working their way up close to the shore. Too soon by several hours for him to expect people to believe he'd been to New River and back. He took his rosary from the pocket of his rolled-up jacket, set his back to a tree-bole in the midst of the island where none would easily see him either from the river or the levee, and gazed blinking into the warm blue-tinted distance. The clouds that had thickened all day formed a solid roof above, and the air was mild and heavy-feeling. Rain before morning, he thought. Maybe even before he could reasonably return to Mon Triomphe.

The thought didn't trouble him. He'd brought the black bandanna with him, that had to be tied onto the tree once it got dark.

It was the first time in many days that he'd been alone, with peace and with God.

"Hail Mary, full of grace. The Lord is with thee. . . ."

Then, because he had worked as a slave and lived as a slave for long enough to recall the priorities of servitude, he stretched out on the ground with his head on his rolled-up clothing, and fell immediately and profoundly asleep.

FIFTEEN

Throughout the following day, as he lopped cane-tops, or carried stalks to the carts, or hauled wood, or played the dozens with the other main-gang men while they rested at noon—"You so smelly the buzzards follow you around thinkin' you got a dead skunk in your pocket." "Yeah, your brother so smelly he's a free man, 'cause he run away and the hounds kept vomitin' and couldn't chase him."—January listened for the arrival of the steamboat that would bring Hannibal back from New Orleans.

The key to the deadly riddle, he was certain now, did not lie on Mon Triomphe itself. Short of catching the hoodoo red-handed, he could see no way farther forward, with the information he had or could reasonably expect to get. That the culprit was a fellow slave he was almost certain. Yet the pattern of the crimes themselves felt wrong.

There was something else going on. Something at once too methodical and too random for rebellion.

When he'd returned last night in the rain, Kiki had made it her business to intercept him on the way back from the big house and let him know she'd found no oil-stained garment in the laundry.

This hadn't surprised him. If the hoodoo had been careful enough to conceal the cut-marks on the mill machinery with pitch, and retreat to the old kitchen at Refuge to boil up the poison from the oleanders, he or she wasn't about to casually stuff an incriminating shirt or skirt or bodice waist into Ti-Jeanne's willow baskets for all the world to see.

Some piece of information lay elsewhere, that would unlock the riddle: Esteban's lover perhaps, or Fourchet's will. January knew the pattern now, the rhythm of these lives. But the breaks and rifts he'd found all pointed to people who had demonstrably been elsewhere when the sheds, or the mill, or the mule barns burned.

There had been a shout last night for the dead children. Rain hammered the roof and dripped from the eaves, and the voices rose and fell against Old Banjo's singing where he crouched in the center of the circle on the floor in Harry's cabin. Standing among these people he was beginning to know and trust, January felt helpless, and angry—felt guilty, too, as if he were defrauding them somehow.

> *"Good-bye, my voice be heard no more,*
> *Good-bye, my voice be heard no more. . . ."*

Juno and Ancilla, weeping for children who would have been lost to them in any case. Kiki holding the bereaved women in her plump arms, tears on her face as she spoke words of comfort. Baptiste handing around food.

Once the wind rattled the door and everyone—even January—had started with fear. *Why fear?* he'd wondered, furious with himself.

He had nothing to fear. He wasn't a slave.

But he had, he now realized, been afraid for a week. Everything he did and felt was tinged with it: fear, and defiance, and the sense that he existed outside the law. That anything he did was legitimate because he was in danger.

The day was moist and humid, smelling of more rain to come. A little before noon brought the rice cart to the fields, Nero came running, to let Thierry know that a flatboat had arrived from Gottfreid's wood-yard just south of Baton Rouge with a thousand cords of wood and a note from Michie Robert. Thierry yelled to Herc to make sure the women finished loading up the carts, then got them all down to the landing. The men were lined up, marched back to Thierry's house where he counted all the knives back in, then set to work hauling wood to the makeshift shelters near the mill.

As he handed off logs from the flatboat's deck to Black Austin, standing on the wharf, January glanced over his shoulder at the river. The *Boonslick* was working upstream over the bar at the foot of Catbird Island, close enough that those on shore could hear the clang of the pilot's bell and the shouting of the leadsman. On the upper promenade deck a fat little man in a black coat was having a furious argument with a tall thin boy; in the coffle chained at the stern deck, a woman combed her friend's hair. The boat made no effort to approach the Mon Triomphe wharf and January cursed Hannibal, wherever he was. *If he spent his ticket money on opium, so help me I will drown him.*

"Rain cloud comin', carry on this day,
Rain cloud comin', carry on this day,
Rabbit in the cane-field, look at the sky and say,
Rain cloud comin', lord."

Hooves at the top of the levee. Esteban ground-reined his lanky black mare and came down to take the note the flatboat's tobacco-chewing captain held out to him. *Where there's a will, there's a relative,* Hannibal had joked. *Esteban was with Agamemnon when the sheds caught fire,* January thought. *I can see him wanting his father dead, but why would he damage his patrimony?*

Why would Marie-Noël?

With his self-pitying smugness and whatever grievance he might nurse for his mother's sake, Robert Fourchet was a tempting candidate, but he had undeniably been out of the country when the trouble started, and as far as January could ascertain he'd had no contact with Marie-Noël since she was a child.

Who did that leave? Jeanette, a voodooienne's daughter? Who might or might not be lying about what her mother had taught her? Then why hadn't she poisoned Thierry?

Reuben's wife Trinette? Why go to Mambo Hera for a gris-gris, if she knew juju herself? Black wax and pins notwithstanding, it was no blind woman who'd drawn the vévés on the walls of Thierry's house.

Cornwallis? The identical copying of the gris-gris, without variation, smacked more of a white man, or someone unfamiliar with the marks, than one who truly knew them—something you'd expect of an American and a Protestant, not raised shoulder-to-shoulder with the worship of the *loa.*

Thierry himself, for reasons that couldn't be fathomed . . . ?

"Bastard!" screamed a woman's voice. "Cunt fucking bastard, I hope you *die*!"

All heads turned. Hair tangled on her shoulders, dress kilted to her thighs and slapping wet on her body, Jeanette stumbled down the levee at a run. Rage and tears transformed her face. Esteban dropped the note he was reading and grabbed her as she threw herself straight at Thierry, dragged her from him wriggling like a cat, clawing and screeching curses. "Damn you! Damn you, may you rot! Damn the mother that bore you, bastard, bastard, bastard . . . !"

Thierry walked calmly to her, caught her by the throat and struck her, twice, with the flat of his open hand across the face. Jeanette's head snapped sideways with the violence of the blows. Blood oozed from her split lip, mingling with her tears.

"Best you watch that mouth of yours, little lady," said Thierry in his quiet voice. "Seems to me I'm going to have to give you *another* lesson in manners. Better to nip these things in the bud," he added, looking over at Esteban.

Esteban's mouth pursed with distaste but he nodded, then looked away.

"God damn it—" Gosport stepped forward, and Ajax was there, his enormous hand on the older man's scarred arm.

"Best stay out of it," cautioned the driver softly, in field hand gombo so thick *les blankittes* could not understand.

Other men had moved when Gosport did, the circle of them tightening, springing down from the flatboat's deck toward Thierry and Jeanette. Thierry had stepped half a pace back in response, his hand close to the pistol at his side, those cold pale blue eyes watching. Picking out this man and that man—touching January, as if he guessed, from January's eyes and the way he stood, that here was a potential source of trouble—moving on to others, the brave ones, the angry ones. Figuring out who he'd have to kill.

"You can't goddam let him—"

"Stay out of it," repeated Ajax. And there was an echo in his soft voice of the creak of weighted gallows-ropes, and children crying as they were sold. The crash of army rifles fired in volleys, the thunder of cavalry hooves.

Don't start down that road.

We all know what lies at the end.

Jeanette moaned, and tried to pull free, but for all his gammy-handed clumsiness Esteban was strong. Beside her, Thierry relaxed a little, understanding what had taken place; seeing the flame that had sparked among the men die back. Seeing them think again, and leave their words unspoken.

He said, "Dice?" and the third driver looked around. "You help me here?"

Dice's jaw tightened hard but he came forward, taking Jeanette by the wrists. January thought about his own decision to help in beating Quashie, his own nauseated awareness that nothing he could do would alter the situation—would only make matters worse.

None of the men looked at each other as Thierry and Dice led Jeanette back up over the levee and out of sight.

Their eyes were on Esteban, the only man present who could have prevented what would now happen to the girl, and as if he sensed it, the planter's son said gruffly, "Get 'em back to work," and strode back up the levee himself.

Ajax's voice was very quiet. "Yes, sir."

The river breeze stirred Robert's letter where it had fallen on the ground, tumbling it like some outsize yellow leaf toward the water's edge. January picked it up, shoved it in his pocket as he stepped back onto the flatboat; if nothing else it would serve him as an excuse to return to the house, should he later need one.

With a sharp kick to his mare, Esteban rode off; Ajax said, "Let's get this shit ashore and under a roof. Gonna rain tonight."

The men did not sing as they returned to their work.

Thierry was back in half an hour, a bandage on the fleshy part of his hand. He looked pleased with himself, like a man who's once more demonstrated his manhood.

They got the wood in, piling as much of it as they could in the mill itself, along the walls and around the grinding-room, so that the women carrying the cane up to the rollers had to edge past it sideways, slowing everyone down. By dark the rain-smell was so strong that Thierry ordered the wood in the shelters to be brought up and burned first, so the supplies indoors could be saved for when the downpour came. As one of the biggest men in the crew January was on that detail, an ox's job. He hoped to hell Hannibal had found out something really damning about Esteban, or Marie-Noël's part in the lawsuit, or about False River Jones. Too much to expect that on hearing the trader's name Shaw would smite his forehead and cry, *False River Jones! My God, the man burned seventeen sugar-mills in Alabama without leaving a track and poisoned fifteen planters! How* COULD *we have been so blind?*

And he'd be able to get his money and go home.

Jeanette joined the women again just after supper. Though she'd washed her face and wore a different dress—a bright green one—she walked stiffly, as if hurt somewhere deep inside, and met no one's eyes. Quashie, who mercifully had been in the mill all day, looked up from stoking the kettles but didn't go to her or speak. A particularly tough knot of cane—rooster-tailed trash that nobody had pulled around straight before loading or unloading—jammed the rollers for the fourth or fifth time that evening. Rodney yelled to stop the mules and hold on to the damn things—January had seen him checking the harnesses regularly, every time they changed teams.

Rodney sprang up to the brick edge of the vat and leaned over to pull the matted cane free, sweating in the torchlight, with moths and bugs rattling noisily around the torches and falling into the kettles. The women on the narrowed stair, their arms laden with six-foot bundles of cane, shifted and muttered, and when everything got started again that bright green dress had vanished.

It was a while before January was sure. Since Jeanette was part of the gang carrying cane, and since he himself was in and out of the mill, he couldn't tell exactly at what point she disappeared. But she was definitely gone. January saw Thierry look around for her once, then twice. Saw the overseer glance sharply at where Quashie still labored stoking the fire, moving stiffly and ashen with fatigue. The overseer spoke to Hope, who shrugged, shook her head, and pointed back into the darkness. January could almost hear her saying, *No, she's out fetching cane, I saw her just a little while ago,* though he guessed Jeanette had been gone for nearly forty-five minutes by that time. Thierry glared at Quashie again and went to speak to Ajax. The men were close enough to January that he heard the overseer this time: "You keep an eye on that Quashie. And you make sure nobody slacks off, and keep those kettles boiling good, you hear? Michie Esteban'll be back from supper any time now and that sugar better not go off its heat."

"No, sir," said Ajax. "Yes, sir."

Thierry strode out into the night.

Later on, January figured Quashie just waited until the big *la grande* had to be struck and skimmed and poured into *le flambeau,* and while Ajax was busy with that, went quietly out the back door.

Thierry didn't return to the mill. At the time January hoped against hope that this was because a boat had arrived at the landing late, bringing Hannibal and some kind of information from town. It would be morning, he thought, before he'd find out. Rain started shortly before the main gang finished its work, hard steady drumming on the roof.

Stepping out the door when the night crew arrived, he could see the glimmer of the house windows through the black curtains of water: a night-light in the nursery, where Marthe would be dozing in a chair beside the children's cots with a stick across her lap, lest rats from the cane-fields creep in and disturb them while they slept. Another light shone in Fourchet's office, probably from the candles in his room. A third, dimmer, in the front chamber on the women's side of the house, marked where Marie-Noël slept since her husband's illness, when she slept at all. According to Kiki she spent most of her time sitting at her husband's bedside, only returning to her own room if more medicine was needed, or to fetch her Bible.

All else was stillness. Behind him the men greeted one another by the wall of heat that seemed to stand just within the doors; the women, headed back to half a night's housework, spoke with one another in soft weary voices asking after their children, or who had fixed a little food for whom. Harness rattled in the roundhouse as the mule teams were taken off.

Vast tiredness surged over January and he wondered for the first time whether Hannibal, who had seemed better when he left Mon Triomphe, had in fact suffered a return of his illness and was coughing blood in some whorehouse attic on Perdidio Street, unable to either see Shaw or locate Monsieur Molineaux.

Virgin Mary, care for him, thought January, his anger and his fear for himself abating. It had been days, he realized, since he'd felt able to feel anything but anger and fear.

Virgin Mary, heal him and bless him and send him the hell back here so we can finish up this mess and get out.

He glanced around to make sure he was unobserved, and set off on his usual circuitous route to the bluff above the landing, to change the bandanna to white before heading back through the rain toward the quarters.

When he thought about it later, he realized that by that time, Thierry was probably already dead.

January woke thinking, *Something's wrong.*

The hush was broken only by the breathing of sleepers all around him. Smoke touched his face like a knife-blade, and in the gray dimness he saw Gosport standing by the opened slit of the door.

"There's something wrong."

"What's wrong is you got the goddam door open and it's freezin' in here," said Kadar, sitting up in his blankets. After the fire all the men had moved down to the floor to sleep, letting the boys have the two beds. Yesterday, without a word being said, Quashie had been given one of the beds, and looking over into that dark corner of the room, January saw that the bed was empty.

"There's no bell," said Gosport.

The men looked at each other in the cindery gloom. By the time it was this light they should have been on their way down the quarters street, to the back steps of the cottage where Thierry would be counting out their knives.

Without a word Parson slid from his blankets and

got a handful of kindling from its box, blew the banked ash of the fire to life. The boys moaned and huddled closer together in their single cot, like puppies seeking in their sleep the warmth of their dam's side, their exhaustion beyond even the power of the bedbugs to disturb. But January knew that if Thierry had overslept, drunk, it would be no favor to let the boys lie in.

The men went out back and washed, quickly, in the trough, and pulled on their dirty clothes. January hated the coarse texture of the filth in the cloth against his skin, the smell of old sweat and old dirt, the creeping itch of lice and the crusty stickiness of dried cane-juice, but there wasn't time to wash them, these days. No wonder the house-servants despised the cane-hands, and the whites wrinkled their noses when they passed. No wonder, after the harvest, men would fall sick as small cuts suppurated and exhaustion long held at bay took its toll.

By gray daylight they hurried along the muddy street toward the mill. They were hungry, but passed by the rice cart under the gallery of the carpenter shop. Minta, spoon in hand, followed them to the open ground between the mill, the jail with its whipping-scaffold, and Thierry's dark and silent house, each man recalling no doubt the overseer's temper and his habit of lashing out at whoever inconvenienced him at the time. Ti-Fred was barely able to work even yet, from Thursday's beating, and Gosport moved slowly, still—though he would not speak of it—in obvious pain.

You bell the cat.

Ajax went up to the rear door of the house and knocked, first gently, then more firmly. "Michie Thierry? Michie Thierry, you all right in there? You sick?" He had better manners—or a sufficient sense of self-preservation—than to call out Jeanette's name.

Minta was already walking back toward the kitchen, her sturdy little form silhouetted against the warmth of its lights. There was no sign of Quashie. A moment later January saw Baptiste hurry from the kitchen to the house, disappearing behind the garçonnière. Above the house—above the oak trees that stood between it and the river—movement caught January's eye, and in the morning's stillness he heard the cawing of ravens far off.

Early as it was, black birds circled in the air over what had to be Catbird Island.

Thierry lay on his back among the roots, about twenty feet from where the damaged boat had been dragged from its concealment. He had not died well. Blood glistened black on exposed intestines, dragged up out of a slit that opened from pubis to sternum—on clothing soaked and saturated with blood and rainwater, as if the overseer had bathed in red paint.

Ravens cawed angrily as the half-dozen men approached. Buzzards spread witch-cloak wings and hopped a little distance away, annoyed harpies cheated of their prey. A fox who'd hung around in hopes of carrion whipped into the shelter of the snags. Ajax said softly, "Lord God"; Esteban Fourchet crossed himself.

The smell of the ruptured guts hung thick above the raw stink of the blood. Someone had stuffed a wad of cloth into Thierry's mouth—and what looked like a handful of leaves—to silence him? And then had cut his throat.

January too crossed himself. Though the man had raped and beaten friends of his, had made life literally living hell for uncounted hundreds, he made himself whisper, "Dear God have mercy on his soul," and tried to mean it.

Because Esteban was there nobody made the observation that God had just had mercy on every African soul on Mon Triomphe, but Ajax, Nathan, Harry, and Samson thought it so loud the words were practically audible in the mist-draped hush.

When Esteban went to kneel beside the corpse January stepped behind him as if he would help, to fix in his mind the way it lay: the head bent forward, chin tucked tight; legs spraddled out, arms fallen to the sides. The rain had washed out any tracks or signs. When Esteban drew the corpse forward January saw that the neck and jaw were rigid, though the back and shoulders and limbs were still mostly loose. The fingers were blue, the eyes sunk and flattened in his head. The flesh was cold to January's touch.

The buzzards croaked again, impatient.

White-lipped but matter-of-fact, Esteban tugged forth the cloth that had been stuffed in Thierry's mouth. A snowy linen handkerchief, fairly new but unmarked. The blood that clotted its inner end looked gummy, and was stuck full of oak leaves, weeds, dirt.

Marie-Noël Fourchet, Madame Hélène, and a small knot of house-servants waited on the shell road from the house. Esteban called out, "Better go back into the house, ladies. This isn't good for you to see."

He was probably referring to his stepmother's pregnancy, but Madame Hélène let out a shriek and sagged into Baptiste's arms, though Thierry's body was being carried in such a way that it was unlikely she could have seen much besides the dead man's shape. Agamemnon, moving very stiffly and not meeting his master's eyes, stepped forward with a bedcover of striped country-work to drape the body, and the two maids crowded forward in frank curiosity to have a look. "Now, you girls stand back and let them lay him out decently," Baptiste admonished. "This isn't a show."

Kiki met January's eyes, her own gaze wide with shock.

"Isn't it?" muttered Cornwallis, standing at the rear of the group. But since he spoke in his native English no one but January understood.

Thierry's house was locked. Esteban made a distasteful move to find the key in the dead man's pocket but Madame Fourchet said, "I have one," and picked it, with a little hesitation, from the chatelaine on her belt. Her narrow face was calm but the marks of sleepless watching by her husband's bed were printed clear in the corners of her mouth and under her pale eyes.

Esteban glanced warily in the direction of the house, as if he expected his father to come storming out and berate him for letting the overseer die.

By entering the overseer's house in the lead, as close behind Esteban as he could manage, January got an instant's glimpse of the floor of the back room—where the knives were kept—and then the front, before the little cortege tracked mud and water all over the bare boards as they laid Thierry on his stained and crumpled bed.

No water, no mud. Thierry had not returned to his house after leaving the mill in the rain.

"Tell Jacko to saddle one of the cobs and put out a flag on the landing," said Esteban quietly to Ajax. "We need to get Sheriff Duffy here. In the meantime, you and Herc get the men out into the field. We've already lost three hours' work. God knows what my father's going to say."

The men filed out. January hung back, guessing Fourchet might not give him permission to examine the corpse and hoping to have the two seconds it would take him to extract the keys from the trouser pocket. Unfortunately Harry seemed to have the same idea, and the sight of two large main-gang men maneuvering to be the last one out of Thierry's bedroom was more than even Esteban could miss.

Esteban halted in the doorway, waiting, and there was nothing for January and Harry to do but to leave.

"Do you know where M'sieu Robert was going to be staying in Baton Rouge?" asked Madame Fourchet softly, as her stepson locked the doors of the little house. "He must be told as soon as possible."

"Gaufrage's, I should imagine." Esteban named the largest hotel in that town operated by a Frenchman. "If he's gone by that time they'll forward it on. Get back to your work now," he added, turning to discover the house-servants still clustered, avid and fearful, around the cottage steps. "There is nothing to see." His eyes met those of his valet. Agamemnon looked away.

"I want to see," piped up little Jean-Luc, who ran forward and would have tried to climb on the steps and look through the window had Esteban not caught him.

"Ben," added the planter's son, after Jean-Luc had been dragged howling away back to the house by Baptiste. "You share a cabin with Quashie, don't you?"

January nodded, knowing what was coming next.

"Did he come in last night?"

"No, sir."

Esteban sighed, as if he'd expected this. "That's all, then. Get yourselves some breakfast and get to work."

And there was nothing to do but go.

SIXTEEN

Remember the Sabbath and keep it holy, God had said. Simon Fourchet, and most of the other planters along the river, would have hurried to explain that God of course didn't understand about *la roulaison* back then and would certainly have made an exception to the Third Commandment if He'd known. There were some—chiefly Americans—who argued that the slaves shouldn't be permitted to work at all on Sundays, but should be required to attend Christian worship instead. These generally retreated from that position when it was pointed out to them how much it would cost them to feed their workers entirely from their own stores, or alternatively, how many hours a day would be taken from plantation work each weekday to enable the slaves to cultivate their provision grounds. The slaves themselves were not asked their opinion on the subject.

Mostly, you found God where you could. A number of the house-servants were Catholics, although some of their beliefs would have startled the Pope. Everyone in the quarters had probably at least been baptized, but when they called on God they did so by His African names. After forty years in America, Mohammed still rose before anyone else on the plantation, to kneel and pray toward the Mecca that he would never visit: *There is no God but Allah, and Mohammed is his Prophet.* Sometimes, coming and going at night, January saw him outside the smithy, kneeling on that faded little rug, when everyone but the mill crew was in bed. His hand found the rosary in his pocket and he whispered the words as he circled through the cane-rows toward the house: *Hail Mary, full of grace, the Lord is with thee.*

Lead us not into temptation and please O God deliver us from evil. . . .

And as always, the words brought him peace.

Cornwallis intercepted him on the gallery. "Michie Fourchet just had his medicine," he said, to January's request. "He's resting now." The dregs of bromide-and-water, not only in the glass on the tray the valet held but in the empty bottle beside it, amply attested as to Fourchet's reaction to the news of yet another catastrophe to the plantation that was his life.

"I won't take but a moment of his time."

The American valet's tobacco-colored eyes traveled up and down January's tall frame, taking in the field dust thick on his tattered clothing, the sweat that crusted and blackened both the shirts he wore, the vagabond raggedness of the second pair of cutoff trousers worn over the first. The filth that, despite a careful wash in the trough, still streaked his face, his hands, his hair.

The short, straight nose wrinkled. "He asked me specifically to let no one disturb him."

My ass, thought January, who couldn't imagine Fourchet making such a request. Sick or well, the old man was convinced that no one could run the plantation as well as he.

There was no getting around the valet's natural bloody-mindedness. "Might I speak to Madame

Fourchet, then?" January asked, and Cornwallis's lips lengthened.

"Madame is lying down. I'm sure field hands aren't even supposed to be near the house, particularly not disturbing M'sieu or Madame at a time like this."

"No, Michie Cornwallis, sir," said January, bowing his head and guessing that an attempt to use the return of Michie Robert's note would just get it taken from his hand. "Of course not, sir. Would you ask Michie Fourchet, as soon as he's able to talk to someone, if I could speak to him something about Quashie?"

"What?" The valet tried to look impassive but his eyes glinted avidly.

"It's kind of a long story," said January. "And you're right, sir, I ought to be gettin' back." And he trotted down the gallery stairs, telling himself that free or not, he could be prosecuted for robbing Simon Fourchet of a valuable slave if he wrung Cornwallis's skinny neck.

He walked back between the laundry and the kitchen and watched the gallery until Cornwallis disappeared into Madame Fourchet's sewing parlor behind the pantry. Then he slipped around the corner of the kitchen.

Kiki should have been in the midst of laying out the lunch dishes for Baptiste to carry across to the big house on his tray, but she wasn't. She sat at the table, small hands clasped before her mouth, staring at the tureens on their shelf across the room. She jerked her head around as January's shadow darkened the doorway and got hastily to her feet; he said, "Is it true Madame's asleep, or lying down after last night, up with Michie Fourchet?"

She nodded, and drew a heavy breath. "Baptiste was just over. He told me she was out the minute her head touched the pillow." Her voice was steady, but she wore the haggard look she'd had since the night of the abortion. "He had a bad night, Michie Fourchet, getting angry all over again at the Daubrays. She gave him medicine so often she near used up those two little bottles Doctor Laurette left, and he wouldn't let her leave."

"Can you get her keys?" asked January bluntly. "I need to get into Thierry's house and have a look at the body before too much more time passes—I take it Sheriff Duffy hasn't arrived yet?"

"I'd be surprised if he came today," replied the cook. "His brother owns a small place on Bayou Va-L'Enfer and they'll be harvesting. Lot of good it'll do him anyway. You know Michie Fourchet won't have an American in the house."

"All the more reason I need to get into the cottage."

"Wait here." Kiki stepped to the door, looked out at the rear of the big house, glanced both ways, and then hastened across with the air of one doing her duty. If challenged, January imagined she'd claim to be looking for Baptiste, but the only person who came out onto the gallery when she climbed its steps and bustled along to Madame Fourchet's room was Ariadne, to whom Kiki merely snapped, "You better not let M'am Fourchet see you wearing those beads," as she walked past. Ariadne hurried away, presumably to remove the offending beads—which January had last seen gracing a peg in Harry's cabin.

Beyond the stables, the steady rustle of activity around the mill had ceased. Far off, January heard the whistle of a steamboat, and wondered if that was the boat that would bring the belated Hannibal back from town. Ti-Jeanne the laundress started across the yard toward the kitchen and January tried to think up a good reason why he'd be there, but halfway there the stooped, elderly woman was intercepted by a voice calling out, "Here I am, honey," and Minta appeared from the candle-room in company with old Pennydip. The three women disappeared back through Pennydip's door.

"Got it." Kiki was breathing hard as she sprang up the kitchen steps. She stopped, pressing a hand to her abdomen, and January rebuked himself for sending her. "What d'you need to see his body for?"

"I won't know," said January, "till I've seen it. Maybe I won't know then."

They took the long way around to Thierry's cottage, skirting behind the laundry and the candle-room and the carpenter's shop, behind the mule barn and the landward end of the mill and thence through the cane. As they pushed heavily through the suffocating rows January asked, "Which way were you going to go? North or south?" and Kiki stiffened, startled, and glanced up at him with fleet fear in her eyes.

"That was your pillowcase I saw stashed with the food in the basket you gave Jeanette. What made you decide to go with them? Was it because of Gilles's death?"

She stammered, "I—no. Gilles . . ." Her face was ashy in the pale sun that fell so straight down through the tall rows, her eyes stricken.

January said gently, "Or was it just that you were scared of what would happen if Fourchet were to die? What would happen to everybody on the place, if the hoodoo isn't caught?"

She turned her face away, catching hold of a nearby stalk of cane for support, and January stopped and put a big gentle hand under her plump elbow. Her breath came in a tearing sigh. "I just wanted to get out of here," she said. "Yes, part of it's because . . . on the night of the fire, seeing Michie Fourchet took sick like that, I thought, *Anything could happen. They could blame anyone."* She shook her head. "They'll do what they want, decide what they want to believe. And part of it . . ."

She hesitated, as if unwilling to speak of what made no objective sense. "When those children burned, it did something to me, Ben. I don't know what. What you said about—about whoever this is, not caring . . ." She fell silent.

January said, "Nobody cares. Not Fourchet, not the hoodoo. Nobody."

"No." Her voice was barely to be heard, though the day was still. "That's why I want to go. A lot of evil comes when no one cares."

They came out of the cane and crossed the rough stretch of deep grass and scythed weeds unhurriedly, and went around to the front door. Kiki automatically started to head for the back, and January had to catch her arm and point—everyone at the mill would be grouped outside eating their lunch. The cook let out a little self-conscious chuckle, and shook her head at herself as they mounted the steps, and unlocked the door.

"Did you know Thierry'd found the boat?" January asked.

In Thierry's bedroom, the body was beginning to smell a little. January thanked God it was winter. Flies hummed around the corpse, and three separate trails of ants stretched from the wall and up the legs of the bed, but it was nothing like it would have been in July.

"I heard about it yesterday." Kiki sighed. "Thierry—well, I knew what he'd do to Jeanette. She told me Quashie hadn't had the first thing to do with that fire but that Thierry'd already made up his mind to put the blame on him for it. If they stayed here, she knew he'd die. And that's when I thought, *They could make up their mind like that about anyone. And nothing anybody could say would change it.*"

She shrugged. "I saw him leave here yesterday afternoon. When I didn't see her come out I came over and found her still tied to the bed." Blood marked the four corners of the sheets on which Thierry lay, where a woman's hands and ankles would have been locked to the bed frame with the spancels that now hung on a peg on the wall. "She told me then about the boat." In addition to Thierry's big driving whip that he used in the field, there was a whalebone quirt in the corner. It was the type horse-trainers used to school recalcitrant mounts.

"That's right," said January softly. Greenflies rose in a cloud when he pulled back the sheet, and he winced. There were a *lot* of ants. Kiki made a faint gagging noise, but said nothing. "So why would he have gone to Catbird Island? He knew he'd scuppered the boat. He knew *she* knew the boat was useless. So when he saw Jeanette was gone, why did he go *there*?"

He crossed himself, and pulled the handkerchief from Thierry's pocket, where he'd seen Esteban thrust it after taking it from the corpse's mouth. The blood was still a little tacky, but it had mostly dried now. He had to strike it several times against the bed frame to clear the ants off it enough to unfold it for a better look.

"Why would Quashie and Jeanette have gone there? They'd escape as soon as it started raining, yes, to cover their tracks, but Catbird Island was the last place they'd want to go. What do you make of this?"

He held the handkerchief out to her. Kiki took it without undue squeamishness and turned it in her hands. "It's good linen," she said. "No initials, but then a lot of men don't have them embroidered—I know Michie Fourchet didn't for years, til he married M'am Marie-Noël and she started doing it for him again. Michie Esteban fussed and fussed at Vanille and

Doucette and Nancy and came near to swearing he'd have them whipped if they didn't embroider as nice as he liked his done, and finally started sending them to some woman in town to do. I think Michie Robert had his embroidered in Paris, or maybe M'am Hélène did it on the ship coming home. I don't remember seeing this kind in the laundry, though."

"Which doesn't mean anything," remarked January, engaged in turning out Thierry's pockets. "Even if it had Esteban's initials on it, or Robert's or Andrew Jackson's for that matter, all it might mean is that Agamemnon or Harry or Ti-Jeanne took one from the laundry to sell to False River Jones."

The overseer's pockets contained, in addition to his keys, which January appropriated, a dozen pistol-balls, a powder-flask, and some wads, but no pistols. There were also two or three Mexican dollars—common currency up and down the river—a tangle of string, the stub of a tallow candle, lucifers in a tin box, a folding penknife, another box containing a fire-steel, flint, and tow. A larger and more serviceable blade was sheathed at his belt.

When January tipped Thierry's body up it came all of a piece, like a clumsy plank. Thierry must have died around midnight, then. The back of his coat was as wet as the front, which only meant that he'd been alive when the rain had begun. No dirt or clay clung to it. With some difficulty January tried to strip and wrangle the coat down the dead man's back and arms, cursing Esteban for preventing him from making this examination when Thierry's muscles were soft enough to maneuver. In the end he pulled the coat up from the bottom, and the waistcoat and shirt after it, examining the skin of the dead man's back.

"What are you looking for?" Kiki spoke from the

doorway, where she was keeping a weather eye on the yard.

"I was looking for bruises," said January thoughtfully. "But what I expected to find—and didn't—is lividity: blood pooled in the back once the heart stopped pumping. Get me a towel or a rag from the other room and douse it in the water bucket, if you would, please. I hate this part." He took a deep breath, and pulled down Thierry's trousers, revealing the nasty mess of caked waste that his body had voided on death.

"Whoa, lord!" The cook put a wet shirt into his hand and fanned the air before her face. "When it comes time for me to die I think I'll drown or something."

"You wouldn't say that if you'd ever seen anyone who had." January sopped and wiped at Thierry's buttocks and the backs of his thighs. "There. See? That's blood that sinks down under the skin to the lowest point on the body, right after death."

"You mean he died sitting up?"

"Looks like it. And someone laid him down later. The way his head's bent forward would confirm that; the neck and the jaw are the first to harden up. Damn it." Having pulled the trousers, shirt, and coat back into position, January laid the body down again and tried to lift the hands from where Ajax had laid them, folded, over the corpse's groin. "The ankles are going to be like wood. We'd need a razor to get the boots off and I'm not sure they'd tell us much. Look at this." He pushed up the coat sleeve, and the sleeve of the shirt beneath it, as far as he could, and twisted and pulled at the fingers, kneeling to peer underneath for a look at the palms. "Can you see the palms?"

"Mostly." Kiki knelt, and squinched herself around. "They look all right to me."

"Exactly," said January. "No cuts. None on the coat sleeves or shirtsleeves either, or anywhere else on the clothing as far as I can tell." Gingerly he probed and separated at the crawling horror of the opened belly, shaking from his fingers the roaches that crawled out. "This looks like it was done with a cane-knife. The intestines are cut through just about to the backbone, far too deep for even a river-rat's fighting-knife. And it looks like a single cut, driven in underhand and pulling up."

"I'll just take your word for that." Kiki went back into the front room and returned with the water bucket, a little pot of Pennydip's soft soap, and another shirt. "But it doesn't take a man from the main gang to be able to do that, you know. Those knives are sharp. A woman could do it, if she was mad enough, or scared enough. You'd be surprised at what a really mad woman can do."

"My guess is," said January, sitting back, "that maybe a woman could do it easier than a man from the main gang. Can you see Thierry letting a man he'd whipped get that close to him, even if he didn't see the knife in the dark and the rain?"

"Hmm." Kiki thought about that. Then she said, "You say that to Sheriff Duffy and he's going to think, *Jeanette*. And probably nobody else." Her eyes met his and she added, "And that might be for the best."

"For everyone but Jeanette," January said. He washed his hands again, then rose and stepped quickly into the back room, to the chest where Thierry would have kept his pistols. None were there now.

That meant nothing, really, he thought, as he went back into the bedroom and wadded the two shirts together. Kiki followed him to the front door with the bloodied and filthy water, which after a cautious glance in both directions they poured out so that it ran under the house. Harry had been in the house, however briefly. He could easily have taken them while everyone else was occupied with the body. Very likely several spare knives and whetstones were missing, and probably Thierry's Sunday stickpin, too.

The shirts January stashed in the long weeds under the steps. The shadows were definitely on the eastward side of the oaks as he and Kiki walked, with inconspicuous swiftness, across to the wall of cane, and stepped inside as through a curtain.

"It was pouring rain last night," said January, as they waded along the rows toward the back of the mill, whence Kiki could cut unseen back around to the kitchen. "Why would Thierry have gone to Catbird Island in a storm like that, when he already knew the people he pursued knew that their boat had been destroyed?"

"To meet someone else?"

January nodded. "It was too much to hope there'd have been a note in his pocket, but that little bay at the south of the island where he was found is only about a hundred feet from False River Jones's campsite. And it seems Jones is back in the area."

"Ben, Michie Jones wouldn't hurt a fly!" Kiki caught his sleeve, looked up into his face with real distress in her eyes. "All right, he'll buy anything that people bring him without asking where it comes from, but he's a good man! Time and again, he's put himself in trouble to bring folks letters and things, news of their families and friends."

"Maybe it explains what Thierry was looking for on the island." January glanced at the shadows of the cane. "Damn it, Ajax is going to welt me for sure. Kiki, listen. I sent Hannibal to town to find out about Esteban's friend Michie Molineaux. He should have been back yesterday, today at the latest. When he comes back, would you ask him to send for me from the fields, at once?"

He paused, seeing the odd light in her eyes, and she said, "*You* sent *Michie Hannibal* to town?"

January opened his mouth and then realized how foolish it would sound to say, *That is, I meant of course that Michie Hannibal went to town and bade me stay here. . . .*

He shut it, and looked down into the woman's eyes. They mocked him, bemused, and she shook her head. "Maybe if Ajax welts you it'll teach you to act like a proper nigger and not some uppity town-bred Ee-thee-opian who's too proud for his own good. And that's all to the best," she added softly, "for everyone. I'll pass your orders along, sir."

"Thank you," said January, "Mamzelle Kiki."

And he loped off fast through the cane, turning over in his mind what he had learned from Thierry's body, and what it could mean. The examination of the corpse would cost him his lunch, but on the whole, he thought, food wasn't something he was interested in, just at the moment.

Through the afternoon, and into the evening, January strained his ears for the far-off wails of the boats on the river, trying to mold the sound into the longer, warping notes of a vessel coming in to the landing. He cursed the singing of the men when it obscured the sound. Yet he knew if a boat came in Bumper and Nero would be out at once with the news.

None came. *It's the wrong time of year for the fever,* thought January. Either consumption, or opium, had tangled Hannibal in its snare.

Damn it, he thought. *Damn it, damn it, damn it.*

I'll have to speak to Fourchet tomorrow.

He wondered what he would say.

Hunger soon enough returned to sponge away his revulsion at the postmortem he'd performed and, more than hunger, exhaustion: He felt like a steamboat trying to paddle upriver without logs in its firebox. Ajax glanced at him once or twice, when the dizziness of sheer fatigue made him stagger, but said nothing. January was aware he was falling farther and farther behind the others—and slowing Gosport down as well—but feared to work faster. *Don't let me lose a finger,* he prayed, aware that the priest who'd taught him his catechism at the age of eight would have pointed out that this was the probable Divine penalty for cutting cane on the Sabbath. And then, as the whetstone slipped from his sweaty, shaky grip, he added, *Or a hand.*

Who had Thierry expected to see on Catbird Island?

And who had he met instead?

And who had come along later and laid him down, saying no word to anyone of his death? January had seen Trinette among the women in the mill but couldn't recall exactly when. Harry had been absent but then Harry usually was. Lisbon and Yellow Austin . . . ?

The following day brought another flatboat, with two thousand more cords of wood. "Three dollars and fifty cents a cord!" Esteban raged, when he got the note from his brother concerning the payment. "My God, he'll bankrupt us!"

"Boy never did have any sense," remarked Old Jules Ney, who had come that morning to take Thierry's place as overseer.

"And I would have bet money he'd have seen Michie Fourchet in Hell before he'd take the job," Mohammed remarked, helping January—as all men on the plantation had been drafted to help, save only the house-servants and those actually working in the mill—unload the wood onto every cane cart and wagon and haul it to the makeshift shelters. "Fourchet made it very clear that the son of a Jacobin *sans-culotte* who'd been deported from France for poaching was no fit associate for his own son, no matter how similar their interest in machines. When Robert would come here during the summers, young Michie Jacinthe used to study with him at the house. I don't think old Michie Jules ever forgave Fourchet for putting an end to it."

"Michie Esteban asked him," provided Gosport, wiping sweat from his face. "Who else would he ask? Every other man in the parish that don't have cane of his own is out riding patrol after Quashie and Jeanette. And anyhow," he added, glancing along the line at the stringy, gray-haired patriarch, an eerie elderly doppelgänger of the scarlet-coated master of the *Belle Dame*, "they're mostly Americans." Behind Old Ney's head, against the damp gray roil of the sky, the red bandanna fluttered from the bare oak tree on the bluff like a streak of blood. "Michie Esteban offered two hundred dollars, for a month's work to finish the roulaison. I should think Michie Ney would forget his pride for that much."

"Forget his pride?" Harry sniffed, and shifted the weight of the wood over his shoulder. "You watch his eyes. He's countin' every man and seein' how the land lies, to sneak a man out of here to sell in the Territories. You mark my words, before roulaison's done somebody's gonna turn up missin'."

The afternoon brought Sheriff Duffy on the *Bonnets o' Blue*, accompanied by an equally hairy cracker deputy. They were met at the bottom of the big-house steps by an exhausted-looking Madame Fourchet, but not admitted to the house. ("Michie Fourchet, he took an' threw a water glass at Baptiste when he asked," reported Bumper.) Whether the lawman considered the matter simple murder or the prelude to rebellion he didn't mention to anyone who later spoke to January, but Duffy didn't spend long in the overseer's cottage. Passing the little building on the way back from changing the signal late last night, January had heard the scratch and scuffle of rats and foxes from its walls. In any house in the quarters, friends and family would have been sitting up with the dead, the men telling stories, the women sobbing and wailing in grief. Their shrieks and tears were a gift to the departed spirit, a token of respect. But even more than that, the presence of friends—by the light of whatever tallow candle-ends and pine-knots could be donated to illuminate the dark hours—was a guarantee that morning wouldn't find the body missing nose or fingers or lips amid a welter of sticky little tracks.

Whatever else Duffy found, January didn't know. The fact that he'd brought a single deputy rather than a posse argued for a calmer outlook than was usual in the district, but then it was roulaison and difficult to muster a force. He and his deputy were offered ale and cornbread in the kitchen—much to Kiki's annoyance, since both partook of the nearly universal American addiction to tobacco-chewing—and departed soon thereafter into the ciprière.

Throughout the remainder of the day, Bumper and Nero brought scraps of news to the toiling men: Michie Duffy had told Michie Esteban there was six posses out lookin' for Quashie an' Jeanette; Michie Fourchet went just about crazy when Esteban told him how much Michie Robert paid for that wood. (January knew that, at least. The train of wood carts followed the carriage track around the side of the house close enough for him to hear the old man's hoarse cursing and the crash of thrown objects.) Little Michie Jean-Luc got into the cottage and stole the dead man's knife and had to have it taken from him. M'am Fourchet and M'am Hélène got into another squabble over whose fault it was that he got the key.

Just after luncheon, Hippolyte Daubray put in an appearance, resplendent in royal blue superfine, and offered one of his many cousins as overseer for the rest of the roulaison—but mostly, January suspected, to poke around for information. Everyone in the wood-carting detail was then treated to the sight of Madame's elegant cousin bolting down the steps like a hunted hare, with Fourchet clinging to the jamb of his bed-room door screaming, "You're all in this together! Pigs! Filth!" after his retreating heels.

From everything January could find out—he spoke to Kiki at noon, before the main gang went out into the fields again under Jules Ney's cold watchful eye—Duffy had been asking after those few old slaves remaining on the place who'd been involved in the uprising of '98. There weren't many of those, for the work was killing and Fourchet wasn't a man to keep a dependent who had outlived his or her usefulness. January hoped Fourchet had spoken to the sheriff about the pattern of the events being wrong for a planned revolt—the men agreed that Duffy was shrewd, and might understand. But after Daubray's visit, it would be useless to try to see Fourchet. January judged by the quiet at noon that Madame had dosed him with bromide again, slowing the heart action and tipping him over into sleep.

And still Hannibal did not return.

When it grew too dark for further work in the field, Jules Ney grudgingly detailed four slaves to bury Thierry. Word had been sent to Thierry's sister, his only relative, in New Orleans, informing her of her brother's death and offering to disinter and ship the remains if so required. At a guess, thought January—as he and Gosport, Nathan, and Mohammed dug the grave—Thierry was going to be on Mon Triomphe til Judgment Day. He couldn't imagine even a sibling wanting the man badly enough to pay for having him dug up and brought to town.

Like the slaves' burying-ground a dozen yards away among the trees, the white graveyard lay close to the river, where the land was higher. Behind the big house you would hit groundwater only a few feet down. The wind made the oak trees curtsey and mutter, and brought the stink of smoke from across the river, where one of the smaller plantations—already finished with harvest—was burning over the fields. This was done to clear away the cane-trash, and fertilize the soil with ash. Whatever bagasse was not dried for kindling would be piled and burned on the levee later. From the top of the levee, January had glimpsed far-off pale ribbons of flame.

Weathered boards marked two other graves in that corner of the little family burying-ground, nearly hidden by weeds and as far from the graves of a former Fourchet sister-in-law, a cousin, and the sister-in-law's three children as space would permit. "Them's Michie Muñoz an' Michie Gansel," supplied Mohammed, nodding toward them. "Michie Gansel was overseer when M'am Juana and Miss Annie was killed. He died then, too, him and his wife and her baby, all buried in the same grave."

"How'd it happen?" January leaned on the handle of his shovel. "It's one thing killin' a man who's caught you tryin' to escape. But a risin'—turnin' on the whole family—they'd have to know the militia'd be on 'em."

"I don't think they cared." Mohammed gazed out into the dark trees. The light of the torches, stuck in a circle around the burying-ground, edged his cropped gray hair with gold. "You reach a point where you don't, you know. And in those days it was different. There wasn't the American Army, as there is now. Back then, there wasn't more than a dozen houses along this part of the river, and no soldiers closer than town. It didn't seem so dangerous then. We just figured—Gowon and his boys just figured—they'd disappear into the woods and never be found. But of course they was."

It was the first time anyone had spoken the name of the only man January had ever learned of who'd refused to do what Simon Fourchet ordered.

The clouds had passed with last night's rain; the day had been windy and cold. The dark that pressed so hard on the fluttering spooky torchlight made it easy to believe tales of platt-eye devils and uneasy souls that could find no rest.

"Was they hanged?" asked Nathan.

Mohammed shook his head. "That wasn't what the Spanish did, to slaves that killed their masters. They tied 'em to stakes and burned 'em alive."

"Lord," whispered Nathan, and January, who recalled those days, and the Spanish rule, crossed himself.

After a time Mohammed went on, "But I don't think Gowon and his boys even thought so much about it as that, or they'd have waited til Michie Fourchet came home. It was summertime, and the moon full, and Michie Fourchet, he'd been drinking a week, and was whippin' mad. He was a young man then and couldn't abide to be crossed, not by God, not by any man. He whipped Gowon twice, three times that week, and the others, too. But it was him beatin' Layla, that was Gowon's daughter, that set it off. She was twelve years old, and she died of it next day, after

Michie Fourchet had ridden off down the river road. That's when Gowon and the others went and burned the house, and cut to pieces all those they met, that none should know which way they'd gone."

And in a soft voice he sang,

"He went, he cut his daughter down,
He carried her to his hut,
He went, he cut his daughter down,
He carried her to his hut.
'Papa, I'm afraid I'm dying,
Papa, I'm going to die.'

"He said, He owe me a daughter,
I got no child no more.
He said, He owe me a daughter,
I got no child no more.
'Papa, I'm afraid I'm dying,
Papa, I'm going to die. . . .' "

The men took up the refrain—softly, very softly, as they cut the heavy soil with their shovels, for even so memorializing one man's rebellion would be, January knew, a whipping offense. But Gowon was owed it, he thought, for the daughter he had lost. For all the children that all of them had lost, Bo and Claire and that infant of Gilles and Kiki who would never be born. For Ajax, untying his own daughter from the whipping-frame, to which he'd surrendered her rather than risk bringing the consequences of revolt down on all those under his care. For January's own father, who had watched his son and his daughter taken away.

"They carry them down to the river,
They throw them in the stream.
They carry them down to the river,

They throw them in the stream.
'Papa, I'm afraid I'm dying . . .' "

The river. The thought clicked suddenly in January's tired mind. Thierry lying on the snags and deadfalls within feet of the river. *Someone gutted him and then cut his throat, and left him sitting up. . . .*

Why didn't they just pitch him into the river?

He was left there on purpose. January had assumed that someone had later come and laid him down, but why was he left there at all?

He was LEFT THERE. Left THERE. Moved from somewhere else, to draw attention to Catbird Island and away from the site of the actual killing.

Moved by someone who had access to a boat.

"Near enough to six feet," decided Nathan. "I ain't gonna waste more sweat on him." The men walked back to Thierry's cottage and from there, while the others were loading the hastily made coffin onto a wood cart, January went to the back of the big house and told Baptiste they were ready to lay Michie Thierry down.

The butler went inside. Lamps burned in the dining room, and January could hear Fourchet's voice, hoarse and incoherent, from his bedroom. Still furious over something, by the sound of it. Then dim forms moved in the shadows under the gallery, and light from the windows caught Madame Fourchet's straight pale hair, and the sheen of Madame Hélène's persimmon-colored silk. "Well, if you find it amusing to go out in the cold like that in your condition by all means do so, but it has never been the custom here, I assure you." The night was not more icy than Hélène's voice. "He was a coarse rude man and I'm sure he got what was coming to him for not controlling himself better around the negresses."

"He must have a Christian burial." Ariadne was helping Madame on with her heavy cloak.

"Oh, honestly, my dear, I don't think the man had been in a church since he was baptized! I'm sure he wouldn't care."

"All the more reason to give him one."

Madame Hélène let out a little titter, but when she got no response she burst out querulously, "If you *must* go, I wish you will tell me what I am to do if Monsieur Fourchet gets restless? He's going to need you. . . ." There was fear in her voice. It wasn't that she didn't think Thierry needed a Christian burial, January realized. She simply didn't want to be left alone with her father-in-law.

The gentle wind lifted Madame Fourchet's cloak as she descended the steps and made the six lights of Lundy's candelabra jerk and dance. The women unloading the cane carts at the roaring orange hell-mouth of the mill, the men dragging wood and stoking the fires, crowded to the mill doors: January heard Old Ney's hoarse shouting and the crack of a whip within.

Madame read the service for the dead in her small, flat voice, and dropped a branch of Christmas roses—the only flowers available at that season in her predecessor's garden—into the grave. Then Lundy walked her back to the house, and the men worked by torchlight in the cold to fill in the hole. As they walked back past the slaves' graveyard, January looked out into the darkness under the trees there where the graves of Gilles and Reuben lay, remembering the fading names on the other graves, the rebels whose names would vanish once Mohammed died. . . .

And a dark scribble on one of the new headboards caught his eye.

"Let me take that," he said, reaching for Mohammed's torch. "I'll follow you along soon."

"Better not." Nathan glanced around him worriedly. "It's not a good thing, to be walkin' in the graveyard on a moonless night. Not ever, come to that. There's witches that wait in the darkness."

"We'll wait for you," said Gosport.

"I'll be quick." Torch in hand, January waded through the weeds to the twin graves. The china Kiki had placed around the new-turned earth glinted in the yellow light, like a black cat's teeth when it mews, tiny and vicious, and the bodies decomposing in the shallow earth filled the air with a musty nastiness. The names, REUBEN and GILLES, were already fading from the wooden headboards.

The new mark on Reuben's board seemed doubly clear.

It was a vévé, surrounded by the crosses and stars of protection and care. The mark of Papa Legba, the guardian of all crossroads, guide of the dead. A blessing-sign, to leave on a grave.

Papa Legba, open the gate, the women would sing in Congo Square, on the hot summer evenings when the slaves' produce market would be set up there, and men would gamble under the sycamore trees, and watch torchlight flicker over the faces of the dancers. *Papa Legba, open the gate.*

Only sometimes they'd sing instead, *Saint Peter, open the gate, Saint Peter, open the gate—gonna pass through, gonna pass through.*

January stared at the symbols for some time, trying to fit times and patterns together in his mind with the memory of a woman's face in the lantern-light of a moss-gatherer's blood-smelling hut. He was very thoughtful as he walked back toward the house.

SEVENTEEN

"Can you get me in to see Michie Fourchet?"

Baptiste, though clearly a little startled to find January in the kitchen yard at noon when he should have been eating lunch with the main gang in the field, at least didn't look down his nose at his filthy clothes.

"I'll do what I can," the butler said, though he sounded doubtful. "But you know Michie Fourchet isn't well."

"Believe me, I wouldn't disturb him unless I felt it urgent," said January. "But if he's thinking he's safe, and the place is safe, because Quashie and Jeanette have fled, he's mistaken. They didn't kill Thierry, and I don't think they were behind the hoodoo. Please tell him that."

Baptiste frowned. In the ten days he'd been on Mon Triomphe, January had seen the little man recover his confidence and settle in as head of the servants, aided largely by the fact that nobody in the household liked his main competitor for the role, Cornwallis. As Baptiste studied him now, January could see he was thinking, not simply of the meaning of the words, but of what they implied in terms of the household—and the plantation—at large. "What do you know about the hoodoo, Ben?" he asked. "You aren't even from here."

"I know what I've heard," answered January. "And I know what I saw, out on Catbird Island and down by the levee on Saturday, when that first lot of wood arrived. And I think if Michie Fourchet thinks he's safe now he's in more danger than ever. And so is every person on this place."

Baptiste bit his lip, and his dark eyes shifted in the direction of the mill. January understood what he was thinking. It was up to the butler to act as gatekeeper of who entered or did not enter the house. Should Esteban return from the mill while January was in his father's room, or Madame Hélène happen to encounter him on the gallery, it would be up to Baptiste to explain the presence of a dirty and stinking field hand in the white folks' sacred purlieus.

He gave January another quick look-over, then appeared to decide there wasn't much that could be done. "All right. I'll take you in through Michie Fourchet's office. But you got to be quick."

"I'll be quick."

They climbed the steps to the back gallery, with Baptiste keeping a watchful eye out toward the mill. He stopped, put his head through the dining room French doors to make sure Lundy was setting the table properly ("Turn those knives over so the blades point in toward the plate, would you? Thanks."), then escorted January through Fourchet's small office, and into the bedroom with its drawn curtains and pale-blue-washed walls. There too was a portrait of the first Madame Fourchet, stiff and odd against a background of banana plants and flowers, leading January to deduce that Juana Villardega had been either born in New Orleans or brought there as a young girl—she looked about sixteen. On the other side of the chimney-breast hung a much-better-executed pastel of the current Madame, its size and the twin houses of Refuge and Mon Triomphe in the background testifying that it had been paid for by her husband, not her relatives.

These January noticed only in passing, for his attention was riveted instantly by the man in the bed, and the smell of vomit and voided blood that choked the close air of the room.

"Michie Fourchet!" He stepped closer, shocked.

Fourchet raised his head like a cornered dog. In the dimness his eyes had a slick silvery gleam. "What do you want?"

January glanced back at Baptiste, standing in the doorway. The table next to the bed was thick with bottles and glasses, a water pitcher and spoons, two or three towels neatly folded. *The man has a heart condition,* thought January. *What are they giving him? That doctor from Baton Rouge isn't puking a man with a strained heart, surely?* But the only bottles on the bedside table among the chewed cigar stubs were bromide—at least three empties—hartshorn, and the pitcher of water, the ammoniac smell cutting the sinuses like a silvery knife.

"I'd like to ask your permission to search the boundaries of the plantation for signs of Thierry's murderer. If you look at where the body was found, sir, and the fact that—"

"Thierry wouldn't murder anyone."

January blinked.

Fourchet rolled his head a little on the pillow. He looked as if someone had siphoned flesh from some areas of his face and pumped water into others, and his hands wavered across the coverlet. "Anyway that was years ago. A man can do what he likes with his own slaves." The words came out in short bursts, as a baby will dribble food. He tilted his head.

"Bitch lied to me," he added. "Too sodden with opium to even turn them over. Thought she was too good for the place. Paris was all she ever thought about."

"Michie Fourchet?" January stepped forward, and Fourchet pulled back his lips in a snarl.

"Get out of my room. What the hell you doing letting a field hand in my room, Gilles?"

Baptiste caught January's arm. "You'd better go."

January pulled free, still staring at the face that was at once sunken and bloated, the puffy pale yellowish bulges beneath the eyes, the line of scarlet along the gums. "How long has he been like this?"

"Get him out of here!" Fourchet snatched up an empty bottle from the table beside him and flung it, subsiding at once with a gasp of pain, hand pressed, not to his side, but to the small of his back. "Esteban! Esteban!"

Baptiste thrust January before him through the office, and the two of them nearly ran into Esteban in the door that led out onto the shade of the gallery. "What the hell is going on?" demanded the planter's son, as more crashes resounded from Fourchet's room. It sounded like the old man had swept the entire contents of the bedside table to the floor. "What the hell is this man doing in here? Didn't I say my father wasn't to be disturbed? Go in there," he added savagely to Baptiste, as the sounds of violent retching followed from the sickroom, and Madame Fourchet, her fair hair hanging disordered about her shoulders, darted along the gallery and into the dining room, and through to her husband's side.

Catching January's arm, Esteban shoved him out onto the gallery. The younger Fourchet's eyes were red-rimmed from want of sleep and his face gray with dust and streaked with sweat. "What did you say to my father?"

"M'sieu Fourchet, I think your father's been poisoned."

Esteban's eyes flared with shock. Then his hand tightened on January's shirt and he slammed him into the house wall. "Who told you this? Where'd you hear this?"

"Hear it? For God's sake, look at him, man! Six days ago he strained his heart! Now he's off his head, he's bleeding from the gums, vomiting . . ."

"You uppity whore!" Fourchet screamed inside. "You think your son's too good to be part of the family? He's not a genius, he's just goddam lazy! Lazy and weak! All he wants to do is play with his worthless machines and his worthless friends. . . ."

"Is he voiding blood? Vomiting blood?" January demanded, as Esteban made a move to go through and into the room. "Has he passed urine in the last day or so? Any at all?"

He realized Esteban was staring at him as if he were speaking Chinese. For a moment their eyes met, then January hastily lowered his, remembering that in this country it was taken as a sign of rebellion, of challenge, for a black man to meet a white man's eyes. "I'm sorry, sir," he mumbled. "It's just one of Michie Georges' brothers was took just this way, from drinkin' salts of mercury. Now I hear as how someone tried to poison your daddy before, and did kill the old butler here, and when he started talkin' so crazy, and with blood comin' out his gums, I thought . . ."

Pick up the hint, you stubborn oaf! Slap your forehead and cry, My God, could it possibly be . . . ?

But Esteban, not an imaginative man, only looked at him with sidelong suspicion, and said, "That's a common—uh—effect of calomel—medicine, you understand? I think you'd better just—uh—leave such things to the doctors. You had something you wanted to tell my—uh—my—my father?"

"Yes, sir," said January. All he could do was try. "How that Quashie, and Jeanette, they couldn't have done that murder the other night, since they knowed Thierry had wrecked their boat; they wouldn't have been on that island." But as the words came out of his mouth he could see Esteban barely heard him, and his own attention was jerked away, again and again, by the tumult in Fourchet's room.

"Goddamned bitch, you will live where I tell you! I'll not pay a lazy whore to have her own establishment . . . !"

At the sound of a blow and a cry, Esteban thrust January aside mid-sentence, and strode through the office to his father's room. January hesitated on the gallery, heart pounding, smelling blood very clearly now as Fourchet vomited again and thinking, *Poison. Salts of mercury. His kidneys must be disintegrating within his body.*

Dear God, what a hellish way to die!

The jingle of bridle-bits came suddenly from the yard, the clatter of hooves. Men called out and laughed. Someone said, "Hey, sweetheart, not home yet!" and someone else, "Hey, the house!" January ran over to the rail of the gallery on the mill side to look.

A posse of the patrollers had captured Jeanette.

The rope that bound her wrists ran up to the saddlebow of a long youth in dirty jean and a low-crowned hat. The girl had fallen, for the front of her green dress was brown with dirt and mud, the buttons torn away and her skirt spotted with blood from her grazed knees. Her head rolled on her shoulders with exhaustion, the curly cloud of reddish-black hair hanging over her face, and, as the men had said, when the horses came to a halt she collapsed among them, sitting in the wet earth of the yard before the mill.

From the gallery January saw Esteban hurry down the back steps and cross toward them, a tall thin figure stiff and awkward in his blue coat, his whip in his hand. He spoke to the men of the patrol, fumbled money from the pocket of his coat to pass among them. Then he bent, took Jeanette's chin in his hand, and forced her to look up at him. January knew what he would ask.

She shook her head, swaying, denying it, her whole body shaken with sobs. Esteban straightened, stood looking down at her for a moment. Then, as if making up his mind to do so, he caught her shoulder and shook her, and she cried in a voice shrill with pain and terror: "He didn't! He didn't! I swear you we weren't anywhere near there!"

No, thought January. The pair would have gone straight inland, across the fields and into the ciprière, striking out toward New River and heading to New Orleans that way. Without a boat they'd be fools to stick to the river.

Esteban looked down at her from his height. He must have asked her something else, quietly, probably where Quashie was now, because Jeanette shook her head again, wrapping her arms around her half-exposed breasts and crumpling slowly to the ground. One of the men still on horseback tilted his hat and said something, pointing inland—that she'd been picked up over toward New River, January learned later—and Esteban's stiff shoulders lifted and settled a little without ever relaxing. Behind him in the house January heard Fourchet cry out, "Not opium! Don't give me that stuff! Oh, dear Christ!"

And from the dining room a bell jangled,

impatiently summoning servants, and a moment later Madame Hélène's voice exclaimed, "Honestly, what is this house coming to? Jean-Luc—Jean-Luc you *will* stay in your chair . . . ! Marthe . . ."

In the cloudy cool of noon, the women sitting on the cane carts before the mill, eating their midday food and suckling their babies, watched silent-eyed as Esteban lurched forward and pulled Jeanette firmly to her feet. Two of the patrollers sprang from their horses and followed man and slave across the mucky ground to the little brick jailhouse, as if they expected Jeanette to turn on Esteban and gut him with her fingernails.

In the doorway Jeanette clung to the jamb for support, turning back to speak to Esteban. Pleading with him to believe her. Swearing that though the dead man had raped her repeatedly, had flogged the man she loved nearly to death, had harried her and insulted her and battered her, still she had not lifted her hand against him.

Her master pushed her awkwardly into the jailhouse, locked the door, pocketed the key. January could almost hear him saying it: *I understand there are abuses but you just—uh—can't have slaves going around murdering their masters. . . .*

In his curtained room, the dying man groaned, "Dear God, save me! Dear God, save me!" as the bloated tissues of his body swelled tight with water he could not void.

January descended the back steps of the house and was on his way to the fields again before Esteban returned.

Through the night Simon Fourchet screamed. The sound carried to the mill doors, where those who hauled cane up to the rollers, or dragged wood in from the shelters through the thin drizzling rain that started at sunset, paused to look at one another with fear in their eyes. Nobody spoke much. Once, when January helped Chuma pick up some cane she'd dropped, the woman said, "Dear God have mercy on him. I'd wear any child of mine out, that gave pain like that to a dog." But January saw she was afraid, too, wondering what would happen to them when Fourchet died.

Slavery, January understood now as he never had before, made you fear change almost more than anything else. Once he looked over in the direction of the jail, and thought he saw movement behind the bars of the single high-set window, as if someone had grabbed the bars and pulled herself up a little, to look out at the torchlight and the rain.

She will hang for his murder, he thought.

And almost certainly, Duffy was going to try to get out of her where Quashie was.

He leaned into the harness and gritted his teeth, to drag the sledgeload of expensive wood—at three dollars and fifty cents the cord—through the softening mud to the mill door.

Bad enough that Jeanette had to sit there in the tiny brick room listening to Fourchet die. What it was like for Madame Fourchet, sitting in the bedroom beside him, he couldn't imagine.

That would still be true, he thought, whether or not she'd given her husband the mercury herself.

"It's in the medicine," he said to Kiki, when, after the night shift men came on, he walked over to the kitchen. The light rain had eased, but the air was full of moisture; rain would start and stop like a seeping wound til daybreak. "It's the only thing he's getting that no one else in the house would touch. Our killer learned a lesson with your husband."

The cook glanced across at him in the muted glow

of the hearth. Her black sleeves were rolled back and she tilted boiling water from the great kettle into the small clay pot that the servants used for their tea; flames reflected in her dark eyes like the sack of far-off towns.

January asked, "Where is the medicine kept?"

"In the birthing-room. Behind Madame's room."

There was a long French door from that chamber onto the gallery that faced over Camille's garden.

"It isn't locked up or anything," Kiki went on. "It sits on the dresser in there. Anyone could come in or go out."

January nodded. He'd seen the room now and then over the past ten days. Small and sparsely furnished, the walls washed a pale cheerful yellow, with its big bed and cypress-wood armoire it could double as a sick-room or lodging for a female guest. Even there, as in the mistress's bedroom next door, Camille Bassancourt had left her mark. The bed was an elaborate confection of pear-wood and ebony, imported from France by the woman who had never gotten over losing her place in Paris society. The armoire, inlaid with slips of pearl and brass, could have contained the garments of a regiment.

Kiki brought the tea to the table. She moved more briskly now, as if the lingering lassitude and cramps that had followed her abortion were departing. When a desperate, moaning shriek ripped the night, more animal than human as Fourchet's strength waned, she did not even check her stride.

January recalled the way Fourchet had said, *Your mother tells me . . .* and the casual glance he'd given to the woman he'd bedded with as little thought as most men would masturbate. To the woman he'd sold as he'd have sold a riding-mare, to a friend who liked her action. It was of only passing concern that he'd included her two children in the transaction. In spite of the law mandating the sale of children under the age of ten along with their mothers—"if at all possible"—it was a far from universal practice.

I wanted this, he thought, wondering at himself. The night he'd seen Fourchet whip the young Mohammed nearly to death, he remembered he'd crept trembling into the corner of the bed he shared with Olympe and his parents. Remembered thinking, *I hope he dies screaming.*

He closed his eyes. *I hope he dies screaming.* He remembered his father holding him, powerful hands comforting him with their strength, and a soft deep voice saying, "God answers prayer. You want to be careful what you ask for."

"Where were you going to go?" he asked after a time, as silence crept over the kitchen. He glanced up, and saw Kiki had been listening. "With Quashie and Jeanette," he answered the question in her glance. "You never did say."

"Quashie wanted to follow the river north," said Kiki softly. "Past Vicksburg and Natchez and St. Louis, and on into the territories, and live in the woods, he said. God knows how he planned to do it. He'd never done nothing but cut cane in his life and didn't so much as know how to make a fish-trap, though I will say for him he was a good shot. Jeanette said no, it'd be better to go to New Orleans, where they could make a living. There's plenty of people in New Orleans who'll draw up freedom papers that'll pass if the police don't look at 'em too closely.

"Me . . ." She smiled a little. "I think I'd go west to the Texas lands, or south to Mexico. I'm a good cook, you know. I was trained up in town. I'd get a little money and open an eating-house, and have my own room with no one to share it."

Her voice broke off and her round little mouth

clipped together hard, as if at a memory. Tears swam in her eyes and she turned her head away fast and cursed as if she'd got a cinder in her eye.

"You loved him," said January gently, and Kiki looked back at him. "Gilles."

After a split second's hesitation she nodded. Then she made herself flash a quick grin. "That's not to say I wouldn't fall in love right away with some handsome Mexican with silver spurs on his boots and silver buttons on his jacket. . . ."

January laughed, Kiki's eyes smiling with him. Then the smile faded, and she asked, "What'll they do to her? Jeanette? Hang her?"

He nodded, sick again with his own impotence. He was sure that one of Thierry's keys, tucked in his blanket in the bachelors' cabin, was to the jail, but it would do him little good. Another of Jules Ney's sons or nephews had been left to guard the jail, keeping an eye on it from the shelter of the mill door. The workers walked wide around him.

"I thought of going out through the ciprière, and finding the cores of those Ashford apples that I know would be out there, proof that's the road they took and were nowhere near Catbird Island or wherever it was that Thierry really died. But no one would listen, and no one would care. I'll have to wait til Hannibal gets back. . . ."

His eyes met Kiki's.

"And he will be back," said January quietly. "Or send someone."

The cook sniffed. "If he thinks of it."

From the darkness came another cry, forming up into incoherent words, curses and ravings. "You're in it with him! You're in it together!" And later, "No goddam opium, you bitch! You want to see me as bad as you!"

"God send that he dies soon," Baptiste whispered, coming in a few minutes later. He crossed himself with a hand that trembled. "God forgive me for saying it, but for both their sakes, for all their sakes . . ."

"He's a tough old man." January poured the butler a cup of bitter, second-brewed tea. He should, he knew, return to the quarters to sleep, for Jules Ney in his calculating fashion was worse than Thierry, uncaring even for a position that wouldn't be his after the roulaison was done. It was nothing to Ney if slaves died to make his two-hundred-dollar bonus.

But he knew he wouldn't sleep.

"I was hoping I'd find you here, Michie Ben." Baptiste sat down on the bench beside him. Having come north with him on the *Belle Dame*—and presumably seen that he wasn't, in fact, a field hand, but the minder of the feckless scion of a well-off planter family—he had never treated January with the dismissive contempt of the other house-servants. Even Cornwallis, who'd also been on the *Belle Dame,* acted as if January were an animal, liable to break something or besmirch the beeswaxed floors at any moment, an attitude that January found in many ways worse than the fiscal—or patronizing—calculations of the whites. "Something Cornwallis said to me about you speaking some other language with Michie Hannibal . . . Did Michie Hannibal by any chance teach you how to read?"

He drew a folded sheet from the pocket of his rain-fleckered black jacket, and January saw written on it BAPTISTE GRASSE——TRIOMPHE PLANTATION——ASCENSION PARISH.

Hope glowed in the older man's eyes. "It's from my wife," he said softly. "Harry gave me this just now. She must have wrote me, same as I wrote her."

"False River Jones is here?"

Baptiste shrugged. "He must be."

Kiki started to speak, then turned and walked quickly away to the hearth, where she sat mending the fire. It occurred to January suddenly that the cook might know of the trader's whereabouts. She had, after all, her own wares to vend.

It was not lost on him, either, that salts of mercury was a town poison, something not obtainable by merely boiling up leaves or bark. It could be bought quickly, and quickly passed from hand to hand.

As January unfolded the sheet he saw again the woman's bright-colored dress, and the way she'd run through the crowd on the levee with her skirts gathered up in her hands.

"Beloved," he read. The spiky French handwriting was clear and the spelling good. Since it was forbidden by law to teach slaves to read or write, it was clear that Baptiste's wife had sought someone to write for her, as her husband had petitioned Hannibal.

"I pray God daily you are well and in a good place, and the people around you are kind. Monsieur Pierre is gone to France now with poor Madame, and I am with Monsieur Norbert on the Rue des Bons Enfants. He and his wife are good people. They wanted me to marry their coachman Emil but because I am married already they say I don't have to. Leon and Aurette are still with me and send their Papa all their love. I pray I will soon see you again. All my love, Odette."

"He's lucky." Kiki came back over to the table after Baptiste left with the letter folded close in the pocket next to his heart. Her hand flinched as she gathered up the used cup and saucer, set them aside.

"That his wife was sold to people who didn't take her children from her?" asked January. "Or make her marry one of their own slaves just to have everything convenient?"

"He's lucky to hear from them at all. So many don't. So many just . . . wonder."

"Do you know where he might be?" asked January. "The trader?"

Kiki hesitated, dark eyes shadowed in the firelight. Then she shook her head. "I have no use for him," she said.

Another howl of pain split the night, the desperate cry of a man pushed to the limit of what flesh will bear. January startled. But only Kiki's eyes moved, sliding sideways, gauging the sound as she would have gauged, by the brisk bubbling of water in the kettle, how long to leave eggs on the boil.

And as she turned away, January thought he saw her smile.

Shortly before dawn on Wednesday, the twenty-sixth of November, Simon Fourchet died. His young widow sent Jacko the groom with a note to Baton Rouge, with orders to locate Robert Fourchet; she dispatched another message to the Waller farm in New River where Sheriff Duffy was supposed to be staying with various members of his posse, giving an account of the new catastrophe.

In the predawn darkness, after the screaming at long last ceased, January climbed the little bluff above the new landing and took down the yellow bandanna from the branch of Michie Demosthenes the Oak.

He did not replace it.

It was time, he thought, to ask for help.

EIGHTEEN

January thought long and hard about going to Esteban Fourchet and saying, "I'm a free man. My name is Benjamin January and your father brought me here to find the hoodoo who murdered Reuben and Gilles."

After he left the kitchen, and before he trekked through the thinning rain to the bluff above the landing to remove the bandanna, he crossed the yard to the garçonnière and checked the underside of the bureau drawer where he'd concealed one copy of his freedom papers, and the underside of the armoire where he'd hidden another.

Both were gone.

He wasn't sure whether Harry could read or not, but almost certainly the official seals on both—beautifully faked by a friend of Hannibal's, who'd forged copies of the original documents themselves—would be worth stealing. The copy he'd rolled up in an empty bottle of Finch's Paregoric Restorative Draught and buried in a corner of Madame Camille's garden shed was still there.

But he thought about Esteban's dark unimaginative eyes, blinking into his when he'd told him his father was being poisoned; about the way the man's mouth had thinned and flattened, not in anger that someone would kill his father but in annoyance that a field hand would take up his time with nonsense. From the dark of the gallery outside the garçonnière he watched that tall, stiff-limbed figure help his young stepmother through the darkened dining room to her own room on the other side of the house, Agamemnon bearing candles behind them. Marie-Noël was still and silent, arms wrapped around herself, blond head bowed.

The papers, and the seal, weren't good enough to stand up to the scrutiny of one who'd assume them to be forgeries. And January could easily imagine Esteban saying—to Marie-Noël or to Cornwallis or to Hippolyte Daubray, who was almost certain to show up with offers to help with the harvest or purchase the plantation—"And one of the hands, that valet or whatever he is that Father's friend Sefton left here, is now claiming he's a free man! Claiming Father brought him here on purpose to spy! Did you ever hear the like?"

January was alone, in the midst of enemy territory, as if he had strayed behind British lines at Chalmette. Worse, he thought, because all the British would have done was impound him, believing no more readily than their American cousins did that a black man could be a soldier.

Whoever had poisoned Fourchet—be it Trinette or Marie-Noël or her uncle, be it Cornwallis or the mysterious False River Jones—was in too good a position to silence him, particularly if someone took it into their heads to lock him up.

He was a rabbit in an open field, he thought, coming down the bluff through the thinning rain. Around him in the darkness he could almost hear the howling of wolves.

Because of the rain, and the black darkness of

overcast sky, he took a small horn lantern from the shed in Camille's garden, to light his way to the bluff. And because he was carrying the lantern, knowing Esteban and probably Cornwallis at least would still be stirring in the house, he made his way to and from the bluff the long way around, through the cane-rows downstream from the house and up the batture, with the levee between the bobbing light and the windows.

The rain, never hard, ceased as he came down the bluff. The smells of the night rose thick about him as he crossed the low point in the levee above the old landing, closed the lantern's slide, and moved cautiously, silently, through the dark among the oak trees until he reached the cane. There was a cart-path a dozen rows in, that he could follow without a struggle. The sweet heavy greenness of the cane, and the cold clayey odor of wet earth; the harsh stink of smoke, where across the river someone had already begun to burn over the fields. The woodsmoke pouring from the doors of the mill, the gritty musk of boiling sugar.

The house was silent now.

Wet jeweled the cane, black walls rising up on both sides of him. Bright angry rubies flashed among the sprawled mess of undergrowth, rats darting, annoyed at the interruption of their suppers. Water beaded on the weeds between the rows, and the reflection of his lantern-light sparkled in the brimming ditches. A raccoon waddled across the row and vanished into the dark, leaving a dark, scuffed trail.

Farther on lay another scuffed line of tracks.

Human.

January froze.

The rain had barely ended—these must have been made since then. The weeds were too thick to hold any kind of edge or print, but the alternating brush of human feet was unmistakable. January followed cautiously to the little dry patch of weeds where the rain hadn't reached. The stalks were pressed down. He saw the place where a heel had driven the herbage into the mud.

Someone had sat here. For hours, it looked like.

Just sitting in the rain.

January felt the hairs lift on his nape. The spot was, he knew almost before he pushed through the cane to check, directly opposite the house.

Whoever it was had listened, since before the rain began, to Simon Fourchet's death-screams. And when he was dead, had gotten up and gone.

When Esteban counted out the cane-knives in the bleak predawn darkness, he announced to the hands that Michie Fourchet was dead. "You're all to pray—uh—for him," he said, holding his whip in those stiff fumbly hands, gloomy down-turned eyes surveying the faces in the mingled rubicund glare of torches and the mill doors. "Pray for his soul."

Behind him, January heard someone say softly, "Oh, yes, I'll do that sure." It was as if Esteban, so long under his father's heel, hadn't the slightest idea of how to behave or think in the face of either his death-agonies, or his total and permanent absence from his life. For the rest of his life, a part of him would still be looking over his shoulder.

And maybe all of them would. January's eyes sought the faces of the house-servants and the yard hands, gathered along the edge of the meeting-ground. Baptiste looked strained; the three maids clung together behind him, genuinely distressed. Agamemnon, holding up a girandole behind the family, had a tense stillness to him, the broken quality he'd borne since his beating almost a week ago.

Cornwallis looked sleek and smug. Kiki, like a bronze idol, but there was a flare to her nostrils and an unholy flicker of bitter joy in her eyes.

"He was—uh—a good master," Esteban went on, as if he knew it was a lie but couldn't imagine what else to say. "Bought you and—uh—cared for you and gave you enough to eat. Madame Fourchet has—uh—taught you all to pray, and I expect you to do it."

Around him, January sensed the tension ease. The worst, at least, hadn't happened. Esteban had told them to pray for Fourchet's soul, not informed them that they were all being held responsible for his death.

Yet.

As the drivers led the men out to the fields, Old Jules touched Esteban on the arm, murmuring something to him and gesturing at the jail. Esteban drew back, shaking his head. Ney shrugged and said more loudly, "It's nothing to me. He was *your* father."

Esteban winced, and looked away. Ney's pale eyes jeered. "Niggers killed your mama, too, didn't they?"

January wondered for the first time exactly where the boy had been, when his mother and baby sister were hacked to death.

At last Esteban muttered, "Have you—uh—done it—uh—before?"

Old Jules Ney nodded briskly. "You want me and my nephew to see to it?"

Esteban shuffled his whip from hand to hand and said nothing. Taking that for assent Ney signed to the stringy youth who'd spent the night in the shelter of the mill door, watching the jail. When January looked over his shoulder he saw Old Jules and his nephew walking to the jail. The younger man held a torch, a rope, and an iron poker.

"They asked Jeanette where was Quashie," Bumper reported later, his thin young face gray with shock. Nero, beside him, was shivering, as if he'd had to stop on his way out to the fields to vomit. "They tied her up by the wrists to the bars in the jail window. First Old Ney slapped her, back and forth on the face, and then he burned some wood and heated up the end of a poker and burned her face and her feet and her boobies. She spit at him."

He swallowed hard, and looked at his father, as if asking whether all white men were that way; whether this was something he'd have to cope with all his life. *Yes,* said the driver's eyes, tired dark eyes that had seen everything. *Yes, it is, my son.*

The men, and the women who'd left the cane carts to gather around the boy, glanced at one another, helpless and shaken. It was mid-morning, and if Jules Ney had been in the field then he'd have cut them all, for leaving the cane-rows to listen to Bumper's news. Esteban was visible, riding between the field and the mill. He'd already observed that Ney was pushing the cutters too fast—the stubble stood a good foot tall, instead of being chopped close to the ground—but instead of speaking to the overseer about it had simply told Ajax to do the best he could. Already the women were behind, from the cut stalks being laid down fast and sloppy any old way, and the carts were filled with cane-trash and weeds.

January stepped back to where Harry stood, arms folded, looking as if he hadn't spent the night tupping one of the housemaids over at Daubray. "Harry, where's False River Jones camped? I need to see him," he added, when Harry widened his eyes in innocence and began to protest that he had no more idea of the trader's whereabouts than the littlest bird in the trees. "You know as well as I do that Jeanette didn't have the first thing to do with poisoning Michie Fourchet. Jones may know something that would save her life."

Harry's wide, friendly mouth curled in wondering bemusement. "And you're going to tell old Duffy, and old Michie Ney, how they got the wrong hoodoo? I'll buy a ticket to that."

"Well," said January deprecatingly, "I'll see if I can get Michie Hannibal to do that part, kind of subtle-like. He's due back today. But we got to do something," he added, as Harry raised his head and scanned the stubble fields. There was movement in the direction of the mill, along the line of the cart path, Ney in his blue-and-red blanket coat returning at a gallop, lashing his horse with the quirt. "Once Duffy gets here, who knows who else they'll light on?"

Ajax had begun to chouse the women back to the carts. They moved stiffly, weary beyond bearing.

"There's a little bayou between Prideaux and Wildrose plantations," Harry said softly. "Bottomland where there was a crevasse in the levee couple years ago. Runs clear back into the ciprière. He'll be about a mile into the woods. Ney'll whip you," he added in a conversational tone, "when you get back."

January sighed, and said, "Fuck Ney."

"I'll tell him that." Harry grinned, and lifted his hand farewell.

"You do that."

They were cutting close to the ciprière that morning, and January had less than half a mile to walk before he reached the trees. He'd been on Mon Triomphe long enough now that he was familiar, by hearsay and instruction as well as actual practice, with the network of pathways, clearings, root-lines, and hummocks in those wet and marshy wildernesses that lay behind the river plantations; he'd heard often enough of the trail that wound north past Lescelles land to Prideaux. Ram

Joe's abroad-wife Nan lived on Prideaux, and Harry was romancing at least two of the house-servants there, plus a girl named Josette on Lescelles. It was a well-trodden way.

He thought about the dry mark between the rain-wet cane-rows. About the long screaming pain of death from mercury poisoning. About the wad of boiled oleander leaves and stems in the kitchen at Refuge.

About the blow-pipe, and the roundhouse below the grinders; about the vévé marks on the bedroom walls of the big house, and those in the kitchen at Refuge, and on the graves of two murdered men.

Thought about the evil that some men do, to all the lives that they touch.

He'd dreamed about the end of roulaison, in the few hours' sleep he'd had toward morning. About the harvesting of the last lone cane-stalk. On the last day of harvest one single stalk was left standing, while everyone went back to the quarters, washed up, and dressed in their best. The women took their hair down from its tignons and out of its strings and braids, combed it, and braided it up. The grooms would put ribbons on the mules, and the men got out all those things *les blankittes* didn't like to see them wear, the fancy waistcoats they'd buy from the traders, the bright-colored shirts. They'd all go out in procession with every cart on the place, singing—his father singing, January remembered, walking at the head of the line. It was his father, in the dream, who cut the last stalk, and rode back to the mill with it upraised like the spear of a vanquished enemy in his hand.

The men would take their turns still at the boiling and the grinding and the hauling of wood, but in the quarters that night they would dance. On some places—not Bellefleur, of course—the masters would set out food, sometimes join in the dancing, to everyone's joshing delight. Tomorrow would be easier. Tomorrow there would be less pain.

In his dream January followed the carts back, and saw that it wasn't a cane-stalk his father bore, but a sheet of cream-yellow paper, like Robert's letter to Esteban from the wood-yard. And he thought, *That's Mohammed's list.* The list of who was where when the mill caught fire.

So he struggled and fought his way through the singing crowd, all the way to the front of the procession, and into the burning mill. He saw by the firelight all the faces he'd known as a child, every one: his mother beautiful and young, with baby Olympe carried on her hip. Mambo Jeanne and clever Django and Uncle Zacky and all the others, and he cried out to his father, "Give it to me! Give it to me! It will save them all!"

And his father, turning, smiling, held out the paper. But when he unrolled it January saw, instead of words, only the triple-cross emblem of the Marasa, the Sacred Twins.

"I don't understand," he'd wept to his father in the dream. "I don't understand."

And his father had smiled.

They were burning over the fields at Lescelles. It was a small plantation, immediately upriver of Mon Triomphe, and the previous night while Fourchet lay dying they had harvested the final stalk and carried it in triumph through the drizzling rain. Fourchet had died, and they had sung and danced for one more defeat of the cane that was their true foe, not knowing of their white neighbor's death at all.

Now the men were burning over the fields. It was a difficult, smoky business. Men walked with buckets from the water cart around each field, to keep the burns small, so they wouldn't run wild, and smoke hung heavy in the air. From the edge of the woods January could see the women and the children skirmishing along the open unburned sides of the fields with clubs, to kill the rabbits and raccoons when they came darting out. Egrets circled above the flames, diving casually through the flames in quest of big lubber grasshoppers, and emerging soot-smutched to stalk about the stubble of the next field like grimy beggars in stolen clothes.

There was something Dantean about the scene, something of Bosch, the way a woman would brain a poor rabbit that was only trying to escape the fire. Or maybe, thought January, it was only a dreamlike horror, shapes seen through smoke.

He remembered wielding a club like that as a child himself.

False River Jones was a tall man, square-faced and potbellied. His lank gray hair hung past his shoulders, braided at the temples and tied with blue-dyed string. January found him by the smell of bacon frying, and coffee bubbling in a pot. He realized he'd been unconsciously expecting a small man, and a younger one. He'd expected a Kaintuck, too, so the mellow loveliness of the Welshman's singsong tones was a pleasant surprise.

"Dear, no, Ben that's a guest at Triomphe?" Jones held out his hand. "And a shabby shabby thing it was of your poor master to leave you that way, and in such hands, and him not returning!"

Jones shook his head. On the prow of the little lugsailed pirogue tied to a cypress knee, a black dog no bigger than a good-sized guinea hen dozed, chin on paws. The boat itself was like a miniature shop, jammed with boxes, packets, rolls of fabric, horns of powder, and firkins of nails. Rush baskets of eggs dangled from bow and stern, and a couple of pumpkins were lashed to the little shelter amidships where, evidently, Jones slept.

"You'd best watch yourself around that old villain Ney, should Master Fourchet grow any sicker. He's a man that wouldn't stick at taking off an unclaimed Negro some night. His brother's a dealer up the river in the territories, and that son of his has been known to run them up the river to him on his boat. An unpleasant family, the Neys, the lot of them."

The Welshman poured out some of his coffee into a pale green bone-china cup, which he held out to January, gesturing him to a seat on a deadfall by the fire. Beside the coarse woolen trousers he wore, and his greasy buckskin coat, his exquisitely fitted vest of purple silk stood out with the ridiculous grace of a lily on a trash pile: like a child's fancy-dress garment, too beloved to put off. "Poor Andy Ffolkes lost one of his men, out looking after Ffolkes's pigs in the woods. Maybe the poor fellow ran for it, but maybe too Ney and those sons of his had something to do with it. So you watch yourself, my boy."

January set the cup, untasted, on the log at his side, until he'd seen Jones drink his. "M'sieu Fourchet is dead," he said quietly, his eyes on Jones's hand, and he saw the fingers jerk with surprise.

"Dead! Dear God." The trader set his cup down quickly and crossed himself. "The poor soul. I knew he'd been taken with his heart, of course, and they got that sanguinary fraud Laurette from Baton Rouge for him. The man thinks of nothing but bleeding! Bleeding and puking, and a blister to draw the blood to the chest so he can bleed again! A disgrace, when modern medicine offers genuine cures like calomel and quinine and the scientific use of magnetism! A disgrace."

Jones shook his head again, and January asked, "Laurette doesn't believe in calomel, then?"

"A Goth," sighed the Welshman regretfully. "A true medieval barbarian." He sipped his coffee again. "Laurette bled him to death, I suppose."

"He was poisoned," January told him. "With salts of mercury, I think—which can be extracted from calomel, by somebody who knows what he's doing." This last statement was purely for the benefit of the trader's obvious prejudices, since calomel was, in fact, nothing more than salts of mercury, administered in whatever dosage the doctor might think appropriate. January had encountered physicians who didn't think the cure sufficiently "heroic" unless the patient's gums bled. If Jones subscribed to this view of healing, he wouldn't take kindly to the suggestion that someone had died of a *genuine cure* that modern medicine had to offer.

"Good God!" Jones scrubbed one surprisingly refined hand over his stubbled chin. "You don't mean it?"

"Did you sell any such thing to anyone along the river?" asked January. "Or know of anyone who bought such a thing? They've caught a girl on Triomphe, the overseer's concubine. . . ."

"Poor Jeanette, yes." His eyes filled with concern and he got to his feet. "And they think she did it? That's foolishness! She and Quashie went east to New River; they hadn't even heard of Thierry's death. . . ." He stepped over the gunwale, bent to extract a small packing box from where it was stowed under a huge coil of rope and a bag of gun locks. "Which was how they were able to catch her so easily. She went to get eggs from the Gallocher farm. . . ."

"Can you prove that? Testify to it?"

"Dear, well, I'll have to word it carefully, so as not to sound like I abetted the poor things. Worse than the

Spanish Inquisition, people are hereabouts when it comes to runaways." The trader opened the packing box, pulled out one bottle after another, holding them up to the sunlight to check the level of their contents. "I'll speak to Duffy tomorrow. He has a warrant out for me, of course, but we have our agreements. Oh, dear, yes."

Had the two bottles of opium that disappeared from Hannibal's luggage ended up here? Several of them looked like it, but Jones probably bought medicaments extracted from the stores of every plantation between here and Natchez.

"No, I don't even have salts of mercury here," the trader said at last, closing the box again. His face was drawn with genuine distress. "It's been quite some time since I had occasion to obtain any. And as for selling it, the planters generally have their factors in town buy whatever they need and send it along by steamboat. The Negroes have no use for the marvels of modern science, if you'll excuse my saying so, my friend. I can tell by your speech that you're an educated man—and as such it's doubly a disgrace that your fool of a master let them use you as a cane-hand, of all things! But surely you know that the average field-worker would rather be dosed with honey and slippery elm by the local mambo, than avail himself of Aesculapius's more standard blessings.

"And speaking of the local mambo," he added, replacing the box, patting the dog, and climbing back over the gunwale, "how is the lovely Madame Kiki? I have missed seeing her, this trip."

"She's well," said January, with a slight feeling of shock, of seeing a fragment of colored stone drop into its place in a mosaic. *Speaking of the local mambo. . . .*

"Is she?" Sadness crossed the expressive dark eyes. "I was so sorry to be the bearer of such news to her. Such a terrible blow to any woman. Please tell her, again, that if there's anything I can do. . . ."

"What news?"

Jones looked surprised. "About her husband and children," he said.

"Children? Husb—Do you mean Reuben, or Gilles?"

The trader shook his head. "Hector," he said. "A dear man with a laugh like Zeus on Olympus. A most amazing fellow—could bring down anything with a blowpipe or an arrow or those little throwing-sticks such as they use in Africa. Looked like he'd mince you up for his breakfast, yet he was as gentle and civilized a man as you could find on three continents. I thought if you were her friend she must have spoken to you of him."

"No," said January, as pattern-pieces shook themselves gently into place. "She told no one. What happened?"

"They both belonged to a Mr. Thomas Bezaire, in town. Five years ago he died, and his nephews sold them, Kiki to Mr. Fourchet and Hector and the children to a man named Bartholomew Lomax who had a lumber-mill downriver near Chalmette. Unfortunately conditions at Lomax's weren't good, and in any case I never thought the boys should have been put to the work—cutting cypress off a flatboat, working waist-deep in water for days on end. There was an epidemic of scarlet fever there last month."

He was silent, big hands toying self-consciously with one of the four watch-chains that measured out his belly in a pendant abundance of fobs. His brown eyes were turned inward, as if he saw that brave and courtly hunter, those lively boys.

Then he said, "I used to bring her news of them whenever trade took me down there. She was most terribly affected. I know her master was an unsympathetic man, but in the end he *was* prevailed on to separate her from that brute Reuben. . . ."

I have made amends where I could, Fourchet had said. But there are some amends that cannot be made.

He pictured what Fourchet's response would have been, had Kiki said, *I will not marry the man you've chosen for me, because I have a husband elsewhere instead.*

Oh, Kiki, he thought, seeing her eyes in the candlelight of the moss-gatherers' hut. Her face as she poured water from kettle to pot, impassive against everything the world had to throw at her.

He'd only sell it. . . .

"What about Hippolyte Daubray?" he asked, though now he knew what the answer would be. "I've heard that on the night of the fire in the Triomphe sugar-mill, he was out pursuing you up and down the river—was this true?"

Jones chuckled richly, almost hugging himself at the memory. "Oh, deary me, yes! My goodness, that was the most fun I've had in years. *Les frères* Daubray have always considered me a pernicious influence on the help—all of them do, of course—so when their coachman mentioned to me, the last time I stopped here, that Hippolyte had arranged a little ambuscade for me, I abstracted one of the old pirogues from the boathouse at the Refuge landing. . . . What a fisherman Mr. Raymond was, to be sure! I did it up with straw and trash to look much like my own vessel, then lit a lantern on the prow and waited just downstream of the landing until I heard Daubray approaching.

"He probably thought he was being so stealthy! Pitiful, really. I started muttering things like 'Why, what'll you give me for this here damask tablecloth, Michie Jones?' " The abrupt shift to field-hand gombo was startling, coming from that white, gray-bristled face.

"And all the while I kept moving the boat downstream, and Daubray followed me along the batture, tripping over cypress knees and getting his trousers wet while the fog got thicker and thicker. He must have pursued me for five miles before I slipped off the end of the boat and left him chasing it downstream for goodness knows how far, while I took a horse I'd arranged to have waiting for me and rode back to my own boat and my own customers."

He chuckled again. "I'm told Daubray forbade any of the house-servants to so much as mention the matter in his hearing. He promised a flogging to the man who made up a song about it, if he could catch him."

Later, January walked back through the ciprière, his mind turning as the buzzards turned in the air high over the burning fields. Circling again and again to Kiki. Others were as much to blame for her pain as Fourchet, but Fourchet was the one closest to her hand. And now Fourchet was dead, and Reuben was dead. . . . And Gilles, who had been good to her, was also dead.

She knew where the oil was stored, he thought. And Rose—who had a surprising streak of matter-of-fact bloodthirstiness in her—had told him enough times about how to make delayed action explosives for him to know that it could be done fairly simply, by one who knew how. The cook had never spoken to him, or to anyone apparently, of her life before she'd come to Mon Triomphe—"Stuck up," Vanille and the other women called Kiki. Meaning that she kept herself to herself.

The local mambo. No one to whom January had talked—not even the other mambos—knew she was that.

Was she clever enough to use the same curse-mark over and over when she'd marked the house, to make it look like the work of one copying by rote, not practiced in the art? She was, but his mind snagged on so intricate a fakery. Why pretend the marks had been made by one ignorant of all the various signs of cursing, if she'd kept her own proficiency hidden? Or was that why she'd drawn the blessing sign, the heaven sign, on Reuben's grave at that late a date? To let him, January, guess that she was, in fact, learned in the old ways?

But why purchase salts of mercury rather than make up oleander poison again? Either one, introduced into the medicine bottles, would assure the man's death, and the purchase—from a trader or another slave—would put Kiki into that seller's hands.

Unnecessarily.

Why break the cane-knives? Why burn the mule barn?

Foolish acts, absurd.

He shook his head. There was something wrong with his chain of reasoning. It looked good up to a point—Kiki certainly hadn't cared what happened to the field hands, at least before the fire—and then vanished when you drew close, like those illusions drawn by Flemish painters centuries ago.

The sun was halfway down the sky when he heard the singing of the main gang across the fields. He watched and waited until Jules Ney rode away, back toward the mill, then slipped from the cane into the line of women, gathering up the cut rows and dumping them in the carts. The woman beside him whispered, "You in trouble," but didn't call attention to him, for which January was grateful. He knew any overseer in the country would be within his rights to whip him—it remained to be seen what Ajax would do.

In moments the driver came walking along the row, whip in hand.

This, January knew, was a bad sign. If Ajax was going to ignore his disappearance for most of the afternoon, he'd stay at the other side of the row and then work him back in among the men, as he'd done before. *Why, Ben been back for the longest time, Michie Ney, I thought you seen him. . . .*

"You in a world of trouble, Ben."

January stepped from the line of women. "I understand that, sir. I'm sorry."

Ajax shook his head, tilted back his high-crowned beaver hat. "I don't know what the fuck you did, but Michie Esteban sent for you to come to the house nigh on to a half hour ago. I told him one of the babies had crawled off into the cane. . . ." He nodded toward the swaddled infants, sleeping restlessly or chewing their fists or bits of their wrappings, in the shade of a patch of maiden cane on the field bank. "That you'd gone looking for it. You better head on back there now. Herc'll go with you," he added, and signed to the driver, who'd paused to talk to Trinette. "Make sure you don't get lost."

There was wariness in Ajax's eyes, and no wonder, thought January. He knew men who took pride in being outlaws or rogues, but he had never been one of them, even as a child. The imputation of shirking, of lying and cowardice, stung him almost as bad as the cut of the whip would have.

But he only nodded, and started back toward the house at a rapid walk. A half hour, he thought, or more. . . . He thought he would have heard a steamboat's whistle, even in the ciprière, but couldn't be sure. It was impossible that it would be Shaw this soon. It had to be Hannibal.

But when they reached the house Cornwallis met them at the bottom of the back steps, and said, "Wait for Michie Esteban in the office."

"Yes, sir." January followed him up the steps and along the gallery as Herc headed back for the fields. A white man in the scruffy corduroy of a cracker was leading old Pennydip across the yard to the jail. The poor old woman was arguing, baffled, but when she tried to pull her arm free the man yanked her nearly off her feet. Two more whites—one of whom January recognized as the tall skinny youth in cheap jean trousers who'd been part of the posse that had captured Jeanette—came around the corner of the stables leading Mohammed. The blacksmith's hands were chained.

"What's happening?" January asked Cornwallis. "Don't tell me those fools think Mohammed had anything to do with—"

"Go on in," said Cornwallis. "Sheriff Duffy is taking in those that were on the place all those years ago, when the slaves rose up."

"That's crazy." January's heart pounded suddenly hard. "After all these years? Pennydip wouldn't have the strength to climb to the rafters of the mill to stuff kindling up there. Do they think she crawled in Thierry's window after the cane-knives? Or carried them to the forge? Mohammed—"

"You just wait in here," said the valet impatiently, and opened Fourchet's office door. "Mr. Esteban will be along as soon as he's done with Sheriff Duffy. And don't touch anything."

"No, sir." He supposed he should be thankful Duffy didn't show signs of hanging every bondsman on the place.

Cornwallis didn't motion him to a chair, and he had better sense than to even think about taking one. When the valet departed in quest of Esteban—whose muffled voice could be heard in the parlor, with another man's—January stepped over to the desk and had a quick look through the papers arranged with such scrupulous neatness on its top.

A half-written letter to Fourchet's agent in New Orleans, requesting that he make arrangements with the bishop for a funeral on the twenty-ninth. Announcements of it were to be posted around the French town accordingly; also the agent was to see to the purchase of the appropriate number of gloves, scarves, and candles to give to the mourners.

Robert's note that had incurred such wrath: Three dollars and fifty cents per cord for wood, indeed!

A list of slaves' names, mostly women and second-gang men, with prices jotted after them: *Nathan, $900. Jacko, $1000 (?). Cynthia, $750 (children?).* Figures in another column, adding and subtracting the sums paid out for cordwood. Esteban, January realized, was planning which slaves to sell to make up the difference.

A letter from an attorney named Dreischoen: *With regard to the evidence to be presented to the Supreme Court on the fifth of December next, regarding Madame Daubray's intention of gifting the Refuge lands outright to her son Gauthier . . .*

The door from parlor to dining room opened and January stepped back quickly, lest he should be seen taking an interest in the affairs of his betters. But it wasn't Esteban. It was young Madame Fourchet, pausing beside the dining table to break the bright green wafers on a folded sheet of cream-colored paper. She stood for a moment in the shadows of the darkening room, reading what was written.

Then she crushed the paper against her chest, her face turned aside, her mouth catching tight to keep her lips from shaking. She stood so, looking out through the French doors into the sunlight of the piazza between the house's wings. Her whole body shivered, and her breath came swift, like one who struggles not to weep.

With a kind of deliberate calm she smoothed the crushed paper out on the edge of the table, refolded it, and passed out onto the gallery as Esteban and Sheriff Duffy entered the room.

January felt his nape prickle at the sight of the sheriff. In the moment it took for the two men to cross the corner of the dining room to the office door, January stepped back, opened the French door onto the gallery, and moved one of the room's plain cypress-wood chairs about a foot, so that it could be seized and flung if, for instance, he had to make a bolt out the door. . . .

"This him?" Duffy's sharp little black eyes sized him up two seconds after January had returned to his respectful stance in the corner beside the desk. "Big bastard."

Esteban nodded. "Ben, what was it you—uh—told me yesterday, about my—uh—my—about Michie Fourchet being poisoned?"

"Sir, I was all wrong about that, as you told me." January bobbed his head, wishing for the thousandth time he wasn't nearly six and a half feet tall and dangerous-looking. He stooped his shoulders and tried to appear oxlike and cowed. "I remembered as how Michie Hannibal's cousin died of drinkin' mercury, and how he puffed up like that, and went off his head, and how his gums bled. And when I seen Michie Fourchet bleedin' from the gums, and him off his head, and I remembered how the folks 'round the quarters was sayin' somebody tried to poison him, and poisoned poor Michie Gilles instead, I just got scared, I guess."

He glanced from Esteban to Duffy, who'd relaxed—the cringing must have worked—and taken his hand from the pistol at his belt.

"But you're right, when I thought about it, that calomel does make the gums bleed, too. . . ."

"I thought you said it was the brother of your master's father-in-law," said Esteban, "who drank mercury."

January thought, *Fuck.* "It was, sir," he said, racking his brains to remember whether he'd given this mythological individual a name. "Michie Jacques and Michie Georges both was Michie Hannibal's cousins on his mother's side—"

"Lock him up with the others," said Duffy. "We'll get to the bottom of this."

NINETEEN

The sheriff was reaching for his pistol as he said the words, but he very clearly didn't expect much resistance. January slung the chair at him and was out the door onto the gallery without seeing whether it struck its target or not. Three long strides took him to the gallery rail and he swung over it, dropping to the ground as Esteban yelled, "Get him! Stop him!" to no one in particular, and Duffy bellowed, "Doyle! Waller! Catch that nigger!"

Because he spoke decent French and was reasonably clean, if shaggy, Duffy had been allowed in the house. But thanks to Esteban's prejudices against Americans, the sheriff's posse had been left on the front steps, chewing and spitting and playing mumblety-peg. If they'd simply run around the corner of the house the minute Duffy yelled, they'd have caught him.

But they didn't. January had bolted across the tree-dotted strip of land between the big house and the cane beyond Thierry's cottage, when they at last emerged around the corner, riding hell-for-leather on the horses that they'd run to, caught, and mounted. It was a good hundred and fifty feet and January leaned into it, legs driving with all his strength, hoofbeats hammering behind him, and a small corner of his heart zinging with the knowledge that there was no way they could catch him before he reached the cane, and he was right.

He plunged into the cane, slithering through the harsh dark green wall of it, praying he wouldn't tread on a snake. They'd expect him to head for the river. That bought him time, for he veered leftward immediately, inward toward the swamp. Once in the ciprière, he thought, they'd have to separate—and then like High John the Conqueror in the tale, he'd be able to take on both the lion and the bear.

He heard the riders behind him, still trying to drive their horses through the cane-rows. They were crackers, not planters, and had never had the occasion to learn that each row of mature cane was, in effect, a wall. He slithered through two or three, like a flea burrowing in a bale of cotton, then hit one of the narrow paths between ditches and ran, their curses fading behind him.

They'd waste time at that, he thought, before turning inland.

His heart was racing, after a week of slavery wild with freedom and with terror.

Two weeks on Mon Triomphe had given him back his old sense of bearings about distances, too. When he worked his way back through the rows toward what he thought would be about the end of the line of cabins, he found he wasn't far off; just opposite Nancy and Boaz's house, two or three only from the end of the row. At this time of the afternoon, the quarters were empty; everyone in the field, except for the sick and the tiniest children under Pennydip's charge. It was an easy matter to spring over the fence in the last garden in the row, to dart to the well-stocked pig-house, slip his hand under the rafters, and find Harry's rifle.

He threw himself under the house, groped in the long weeds there for the boards that covered holes. He was looking for powder and ball, and found none, although he did find a bullet mold and seven or eight small bags of lead scraps such as he'd collected from Arnaud on Daubray. Also three gourds of liquor, a bag of salt, a woman's blue silk dress, and two cane-knives. He took one gourd of liquor and the salt, in case he needed something to trade, but didn't dare stay to hunt more thoroughly. He was thinking very fast, like a hunted animal—aware that they would indeed hunt him like an animal. What he meant to do had to be done swiftly, in the hunt's first rush, before men came in from all over the parish. Already he could hear the voices of the pursuers, far distant and still near the river. But with rumor and fear of rebellion capping three years of accounts of Nat Turner's depredations, it wouldn't be long, he thought, before more men joined them.

He paused only long enough to help himself to the ash-pone and yams Cynthia had laid out under a pot, then slipped back into the cane, and started to run along the rows—Harry's liquor gourd bouncing and knocking against the small of his back. Once the men turned their horses toward the ciprière, they could travel faster than he.

Once they got Tim Rankin's dogs, he reflected, he had better be able to lick all four feet and JUMP . . . and thereafter keep his feet off the telltale earth.

A rider bound for Tim Rankin's would take the cart path that turned into the little trail he and Harry had used, that ran along the edge of the slough.

The initial search would be downstream, in the direction of Refuge. If he swung upstream—if he obtained a horse long enough at least to lose the dogs—there was a good chance he could work his way to the river in the next parish. Thereafter he could hide out on Catbird Island and wait for Shaw.

If Shaw was coming. January had been angry at Kiki for saying Hannibal might desert him, but now—on the run for his life—he wasn't so sure.

They would hang Mohammed, he thought, as he reached the shelter of the woods with barely three hours of daylight left and the riders close enough that he could hear their voices, sharp in the distance like bells. Jeanette, too, of course, and Parson and Pennydip. Probably old Banjo as well. Anyone who'd been on Mon Triomphe thirty-six years ago, when Gowon and his friends had burned the house, murdered the overseer and his family and Fourchet's young wife and infant daughter. Duffy was looking no farther than that, seeing nothing but the specter of slave rebellion, without examining the pattern closely to see whether it fit or only appeared to fit.

Well, you can't tell about niggers. Settling himself in the long grass of the slough, January could almost hear the man saying it. Reason enough not to search for motive, or logic, or any coherent chain of likelihood. A white man had been murdered by his slaves. Every man of them who held slaves—or hoped to hold slaves in the future when he was richer—would be uneasy, too frightened by the recent events in Virginia to consider that January hadn't even been on the place when the trouble had started.

And by flight he had branded himself guilty. Reasonable or not, there was little likelihood he'd survive capture.

You can't tell about niggers.

Well, he thought, leveling his gun on the path that led toward Tim Rankin's house, *you can sure tell about this one.*

He would have, he knew, only the one shot.

And the shot, if it failed, would give away his hiding place to the rider whose hoofbeats he could feel through the vibration of the ground.

Virgin Mary, help me get out of this. He was back in New Orleans, the mob of white men around him roaring with laughter as they razored his clothes off him with their knives. *Help me get that horse.*

There was an oak tree the rider would have to swing around, a low branch he'd have to duck, not twenty feet from where January lay. Smoke from the burning fields of Lescelles stung January's eyes and he blinked the tears away. His mind focused, narrowed, his whole being relaxed and waiting, concentrating on the single shot he'd have. He propped his arms on the elbows, leveled the barrel. *Virgin Mary . . .*

. . . help me kill this man?

As if someone had pulled the bung from a keg he felt the fire of concentration, the focus of his mind, leave him in a rush.

Virgin Mary, help me kill this man, who is your son as I am your son.

The hoofbeats were audible now.

He's a white man. He'll shoot me running, shoot to kill.

I need the horse. They'll have the dogs on me, hang me. This is my one chance. He tried for a split second to tell himself that he didn't really intend to kill the rider, but of course he did—he'd already figured out where to hide the body, in the long grass of the slough.

Anonymous rifle, anonymous bullet. Shaw's not coming, and even if he guesses he'll understand. No one will know for sure.

Except you. Will you speak of it to your son?

He wanted to yell at her, *Shut up! I don't have time for this!* But you didn't talk that way to God's mother.

And she was right.

Trembling, he closed his eyes. Heard the hoofbeats check and slow as the man passed under and around that perfectly extended tree limb. Heard them pick up speed.

They're going to get the dogs. The afternoon air hung silent, even the singing in the fields hushed. Bumper and Nero must have come out with the news that Ben had run away and they were sayin' at the house as how it was him that poisoned Michie Fourchet. . . .

Here in the ciprière the smell of cooking sugar was less, the smoke of the burning fields at Lescelles stronger, like sand in his lungs and eyes. *Blessed Mary ever-Virgin,* he prayed helplessly, *show me the way. If I'm not going to turn outlaw—if I'm not going to become the man who steals other men's food and liquor and salt just because I might need them to trade, who'd kill a man from ambush just to steal his horse—please show me what I need to do.*

The smoke and the scent of ashes grew stronger, a hot reek that stung and burned and drowned out all other scents.

January heard the dogs behind him as he strode north through the ciprière. He stuck to water where he could, wading knee-deep and thigh-deep and waist-deep in green stagnant ponds, the few turtles not sleeping in their burrows turning to regard him somnolently from the branches where they sat. Sometimes he could cut across the drier ground by making stepping-stones of cypress knees, or wading through hackberry brambles. Sometimes he was able to climb a tree and work his way through the branches monkey-wise.

But all this slowed him down. What he needed now was speed.

Sun slanted through the thinning western trees, sun blurred with smutty yellow veils of smoke.

January dropped from the trees and raced over the dry ground, the pack howling behind him. Through the trees he saw the air wavering as heat beat on his face, saw the quarter mile of ash-covered, smoking stubble-rows where the fire had already passed. The smoke nearly hid the men working far out to the sides with the water buckets, dim shapes, like demons in a nightmare. Smoke veiled the hot ruined carpet of earth and ash.

There was a ditch filled with last night's rainwater just beyond the edge of the trees, like a little moat delineating white man's land from the territory of runaways. January lay down in this and rolled, soaking his clothes; got up and shoved his stolen food and stolen salt into his shirt again, his little bundle of passes. He remembered Rose's experiments with alcohol, and regretfully left the liquor by the ditch after taking one big hard swig of it.

Then he picked up the gun again and ran.

His cheap brogans smote the hot ash and cinders of the field, kicked live embers, like High John the Conqueror striding through Hell. The buzzards ascended like cinders themselves on the columns of heat, grasshoppers bounced and buzzed around him, and the smoke wrapped him in scorching veils, rendering him unseen.

Virgin Mary, guard me, he thought, with the pounding rhythm of his flight. *Hide me in your cloak and keep me safe.* The wall of fire loomed ahead of him, heat growing, hammering. *As you covered over Shadrach, Meshach, and Abednego in the fiery furnace, so cover me. . . .*

He could hear the dogs barking among the trees as he plunged into the flame.

Heat and smoke and suffocation all around him and then he was through, with the leaping wall of gold and crimson flame behind him now, following him, and panicked rats and squirrels skittering madly around his feet. He ran along the row through smoke thick as muslin curtains, watching the fire that raced and crept over the litter of leaves, weeds, trash, and maiden cane. The long lines of fire extended before him on either side. Through the smoke he could make out shapes moving in the gloom, women and children waiting with clubs for the small game to flee before him, men with water buckets, ready to douse down the fire if it looked to be growing too big to control. Through the licking flames on his left January could see them, a hundred feet or so ahead. On the right the fields had been burned that morning. Last night's rain set up a smolder and smoke. Night was drawing in.

Before he got close enough that anyone could say for certain what they saw through the smoke, January veered right, springing over the spear-points of the cut cane-rows, dodging through the oncoming stringers of the fire. On the sides of the field, the line of fire was a reef of heat and flame, scorching his skin and making the water steam in his clothing as he dodged through its channels and plunged into the smoky world of ash and burned earth beyond.

There he dropped immediately to the ground, stretching out in one of the ditches that had bordered the cane-rows, so close to the burning field that sparks fell on him. He could hear the hounds baying, frustrated, in the distance, nearly a mile behind him now at the borders of the ciprière. Ash and burning buried his scent. Now and then a leaf of flame would gyre lazily above the retreating inferno, spin and loop as it was consumed and drift, still burning, to the ground.

"Sovra tutto 'l sabbion, d'un cader lènto," whispered

January, the words of Dante coming back to him. *"Piòvian di fuoco dilatate falde/ cóme di néve in Alpi sènza vènto."*

Flakes of fire falling like snow in the Alps when no wind blows.

Like the damned beneath that endless snowfall of fire he lay on the burned earth, waiting for the darkness to thicken. Dante had written those words concerning the Hell of the Violent. Those who kill without thinking. Who feel that their fear or their rage entitles them, and do not ask the names of those they kill.

The baying of the dogs faded. The voices of the women and children disappeared as their frightened game took shelter, like January, under night's protecting veil. Only the voices of the men remained, those few who stayed out in the night with the water cart, making sure the fires didn't get out of hand.

But he'd accomplished one thing, he thought, the red-hot goad of panic subsiding in his gut. Two, if you counted saving his own neck from the noose.

He'd laid a trail that definitely led north. Any escaping slave in his senses would keep on heading in that direction, instead of doubling back. The waning moon wouldn't rise til late, and in any case the sky was still densely overcast, with the promise of fog by morning.

Despite the darkness he had little problem in following the cane-rows riverward. The Lescelles hands were burning the bagasse from the mill in great heaps all along the levee, as was the custom at the end of roulaison. The yellow glare of the flame led him on, through thickening mists that held and condensed the smoke, until he seemed to be passing through another of Dante's landscapes, night sulfurous with distant fires.

Through the darkness came voices, singing, incongruously gay. Hands clapping time, and January's own heart involuntarily lifted. For these people, the worst was over. The backbreaking part of the job was done. Michie Sugarcane had been carried to the mill, defeated, as his father had carried that last captive enemy in the dream. They'd made it through again. They'd survived another year.

"Jump, frog, your tail gonna burn,
Jump, frog, your tail gonna burn,
Jump, frog, your tail gonna burn,
Be brave, it'll grow again. . . ."

Men and women called out, laughing, their breath gold clouds in the raw night. A woman danced between two blazes on the levee, waving her red tignon like a flag, and the mists glowed around with the fires. Everyone would get more sleep. Someone at least from every family would be able to get the overgrown garden-patches cleared, get the yams dug, spend a little more time cooking so there'd be the comfort of eating good food on your own doorstep again. There'd be time—January remembered, standing in the darkness beyond the range of that hot woolly light—for his mother to sing him and Olympe songs again, before they fell asleep. Time to wash clothes and air bedding, and keep the cabin clean. He heard the voices of children, darting and running around the fires and in and out of the darkness, and an ache came back to his heart for them, remembering his own joy at such times.

Joy more precious than gold, he thought, because there was so little of it, and it was so hard won.

Careful to stay beyond the range of the fire, cloaked in the darkness and the mist, he climbed the levee's shallow breast, to where the river's curve deposited a huge tangle of snags, grown up with brush during low water. The fog lay thick, and with luck would hide him, though the firelight from above let him pick his way among them, the voices on the levee a comfort.

Keeping just outside the range of the fires' smudgy light, he settled himself among the snags.

He'd have to wash out his clothing, he thought—it was black as any Miltonian devil with soot and burned dirt. That meant a fire, probably on the far side of Catbird Island and sheltered from sight of the river, to keep him warm through the night while it dried. With any luck Shaw would arrive tomorrow, possibly with Hannibal in tow. . . .

If Hannibal was capable of travel.

January's jaw tightened. In some ways, he admitted, Simon Fourchet had had a point about trusting those who used opium. Still . . .

He dug from his trouser pocket the wallet containing the passes Hannibal had written. As he took them out he toyed with ideas of how to slip onto the levee come morning and mix up soot and tree-gum into something resembling ink. It would take a clever line of talk, however, to convince a posse he wasn't the man they were looking for, if he happened to be cornered. There weren't a lot of six-foot, three-inch coal-black Negroes wandering free about the countryside. From the island he could keep an eye on the landing, always provided Duffy and his stalwarts didn't decide that the island was a good place to look for a fugitive.

In that case . . .

A flash of virulent green among the packet of papers caught his attention. January frowned, the color half-familiar, and flipped back among the tight-folded sheets. He'd thought the packet was a little thick.

Between the two undated passes a crumpled sheet was wedged, whose handwriting didn't match the fiddler's graceful Italianate script.

French handwriting. The sort of script, in fact, that

had been beaten into him at the St. Louis Academy for Young Gentlemen on Rue St.-Philippe, and nothing like Hannibal's very English hand.

January held the paper up, so that the light from the bonfire showed up the writing more clearly.

It was only Robert's first note to his father, explaining that he'd had to pay two dollars and forty cents a cord for wood from the woodlot of M'sieu Gottfreid in Baton Rouge. January remembered the stiff cream-colored stationery; remembered Esteban dropping it as Jeanette came stumbling over the levee, screaming her hatred at the man who'd raped her. Broken fragments of the seal still clung to the paper, not wax, but a cheap gum-and-flour wafer the color of an unripe lime.

. . . such a SHOPGIRL method . . .

Precisely like the second letter, which January had seen on Esteban's desk that afternoon.

The fastidious Robert might conceivably use seals that color if they were all that were available at a place of temporary lodging, but would he carry them in his luggage?

The first of the line of bonfires was about thirty feet from where January crouched among the deadfalls. Most of the singers were gathered around the second and the third, watching the woman with the red tignon dance. Carefully, January crept closer, prodding among the wet dark hollows for sleeping gators or snakes. In time he came directly beneath the blaze on the levee, the light of it brilliant above him as day.

The ink on the letter was black and even. He remembered thinking, in Esteban's office, how unusual that was, for the ink in a public lodging to be so expensive and so free of grit.

He's traveling north, thought January, turning the stiff sheet back and forth to the light. Going from woodlot to woodlot, from plantation to plantation, during the roulaison, in quest of wood, at this time of the year the commodity most in demand. He's staying in whatever inns and lodging-houses he can find. Presumably he's carrying his own notepaper. Maybe even his own wafers.

But he wouldn't carry his own ink, unless he wanted black splotches all over his nice white Parisian ruffled shirts.

And if he wouldn't be caught dead with colored wafers on his letters, and is using them only in the emergency of not having anything else, how conceivable is it that two separate establishments would have the same colored wafers? Or ink of the same color and consistency in its standishes?

At the same moment that he saw in his mind Marie-Noël Fourchet crushing a letter to her breast—a letter written also on cream-colored notepaper, sealed with a green wafer—he thought, *He wrote all three of those letters in advance.* Wrote them all in the same place, at the same time, and sent them north with someone else to buy the wood.

You're in this together, Simon Fourchet had said, dying.

You're in this together.

And January thought, without further conscious train of one idea to the next, *Refuge.*

It had been in his mind already, to find a plank or a snag or a floating trunk, and so paddle and drift south with the current to the boathouse at Refuge. False River Jones had spoken of M'sieu Raymond's pirogues stored there, and if for some reason Shaw did not make an appearance in the morning, a boat would be a useful thing to have.

Always supposing, thought January, as he poled

along close to the shore of the outward side of Catbird Island, there's a vessel there without a hole in the bottom.

And if there was, January very much wanted to have a look at the planking of its seat and floor.

The house Gauthier Daubray had built to separate his spouse from the rest of the family was dark. The boathouse lay a little distance from the weedy remains of the plantation landing, and January slipped off his drifting log and swam to it. Once inside, he removed his shirt—shivering in the cold—and covered the single window before striking a lucifer to locate the boat, then another to have a look at the planking.

As he had suspected, there were dark smudges and stains in two places on its bottom, about eighteen inches apart and much blurred and blotted with water.

Precisely the distance, thought January, from a man's throat to his belly. Slashed open with a cane-knife because Thierry, out hunting for Quashie and Jeanette, encountered someone who shouldn't have been anywhere in the vicinity last Saturday night.

The old landing, thought January. Easy to tie the pirogue up there, and walk to the house where Simon Fourchet's medicine bottles sat unguarded in the birthing-room. And of course Thierry had gone to that landing thinking to intercept the fleeing lovers. Robert Fourchet had slashed him, stuffed the handkerchief in his mouth to stop his cries, cut his throat, and left him sitting up on the batture while he went to the house; his neck and jaw had begun to stiffen by the time he returned.

The body had been taken up to Catbird Island for precisely the same reason January had run north, to lose himself in the fire of the burning fields.

To get everyone looking the other way. Upstream, not down.

You're in this together. . . .

The only question now was, *With whom?*

He groped his way through the pitch dark to the window and slipped his clammy shirt back on. The boathouse door was locked: He had to lower himself into the water again, and wade and swim around to the nasty mess of cypress knees and clinging weed that fringed the batture. Something moved in the water and he backed off to circle around and wade in at another point, and this was what saved him.

For in that moment he heard the quick scrunch of hooves on the oyster-shell road that ran along the top of the levee. Immediately opposite the landing and the boathouse the wheels slowed, and a woman's voice said, "To the left. There between the trees."

And there was no mistaking the soft, gruff tone of Marie-Noël Fourchet.

The vehicle—by the sound of it the gig rather than the Fourchet carriage—bore no lights. When January cautiously ascended the levee a few minutes later, no glimmer of any lantern showed up among the cane that had been planted before the house, though in the dense blackness he could sense a stirring, a restless thrashing as the groom led the horse along the narrow path. The house itself, small though it was, stood near enough the levee that even in the dense postmidnight darkness its pale shape could be discerned.

Even as he had seen it, thought January, twelve days ago, when the *Belle Dame* had passed in the darkness, and he had stood on the boat's deck, observing each isolated house, each rider on the levee, the stir and movement around the door of each mill, ignorant of what he was going to meet.

The intervening cane was too high for January to see the gig, but like the house at Mon Triomphe, this one was built high, a pale blur easily seen. The stillness of the foggy night was such that he could hear the faint, distant tap of Marie-Noël Fourchet's knock on its door.

Then the bright hot star of candlelight as the door was opened from within. It dimmed and wavered as she passed inside, died as the door shut again, closing her into blackness.

TWENTY

Not knowing how many servants Robert might have with him at Refuge, January spent the night in the farthest cabin of the quarters, working out times and dates, events and causes, in his mind. He devoured the ash-pone and yam he had with him, but was still almost sick with hunger when he woke in the chill black of morning. The fire-scorched skin of his face and throat and arms had begun to blister.

Only his trust in Shaw, and his faith in the parsimony of white men, kept him from risking a jail delivery that would almost certainly result in his own death. Whatever Esteban and Duffy might surmise about the guilt of Mohammed, Jeanette, and the others connected with the '98 revolt, it was extremely unlikely that Esteban would have potentially salable slaves hanged out of hand. He would hold them for a trial, in order to claim financial reimbursement from the state if the state ordered them executed. *By that time,* January thought grimly, *I'll have the evidence I need to convict Robert.*

And Kiki, he thought, with a stab of bitter regret, as

he slipped out into the overgrown garden-patch behind the cabin in quest of whatever he might find.

But if justice was his aim, he understood that it would have to be both. The Heavenly Twins, as in his dream. Alike in their hatred, alike in their crime, and in their punishment.

He had Hannibal's passes: They might get him by if his clothes weren't in rags. The surviving copy of his freedom papers was still buried behind the shed in Camille's garden. With the countryside up in arms at Fourchet's murder—and with operators like *la famille Ney* in the vicinity on the prowl for unattached human cattle—he couldn't risk it.

Shaw should come today, he thought.

Then he recalled Hannibal's extended absence, and his own days of waiting, and his empty stomach clenched with dread.

And if they don't?

If Shaw was sent out of town on some other duty? Or killed in a tavern brawl?

And a part of him whispered—the part of him that distrusted the white man because he was white, that had reacted to yesterday's panic, yesterday's wild flight—*Or just forgot?* Like the child with the hoop in the Place d'Armes, leaving his little black friend to weep.

Don't think this, January told himself. *Don't do this to yourself. Or don't do it today, anyway. He'll come.*

They'll both come.

It had been six or seven years since the provision grounds had been cultivated. But two cabins over, among the wild tangle of yam-plants and gourds, he found a couple of apple trees, and every garden had a half-dozen ground-nut vines whose coarse-shelled, oily fruit he husked and devoured by the handful. He remembered Rose saying, *I don't think I could pass myself as a slave because I don't know all those little things, the things you learned as a child. . . .*

Like how to run from men with dogs and guns, he thought. Like what to eat if you're on the dodge, and how to get yourself alive through a bad night.

But with that knowledge, he understood now, came other things. Things terror did to you, and the pent-up rage of the unfree.

He hadn't yet found anywhere near as much food as he wanted when he heard the clank and jingle of harness chains. From the direction of the deserted stables torchlight flickered, and in the foggy stillness a hinge creaked. Someone was getting out the gig. Cautiously, burningly aware of the single shot in his rifle, January worked his way along the line of overgrown gardens and corn run to seed, until he was within sight of the rear of the house.

Jacko came out of the stables pulling the gig, went back, and brought forth the small bay mare January recognized from Fourchet's stables. A few moments later Robert Fourchet escorted Marie-Noël down the rear steps of the house, the swollen-bellied young woman in her black mourning gown leaning heavily on his arm as if dazed or beaten down with exhaustion. *For Jacko's benefit? Or because the widow was truly overwrought?*

Robert helped her into the gig and sat beside her, leaving Jacko to take the reins. Simon Fourchet's younger son was neatly barbered and point-device as usual, bright green long-tailed coat pressed, his hat without smutch of dust, black silk cravat in a modish little bow beneath his chin. He carried a cloak folded over his arm, which he partially spread across his young stepmother's knees. Marie-Noël had drawn her widow's veil already over her face, and sat without speaking as the gig moved off.

That leaves Leander at the house. January shivered in the cold. *Always supposing the conspirators trust him with this kind of secret.* He remained where he was, watching the shuttered windows, the rear gallery, and especially the cistern beside the kitchen, for nearly an hour without seeing further sign of life, before he crept up to investigate.

In the kitchen January found evidence of many days' stay. A small sack of rice and another of cornmeal were stowed in the bin-table. A few half-burned candles had been left as well. A great clutter of dishes had been roughly scraped and left in the laundry room, alive with ants and mice. *No Leander.* January tried to imagine the valet being sent off to Baton Rouge with a pass and instructions to purchase the wood and dispatch Robert's letters, and couldn't. Robert Fourchet was pompous, vain, and greatly enamored of his own intelligence and erudition, but he wasn't foolish, and Leander had never impressed January as being trustworthy.

Hunting by candlelight behind the kitchen, January found cheese and fruit in a sunken oil jar, and these too he devoured. The vévé still on the wall made him uneasy, but it was better than the laundry room's stink. He wondered if he dared light a fire, for he could not stop shivering. The fog, at least, would hide the smoke from the chimney. He opened the cabinet door and brought in a few sticks of wood, but there was no kindling in the box.

Returning to the cabinet and skirmishing around the piled cords in quest of bark and twigs—there was no hatchet either, as he'd earlier observed—he became slowly conscious of the smell of decay.

No hatchet, but January remembered glimpsing a shovel near the back door. He got it, and saw that the earth that clotted its blade—of course Robert wouldn't clean it or probably have any concept how to clean it—was fairly fresh, within the last week. January stood thinking about that for a moment, then set his rifle in a corner and began to move the heavy cords of wood aside.

It didn't take him long to find the grave beneath them. It hadn't been dug deep. A few feet only; it was the wood that had kept rats or foxes from trying to dig up the carrion. January guessed at which end would be the head, and guessed wrong, uncovering in a short time a pair of natty shoes and slender ankles clothed in gray trousers that were unmistakably Leander's.

Bundled up beside them was a man's ruffled white shirt liberally stained with oil, and another one splashed with dried blood. An empty bottle labeled *Concentration du Calomel Spéciale, Solution d'Hericourt.* A careful drawing of the now-familiar vévé of coffin and knives. . . .

And a violin case.

January's breath stopped in his lungs.

Hannibal. Hannibal had been here.

His blistered hands stiff and cold, he tore the little black casket out of the earth. Inside, the battered Stradivarius was wrapped in its customary cocoon of faded silk scarves, with a hideout bottle of opium.

Damn them. Moving almost automatically he cached the instrument in the rough rafters of the shed, and bent to digging again. *Damn them to Hell.* He worked fast, illogically, as if his friend had been interred alive and he could somehow save him by finding him quickly. While he worked his tired mind probed and twisted at what might have happened, how Hannibal had come to get off the *Heroine* here, what would have made him stop and investigate Refuge. Under Leander's body the hard clayey soil was untouched. Still, he cleared up to the valet's waist in order to satisfy himself that no second body had been crumpled into the grave.

Nothing. He straightened, sweating, trembling with exhaustion and hunger, guilt and grief, and bewilderment.

I will see them hanged, he thought. *Robert and Marie-Noël. Whoever did this . . .*

He cast the shovel into the corner and pulled out the two shirts, the drawing, the calomel bottle, concealing them in a dry corner for Shaw. He paused for a moment, turning the bottle over in his hands. The label—one he recognized—was only confirmation of what he'd already guessed. Then he dragged the wood back over the grave, knowing enough had to remain of the valet's body to serve as evidence but too weary, too fatigued, to replace the soil.

Shaw will be coming to Mon Triomphe, he thought. *Robert will be there, and Marie-Noël. Shaw needs to be warned.*

Bone-tired, hands and face smarting from yesterday's burns, he flinched from the thought of getting the pirogue out of the boathouse in the dark, of rowing upstream and lying in wait off the island again. January left the woodshed, crossed through the kitchen to get the rest of the bread and cheese, and thought, *the rifle. . . .* And stepped out into the yard straight into the midst of Captain Ney and the crew of the *Belle Dame.*

Jacinthe Ney and the rotund little Spaniard who was his first mate had their pistols out already, watching the cinder-gray fog that enclosed the yard, and there wasn't a hope in hell of flight. January flung up his hands as the pieces were leveled on him, widened his eyes in astonishment—which was genuine—and terror—

feigned—and cried in what he hoped was a disarmingly frightened voice, "Don't shoot, Michie! Don't shoot poor Ben!"

Which almost certainly saved his life. That and the fact that he'd left the rifle behind. It stopped them pulling the triggers at once, and as two more men ran up, with dark-lanterns and guns leveled, January added, "I'll go back! I wasn't runnin' away! I swear it!"

Ney glanced toward the lightless house. The mate said, "The door was still locked."

"I didn't go near that house!" January protested, as his hands were seized and bound behind him. *Oh, please, God, don't let them look in the kitchen woodshed. . . .* "I was just lookin' around for somethin' to eat." With his soot-stained clothing, blistered face, and the dirt and grime that covered him, he hoped he looked sufficiently like a runaway, but he had to fight to maintain the look of wide-eyed innocence when, in the course of searching him for weapons, they found the packet of passes, and Ney pulled Robert's letter from it and held it up to the lantern's narrow beam.

"What's this?"

January shook his head. "It's a pass, sir. Michie Hannibal, he gave me a bunch of passes 'fore he left."

Ney and the Spaniard exchanged a glance. Behind them, three or four of the steamboat's crew were hurrying back and forth to the levee with wood from the mill's sheds. The boat itself must have been stripped to a skeleton crew, January thought through a sickened haze of dread—stevedores and stewards and handlers of cargo left elsewhere. The only men he saw now were ruffians, grim-eyed men whose interest quite clearly lay in making a dollar wherever and however they could.

"Get him on board," commanded Ney. "Get them both on board."

January was chained in the cargo hold, a good-sized

area immediately in front of the engine room. His hands were still bound behind him, his feet joined by a short shackle whose central chain was run through a ring in the wall about three and a half feet above the floor. This was a position favored among dealers and owners of rebellious or uncooperative slaves, for in addition to rendering the captive completely helpless, it was a position of total, almost childlike, humiliation. Only the thought that Shaw would be looking for him—that Shaw would in all probability be able to figure out from tracks and signs at Refuge what had happened—kept him from attempting to break away from them in despair.

Don't be stupid, he told himself, as the men gagged him and left him. Panic had nearly betrayed him once—*Don't let it do so again.*

They're in a hurry. Ney hates to dump steam. With the engine stopped they're risking a boiler explosion if they stay here a moment longer than absolutely necessary. They have wood from the mill sheds and there's no reason for them to open that kitchen porch.

And don't let Senecan aphorisms seduce you into thinking that the only alternative to slavery is death. You're worth a thousand dollars to these people. And unless they find Leander's grave, the VERY *worst that can happen is they'll sell you somewhere along the river. You'll smile and bow and look "likely," as the Americans say, and at the first opportunity you'll head for New Orleans, where there are people who'll testify you're a free man.*

And then you'll come after Ney and his crew with everything you have.

The thought allowed him to lie still, though the hammering of his heart left him short of breath. To listen and to watch.

On the voyage upriver from town he'd put his head through the cargo-hold door out of simple curiosity, in the same spirit in which he'd investigated the rest of the boat: One had to do something for eight hours besides maintain a running mental competition for the most ostentatious American dwelling on the lower river. The hold had been filled with crates, bales, and passenger luggage then, piled around the two long walls in such a fashion as to completely conceal the heavy wooden beams that ran, like chair-rails, along the middle of the wall. Exposed now, it could be seen that these beams supported iron rings every three feet or so, through one of which his own ankle chains were fastened. More chains hung from each of the other rings, long chains bearing many manacles: large ones to fasten around the neck, smaller ones for the wrists.

Other than that, and a couple of latrine buckets in the corners, the hold was bare.

January counted the chains. There were enough for a hundred and fifty, maybe a hundred and seventy-five souls.

"Stow those in the stateroom." Captain Ney's voice spoke very close to the open cargo-hold door and lantern light splashed through. "Make sure every man gets a pistol and a rifle. We don't want to take chances. And tell the men to step lively. We need to make Triomphe before daylight."

He strode past the door, pistol in hand. Two men followed, bearing a crate whose open lid leaked straw. As they passed the door one of the other men came by and took a rifle from it, and hurried on his way. "What about him?" asked a voice, and Ney replied something indistinct. *The stateroom,* it sounded like, so there was little chance, reflected January wryly, that they referred to him. "I mean, what the hell do we do with him? Why'd Fourchet keep him around? Why not just dump him overside?"

"Because, you imbecile cunt, his family knows he

was staying at Triomphe." Anger made the young boatmaster's voice clearer. "So that's where he'll have to be found."

For a moment January didn't understand whom they meant. Then the Spanish mate passed the door with another man, carrying Hannibal slung between them like a parcel. January heard the door of the stateroom next to the cargo hold open, the muffled creaking as Hannibal was dropped roughly onto the bed there. A man asked, "He be all right?" and the Spaniard replied, "With that much opium in him he'd better be." At the same time Captain Ney passed the door again, this time with a man dressed as a fireman or engineer, whose face bore the same long jaw, the same wide-lipped heavy mouth and pale eyes as his: a cousin or brother, part of the clan. Boots creaked, and above the jarring racket of the engines, which had all the while shuddered the ship's bones, January heard the roaring hiss of a release-valve venting steam.

"Idiots," said Ney, so close to the opposite wall it sounded as if he stood at January's side. "Is it so difficult to put in a pump that will take on water without the engine running? Make sure she fills properly on the way, and when we get running fast, you come in every five minutes. That's the pitch-pine wood over there. When we use it—if we have to use it—keep a weather eye on her."

"Think we'll have to, Jac?"

"I doubt it. But it's as well to be prepared to make a run for it. And as hot as pitch-wood burns, I don't want to end up scattered all over the territories in little shreds."

And from behind the opposite wall, Hannibal abruptly began to declaim Shelley's "The Cloud" in his hoarse, fragile voice.

"That's it!" shouted a voice from the deck. Juddering lantern light, and Ney passed the door again, striding toward the stair that led to the pilothouse on the hurricane deck above. January resumed breathing. Hannibal was alive. And they hadn't found either the rifle or the open grave.

More men passed, bearing the long poles with which the sternwheeler would be thrust from the landing and turned out sufficiently that the paddle could be engaged. The trees of the batture, mere sable cutouts, vanished at once. *Mon Triomphe,* thought January, wriggling tentatively in his bonds. To rendezvous with Robert—and possibly Marie-Noël. . . .

The chains on the wall jingled with the stomp and jerk of the engine. "River's rising, piss on it," said the Spanish mate, pausing by the rail outside the door. "Just what we need in the fog."

And turning, he banged shut the hold door, leaving January in darkness.

Robert, thought January, as he had last night.

Camille's son.

You're in it together, Simon had cried, dying, though it was clear to January that whether or not Robert had seduced his stepmother into complicity after his arrival, his original partner had not even been aware of him when she'd started *her* revenge.

But Robert had been aware of her.

And that was all that he'd needed. Even the dates fitted, the deeds that had seemed so senseless—the mule barn fire, the second and third time the harness had been damaged, the marking of the house with those childishly identical vévés, the knives damaged—all had taken place after Robert and his family had returned on the seventh. And they were senseless, if you actually were a slave.

But not if you only wanted people to think you were.

Not if your motive wasn't property, but vengeance.

The sign of the Heavenly Twins. Double vengeance. A double crime.

You sow the wind in your hatred, but somewhere a whirlwind is listening. Robert had stepped off the ship from France to be met on the dock by his older brother, with the news that the father he already intended to murder had remarried, to a young girl capable of bearing many more sons and daughters with whom the inheritance of Mon Triomphe must be divided. . . .

And that there was slave unrest afoot, to take the blame if one, or some, or all of the other heirs were to die.

It had, after all, happened before.

That Robert had returned from France with the intention of killing his father, January was almost certain. He'd have to ask Shaw—and he *would* see Shaw again, he reminded himself firmly—to get in touch with authorities in Paris to confirm the identity of the aged, opium-soaked prostitute whose apartment Robert had visited, not once but many times. . . . Scarcely the sort of girlfriend the young dandy would choose. Scarcely the neighborhood he'd select to visit, if it weren't to see his mother.

A good thing too that she did turn out to have died, the cook Arnaud had said. *He went nearly crazy tryin' to find out. . . .*

And of course, thought January, *in the end he couldn't. And he hadn't let that stop him.*

Saw her on the bed, and Michie Robert holding her in his arms. . . .

Had she died then? he wondered. Of drink and opium and the sheer ill-usage a woman endures, when she's forced to whore for her living? Or was Camille Fourchet still alive in that filthy Paris room, waiting for her son's revenge?

All she wanted was to go back to France.

Hericourt's Concentrated Calomel Solution was a proprietary brand, bottled by one of the large apothecaries on the Right Bank. Robert must have bought it shortly before embarking for New Orleans again. Had his father not been ill, there were a dozen other places where it could have been put, once Robert had arranged to be officially out of the area, with little notes from Baton Rouge and points upriver to prove it.

A young man who, when staying at Mon Triomphe as a child, had shared his studies with the brightest scion of the disreputable Ney clan would have no lack of accomplices.

In the darkness of the hold, with the lurch and jerk of the engine rattling his bones and the stealthy scurrying of the inevitable rats along the walls, January thought about Marie-Noël, clutching Robert's clandestine note to her chest. Bidding her come to Refuge, of course. Baiting the hook with words of love.

Did she really think he'd let her unborn child live? Or was she so eager to extricate herself from that violent and abusive old man that she didn't consider what risks involvement with so calculating a murderer might entail?

Kiki had said, "I wouldn't be surprised if those children of hers that died didn't die of something else. . . ." Little knowing how truly she spoke.

Even then Robert had hated his father and his family, for his mother's sake. Even then he had wanted her love—and his father's money—all to himself.

The bone-jarring rhythm of the engine shifted and eased. With a howling hiss of steam the boiler was dumped—January had heard many times that engineers could tell the state of the boiler merely by the sound, scorning those fearful souls who argued for the installation of gauges. The jolt of the pistons and the heavy splash of the wheel ceased; the wheelhouse bell clanged distantly. They'd come opposite the Mon Triomphe wharf, and were being towed in.

He twisted against his bonds. The leather thongs around his wrists were cuttingly tight and double-wrapped between them in a figure-of-eight—feats like "wriggling free of his bonds" and "finding a convenient fragment of broken glass," performed with such aplomb by the likes of Leatherstocking and Ivanhoe, were clearly the province of mighty-thewed, younger, and gray-eyed men. In any case neither the Deerslayer nor the Knight of the Oak had ever been chained with his feet above his head, a position in which it was difficult to do anything except hope that the beautiful Indian maiden (or Saracen girl) whose eyes he'd met for an unforgettable moment during capture would hurry up and steal down those dungeon stairs. . . .

"And make it quick," snapped Ney, from the stateroom door nearby. "We can't afford to let the engine go off its steam."

Within a very few minutes January heard the scuffling tread of feet on the deck. Bumper's voice asked, "Mama, what's goin' on? Michie Esteban wouldn't really sell off everybody on the place. . . ."

The door was opened.

"Ben!" cried Hope, the first one through, with her boys at her sides and her youngest baby tucked in the fold of her shawl. Washed-out dawnlight flooded in around her. "Ben, what . . . ?"

"Don't mind him," said Jules Ney's nephew who'd guarded Jeanette. "Get over there. You—next to her. You . . ."

They were pushed into line. Chained, neck and

wrists. Even Marquis, gasping with the pain of his burns, and Boaz, carried by his wife and his friend Philippe. The other sick men, Java and Dumaka, staggering. January counted, tallied in his mind, as each slave was herded through the door by men with rifles and pistols in hand, men who locked them into their manacles, shoved and thrust them as if they had been sheep.

All of them were there. Cornwallis speechless with outrage, Agamemnon trembling with silent fury at this second betrayal. Eve shrinking fearfully from the men who pawed and fingered her. Ancilla holding close to her surviving son Ti-Rod and trying to catch her husband's eye. Ajax and Rodney and Herc doing their best to keep everyone in order, knowing that to do so was often the only way of averting wholesale, unpredictable retaliation.

Mohammed and Parson, half-carrying old Pennydip. Jeanette stumbling in chains, her face and half-bared breasts marked with burns. Mohammed and Baptiste went immediately to move January out of the way of the crowding feet, the shuffling bodies that filled the hold more and more tightly. "Get away from him!" snarled the mate. "You leave him gagged, you hear?"

"Yes, sir," said Mohammed, stepping back. His face was swollen and caked with blood and his nose had been broken. "Yes, sir."

"Can we take a couple, sir?" one of the deckhands asked discreetly, running a hand over the back of Eve's neck. "Just for an hour or so?"

"I'll ask." He might have been speaking of books in a lending library. "Let's get under way first."

"You trust that Napoleoniste's brat?" Old Jules Ney paused outside the door with his son, watching someone outside the range of January's sight.

"Shouldn't I?" retorted the younger man. "All Fourchet wants is to be out of this country. A man may live comfortably enough in Paris on fifty thousand dollars, if he invests it wisely. And if he doesn't . . ." Captain Ney shrugged. "They're all healthy and strong, except for a few old crocks. Those we can just drop off the back of the boat. Where else would we get prime blacks for three hundred dollars apiece? Revenge is a wonderful thing, *mon père*."

And old Ney sniffed, as Robert's voice said, "Jac," and both the captain and the old man stepped away. January strained his ears to listen, but the noise in the hold was too great, children crying, men muttering and whispering.

"This is ridiculous!" Agamemnon sobbed, "Absurd! I don't care how much damage has been done by this—this hoodoo! Michie Esteban wouldn't sell all of us! I tell you that woman is forcing him to do it!"

"How would she do that?" demanded Ajax, exasperated. "I suppose she's forcing Michie Robert to do it, too. . . ."

"He wouldn't sell his own children's mammy!" raged the valet. "His wife's maid!"

"You shut up in there!"

There was quiet, through which January heard Robert say, ". . . found her in Paris. In a garret in a street in the Saint-Antoine district, near the Halles, the worst of the worst. She was so sodden with gin she barely knew me! I was with her when she died. I swore then . . ."

"I'd have heard something of it, if they were planning this!" hissed Agamemnon.

"Like they tell you everything?" demanded Cornwallis scornfully.

"What's gonna happen?" pleaded Yellow Austin's

daughter Tanisha, clinging to Baptiste's hand. "We all gonna get sold?" Boaz coughed desperately, and those around him propped him gently so he could breathe.

Boots clunked on the deck; the stateroom door creaked again. Two deckhands carried Hannibal past the cargo-hold door, and those standing nearest the door looked back fast at where January lay in his corner, eyes asking, scared. Ney, Old Jules, and the engineer walked over and gave some low-voiced instructions, then followed them out of sight, and a voice called, "Get ready to cast off. Let's get out of here." From the engine room came a sharp clanging, the hiss of steam immediately cut off, and through the wall January heard the engine room door open and a deckhand say, "We're ready to cast off, M'sieu Fourchet."

"I'll be along," yelled Robert, over the dense rattle that shook the engine, and another hiss of steam.

The deckhand's boots retreated. More steam, thinning away to a frail piercing whisper.

What's Robert doing in the engine room?

" 'Sieu Robert, the Captain's gone ashore," said the engineer's voice, and January saw him outside the cargo-hold door, looking back toward the stern as Robert, evidently, emerged from the engine room. "You want to help him finish at the house?"

"Good Lord, why should I do that?" The young man's voice was thick with revulsion. "The place was a purgatory to me. I was married to the silly bitch against my will; her brats were spoilt little grubs, and the world will be well rid of the lot. Let them all roast together."

There was silence, or as much silence as there could be with everyone in the cargo hold whispering among themselves, murmuring fear and apprehension under the deckhand's eye. Outside, evidently speaking to the look on the engineer's face, Robert added, "Behind every great fortune there is a great crime, my dear Theo. Surely you know that."

And Ney's voice: "Done." The gangplank creaked. "You coming with us?"

"I think not. I have tickets on the *Anne Louise* Saturday, for Bordeaux. Adieu, my dear Jac, and thank you for everything. You have truly been the agent of my liberation. Given my overwhelming grief at the loss of my family, I think I'm not going to be able to bear to return to this benighted province anytime soon."

Cries on deck. Men running past with poles, and then the soft jostling as before, as the boat was thrust away from the landing. Ajax, standing nearest the door, gasped, and at the same moment the deckhand shoved him deeper into the room and went out past him, closing and bolting the door.

"What is it?" asked someone softly.

The driver whispered, "My God. That white man shut the door quick so I couldn't see for sure . . . but it looked to me like they set fire to the house."

TWENTY-ONE

"Ben, what the hell's going on?" Kiki knelt beside him, wrenching and picking at the knots of the bandanna they'd gagged him with. "Michie Robert and M'am Fourchet drove up in the gig early this morning. . . ."

"M'am Fourchet come to me late last night and told me to take it out." Jacko crowded as close as his chains—fastened to the opposite wall—would allow. "We drove over to Refuge and Michie Robert was there. . . ."

"Old Michie Jules had us all out and waiting," put in Gosport. "He knew that boat was coming. He had to, the way he wouldn't bring out the cane-knives, and wouldn't have the second gang go into the mill, nor let the night gang go back to their cabins."

The knots were tough and had been tied by experts. January, whose mouth had been stuffed with another rancid and sweat-stained bandanna before the gag was tied on, wanted to scream with frustration.

"I swear Michie Esteban didn't know what was going on." Baptiste knelt beside Kiki, gently working at the knots in the thong around January's wrists, so that the two servants' elbows got in each other's way and January felt like everyone in the hold was standing on top of him. "He asked me what was going on out there, when he looked out and saw the men still standing."

"Michie Robert and M'am Fourchet came up to the door and spoke with him alone," offered Ariadne, almost invisible in the dense gloom of the hold. Her chains clinked as she tried to get nearer. "They had us all leave the dining room, and when we came back in, Michie Esteban said we was to get all the house-servants down to the mill. I don't understand . . ."

"You little imbecile, he had a gun on her," snapped Cornwallis.

Everyone fell silent in momentary shock. The valet's chains jangled with his gesture of annoyance.

"He has to have," Cornwallis went on. He was barely to be seen in the dimness, but his neat cravat had come awry and his sleek hair was mussed. "You saw the way he stood next to her, the way he never let her away from him. You saw the cloak he had over his arm. He had a gun under the cloak and I think he told her—and Mr. Esteban—he'd shoot her if they didn't cooperate. She wasn't herself, you could tell that. I'd say he gave her opium last night to keep her quiet, if as you say she went to meet him at Refuge. You've seen how he's been making up to her, making love to her. . . ."

"Tcha!" said Hope, and Henna said, "I thought it was sad. That he loved her—"

"He no more loved her than he loves his wife," said the valet disgustedly.

"He came in the nursery himself." Marthe's voice sounded shakily from another part of the dark room. "He had M'am Fourchet with him then, too, and yes, like you said, he held onto her close so that cloak he carried was right up against her side. The children were sleeping and I said, did he really want me to leave them? Their mama's mighty particular about that. But he said yes, he'd see to their mama. You don't think he'd harm his own children? I know what Ajax says he saw, but he wouldn't—"

"You know as well as I do how he hates those children," said Vanille's sullen voice. "You watch him with them sometime. He doesn't even want to touch them."

"I know," said the nurse, grieved that it had been so. "Poor things. I know Jean-Luc can be a trial, but . . ."

"Jean-Luc is a nasty little beast." That was Agamemnon. "And Fantine . . ."

"Fantine's just timid."

"We can't argue about that now." Ajax's deep voice cut through the rising tones of frightened anger. "They're burning the house, I tell you! I saw one of those white deckhands throw a lighted lamp in through the window of the parlor. I saw the smoke rising."

"But not with the children in it!" Marthe's voice was pleading. "He wouldn't. . . ."

"He would and he did." January gasped as Kiki dragged the bandannas out of his mouth. "He came back from Paris wanting revenge on his father for his mother's death—Who here knew his mother? Did she really die in New Orleans, or did she go to France?"

"She went to France." Old Pennydip's voice came shakily over the stirring and the din around Marthe and the handful of others—Mundan the gardener, Musenda the groom, Henna and Ti-Jeanne—who had begun to cry out, trying to come up with a way to go back and save the women, the children, the men who had been left behind in the burning house.

"We've got to do something! We can't let them die!" they kept saying, though January was grimly aware that, chained in the hold of the fast-moving steamboat, already several miles upriver, there was in fact nothing any of them could do. That the Fourchets—and Hannibal—would die. Were probably dead already.

There remained only retribution.

And he, January, was the only person in the entire room who would have even a chance of testifying in court as to the sequence of events.

"After that summer when her two babies died, her two little sons, M'am Camille wouldn't live on Triomphe no more, and she went with her daughters to New Orleans," Pennydip went on in her soft slow voice. She was probably as old as Mambo Hera and had seen too much of death to be drawn into the clamor around her. "She lived in the town house there for a year or two or three, until Michie Robert was married—and my, what a to-do there was about that!"

"Michie Fourchet made some kind of deal with Michie Prideaux, M'am Hélène's daddy." With one eye swollen shut and blood caked on his nose and mouth Mohammed looked like a nightmare, but his voice was still steady and calm. "They were going to buy out Lescelles and divide the land between them, or some such plan, only it never came off."

January gritted his teeth, trying to listen, trying to focus his mind on the pieces of the puzzle, instead of thinking of his friend lying like a pagan sacrifice on Fourchet's pyre. They'd drugged him—probably forced everyone in the house to drink opium before they fired the place. . . . *There was nothing I could have done,* he repeated to himself, over and over, above the creaky run of old Pennydip's voice. *Nothing.*

Except check the house first instead of the kitchen.

Even then, he thought, that would only have meant Ney and his men would have killed him the moment they caught him, instead of keeping him to sell.

It crossed his mind that, opiated as Hannibal was when they'd carried him ashore, he had probably not suffered.

But his whole body hurt with it, with sorrow and fury.

I will kill him, he thought. *Somehow, I will destroy Robert Fourchet. For all that he has done.*

"Well, just after the weddin' M'am Camille took all the jewelry old Michie gave her and sold it, and ran off to Paris," continued the candle-maker. "I never heard such a yellin' and cussin' and carryin' on in my life. He say, 'She dead to me. I have no wife.' "

"Easy enough to say," put in Mohammed, "until you want to have a wife again. When he was courting the young Madame—if you can term it courting—he asked his lawyers to find out whether Madame Camille was alive or dead."

"For a long time they couldn't, I remember that." Kiki remained squatting beside January's head. "Gilles told me it drove Michie Fourchet just about crazy, that he couldn't marry the girl he wanted. 'What's it to me, if the other bitch is alive or dead?' he'd yell. I'd hear him, clear across the yard. Then all of a sudden everybody was saying, *Oh, yes, M'am Camille's really dead, it's all all right.* Myself, I think Michie Fourchet might have just made that up."

"He did, or his lawyer," said January grimly. "Because Robert found his mother in Paris in September. Dying."

"Oh, my lord, was that M'am Camille?" gasped Vanille. "That nasty old whore he went to see?"

"I think so, yes."

In the darkness Marthe's sobbing sounded very

loud, and Henna cried out, to no one in particular, "Is that all you can think of?"

"They took the horses," said Musenda, his voice shaking with hurt, for the carriage team and the riding-horses were like his children. "Just led them away like cattle. That Jac Ney, he has no care for a good horse, he'll sell them for what he can get, to Americans. . . ."

"Then you're saying it was Mr. Robert who poisoned his father?" Cornwallis looked down at January, his long arms folded over his black-coated chest. "Out of revenge?"

"Yes. Knowing that there was already unrest on Mon Triomphe. Everyone in the parish can testify about the voodoo marks, the destruction, maybe a rebellion brewing. When the house is found burned, and the family dead—all except Michie Robert, who as everyone knows was away in Baton Rouge—and every slave on the place missing, what do you think Sheriff Duffy's going to say? Thank you!" January added, pulling his newly freed arms around from behind him and rubbing the deep welts on his wrists.

"That's why he's selling us?" asked Ajax, squatting beside January. He moved his hand, to reach out to where Hope and Eve stood, but could not stretch his arm so far. "Just to make us all sort of disappear so he can say it was a slave revolt?"

"But what are we going to do?" pleaded Marthe, twisting her hands. "What about the children? About poor Madame? Poor Michie Hannibal? We have to do *something*!"

"Like what?" demanded Jeanette roughly.

"If Ney sells you off far enough," said January, "who's going to hear? Who's going to come around and ask?"

They looked at one another. Held one another close: husbands and wives, mothers and children. A man's footsteps creaked past the door: Eve flinched, as if at the memory of a man's hand on her neck.

"You know a lot about it," remarked Cornwallis.

January nodded, wishing it were possible to stand and confront the man's sardonic eyes, rather than remain, perforce, on the floor with his feet chained in the air. He'd never liked the valet. "That's why we were there," he said. "Michie Hannibal and me." And his voice stuck over the name. "Tell me one more thing, Mamzelle Pennydip. Was Robert on Mon Triomphe, the summer those two babies died?"

"Robert was there, yes," mumbled the old woman promptly. "He'd been left in school in town but he came up on the boat, summers. He spent most of his time there runnin' with Jac Ney, no matter what his daddy said of them Neys bein' no good."

There was silence, as men and women mutely pieced together the evil details of the whirlwind they'd seen only from the outside.

"And did you ever find who else was causing the trouble before Michie Robert came home?" Cornwallis tilted his head, managing to look superior in spite of the chains on his wrists and neck. "Who caused the fire in the mill? And poor old Reuben to die?"

"I think a lot of people wanted revenge," January replied. "But that's not the problem now. The problem is: Michie Robert is too smart to think he's going to get away with this, if any of us survives."

In the shocked hush that followed, the clatter and jerk of the engines was horribly loud.

"Is there any water in here? Any food?"

But the cargo hold was bare, save for the two latrine buckets—chained into the corners where they stood—and the wall-rings and chains themselves.

Gosport volunteered, "I saw barrels of water and what looked like food—pots of beans and rice and that—when we come past the galley doors. You think he'd put poison in that?"

"I wouldn't put it past him." But as the words came out of January's mouth he didn't believe them. Poisoning one man was one thing. Poisoning a hundred and fifty—or, if Robert planned to deal with the crew as well, nearly two hundred—was chancy, uncertain, and would probably take more time and certainly more poison than Fourchet had at his disposal. Robert would need to be sure, if he were doing anything at all. It would be better to—

"Fuck damn!" said a voice on the other side of the wall. Metal clanged harshly in the engine room. "Roger? Roger . . . Let Jac know we've got a problem with the pump, and with the steam cutoff to the boilers."

Quick-striding feet. The recollection of the sound of steam venting in the engine room not long ago, of rattling pipes . . .

Robert's voice on the other side of the wall.

January turned absolutely cold inside.

At the same moment the footfalls, coming from the engine room door and heading for the steps, checked, scuffled, and there was a thump, as if someone had kicked the wall near the door. Then the slap of the bolt shooting back, and the door opened to frame Abishag Shaw's gawky figure against the light-soaked fog of morning.

The American had a rifle slung over his back and another in his right hand. In his left was a skinning-knife, and his left arm was hooked around the chest of a dying deckhand whose cut throat spouted blood, which dribbled down his forearm. Those nearest the door—Ajax, Juno, Agamemnon, and Nathan—all sprang back as the red liquid splashed their clothes, and Nathan cried out, "What the—?"

"Shut up!" hissed both January and Cornwallis at once, as Shaw dumped the body onto the floor, set his rifle against the wall beside the door, knelt to reach into his victim's pockets. . . .

Eve screamed.

Another deckhand appeared in the doorway, leveled a pistol at the back of Shaw's head, and fired.

The hammer clacked noisily and harmlessly in a misfire and Shaw came up off the floor like a mountain-cat, catching the man's shoulder in one blood-slick hand and striking upward under the chin with an elbow like a corncob, full force. The deckhand's feet lifted off the planking with the impact of the blow and January knew the man was dead before he landed.

"Search him," ordered Shaw, turning as shouts rang out overhead. The door at the other end of the hold flew open and two rifles were thrust in. One misfired; the other, aimed over the first shooter's shoulder, tore a hole in the panels of the wall to the right of Shaw's head. Shaw brought up both his rifles like pistols, firing each one-handed—January was amazed he didn't break his wrists. He flung one to January and a powder-flask with it, pulling out his pistol as a man appeared in the doorway behind him; there was a deafening report from somewhere outside and the man fell. A moment later Quashie swung through the door, one of Harry's rifles in his hands.

Harry was already loading Shaw's other rifle, as January, propped awkwardly on his elbows, measured out powder, ball, wadding . . .

"Engine room!" yelled January. "Robert disabled the pump to the boiler!"

Shaw said, "God bless it," and tried to duck out the

door, only to be driven back by a shot from outside. Meanwhile the hold was pandemonium, men and women flattening to the floor, to the walls, clutching children to them or pressing them to the boards beneath them, defending them with their bodies.

"Does that mean the boat can't go, if there's no steam?" Baptiste crouched against the wall as Quashie ripped one of the dead slavers' pistols from the man's belt, fired as the opposite door started to open again, the ball tearing a hole in the wood. Two shots from outside cracked through the wall over January's head; he heard one of the balls clang against something metal.

"It means the boilers will blow." January held out the loaded rifle to Shaw by the barrel, tugged one of the corpses closer to him, and relieved it of two enormous scalping-knives. "Ajax, Random, start cutting at the beam over the bolts. Engine room's on the other side of that wall," he added, as Gosport relieved another corpse of its blade. "Score the wood and maybe we can ram or kick through. . . ." He dodged and twisted as another shot from outside holed the wall again. Ancilla screamed, the splinters driven by the ball piercing her leg like darts. "They fired Mon Triomphe. . . ."

"Been there." Shaw had shoved one of his corpses into the doorway to prevent the men outside from simply slamming it and shooting the bolt, something that had been done on the other side of the room, though Quashie, grim-faced and filthy, remained there to guard against a sortie. "They's all all right. Ney!" he yelled. "Ney, God damn it!" and returned fire against two shots and a clicking fusillade of misfires, as if three-quarters of the rifles and pistols in possession of Ney's men had been bewitched. "Damn you, cut your engines! Draw your fires! Your pump's out!"

"Lying American whoreson!" And then, as an aside, "Son of a whore, what is with these rifles?"

"Your pump's out and your goddam engine's going to blow—"

Another shot; two men tried to rush the door, Shaw waiting until they were almost inside to return fire. Gosport, who'd managed to hack and saw all the way through the beam that held the chain, sprang forward, looping the chain around the neck of one attacker as the man's pistol—inevitably—misfired, and the whole dozen or so men and women attached to that chain dragged the man down, ripping the weapons from his hands, his belt, his boots . . .

"Here's keys!" yelled Nathan in triumph. At the same time, January heard dim pounding on the engine room door, voices calling:

"Theo? Theo! Open up in there! Theo!"

One of the shots through the wall, thought January, feeling very calm about the whole business. The man must have bolted himself in when the commotion started.

Nathan, hands trembling, was trying key after key in the manacle locks, while men threw open the opposite door again and Quashie fired with every piece he possessed—quite a number, now. Harry, who'd been reloading for him, had tossed aside at least four pistols, and when Kadar grabbed for one said, "Won't work. Flint's busted."

"Get 'em out of here," said January quietly, rolling gratefully to his feet as Nathan found the key to his ankle chains and let him, finally, scramble right side up. "Just get 'em out, over the rail. Risking a bullet's better than getting blown up."

"I suspect you're right, Maestro." Shaw fired again at another sortie. "River's rising and full of trash, floaters and logs and branches. Since we're bound upstream we're close to shore, too."

Outside men were shouting, arguing, and Jac Ney's voice rose above the rest: "I'll shoot the man who goes over-side!" There was a crashing, a thudding, from the door, and, January fancied, over the clank and lug and rattle of the engine another sound, the strangled desperate keening of steam escaping from too small a vent, trapped too long and too tightly. . . .

"Now it may so be," Shaw added placidly, blasting away as the far door jerked open yet again, "that I might get myself blowed up or knocked out or washed down the river a ways, and not be able to get all these folks back to the people that owns 'em. I'm leavin' that up to you, Maestro." His gray eyes met January's, completely without expression. "If so be any survives."

"I doubt anyone will," said January, warning him.

Shaw nodded. "Well, we can only do our best. Was it Seneca that said Death is Freedom for a slave?" He pulled a packet of waxed silk from his shirt, and shoved it into the front of January's—his freedom papers, January guessed. "You watch out for that wheel, when you go over-side."

Shaw and January slammed the door open, firing in both directions, clearing a path. Return fire was sporadic—January could see only about a dozen men still on deck, Ney and his father among them. Dark heads bobbed already in the quicksilver current of the river, clutching at the snags and branches that the rise was bringing down. The boat itself was farther from the shore than January had reckoned, swinging with the current already but plowing hard. Even as the first of the newly freed men and women plunged from the hold, threw themselves across the narrow space of deck to the rail and over, he felt the boat lurch and hitch, felt the rhythm of the engine jar, jolting as the wheel picked up a snag. The huge tree-trunk caught, jamming the already overburdened machinery. . . .

Men's voices yelling the dead engineer's name outside the locked engine room door.

Jacinthe Ney screaming at the Spanish mate as the man plunged over the rail, firing his pistol at his head and getting nothing but a broken spark from its damaged flint.

Hope flinging herself over the rail with her infant tied to her back with her shawl, Bumper and Nero following, holding hands tightly.

Jeanette and Quashie side by side, both firing rifles and pistols and everything else they could lay hands on to keep the white attackers at bay, Quashie like a filthy animal, bearded and bushy from five days' hiding, five days' watching. Five days, waiting his chance.

Disappearing Willie, amazingly, sat a dozen yards off in the pirogue that had brought Shaw and Quashie, already fishing children and the weak from the flood. His eyes met January's and he grinned, as if this were a game.

The *Belle Dame* lurched, swung with the current, even its own crew springing over-side like rats now, dark and sleek and wet in the water. Jac Ney fired at them, and hurled the useless pistols at their heads when they misfired, cursing like Satan in Hell.

January strode from the door of the empty cargo hold and swung up on the rail. He had a flashing glimpse of Ney's wild eyes, the dark muzzle of a pistol brought to bear, flame bursting and a ball skimming his shoulder like a hornet's hot kiss—

—And then the entire world went up in a bellowing roar of earsplitting fire. The concussion drove him down into the river's heart, drowning him, hammering his ears, the impact whirling him away. He felt the heat of it, struggled blindly upward, eternities without breath.

Sickened eons later, his head broke water. Burning hunks of wood, slobbering bubbles, floating shutters and benches and doors strewed the surface. He grabbed a door, for the current was strong, turned a little in the water and saw the hulk of the *Belle Dame* riding the stream like a floating bonfire. Heat pounded his face. Weak with shock and hunger and sheer fatigue, for a long time all he could do was cling to his isolate planet of flotsam, the sole life in a universe of wet gray.

In time the river sent him a plank, and he used this to paddle slowly to shore.

TWENTY-TWO

January fully expected that he'd have to haul himself out of the river, limp somehow to the nearest house, convince its inhabitants of his freedom and his bona fides, and make his way into Baton Rouge and hence back to New Orleans—staying one step ahead of Sheriff Duffy's posses all the while—entirely on his own. But as he paddled, trembling with exhaustion, in to shore, two figures waded out to meet him, Gosport and one of the second-gang women, Giselle. They dragged his makeshift raft in among the tangle of the flooded batture, and helped him up to the dry ground of the levee: "We must be ten, twelve miles down from where that boat blowed up," said Gosport. "We're clear round the other side of Duncan Point."

On the other side of the levee, dark fields of cane disappeared into the fog. Somewhere voices sang:

"Day zab, day zab, day koo-noo wi wi. . . ."

The darkening air stank of burned sugar.

Thank you, Mary, Mother of God. His fingers touched the rosary in his soaked pocket. *Thank you God, for bringing me alive out of the fire and the flood.*

He wondered if in fact Shaw had survived.

"You all right, Ben?" Giselle had her baby girl with her, tied to her back with a shawl when she'd gone into the river. The child blinked over her shoulder at January with huge liquid unsurprised brown eyes.

January sighed, and touched his forehead with one hand, wincing at the mingled pain of bruises and blisters. "I feel like I did twenty rounds with an iron stove and lost."

Gosport asked, "Will you *be* all right?"

January reached into his shirt, and smiled. The waxed silk was intact. "I'll be all right."

"You know," said Gosport, "I never did believe all them songs Mohammed used to sing about High John the Conqueror, beatin' all the white men and gettin' his people to safety. I'll believe 'em now. I know they're true."

They walked January to the oyster-shell road that ran along the top of the levee, and made sure he was well enough to stand on his own, before they faded like ghosts into the mist. January never saw either of them again.

Monsieur Conrad, of Le Chenière plantation, had already gotten word that a boat had blown up on the other side of Duncan Point. He ordered his butler to make up a bed for January at once in one of the several cottages shared by the house-servants; only when January offered to show him his freedom papers did the planter say, "Janvier? Benjamin Janvier? Your wife is here. It was she whom my people first brought from the river with the news. . . ."

January just stopped himself from gaping and said instead, "Kiki?" with what he hoped was a blossoming smile.

Monsieur Conrad's face broadened into a grin. He was a gray-haired, pleasant man of German Creole extraction and quite clearly reveled in being the reuniter of lost families. "Even she."

January crossed himself. "Thank God," he said simply. He wasn't quite sure what else to say, not knowing what the cook had told this man; he felt annoyance that she'd manipulate him in this fashion. "I didn't dare hope. . . ."

Kiki was sitting on the edge of the bed in one of the house-servants' cottages. She was wrapped in a quilt, and one of the maids was combing out her mahogany-black hair. She looked up as January came in, and made her eyes melting as she held out her arms. "Oh, Ben!"

"Thank you," she said, after they'd been served with food and left alone. A small fire burned in the cabin's little hearth, making the borrowed refuge warm and pleasant. The servant had helped her braid her hair into strings, and Kiki finished tying them as she spoke. "I was almost unconscious when Monsieur Conrad's people found me. I was gambling that you'd get ashore all right, too. You might have gone anywhere, but at least you wouldn't be hiding like the others. And if you *did* come here. . . ."

"How did you know my name?"

And her dark eyes twinkled. "If you were a free man," she replied, "I knew you had to have your papers hidden somewhere. And since Michie Hannibal was like your white kid glove, the place to hide them would have been in his room."

January sniffed. "You're lucky you're here in this room with me instead of Harry. Or whoever Harry sold the other set of my papers to. Now I'll have to deal with having a duplicate Benjamin January at large, stealing pigs and trading guns. . . ."

"Don't be silly, Ben, in a year his credit will be better than yours."

January sighed, and leaned his back against the pillows she'd heaped between the wall and his shoulders. He ached all over and wanted only to sleep. Outside, the fog was losing the light that had filled it all day.

Where would Marie-Noël Fourchet spend the night? *They're all right,* Shaw had said, meaning he'd gotten to Mon Triomphe in time. If he knew Shaw, the man had come up on a boat to another landing, and checked the lay of the land before going in. Disappearing Willie had probably gone to ground the same time Duffy had imprisoned Mohammed and Pennydip, and Quashie had been waiting, all that time, watching for his chance to rescue Jeanette. . . .

And a good thing, January thought. Otherwise, preoccupied with their own harvests, the other planters wouldn't have seen the burning house until too late. Would have attributed the smoke to the burning of the cane-fields.

He had a mental image of Hippolyte Daubray riding up on the heels of the disaster, offering hospitality with one hand and three dollars and thirty-five cents for Mon Triomphe and everything on it with the other.

In the stillness he was aware of Kiki watching him.

"False River Jones told me about your husband," he said. "And your sons."

Kiki turned her face away, and tied up the last of her many braids with string. Her plump face looked haggard in the warm hues of the fire, as if she understood that from those deaths—deaths she'd learned of at the trader's last visit in the dark of the moon—he had guessed all the rest.

"I should say I'm sorry," she said at last. "But I'm not. About Gilles, yes. He was a kind man, a good man. Even when he was drunk he hadn't an ounce of harm in him. I should have realized, after Michie Fourchet beat him for stealing liquor. But I didn't."

"Did you love him?"

"Everyone thought I should have," she said simply, "so I said I did. And then, M'am Fourchet wouldn't have put in her word for me, if I hadn't said it was love. It wasn't enough that Reuben was a wild pig in his soul. It was the love story that fetched her heart. Well, she's only a girl. But Hector was the only man I ever loved."

January was silent, thinking about how a man dies, who drinks the boiled roots of Italian oleander. Thinking about the stripped leaves beneath M'am Camille's dark hedges, and the mashed bolus of boiled vegetable matter on the midden at Refuge; the vévé of hatred drawn above the stove. The dead rats beneath the house.

"I am sorry," Kiki said.

His eyes met hers again, and he read in them her regret, and her understanding that he would have to take her in to the law if he could. Yet he understood, too, that having told Conrad they were husband and wife, there was no way that he could now announce that this woman was a murderess and his prisoner. It would mean a contest of lies, and Conrad might believe her, or call January's freedom papers into question.

All he wanted to do now was ascertain that Hannibal and the others had indeed survived the fire, and then go home.

"It sounds silly," Kiki said at length. "I am sorry. I didn't think of what it would mean—that others would be blamed, and maybe punished, for that horrid old man's death. And at the time I didn't care. I was so—so angry. So crazy with grief."

January said nothing. He remembered the madness of his own sorrow at Ayasha's death. Remembered too the sick helpless fury he'd felt, his whole time at Mon Triomphe, as if everything beneath his skin were being consumed by slow fire.

"Reuben was easy," Kiki went on, her voice matter-of-fact. "We all of us, as children, played with blow-pipes. There was an old mambo in the quarters where I grew up who made them out of maiden cane or straws, and my brothers and I could hit near anything with thorns or slivers as well as peas. Hector and I used to have contests—I was a better shot than he. Even though I marked the walls for Shango and the other spirits of the fire to help me, I didn't really think I could trap Reuben long enough in the mill for him to smother or burn, but nobody would question, then, if the machinery broke."

She drew the blanket more closely around herself. One of the Conrad servants had lent her clothes, a faded yellow calico gown sewn for a woman even more amply built than she, and the bright color warmed her face more than the blacks of mourning that she had worn. *Proud,* January remembered Mohammed calling her. *Proud and strong.*

Of course a man like Reuben would take it as a challenge, to break her.

Someone—Mohammed?—had told him how Kiki had nursed her former husband in his injury, when Trinette would not. Looking at her calm somber face he understood now why she'd volunteered. What the rollers, and shock, and loss of blood hadn't accomplished, she would have made sure of, one way or another.

"When the mule barn caught fire I thought it was an accident," she went on. "Baron was always a little careless with his lantern. But then the vévés showed up in the house, and the other things started to happen—the axles sawn, and the harnesses rubbed with pepper again and again, and I knew someone else was doing it. But I never thought it was Michie Robert."

Her round, powerful hands toyed with a frayed place in the blanket, her dark beautiful eyes downcast. "I thought I'd best stay quiet and wait. I wanted to kill Michie Fourchet and I knew when I did I'd have to run, and I couldn't do that carrying a child. I'd already got rid of the baby Reuben put in me, a few years ago. . . . And then the sheds burned. And so many people hurt, and those poor babies killed, and it was as if I woke up after a bad, bad dream. Maybe what you said to me, about how a man will burn down a house just to cook eggs, made me think. And I understood I just couldn't do it. After that, all I wanted was to be away."

"And that's when you offered to help Quashie and Jeanette escape, if they'd take you with them?"

She nodded. "I was scared. I can't tell you how scared I was. I wouldn't have done it, if I'd known someone would come along after me, masking his footsteps in my own."

"Wouldn't you?"

Their eyes locked. For a moment it seemed to January that a man's body lay between them, a man who she knew was likely to drink his master's liquor, if he couldn't get his own.

It was her gaze that fell.

She said, very softly, "I don't know. That's the honest truth, Ben. I don't know. I know for five years I got by on hearing those little notes Hector would send me by False River Jones. I know I have them memorized, every word, about what Daniel and Adam looked like, and what they loved, and all the things they did in those five years. I have a hole in my heart a thousand miles deep that it doesn't feel like anything is ever going to fill. And that's all I know."

When January woke—with a splitting headache—Kiki was gone.

"She said you'd know where to catch her up," said Monsieur Conrad's butler, who knocked while January was still lying in his borrowed bed wondering where the woman had managed to secrete a bottle of opium on her person. "She said you'd talked about it last night." He regarded January doubtfully, as if rethinking the whole tale of freedom papers and matrimony, and January put a hand to his head and said, "Of course we did. I have such a headache this morning I can't rightly think."

The butler smiled. He was young and businesslike and had the air of a man who ran the entire household with neat efficiency. Like Esteban, not imaginative, but greatly desirous to have all books balance at day's end. "I understand that. Your wife said you was one of the last ones off the boat, and those blisters look like you was burned bad. Why don't you rest here for another day? She said she'd stay with your brother in town til you came."

January was very tempted to avail himself of the offer, for he ached all over and the lassitude of shock pressed on him, physically and mentally. If Shaw had survived—and January prayed that he had, and not simply because Shaw could vouch for his identity—the policeman could keep Duffy and his posses at bay. If he hadn't, if he'd been badly hurt, January was still a fugitive. In any case it would take weeks for the garbled tales of slave revolt, house-burning, poisoning, and kidnapping to sort themselves out, if they ever did.

It was best, he thought, that he exit the whole situation through the first door that opened, and not ask questions that would cause delay.

Though frantically busy with his own harvest and boiling, Monsieur Conrad lent January money to take a boat south that afternoon, as, he said, he had lent money to Kiki. The river's rise brought several boats a day past La Chenière. The butler recalled that Kiki had taken the *Achtafayala.* January was willing to bet she wouldn't be aboard it when it docked in New Orleans.

When the *Boonslick* passed Lescelles plantation there was a flag out on the landing, and Hannibal, Esteban, *les deux* Mesdames Fourchet, and the children boarded. January concealed himself in the stern section of the deck where the poorer free colored and the slaves were relegated, and it was there that, much later, Hannibal sought him out.

"All I can say is, for a man raised by an opium addict, Michie Robert has only the dimmest possible idea of how much Patna Naptime the really hardened system can absorb with impunity," said the fiddler, perching like a rather worse-for-wear grasshopper on the top of a hogshead of nails. "They dosed me with enough so that I didn't really feel up to much derring-do—not that I'm much in the derring-do line to begin with—but I had plenty of leisure to chip off the business edge of every gun-flint in their boxes there, and dump most of my ration of water into the powder. As I observed before, *Solus pro virili parte ago:* I can only do the best I can."

"And what you did saved all our lives," said January. "I don't think Shaw and Quashie would ever have gotten on board if the crew had been fully armed. How did you happen to end up as a guest at Refuge anyway?"

"Silly bastard came out onto the gallery as the *Heroine* went past. There aren't even any trees in front of the house nowadays, just cane. I don't suppose it would have mattered if it wasn't me on board, or if I hadn't seen him board the *Belle Dame* that morning bound in exactly the opposite direction. That green coat of his stood out a mile. We stopped at Daubray to pick up a letter, and I disembarked and walked up the river road. I hid my luggage in the cane—they must have found it after Jules Ney caught me behind the kitchen that evening."

The fiddler unfastened the clasps of his violin case for the fifth or sixth time, peeking inside as if to reassure himself that the instrument was safe and undamaged; touching the varnished wood as a lover would have touched his lady's cheek. He looked desperately thin but surprisingly well, despite singed hair and an angry burn on his forehead, earned when he'd dragged young Fantine Fourchet out of the inferno of smoke and flame that had been Mon Triomphe.

January could see the charred ruin of the house as they passed it, veiled in the smoke-clogged white mists that still blurred the river. Through the trees his eye picked out the pale tumbledown planks of the slaves' graveyard, the broken crockery and bottles around the graves slowly sinking into the earth.

Mon Triomphe.

Simon Fourchet's pyre, consumed like a barbarian prince with all he owned.

Look on my works, ye mighty, and despair.

"Papa Ney was all for scuppering me on the spot, but Robert argued that as I'd written to my fictitious cousins on New River—thank God!—if my body wasn't found among the victims of this slave revolt there'd be a search. After romancing his father's wife for weeks—unsuccessfully, as it turned out—Robert brought her to her father's old house with a note swearing he'd kill himself for love of her if she didn't see him. . . ."

"And Marie-Noël *fell* for it?"

Hannibal gestured forgivingly. "She's only sixteen. In any case he forced her to drink paregoric that night, and she was still logy from it the next morning, not that any woman's going to endanger the life of her unborn child when a man has a pistol to her side. After Robert forced her and Esteban to tell the slaves they were being sold, and to cooperate, Ney and his father drugged everyone in the house—as you guessed—then put it to the torch. They didn't tie anyone, because we were all supposed to have been driven into the house before it was fired by rebelling slaves. God only knows what possessed me to rescue the children. I quite agree with Robert that murdering the pair of them—and their mother—was not only necessary to his scheme but intensely gratifying as well."

And from the upper deck, Jean-Luc's voice called shrilly, "You give that here! That's mine! It's MINE!" followed by strident and uncomforted tears. Madame Hélène remained in the women's cabin, prostrate with shock at what she had undergone.

She recovered sufficiently to go down to the ship wharves the following day, however, in company with January, Hannibal, a slightly singed and bruised Lieutenant Shaw, Madame Fourchet, and a trio of stout, blue-clothed City Guards, and intercept her husband as Robert was boarding the steam packet *Anne Louise.* January went with Shaw and his minions along the crowded levee, while Hannibal and the women waited in the market arcade, at the same little table by the coffee-stand where January had so often sat with Rose. It was unlikely, Shaw said, that Robert Fourchet would recognize a tall, well-dressed gentleman of color as one of his father's field hands.

But January would certainly recognize him.

The sailing-ship wharves lay downstream of the French town, the levee jammed at this time of the year with the world's commerce. Hogsheads of sugar, pipes of wine, bales of cotton; voices clamoring in every language God distributed at Babel: whores and Yankee sailors and Greek oyster-fishers and market women selling bandannas. Clothed in his high beaver hat and new black nip-waisted coat, January strolled toward the *Anne Louise* and scanned the faces, looking not only for Robert, but for Kiki.

January was still not entirely certain what he felt about Kiki. She had murdered an innocent man, and had calculatedly and coldly murdered a guilty one, not to free herself from him, but out of pure revenge. *If you cut us, do we not bleed?* Shylock had asked of men who, later in the play, had put their boots on his neck and made him eat filth. Having only sipped the cup Kiki had drunk of all her life, January understood exactly why she had done what she had done.

But he understood too that pain and fear are no pardon for murder. On the whole he was glad that Kiki had drugged him—in his exhaustion it had not taken much—and made her escape. He was fortunate, he supposed, that she hadn't killed him as he slept. She was quite capable of it. If he saw her on the wharf he knew he must—and would—raise a hue and cry.

But he did not. He did, however, see Robert Fourchet, decorously clothed in mourning black, hastening along the levee toward the *Anne Louise,* with a new valet carrying his valise in his wake. January raised his tall beaver hat and wiped his forehead, which was the signal, and Shaw and his myrmidons closed in.

He was close enough to hear Shaw say, "Mr. Fourchet?"

There was a momentary hesitation; January thought he saw the young man's eyes dart among the crowd, pick out the blue-clad forms of the City Guard moving in on him. "I'm Robert Fourchet, yes."

"If'n you'd care to come along here to the market for a minute, there's a couple ladies would like to have a word with you."

TWENTY-THREE

"Thank you." Marie-Noël Fourchet rose from her seat after Robert had been led away, and walked across to where January stood, unobtrusive in the curious silent way he'd practiced since early adolescence, against the brick pillars of the market. She'd put back her veils of mourning crêpe to speak the few words that identified her stepson as the man who'd held her at gunpoint, forced her to drink opium, left her and her family unconscious in a burning house. In their sooty frame her triangular, homely face looked even paler and more lashless. She held out a black-gloved hand.

"M'sieu Sefton tells me you were working for my husband." She nodded back toward the table under the arcade, where Hannibal was charming Madame Hélène out of the hysterics that she'd considered an appropriate accompaniment to her husband's arrest. "That you tried hard to save him."

At the table, the dark, florid woman—in crêpe and jet beads and veils to her knees despite the fact that she was mourning only a father-in-law—clutched Hannibal's hand and sobbed, "We have been left destitute! Destitute!"

"Will you be all right, Madame?" asked January. Whatever the courts decided to do with January's evidence from the slaves and Madame Fourchet's account of an attempted murder, Robert's valise had contained two of Thierry's pistols, which could have come into his hands no other way. The rest, January surmised, could safely be left to Shaw.

"I think so. Robert had most of the fifty thousand dollars those men paid him for the slaves. . . ." Marie-Noël raised her glance to January's face. "Were all of them killed?" Tears glimmered in her pale eyes.

"I think so, Madame. Some of them got into the water before the boat blew up, but not many, I don't think. And the boat was out in mid-river by then, and rolling with the current. I myself barely got to shore."

She bit her lips and crossed herself. "Those poor people," she whispered in real distress, that had nothing in it of sorrow over the loss of an investment of a hundred and fifty thousand dollars. "Those poor people." A gawky, familiar figure edged its way toward them through the gaudy press of market women and keelboat thugs, stevedores and flâneurs, and January recognized Esteban, followed closely by a tubby, pleasant-faced little gentleman wearing an overly elaborate lilac-striped cravat.

The pair paused by Hannibal and Madame Hélène, and Hannibal gestured toward where January and Madame Fourchet stood. January heard Esteban say, ". . . settlement out of court . . . sixty thousand dollars plus help to get the rest of the harvest in . . ."

Evidently, January thought, in spite of losing all their slaves, Marie-Noël—and the child she carried—were not going to starve.

"Hannibal tells me my husband agreed to pay you for your time and your pain." Madame Fourchet opened the beaded reticule at her belt, and drew out a stiff piece of pale brown paper—a draft on the Louisiana State Bank for five hundred dollars. "I'm sorry it cannot be more, for we owe you more than we can say, Esteban, and my . . . daughter-in-law . . ."—her voice stuck on the words—"and myself. But we've lost most of the crop, and it will take everything we have to keep the plantation itself. I hope you understand."

January took the paper from her black-gloved hand. "I understand, Madame." They'd probably sell the town house, he guessed. And use the proceeds, and the settlement, to buy more slaves. And after everything that he had passed through, to save the people who'd plunged into the river, the people among whom he'd lived, nothing had changed.

Vast weariness crushed him and he wanted to tear the bank-draft up and walk away, rather than have anything further to do with the Fourchet family. Even that five hundred dollars, he understood, had come from human sweat and human blood. His mother's and his friends' and his own.

But he put it in his pocket.

"You must not think too harshly of my husband," said Madame Fourchet, in her soft, gruff voice. "He was a man who lived with a great deal of pain in his heart. He did the best he could."

January recalled the dark face creased with rage, that yelled at him in nightmares. The sickening slap of a broom handle on his flesh and the sound of his own ribs breaking.

Screams in rainy darkness. The stink of cigar smoke. *I have tried to make amends where I can.*

This woman, he thought, looking down at her, had sat beside his bed all through that night, while his son sat out in the rain for the pleasure of hearing him die. "Did you love him, Madame?" he asked.

"Yes," she said. "Yes, I did," and there was no

mistaking the warmth in her eyes, as she drew her veils down.

She turned and walked back to her family, leaving January alone.

"So they all live happily ever after," said January a few nights later, as he walked Rose home from supper at Dominique's house. His sister's white protector was still on the family plantation, seeing to the last of the harvest, and Minou was taking advantage of the chance to entertain friends of color who would not, of course, be admitted to her house when a wealthy white gentleman was either there or expected to arrive. "Esteban with his dear friend M'sieu Molineaux, Madame with her child, Madame Hélène as a poor relation among the Prideaux clan. . . . She's apparently suing her mother-in-law for upkeep, on the grounds that they had enough money to give me five hundred dollars."

Rose laughed at that, a joyous whoop at the absurdity of humankind, and January shook his head. He had found rooms of his own that day, in what had been the garçonnière of a neat cottage on Rue Ursulines: slightly more than he could afford, but the woman who owned the house, a former plaçée like his mother, would allow him to use her parlor for piano lessons three days a week.

"What did your mother say?"

"Nothing. She thinks I'm a fool for leaving, and points out—quite rightly—that I'll be paying twice as much for the same accommodations and no meals thrown in. I suspect she's going to rent out my old room to someone else for three times what I was paying her. She doesn't understand that what I'm paying for is freedom."

"Of course she doesn't," said Rose. They passed the lights of the Café du Venise, and for a moment the music of Hannibal's fiddle flowed through the illuminated doorway to infuse the mist around them. "Because of course you're no more free of her than you were before."

"I may not be free," he said, "but at least I have choice. And that's something."

She smiled. "With your mother, that's a great deal."

"But I'm angry, Rose." Their steps turned along Front Street, toward Rue des Victoires where her rooms were. To their right the levee spread out in the cobalt luminance of the winter night, torches blazing like golden footlights, outlining some incomprehensible spectacle on a stage. The smells of the eating-houses swirled around them—oysters frying, onions, syrup—meeting the stinks of salt and fish and tar and engine smoke from the wharves like a tidal river, and from somewhere close by a woman sang, *"One cup of coffee, just five cents/Make you smile the livelong day. . . ."*

"The way the people in the quarters were treated—the way *I* was treated—I can't forget it. I thought I'd left it behind when I was a child and I found I hadn't. I'd just buried it, deep. And now it's come up out of its grave like a dead man's haunt, and it speaks to me all the time."

He shook his head, as a hobbled animal does when tormented by summer flies. "I see Quashie tied and beaten for no better reason than that he loved Jeanette. I see Kiki given in marriage to a man she hated just because Fourchet wanted Reuben to do his job well. I know there are good masters and bad masters and that the poor in the big cities are treated just the same, and yet I walk down the streets now and I see white men—strangers—and I hate them, I feel rage at them, killing rage, and this isn't a good way to feel. I know, because I saw what it did to Simon Fourchet. And I don't know what to do."

He spoke desperately, words he had not voiced to anyone, and as he spoke them he felt anger all over again at Simon Fourchet for having changed him, put this in his heart. Anger and helplessness and burning shame.

"Have you spoken of this to your confessor?" Torchlight flashed across her spectacle lenses as she turned her head, made a golden halo of the white tignon she wore. He knew that Rose was not a religious woman—a logical Deist, whose God was mathematics—but in her voice he heard her understanding of his own faith.

"He told me to pray. To pick out one white face—and one black face—from all the strangers I see, each day, and to burn a candle, and say a prayer, for those two every day. But I'm still angry. I think I may be angry for a long time."

"Are you sorry you went?" she asked. "Sorry you lived among these people? Sorry you remembered?"

He said, "No."

"It's an injury," she said. "A wound. There will be a scar, and the scar will hurt—mine certainly do—but wounds do heal." Her long slim hand, cold within its glove, slipped into his.

Shortly after the New Year, January was passing a blacksmith's yard on the Rue St.-Pierre, coming home late from rehearsals with an opera company visiting from Italy, which would open in the Carnival season. The mist lay thick in the wet streets, and his head was filled with arias and duets and the precise placement of half-notes, but out of the dark he heard a man's single voice lifted in wailing, gentle song:

"They carry them down to the river,
They throw them in the stream.
They carry them down to the river,
They throw them in the stream."

He stepped into the torchlit yard, and saw the smithy brimming over with the warmth of lamps. A small broad-shouldered man bent over an anvil, like a bee in the center of a rose of crimson light, drawing out an iron bar flat for some future project, the forge-light edging his cropped gray hair with gold. From the yard gate January added his voice to the song:

"Papa, I'm afraid I'm dying,
Papa, I'm gonna die. . . ."

Mohammed looked up, and his teeth glinted in a smile. "Ben!" He laid his hammer aside, and his hand was rough and hard as the forged iron as it clasped January's. "I'm glad to see you well."

"And I you."

"It *is* still Ben, isn't it?" asked the smith. He'd grown a beard, which with the broken nose and the scars left by Duffy's beating altered the look of his face. "I go by the name of Moses these days. Moses LePas. M'sieu Theroux, that's the owner here, speaks of taking me on as a partner."

"He couldn't get a better," said January. "Man, it's good to see you. Are any of the others in town, do you know? Are they well?"

"Just about everyone's well," the blacksmith said. "I heard from Herc only last week—he and Trinette are in New York. Ajax has his own gang of stevedores on the waterfront there, and Bumper and Nero are in school. They come home and teach Hope what they've learned, to read and to figure. Marquis—you remember how bad he was burned—he's got a little farm on Cane River, and a Chickasaw wife. Agamemnon's up there, too, working in a tavern; old M'am Pennydip cooks for him and keeps house. Quashie and Jeanette are expecting a child, over in Mobile."

"And Kiki?" asked January, and the look Mohammed gave him, sidelong, told him what the blacksmith guessed.

"I've heard no word of her," he answered. "Mostly everyone else, though. Not many are here in town, of course, for fear of running into Michie Esteban, but there's some. They all ask after you, you know."

And what did they feel? January wondered. Did they feel that hideous, despairing sense that whatever they did, it would accomplish nothing? Did they feel hate every time they saw a white face, or wake in the night with memories that would be part of them forever?

But it *would* be forever, he thought. And it was a part of them, and a part of him as well, a blood-link that joined them. At that realization some of his anger shifted, and sorrow and understanding entered to ease a little of its pain. Joy warmed him at the thought of all those friends, as if he'd received word of a family long lost.

"Tell them I'm well," he said, smiling then. "Tell them I'm fine." He filled the blacksmith in on what he'd heard of Esteban's activities, and those of Madame Fourchet; "Not bad," he said, "for one who had to start all over again."

"No." Mohammed grinned. "No, that's a woman who'll go far. It was a good thing that you did, you know," he went on. "I always meant to tell you at the time. So many men say to Allah, 'Show me your will and I'll do it,' and then when Allah says, 'Take this staff and go save that flock of sheep from wolves,' they say, 'Show me your *other* will.' We weren't your sheep. You didn't know us at all. I wanted to tell you how proud your father would have been of you."

January had been about to speak, to deprecate what he had done, but he found he could not. He stood with his breath indrawn, looking at the *griot*'s face in the lamplight, unable to say a word.

Mohammed went on, "You are Jumah's son, aren't you?"

Jumah.

Up until that moment January had never recalled his father's name. It had been buried under the pain of losing him, under the terrors of being taken away from the only home he had known; under the fear of his mother being taken from him as well. But now the name came back to him, not as a new thing, but as something always there. He said, "Yes. Yes, Jumah was my father."

And something cracked inside him, like ice breaking on a river in spring. He put his hand to his mouth but could do nothing else. Only stand in the lamp light of the smithy, sudden tears running down his face.

Old scars hurting. Dried wounds opening with life-giving blood. Old memories singing from out of his dreams.

"No," said Mohammed gently. "Here, no, it's not a thing for tears, Ben. Your father was a good man, a righteous and upstanding one. He'd have done what you did."

And January shook his head, his shoulders shuddering as he fought to steady his breath. "Why didn't he come?" he asked, when he could speak. "All those years. Bellefleur was only a few miles from town, an hour's walk at most. Why didn't he come?"

"But he did," Mohammed said. "He came every week, whenever he could get a pass and many times when he couldn't. He'd walk into town and stand across the street, or around the corner, watching you come and go sometimes, or listening while you practiced on the piano. He said you played music like the spirits all praising God together, music like the sun coming up. He'd come back all glowing with it, and whether he spoke of it or not, we knew he'd been to see his son."

"He never spoke!" The words came out of January like broken potsherds working up through the earth of a grave. "He could have stopped me on the street, he could have come around the corner. He didn't have to let my mother keep him away. I used to sit on the gallery behind the house, waiting for him at night. And he never came."

"Ah, Ben." The smith spoke, not to the musician standing before him, with his new black coat and his music satchel, but to the child on the gallery, the child who dreamed of the tall naked man with the country marks on his face. "Ben, he would not have done that to you. 'My son is a free man,' Jumah would say—to us, those days when we'd ask him the same thing. 'Ben has to learn to stand like a free man, and to look other men in the eye. He has to learn to speak like a free man, so that no one will even have to ask him to prove he's free. They'll know it. And he can't learn that from a father who's a slave.' "

January was silent for a long time. Thinking about those nights, and the stillness and peace of the country. The silence of the sunlight, lying on the cabin floor.

"What happened to him?" he asked at last. For he knew then that the *griot* would know.

"In time Fourchet had him moved up to Triomphe."

"Because he'd run away all the time?"

Mohammed hesitated, then shook his head. A lie, but January understood. "I think he just wanted more hands there, or maybe it was after he sold Bellefleur. I don't remember."

As if, thought January, there wasn't a lost pot or a cast horseshoe that Mohammed didn't know about the people of the quarters in thirty-three years.

"He ran away from Triomphe, and three days later they found his body in the ciprière. He'd been bit by a snake, and he died there underneath a sweet-gum tree, about a hundred feet from where Disappearing Willie had his house. By what we could tell, he'd made no effort to cut the wound, or suck the poison clean. He was just tired, and had lived enough, and so he fell asleep."

January closed his eyes, the tears still running down his face.

"There's no call to weep," said Mohammed gently again. His hard hand rubbed January's arm as if to remind him of his own bone and flesh. "It was a long time ago—nearly twenty-five years. He died a proud man, and a happy one."

"He died a slave."

"He died knowing his son was a free man, and a man who could make music that the angels in Heaven would sneak away from their work to listen to. He died in the wilderness, where it was quiet and green. We all sang a ring-shout for him, and laid him to rest, there on Triomphe, for his dust to mingle with the dust of his friends. How many other men die that happy?"

January nodded, and drew in his breath, remembering the burying-ground near the levee. Recalling those anonymous marker-boards, and the still silence where hundreds lay unmarked, reabsorbed into the womb of the earth. His father was buried, he realized, with Reuben and with Gilles, with those others who were little more than names—LAVINNIA and PUSEY. He could say now to Olympe's children, *This was your grandfather, a good and wonderful man.* Maybe one day say it to a child of his own. He had seen his father's grave, and that gave him peace.

"How did you know it was me?" he asked Mohammed. "I couldn't have been eight years old when I left Bellefleur. You couldn't have known me."

Mohammed almost laughed. "Ben," he said, "you're the mirror of him, his living double. I knew your name was Ben. And like you he was a music-maker, with his hands and his voice and his heart."

"Thank you," said January softly. "I didn't know all that. And I'm glad now that I can tell my sister and her children."

"That's good," said the smith, nodding. "He'd want his grandchildren to know his name."

January stepped into the dense lapis midnight of the streets, and though he'd spent the evening playing Bellini's bright flamboyant airs—and those airs still resonated golden within him—as he walked he raised his voice in a wailing field-holler with all the joy in his heart. And as he passed each dark alleyway, each slave-yard or carriageway, voices answered him, as they would have out in the cane-fields, lifting in harmony, catching and twirling his notes like a dancer. The reverberance of sorrow and joy echoed around him, and followed him all the way home.

WORK SONGS AND SPIRITUALS

All accounts of travel through the Deep South in the 1830s make mention that the slaves sang as they worked in the cane-fields. When it came to researching this book, the question of *what* exactly they sang proved to be a difficult one.

Until almost the eve of the Civil War, most rural plantation slaves were only nominally Christian, if that. House-servants were probably given some instruction in Christianity, depending on the master. Many urban slaves attended Christian worship, though in New Orleans particularly, the legally mandated Catholicism was frequently blended with voodoo. In the countryside, most small slaveowners—not of the planter class—who owned one, two, or possibly half a dozen slaves who divided their duties between farm work and the house, might convert, or instruct, their bondsmen.

But the majority of rural slaves—and a goodly number of urban ones—did not become Christians in any real sense of the word until the Evangelical movement of the 1840s. Up to the 1830s many whites refused to tolerate black congregations, arguing that any gathering of blacks would provide a seedbed of rebellion and pointing out that the two great leaders of early-nineteenth-century rebellions, Denmark Vesey and Nat Turner, were both preachers.

Spirituals—the quintessential form (with blues) of black music in America—did not exist until the late 1840s or 1850s.

So what did they sing?

I've done the best I can in assembling what phonetic fragments of presumably African songs survive in the works of such writers as George Washington Cable, and the old Creole songs that were popular then. There are contemporary or near-contemporary (1840s and 1850s) accounts of both ring-shouts and the field hollers, and the similarity of these hollers to descriptions of street-vendors' cries is striking.

Descriptions agree that the songs were extremely odd and frequently unpleasant to Western ears: words like *wailing, monotonous,* and *caterwauling* are used, and frequent reference is made to the call-and-response form that was later absorbed into spirituals. Accounts agree on the very African emphasis on rhythm—in fact on many plantations possession of a drum was a whipping offense.

What is clear is that music played a critical part in the lives of the displaced Africans; that it was a vital link to the world from which they, or their parents or grandparents, had been ripped. When plantation blacks did come to Christianity, either through camp-meetings in the 1840s or through the often-secret efforts of preachers from urban black congregations, they naturally adapted Protestant hymns to African needs and African modes of song, giving rise to spirituals in the same way that European cotillions and Irish clog dancing morphed into characteristic black dance. Field hollers blended imperceptibly into the blues, the casual weaving of songs from and into everyday activities.

"Playing the dozens," the game of insults and counter-insults, is attested to in slave-related literature well back into the eighteenth century.

MASTERS AND SLAVES

What struck me most clearly, in reading first-person accounts of slavery, is the enormous variety of personal experiences in what was by definition a hideously dysfunctional relationship. Some masters were very nice to their slaves. Some slaves were maliciously rebellious and manipulative. Some masters nailed their slaves up in barrels and rolled them down hills. Some masters sold families as units and others didn't think twice about splitting them up. Some slaves poisoned their masters, sabotaged farm equipment (though the word "sabotage" didn't exist until the early twentieth century), deliberately injured work animals or their masters' children.

In some ways, *Gone With the Wind* is as accurate as *Uncle Tom's Cabin.*

Men and women, both white and black, reacted to these conditions with the entire conceivable (and in some cases inconceivable) spectrum of emotions and behaviors: loyalty, resentment, kindness, patronization, uncaring.

The critical thing about all these accounts is, that if you were a slave, you could just as easily get one sort of master, and treatment, as you could another. What happened to you was entirely arbitrary.

There was nothing you could do about it.

And there was no redress.

One of the most amazing things I've encountered in my research on slavery was that any slave, male or female, was able to remain reasonably cheerful, survive emotionally, raise children, sing songs of any sort, and get on with their lives under the conditions described. I am recurrently and repeatedly astonished at the adaptability and strength of the human spirit.

Naturally, in writing a murder mystery involving slavery, I've written about a harsh master who treated his family as poorly as he treated his slaves. If he was a nice person I wouldn't be telling this story. He had plenty of spiritual brothers out there, and plenty of fellow-slaveowners who would have been horrified by his behavior—although quite possibly they wouldn't have considered it their business to do anything about it.

In writing any work of fiction about a condition like slavery (or Nazism, or child abuse, or the enslavement of women) one runs the risk of trivializing horrors by weaving them into the background, by making them part of the scenery—part of the game. I've done my best to portray conditions and attitudes as they were, insofar as I have found them in my studies of the period. If I have offended those whose families actually endured the conditions I've described, or belittled their experience and suffering, I apologize, for the offense was unintentional. I'm not seeking to make anyone into a saint, or anyone into a monster—only to tell a story as it might have taken place, and to stay as close to the truth—and to human nature—as I can.

ABOUT THE AUTHOR

BARBARA HAMBLY attended the University of California and spent a year at the University of Bordeaux, France, obtaining a master's degree in medieval history. She has worked as both a teacher and a technical editor, but her first love has always been history. Ms. Hambly lives in Los Angeles with two Pekingese, a cat, and another writer. The fifth Benjamin January novel, *Die Upon A Kiss,* is now available in hardcover.

If you enjoyed Barbara Hambly's

SOLD DOWN THE RIVER,

you won't want to miss any of the superb mysteries in the Benjamin January series.

Look for

A FREE MAN OF COLOR,
FEVER SEASON,
and
GRAVEYARD DUST

at your favorite bookseller's.

And don't miss

DIE UPON A KISS,

the newest Benjamin January novel, now available in hardcover!